SEEKING THE TRUTH

RACHAEL C. DUNCAN

Seeking the Truth
by Rachael C. Duncan

Copyright © 2023 Rachael C. Duncan

Paperback Edition

Published in the United States by Wolfpack Publishing, Las Vegas

CKN Christian Publishing
An Imprint of Wolfpack Publishing
9850 S. Maryland Parkway, Suite A-5 #323
Las Vegas, Nevada 89183

cknchristianpublishing.com

Paperback ISBN: 978-1-63977-463-0
eBook ISBN: 978-1-63977-462-3
LCCN: 2023942016

NOTE FROM THE AUTHOR

When I began researching for my first novel, I was blown away by the vast array of resources available concerning anything and everything biblical! It was thrilling to discover such a wealth of information regarding topics that have always intrigued me.

Because I write Bible-based novels, please allow me to state this simple disclaimer: The novels I write are categorized as biblical fiction, which means I have taken some literary license in instances where the Bible story itself remains silent, unclear, or disputed. As you can imagine, there's a LOT of controversy and differing opinions regarding certain biblical characters, settings, dates, etc. As we dive into the book of Acts in the *Crowning Crescendo: A New Era*, exact dates pertaining to certain events remain unclear, disputed, or unknown. I've also encountered tricky questions such as, *How do we know if every story in Acts is listed in chronological order?* Especially as the narrative passes back and forth between multiple characters and settings, these questions tend to surface. So just a reminder, while based on the biblical narratives, this is indeed a work of fiction.

So as I tackled this exciting new project, I sought to honor the Word of God and then I asked the Lord to help me fill in the blanks in a way that will reach my readers, touch their hearts, draw them closer to Him, and bring these beautiful Bible stories to life, inspiring each reader to dive headfirst into the precious Word of God!

Thank you for purchasing this novel. I hope you are blessed page after page!

SEEKING THE TRUTH

CHAPTER 1

Tabitha

A.D. 33, Jerusalem

"Tabitha? Tabitha, my love."

Stirring slightly, Tabitha drew the soft blanket under her chin, drifting blissfully upon the airy, cloudlike sensations of sweet slumber and even sweeter dreams, her entire being resisting wakefulness.

"Beloved, are you awake?"

Tabitha grew still, clutching the warm blanket even more tightly about her. As consciousness dawned, her hazy mind began to clear. With the soft rustle of blankets, Tabitha turned on her side, propping herself up on one elbow and squinting slightly as the faint rays of early sunlight slanted through the open window. Glancing up, she saw the curtains fluttering lightly in the cool spring breeze, felt the delightful warmth of sunshine upon her face, streaming in through the open window.

"Ah, good morning, love." Stephanos was kneeling beside their pallet, watching her, his dark eyes filled with warmth.

Offering her new husband a lopsided smile, Tabitha held out her arms to him.

Stephanos didn't need a second invitation. Slipping onto the bedroll, Stephanos stretched out beside his young wife, drawing her close to him. Smoothing back Tabitha's wayward honey-gold curls, Stephanos smiled indulgently. "I love you."

Tingling at his closeness, Tabitha nestled in his embrace, reveling in the God-given gift of marriage. Drawing her husband's head down, she kissed him deeply, glorying in the peaceful bliss of these early morning hours before the responsibilities and demands of the day vied for their attention, requiring them to part.

"How am I to tear myself away from you, beloved," Stephanos teased, fondly tipping her chin, "when your presence is so inviting?"

"Perhaps that's my aim," Tabitha responded, her hazel-green eyes sparkling mischievously. "To keep you here with me all day."

"I must confess," Stephanos grinned, kissing her gently, "you are dangerously close to succeeding."

Sighing wistfully, Tabitha allowed her husband to help her sit up. "But I suppose we must begin another day."

"*This is the day the Lord has made*," Stephanos reminded her tenderly, "And—"

"*We will rejoice and be glad in it*," she finished along with him, laughing musically.

Accepting Stephanos' proffered hand, Tabitha rose from their comfortable sleeping pallet. Tomorrow, she would accompany her husband to the house of Mary, her former mistress. The thought was enough to put a bit of a spring into her step, although she would have liked to join him *today* rather than staying home alone to keep house. But there would be plenty of sewing and housework to busy her mind until the following day.

Within the first week of Tabitha's marriage, practical Mary had suggested her former maidservant accompany Stephanos several days each week, resuming her chores at the magnificent villa in exchange for pay. It was a wonderful arrangement, for Tabitha rejoiced at the opportunity to fellowship with her beloved mistress and former household— the only *family* she had known since being orphaned as a child. The salary she earned generously supplemented her husband's income, which was an added bonus. Since Tabitha worked but a few days each week, she had plenty of time to keep her own house, and her ministry to the widows and orphans of Stephanos' jurisdiction in the City of David, an ancient district just south of the Temple Mount in Jerusalem's Lower City, continued to flourish. As a newly appointed deacon in the Jerusalem church, Stephanos—along with his dearest friend Philip and five others—oversaw the distribution of food, clothing, and necessities for those in need. Tabitha, a skilled seamstress, delighted in weaving beautiful garments and warm bedding for distribution.

Smiling to herself, Tabitha's gaze traveled past the sheer tapestry serving as a bedroom partition, toward her cherished loom at the opposite end of the one-room house. Mary had issued strict orders that the impressive piece of machinery be delivered to Tabitha's new home shortly after her wedding, several weeks prior.

"Why are you smiling like that, beloved? Not that I object."

Drawn by her husband's good-natured inquiry, Tabitha turned to face him. He stood near their pallet, dressing quietly.

Blushing slightly, Tabitha admired his handsome looks and build. "I was just thinking about how blessed we are, Stephanos," she admitted, crossing the distance between them. Reaching for his outer tunic, she held it out to him.

Shrugging his arms into the simple shirtsleeves, Stephanos' dark eyes conveyed his agreement. "God is gracious."

"He is, indeed," Tabitha said with great feeling. Taking up her husband's leather belt, she fitted it carefully around his lean torso. "He has granted us a beautiful life together."

"A small taste of Heaven," Stephanos admitted, taking his wife's delicate hands in his. "We cannot even comprehend what God has prepared for those who love Him. Even the most breathtaking moments we experience on this earth are but fleeting glimpses of the glory yet to be."

***

Candace

It had been a rather trying morning. Her young sons, Alexander, age nine, and Rufus, at nearly eighteen months, had been uncharacteristically stubborn and petulant. Rufus was clearly enjoying a somewhat recent discovery called *walking*, which he utilized with alarming speed and maddening regularity. Not only was this newfound ability clearly liberating, it also inspired him to explore every possible nook and cranny in the old stone house—often prompting him to stick his nose and his fingers in places they didn't belong.

Just this morning, as Candace combined freshly milled flour and olive oil for breadmaking, young Rufus had burned two of his chubby little fingers on the hot clay oven in the outer court. Before that, he had taken a hard fall off the bottom step, valiantly attempting to climb the steep stone staircase leading to the flat, open-air rooftop. Candace felt as if she had spent the entire morning chiding him, and it was obvious Rufus disagreed with her parental instructions, expressing his frustration with shrill, ear-splitting screams.

At this point, Candace was sorely tempted to follow suit.

Poor Alexander, wearying of his younger brother's inexorable antics, grew petulant and exasperated rather than helpful. Clambering up the rickety ladder propped against the wall at the far end of the house, he retreated to the hay-strewn loft above—his place of safety.

Candace didn't blame him. In fact, she was rather tempted to join him in his safe respite.

Suppressing a sigh of discouragement, Candace lifted baby Rufus off his active little feet, perching him carefully upon a large wooden chest. She knew she must examine the burns she had lovingly doctored earlier that morning but didn't relish the thought. Fiercely protective of his throbbing fingers,

Rufus would undoubtedly throw back his curly head and howl his angst at her unwanted intrusion.

Kneeling before her protesting son, Candace straightened at the sound of a firm, unexpected knock at the door.

It wasn't unusual for women of the Way to visit unannounced. Perhaps Tabitha had arrived to collect the garments Candace had been piecing together, honored to participate in her friend's ministry to the many poor. She could also think of a dozen different women who may have had an opportunity for a social call, although Candace couldn't help but consider the fact that this was far from an opportune time to entertain guests.

Releasing a sigh of frustration, Candace swept Rufus off the wooden chest, balancing him carefully on one hip. Detesting his captivity, he writhed and squirmed, but Candace held him firmly in place, refusing to be cowed. Her willful son *must* learn obedience—even if she lost her sanity in the process!

Unbolting the latch, Candace swung open the rough wooden door, wincing as it creaked upon ancient, protesting hinges. Catching her breath sharply, Candace's hand flew to her heart at the sight of the unexpected visitor on her doorstep.

A young, breathtakingly beautiful African woman stood poised on the threshold, slender arms outstretched, her radiant face alight with joyful exuberance. "Surprise!" she squealed, throwing her arms around a stunned Candace and eliciting whimpering protests from baby Rufus, who didn't appreciate being stifled in the arms of a complete stranger.

Drawing back in stunned silence, Candace's eyes

swept over the brightly clad, graceful form of her youngest sister.

"Kelila?"

"Did you miss me?" Kelila exclaimed, her shining brown eyes bright with enthusiasm. "Well, of course, you did!" she declared in answer to her own question. Sweeping up several heavy leather bags, she toted them into the house, dropping them rather gracelessly upon the earthen floor. "My," she exclaimed, her beautiful brown eyes taking in the small house with unveiled disappointment. "You live *here*?"

Still too shocked to be insulted, Candace cradled baby Rufus close to her breast. Instantly shy, the child buried his face in his mother's shoulder.

"Well?" Kelila declared, her radiant features awash with excitement. "Say something, sister!"

"I…" Candace faltered, attempting to locate her tongue. "I'm…speechless."

"Clearly!" Kelila laughed, the silvery sound filling the house. "I wanted to surprise you!"

"And you succeeded," Candace admitted, slowly regaining her composure. "Kelila, forgive me. And do pardon my manners—or lack thereof. You simply gave me a terrible shock."

"A terrible shock?" Kelila repeated, her dark eyes dancing in merriment. "I was aiming for a *delightful surprise*, but oh well. Maybe next time!"

Next time? Candace thought faintly.

"You must be wondering why I am here."

Candace nodded weakly, taking note of the quantity of heavy bags her sister had lugged into the house. Now they lay strewn upon the narrow, lower level of the small house, near the threshold.

Clearly, this was no brief visit or social call. Her sister intended to stay...and by the looks of her baggage, possibly forever!

"So why am I here? Well, I missed my sister, that's why!" Kelila declared in her characteristically exuberant tone. "And I longed to meet my beautiful nephews!" she added, pinching Rufus' ample cheek. "Surely I needn't a better reason than that!"

Somewhat startled by the zesty stranger's rapturous enthusiasm, Rufus again buried his face in his mother's comforting shoulder.

"You shy thing, you!" Kelila crooned, ignoring the fact that Rufus' entire little body stiffened when she attempted to rub his small back.

"Ah, yes, your nephews," Candace supplied, suddenly remembering her eldest son still hiding in the loft. "Alexander, come down, sweetheart. Come meet your aunt."

"Your *favorite* aunt!" Kelila exclaimed with an expressive flourish of her graceful hand.

Surprised by the appearance of this fascinating new relative and somewhat startled by the great commotion, Alexander peered nervously over the side of the loft.

"Come on down, sweetheart," Candace prodded him gently. "It's all right."

Hesitantly, Alexander clambered down the ladder, shyly presenting himself before his long-lost aunt.

While Kelila's attention was temporarily diverted toward her older nephew, Candace allowed herself a moment to observe her sister. It had been years since she'd last seen her. Kelila had been but a girl when Candace and her husband, Simon, relocated to Jerusalem. Now, as Kelila gathered her slightly resistant older nephew in eager arms, crooning about what a "big, strong boy" he was, Candace couldn't help but smile softly. Though she had blossomed into a lovely young woman, Kelila remained the same laughing, dancing girl she had always been.

Amused, Candace conceded that she and her sister presented a rather interesting study in contrast. Candace—quiet, elegant, and poised—had learned to shoulder responsibility and motherhood at a very early age, having many younger siblings to look after while growing up. Kelila, on the other hand, was the youngest of the large brood of children. Flighty and whimsical, Kelila was carefree, a bit spoiled, and breathtakingly beautiful. Her bubbling enthusiasm and zeal for life emphasized her dusky, exotic beauty. While growing up in Cyrene, Candace often felt forgotten and overshadowed the moment her lively younger sister walked into a room, effortlessly capturing the attention of all within a Roman mile of her delightful charm. The fact that their parents had coddled and doted on their youngest had only increased the tension in the sisters' somewhat strained relationship.

Breathing a silent prayer, Candace asked the Lord for His guidance in this situation. How would her husband feel about this lively young woman moving into his home? Would he even permit it? And how did *she* feel about sharing her home, her family, with an entitled younger sister?

For where envy and self-seeking exist, confusion and every evil thing are there... Candace caught her breath, for the wise words spoken by James, the brother of Christ, in last night's prayer meeting hit her as forcibly as a ton of bricks, searing her conscience and reminding her of her sacred calling in Christ. James had warned the believers against the dangers of envy and self-seeking, for such things were earthly and demonic. *But the wisdom that is from above is first pure,* James had explained, his gentle features glowing with conviction, *then peaceable, gentle, willing to yield, full of mercy and good fruits, without partiality and without hypocrisy...*

Sensing the Holy Spirit's gentle prompting, Candace examined the motives of her own heart, evaluating her response to Kelila's unexpected arrival. Convicted, she realized she had responded according to her former nature—in envy and selfishness.

Precious Lord, forgive me, Candace prayed, ashamed. *How long have I prayed for the salvation of my family, Lord? And then, when You led my dear little sister right to my doorstep, granting me the opportunity to share Your truth, did I rejoice in Your great mercy? No, I reacted in petty jealousy like a selfish, willful child! Forgive me, Righteous Father. Enable me to reflect Your unfailing love, to accept Your will with gladness.*

"Your children are beautiful, dear sister," Kelila declared with great feeling, interrupting Candace's silent confession. "I love them already!"

In that moment, a very strange thing happened. Candace's former feelings of bitterness, resentment, and envy evaporated as swiftly as the morning mists upon the River Jordan, replaced instead with a love so radiant, so pure, it nearly stole her breath away. Emptied of herself and her own contrary emotions, Candace realized she was now a worthy vessel, ready to be filled with the good fruits of the Spirit of God—ready to accept His calling, whatever it may be.

Smiling warmly, Candace took her sister's hand, giving it a gentle squeeze. "I am overjoyed to see you, dear one. We have quite a bit of catching up to do, don't we?"

Squealing her delight, Kelila threw her arms around her sister and baby Rufus, receiving the same unhappy reaction from the reticent child. Laughing merrily, Kelila drew back, her countenance shining like the sun. "I must admit, I was a bit concerned you wouldn't wish for me to stay."

"I am delighted to receive you, Kelila," Candace said, and she meant every word. "I shall speak with my husband as soon as he returns so we can make the proper arrangements."

"Arrangements?" Kelila repeated blankly.

"Obviously, we will need to discuss where you shall stay—"

"Oh, but I haven't money for room and board at an establishment," Kelila stammered, alarmed. "I'd planned to stay with you." Scanning the simple, one-room structure, she added with a hint of accusation, "I hadn't realized your home was so...cozy."

Smiling ruefully, Candace led her sister up two stone steps to the main level of the house. She supposed her modest home was a bit of a shock to Kelila, as the sisters had been raised in an elegantly pillared Greco-Roman style house in the illustrious city of Cyrene. Their father's magnificent house reflected the prestige of his great city—the chief city of North Africa, the capital of a Roman province, and a great intellectual center of learning boasting its own medical school and a thriving forum teeming with renowned philosophers and scholars. Abounding with marble temples, sacred tombs, a glorious amphitheater, and even a gymnasium, the great city was brimming with magnificent structures rivaling the breathtaking marble wonders of Delphi.

"Please, do be seated," Candace said invitingly, gesturing toward a simple wooden bench near the hearth.

Kelila did so, gingerly brushing at the rough wooden surface before seating herself.

Hiding a smile, Candace supposed the privileged young woman was concerned about her expensive garments. But she needn't have concerned herself—Candace was a fastidious housekeeper. To allow dust to accumulate upon any surface was unthinkable in her opinion.

Lowering herself to a comfortable mat on the floor across from her sister, Candace planted young Rufus in front of her. Shyly, he pushed himself up on chubby legs, clinging to his mother's hands. Clearly, he remained a bit uneasy about the vibrant newcomer seated primly on the bench across from him. Alexander stood politely behind his mother, one small hand resting upon her shoulder.

"So when is Simon expected to return?" Kelila asked rather artlessly. Clearly, she wished to settle the matter about staying in his home.

"Not until later today," Candace replied, "but you needn't worry, Kelila. Simon is a good man. He won't turn you away."

"I certainly hope not," Kelila huffed, her tone indicating that she was accustomed to getting her way.

"I must admit," Candace observed, dismissing her initial irritation, "I am surprised Father permitted

SEEKING THE TRUTH | 13

you to travel alone, all the way to Jerusalem."

Kelila waved a hand as if in dismissal. "Oh, you know Father never could deny my wishes," she teased, playfully batting her eyelashes. "I have always been his little angel."

Don't I know it, Candace thought, peeved. But she quickly repented, focusing her mind on the mission at hand. The Lord had faithfully presented her with this opportunity to win her sister, to share the truth about Jesus. She would not squander it by wallowing in envy or self-pity. True, rebellious thoughts were sure to crop up now and then, but Candace knew the Holy Spirit would enable her to dismiss negative emotions, staying her mind on the will of God instead.

"I am honored you traveled all this way just to visit us," Candace said warmly.

Kelila's dark eyes flickered slightly, revealing the briefest moment of vulnerability. But then she smiled brightly, expertly masking an obvious inner struggle. "I've always admired my big sister," she declared, opening elegantly clad arms with a dramatic flourish. "And now I'm here to stay!"

Candace tilted her head, studying Kelila's lovely profile. She and Kelila had never been close. So why this sudden urge to forsake the privilege and luxury of Kelila's childhood home to abide with a distant older sister?

True, Kelila had always been flighty and impulsive. Perhaps she had simply embarked upon this unlikely journey on a whim...

Somewhat disquieted, Candace sensed in her innermost spirit there was far more to it than that.

CHAPTER 2

Candace

Hearing the outside gate protesting on ancient hinges, Candace hurriedly met her husband in the outer court. She didn't wish to stun him by ushering him inside, where Kelila had already made herself quite at home, scattering her belongings throughout the entire house.

"Simon, how I missed you, my husband."

Simon was a stoic man of both African and Jewish heritage. Like Candace, he was reared in the thriving Hellenized community of Cyrene. He was a fair-minded, quiet man, and Candace had always admired the way he bore himself with strength, humility, and confidence.

Closing the short distance between them, Candace shifted Rufus' weight upon her hip, pausing nervously before her husband. "May I speak with you, Simon?"

Sensing that something was amiss, Simon's eyes betrayed questions even while his mouth curved in a slight smile as his young son held out both arms to him, squealing in delight. Taking Rufus in strong arms, Simon raised him high above his head, smiling fondly. Rufus, in turn, gurgled his delight.

Smiling at their antics, Candace touched her husband's arm. "Kelila showed up on our doorstep today."

Lowering his son and holding him close, Simon's eyes flickered with surprise. "Your youngest sister?"

"Yes. She has asked to stay with us."

Simon's jaw stiffened slightly. "For how long?"

"Indefinitely, I suppose."

Simon's expression was not encouraging. "You were never close."

"No," Candace admitted, her tone tinged with regret. "I suppose we weren't."

"Then why has she come?" There was no condemnation in his quiet tone, simply concern.

"Quite frankly," Candace admitted honestly, "I'm not sure. But I sense the Spirit's leading in this, Simon. I sense it with my entire being."

Simon's lips formed a grim line even as he rocked his young son. Raising solemn eyes to his wife, he sighed. "I would be less than honest if I said this situation was of my choosing."

"I understand, Simon," she said gently. Her husband was a very private man. To plant a boisterous and energetic young woman right in the midst of his home—his place of refuge—was almost unthinkable. "And you are the head of this household, Simon. Obviously, this decision belongs to you, and I will support your decision, whatever it may be. But I, too, would be less than honest if I said I didn't believe the Lord was leading in this."

Simon's countenance sobered, for Candace was not one to make such claims lightly. Trusting his wife implicitly, Simon knew she would never assign the Spirit's leading to a situation simply to obtain the result she desired. She was far too reverent to even consider such a thing.

Sensing his father's hidden tension, Rufus leaned toward his mother, arms open. Receiving the young child, Candace rocked him gently, planting a kiss on the top of his curly head while awaiting her husband's verdict.

"Where will she stay?" Simon finally asked, anxiously rubbing the back of his neck.

"Here, with us," Candace supplied.

"Well, yes, I gathered as much," Simon replied, releasing a sigh of frustration. "But is there room enough?"

"I've considered that," Candace said quickly. She'd had the entire afternoon to stew over it, eventually remembering to ask the Lord for guidance. "As a young woman, she should have a bit of privacy. I was thinking—"

"I suppose she could have the rooftop. We could construct a canopy, of sorts—"

"She can hardly sleep on the roof, Simon," Candace responded a bit more sharply than she intended.

"All large families utilize the rooftop for sleeping quarters. Half our neighbors' children bed down on the roof each night, under the shining stars."

"Simon," Candace reasoned, striving for patience, "can you imagine *my sister* sleeping on the roof? She is accustomed to a private suite with her own plush, canopy bed."

Simon was not amused. "Clearly, we are unable to provide such amenities."

"That's true," Candace acknowledged with a wry smile. "But I have considered the matter, and I believe I have a workable solution."

Simon met her gaze. "I'm listening."

"Alexander will gladly relinquish his loft. He's only recently begun using it, and I think he secretly misses sharing his brother's bedroll each night. We can section off a private bedchamber for ourselves using a partition like the one in Stephanos' house. That would allow for a bit of privacy for all of us."

Simon smiled slightly, stroking his clean-shaven chin. "I must admit, I have a rather difficult time imagining your prim little sister clambering up that rickety old ladder each night."

"Better that than on the roof, open to the elements," Candace supplied, her eyes sparkling with a hint of mischief. "Another thought to consider," she plunged ahead, her tone hopeful. "Should Kelila remain with us, wouldn't it be wonderful to have someone to watch the children when we engage in the Lord's work? After all, it is becoming increasingly hazardous—"

"You would entrust our children to her care?" Simon's wide eyes betrayed his alarm.

"Not right away," Candace said quickly, sensing her husband's disapproval. "I know she's always seemed terribly flighty and carefree, but she is quite intelligent—an avid learner when she sets her mind to it. I know she could learn to mind the children. It will be excellent training for her, as she is of age to marry and begin a family of her own."

"To marry and begin a family?" Simon repeated in shock. "Our little Kelila?"

"Just wait until you see her, Simon. She has blossomed into a lovely young woman in our absence."

Simon released another sigh, his eyes searching. "You really want to do this, my love?"

"Honestly, I'm not entirely sure what I want," Candace admitted humbly. "But what *I* want doesn't matter. What matters is what *God* wants, and I believe He has brought Kelila back into our lives for a purpose."

Shaking his head, Simon smiled faintly. Tipping his wife's delicate chin, he gazed deeply into her warm brown eyes. "It won't be easy, beloved," he admitted, warmed by her desire to honor the Lord above all else. "But if this is the will of God, He will provide the grace we need."

Reaching for her husband, Candace pulled him close, thanking God for such a wonderful man. Simon was humble and selfless, obedient to God above all else—even at the expense of his own comfort, his own convenience, his own pleasure. Silently, Candace resolved to show her husband how very much he meant to her, how very much she loved him. "You are too good, my husband."

"Only God is good," Simon said ruefully, kissing his wife's smooth forehead. "May He grant us *His* goodness as we navigate this unexpected new season." Considering his wife's vivacious sister, Simon's firm mouth curved in good humor. "Heaven knows we're going to need it."

***

Mary

"My lady!"

Turning a regal head, Mary's serene countenance brightened as her former maidservant emerged at the top of the broad marble staircase, hastening toward her with arms outstretched.

"Tabitha!" When the enthusiastic young woman enshrouded her with soft arms, Mary returned her embrace. Pulling away, Mary touched the top of Tabitha's modestly covered head, smiling warmly. "How often must I remind you to call me *Mary* now?" the young widow teased, adjusting Tabitha's flyaway head covering. "I am no longer your lady."

"And how often must I remind *you*," Tabitha shot back, hazel-green eyes flashing devotedly, "you will *always* be my lady?"

Mary had long since learned to mask uncooperative emotions. Even so, her lovely gray eyes flickered in response to Tabitha's unwavering loyalty. How she loved this dear little sister in Christ! "And you will always be like a daughter to me, beloved. Now, where is that dashing husband of yours?"

Tabitha laughed, allowing her former mistress to guide her toward one of the empty benches within the large Upper Room where the believers gathered for church meetings. Already, attendees were beginning to take their usual seats. "He is still downstairs, greeting the believers as they arrive for our prayer meeting."

"You look radiant," Mary commented, gracefully lowering herself onto the bench beside the young bride. "Married life suits you well."

Blushing slightly, Tabitha considered the blissful weeks she had shared with her fiery evangelist. He was so powerful, and yet, tender. She loved him fiercely. "Stephanos is everything I could have possibly hoped for in a husband, and so much more."

"You trusted the Lord to provide a worthy husband, beloved, and God often exceeds our wildest expectations."

Color deepening, Tabitha had to admit the Lord had most certainly done so. She was deeply in love with her husband and couldn't imagine life without him now. "Stephanos is excited to address the brethren tonight."

"He is an excellent teacher," Mary said honestly. "The way he brings the Scriptures to life is truly thrilling. I always leave his meetings quite convicted, and often with a whole new perspective."

Tabitha beamed, basking in Mary's praise of her husband, nearly bursting at the seams with pride for him.

"Does Stephanos continue to instruct the Hellenists at the Synagogue of the Freedmen?" Mary asked casually.

"He does," Tabitha replied slowly, her eyes flickering slightly as she attempted to mask her emotions with a somewhat veiled expression.

Mary recognized that look. "What troubles you, dear one?" she asked frankly, lowering her voice as believers poured into the Upper Room, talking in hushed, reverent tones, clearly eager to begin evening prayers and worship.

"I admire Stephanos' boldness, I really do," Tabitha said, leaning in a bit closer to avoid being overhead. "But I must confess, it frightens me at times, Mary. The way the religious leaders watch him, skulking in the shadows, hatred burning in their eyes…and that incorrigible Saul of Tarsus is the worst of them all! He never misses a meeting, glowering through the entire teaching when Stephanos dares to address the gathering."

Mary nodded her understanding.

"Do you still pray for that man?"

"For Saul?" Mary repeated, a faint smile playing at the corners of her soft mouth. "Of course, I do. Every day."

Feeling a stab of guilt, Tabitha clenched tightened fists in her lap. Would she *ever* possess Mary's faith? Just the thought of praying for that pompous Pharisee made her skin crawl!

"The Lord has placed a burden upon my heart for him," Mary expressed with great conviction. "For what purpose, I cannot know. But Saul is not beyond the Lord's reach, nor are his brethren, the Pharisees, or their religious rivals, the Sadducees."

Tabitha harrumphed her bitter skepticism.

"It's true," Mary said, smiling at her former maid's ire. "We've already seen many Pharisees embrace the Way, haven't we?"

"Only those humble enough to admit they need a Savior," Tabitha conceded grudgingly. "But I hardly think Saul falls under that category. He considers himself holier than all the ancient saints combined!"

"He is a brilliant scholar. Unfortunately, when such men do not have the Holy Spirit, pride often rages unchecked," Mary acknowledged sadly. "Both Nicodemus and Joseph of Arimathea say he is being groomed for the Sanhedrin."

"God help us should that ever happen!" Tabitha said forcefully, drawing the attention of several chatting believers nearby. Color deepening, she lowered her tone. "Isn't Saul far too young to become a member of the Sanhedrin?"

"Not necessarily," Mary said, recalling a recent conversation she had shared with Nicodemus. She, too, had voiced the same question. "Apparently, it's preferable for men to reach the age of forty before joining the Sanhedrin, while the president of the Sanhedrin must be at least fifty years of age. And though anyone under the age of eighteen is forbidden to join the Council for any reason, young men are received if they show exceptional promise in their studies of the Law and the sacred texts."

"Well, I suppose we needn't concern ourselves yet," Tabitha said, unwilling to concede defeat. "Saul can do nothing unless a current member of the Council dies."

"Or resigns," Mary reminded her. "Even so, we needn't fear. God is in control, Tabitha. Nothing can happen without His permission."

"I wish I had your faith," Tabitha admitted for what felt like the umpteenth time. "Hostility against the Way increases with every passing day. I fear for those I love. Even though I remember to place them in God's hands, I snatch them right out of His grasp the moment a threat arises."

"You are not alone in that," Mary assured her, patting Tabitha's knee in a motherly fashion. "Thankfully, God's mercies are new every morning. He knows our frame, Tabitha, and He loves us despite our weaknesses. When you begin to fear for those you love, simply entrust them to God again. And again. Faith is a daily exercise."

Acknowledging the truth of Mary's words, Tabitha's gaze flickered toward a familiar, cloaked woman emerging at the top of the stairs, hastening toward a lone bench at the back of the Upper Room. She had been attending meetings for quite some time now, shrouded in silence and secrecy. "It's people like *her* who most concern me. Who is she *really*? Why does she continue to show up at these meetings, disguised as a pauper, secretive and reclusive?"

Mary remained unperturbed. "I'm glad she has found solace here."

"And how can you be so certain it is solace she seeks? She could just as easily be a spy for the San-hedrin, or even the Romans!"

"I believe she is sincere," Mary responded, offer-ing the evasive woman a genuine smile from across the room.

"As always, she is here on the heels of the Pass-over, a festival season. And then she will disappear for several weeks, cropping up again at Pentecost. Not once has she bothered to disclose anything more than her name—Sarah—a name that is most likely an alias."

"She doesn't owe us an explanation of her past or present circumstances, Tabitha," Mary reminded her gently.

"True believers are open with one another, not distant and aloof."

"You don't like her," Mary observed sadly.

"I don't *trust* her," Tabitha responded vehemently, feeling somewhat reprimanded. "There's a differ-ence."

"I am not asking you to trust her, dear one," Mary said, gently squeezing Tabitha's stiff shoulder. "I'm asking you to trust in *God*. He is the one guiding all who set foot here, regardless of their motives or initial intent."

Conscience pricked, Tabitha watched as Mary rose gracefully, purposing to welcome the believ-ers milling about their meeting place. Glancing down, Tabitha noticed her own hands still balled into white-knuckled fists in her lap. Embarrassed, she swiftly released them. Lifting her gaze, it swept toward the unwelcome stranger once more, seated alone at the back of the gathering. Slender brows drawing together fiercely, Tabitha committed the woman into the hands of God, just as Mary advised. God already knew everything about this woman, even if *she* didn't. And He was fully capable of drawing her to Himself.

Perhaps there was a purpose in her presence.

CHAPTER 3

Tabitha

Opening the door upon protesting hinges, Stephanos stepped back with a dramatic flourish of his arm. "After you, my lady," he teased, allowing his pretty young wife to step into their modest house before him.

Striding somewhat stiffly past her husband, Tabitha removed her shawl and tossed it rather heedlessly upon a convenient peg hanging behind the door. She didn't look up when Stephanos strode into the house, closing the door softly behind him. Presenting a rigid back, Tabitha loosened her long honey-gold braid, raking slender fingers through lush, wavy tresses.

Noting his wife's obvious chagrin, Stephanos hid a knowing smile. "You seem upset, my dear," he quipped, his tone tinged with amusement rather than concern.

"Upset?" Tabitha muttered, refusing him the courtesy of turning around. "Now why would I be *upset?*"

"Tell me." Reaching for her shoulders, Stephanos felt her resistance as he turned her slowly around to face him. Lowering his head to look directly into her flashing eyes, he caressed the gentle curve of her face. "If I didn't know better, I'd assume you were dismayed with your husband," he teased.

Folding stubborn arms across her chest, Tabitha resisted his charm. "You certainly caused quite a stir back there, didn't you?"

"During my instruction at the synagogue?"

Ruffled, Tabitha returned his inquiry with a well-deserved glare, followed by stony silence.

"I always cause a stir," Stephanos teased, lightly running his hand over her golden hair. "So what's the problem?"

"The *problem*," Tabitha huffed rather hotly, "is the fact that you don't even recognize the problem!"

"All right," he conceded, drawing her a bit closer despite her stout resistance. "Then tell me about this problem I'm not seeing."

Tabitha rolled her eyes. "You baited the religious leaders. Again!"

"I'm not following."

"I shouldn't have to spell this out for you!" Tabitha exclaimed, exasperated. "Stephanos, you place yourself in harm's way every time you challenge Saul of Tarsus or his colleagues! Can't you see that?"

"I didn't challenge Saul," Stephanos stated simply. "He challenged the gospel, and I defended it."

"Yes, you *defended* it," Tabitha snapped. "With the subtlety of fire and brimstone! You infuriated every Pharisee within ten miles of that synagogue!"

"Well, then, I've certainly outdone myself this

time."

"Stephanos! It's not funny!" Shaking free from his grasp, Tabitha stormed away, miffed.

"Tabitha." Stephanos sighed, following her as she stalked over to her loom. He watched her as she seated herself behind the large loom, rummaging through a wicker basket brimming with colorful fabric. "You know my calling. I cannot forsake it."

"And I'm not asking you to!" Tabitha shot back, meeting his gaze in challenge. "But must you be so bold? So brash? Must you raise the ire of every Pharisee and Sadducee in the city? We have enemies enough, Stephanos. Must we create even more?"

Releasing a sigh of frustration, Stephanos went to her. Kneeling before her, he took her hand. When she attempted to withdraw it, he clasped it even tighter, holding it captive between his own. His gaze traveling over her taut form, Stephanos whispered poignantly, "I didn't expect this to happen so soon."

"What?" Tabitha demanded hotly.

"Our first fight," Stephanos quietly responded.

His words were like a hammer blow, snapping Tabitha's rebellious thoughts into focus. She reached for him, hot tears springing to her eyes.

Gathering his wife in strong arms, Stephanos rocked back on his heels, cradling her like a disconsolate child. "It's all right," he whispered softly, burying his face in her neck. "It's all right, love."

Dashing at her tears, Tabitha drew back slightly. She wanted to look into those dark, telling eyes of his. "If I didn't love you so fiercely, I wouldn't care. I wouldn't care what might happen to you."

"I know," he whispered into hair.

"I fear for you."

"I know that, too," he said gently. "Trust in God, beloved."

Cupping his clean-shaven face, Tabitha looked directly into his eyes. "Couldn't you host private meetings at Mary's villa—without drawing the religious leaders' attention?"

"I must obey God, Tabitha, and I believe He has called me to the Synagogue of the Freedmen."

"But why?"

"Does God owe us an explanation?"

"Well, no," Tabitha admitted, draping her arms lightly around her husband's neck. "But it sure would be nice to have one."

Stephanos released a low chuckle.

"It's so hard to trust when you don't know what lies ahead," she confessed, disheartened.

"But isn't that what faith is all about? Trust in the face of uncertainty? Faithful obedience to God without demanding an explanation?"

Releasing a long sigh of resignation, Tabitha leaned forward, her own forehead pressed against her husband's. "Why is it so hard to trust?"

"Faith is like any other skill—the more we practice, the more it grows. Consider this a blessed opportunity to trust our faithful God even more."

Gently raking her fingers through her husband's jet-black hair, Tabitha's mouth tipped a bit ruefully. "You always have an answer for everything."

"You look unsure," Stephanos teased, his dark eyes sparking mischievously. "How can I convince you? Shall I prove I have the answer to cure your troubled countenance? Because I do."

"Oh, do you?" Tabitha returned, enjoying his playful banter. "And what exactly do you propose, good sir?"

"Maybe something like this." Pulling his young wife even closer, Stephanos cupped her face in one strong hand, kissing her deeply.

Temporarily distracted while lost in a sea of pleasurable sensations in the arms of her beloved, Tabitha resolved to dismiss her husband's misdeeds.

For now.

***

Midway through her supper preparations that evening, Tabitha noticed Stephanos seated on a straw mat on the floor, parchment paper spread out over the chest before him, a writing utensil poised above a small clay pot of ink.

Feeling contented after sharing a cozy afternoon with Stephanos, Tabitha restrained herself from hounding her husband with questions about his mysterious doings. Even so, she couldn't help but peer over her shoulder several times as she poked at the fire in the hearth, stirred a pot hanging over the licking flames, and reached for two simple stone mugs from the shelf.

Passing by him for the third time, Tabitha feigned disinterest even as she attempted to decipher the flourishing script upon the parchment page. Was he composing a letter? Writing a sermon? Making notes pertaining to his responsibilities as a deacon? She couldn't be sure.

Slipping casually past him, Tabitha returned to the small area designated as her cooking space. She could have also utilized the simple clay oven in the outer court but had decided against it. After all, she preferred her husband's company indoors this evening, and the neat little vent behind the oven was quite effective at channeling the haze from the cookfire outside.

Glancing toward her husband once more, she realized Stephanos' gaze rested enigmatically upon her. Lips tipping upward in amusement, Stephanos tapped his writing instrument upon the large chest before him. "Go ahead."

"Go ahead and what?" Tabitha responded a bit tersely.

"Ask me what I'm doing. I know it's killing you."

Toting a tray of fresh flatbread across the room, Tabitha dropped it upon the small wooden table. "Why should I care what you're doing?"

"Because your curiosity is relentless and insatiable." Stephanos grinned, entertained by her antics.

A sharp retort teetered upon the tip of her tongue when Solomon's unwelcome proverb danced across the forefront of Tabitha's mind. *Better to dwell in a corner of a housetop than in a house shared with a contentious woman...* Inwardly resolving not to quarrel twice in a day, Tabitha bit back her irritation and responded with a forced smile. "It's none of my concern, dear husband."

"Oh? Then you haven't been wondering what I'm up to?"

Biting her lower lip, Tabitha resisted the urge to deny it. After all, to do so would be dishonest. "The thought may have crossed my mind a few times," she admitted, swooping down beside her husband on the hard-packed earth. "So?"

"So what?" Stephanos' eyes glinted with mischief.

"*So...*what are you working on?"

"I thought it was none of your concern?"

"Stephanos!" Tabitha swatted his solid shoulder. "Tell me!"

"Well, I thought you'd never ask," Stephanos said rather ceremoniously. Lifting the sheet of thick parchment, he explained, "I'm writing a letter to my father."

"Your father?" Tabitha repeated blankly. "You keep in touch?"

"Well, *I* keep in touch," Stephanos replied wanly. "It's a bit of a routine we've established. I write him, then he returns the letters to me, the seal unbroken. I've come to think of it as a game of sorts. Eventually, he'll soften. If not, curiosity will surely take its toll and he'll open my letter simply to appease it."

Sensing the pain behind her husband's sparkling humor, Tabitha touched his knee. "I am so very sorry, my husband."

Placing his hand over hers, Stephanos smiled. "All in God's good timing."

"What do you write about?"

"I share the gospel. I beseech him to examine the ancient texts, comparing the Messianic prophecies against the life and message of Jesus Christ."

Tabitha's eyes softened in understanding.

"And then I tell him about life here. I've written to him all about you, beloved, not that he's ever read it. And I tell him about average, everyday things. My prayer is that, in time, he will accept the truth."

"Have you considered visiting him? I could go with you—"

"I would love nothing more than to take you to Athens, to introduce you to my gentle mother and rather belligerent father. But he's made it perfectly clear I am not to set foot upon his estate until I relinquish my faith in this 'bizarre new cult' I've embraced," Stephanos explained with a knowing smile. His expression sobered a moment later. "On those terms, I may never see him again."

Tabitha took his hand. "Don't lose heart, my husband. We will pray about this together every single day without fail. No one is beyond our Savior's reach. And He knows exactly what it will take to soften even the hardest of hearts. I believe your father—and your mother—will be won, Stephanos. As you said, all in God's good timing."

With a tender smile, Stephanos tucked a stray tress of golden hair behind her ear. "Amen to that, dear one."

CHAPTER 4

Mary

"I knew his father had disinherited him when he became a believer," Tabitha said, shaking her head in dismay. "But I hadn't the slightest idea Stephanos was hurting so. He's always been so confident and optimistic. This is the first time he's even mentioned his father since I've known him."

"I don't believe Stephanos has ever been close to his father," Mary supplied sadly, strolling arm-in-arm with Tabitha as they traversed the broad, palm-lined avenue just beyond her exquisite villa. The pair had slipped out a quiet back exit to share this private conversation after Tabitha completed her allotted tasks in Mary's impressive house. "If my memory serves me well, Stephanos' education was his father's utmost concern."

"His father sent him away to study in Alexandria at the feet of Philo and the world's most renowned philosophers," Tabitha agreed. "I don't think he invested much time in establishing a relationship with his son."

"A pity," Mary said, considering her own good-natured, easygoing son, John Mark. She treasured their relationship and couldn't imagine forfeiting the mutual trust and companionship they shared. "Stephanos' father hasn't the faintest idea what he has lost."

"May the Lord grant both Stephanos and his father the gift of restoration," Tabitha said with great feeling. "And even more than that, may his father be restored to the Heavenly Father, accepting the truth about Jesus."

"I shall join you in prayer for this, dear one," Mary said, sensing how very important this was to her maid. "The Father desires restoration even more than we do, though that fact is hard to fathom, at times."

"Thank God for His mercy," Tabitha murmured, deep in thought. "Stephanos told me his father, a wealthy Hellenized Jew firmly established in Athens, has always gravitated toward the Greek way of thought. Though he's proud of his Jewish heritage, he leads a very secular lifestyle. As we spoke about this, I could see the torment upon Stephanos' features. As an evangelist, it must pain him terribly—leading hundreds to Christ each day, yet unable to reach his own father."

"I can see how that could be very difficult for him," Mary said honestly, deeply saddened for Stephanos. She had always admired his stalwart courage and his passion for the truth, but now her admiration for him heightened even more. Despite his own secret pain, Stephanos had embraced his calling wholeheartedly, unwilling to allow regret or self-pity to hinder the Spirit's leading.

"Frankly, my lady, I'm terribly disappointed in myself," Tabitha confessed, her lovely countenance falling as she considered her own shortcomings.

"What do you mean, beloved?" Mary asked, sensing Tabitha's inner struggle.

Pausing mid-stride, Tabitha turned to face her former mistress, her expression etched with remorse. "I am married to the most wonderful man in the world, my lady. But what kind of wife am I? We have been married for over a month, and I hadn't the slightest idea he was in pain."

"You couldn't have known, Tabitha."

"But couldn't I?" Tabitha demanded, shaking her head in disgust. "Had the roles been reversed, had I been the one silently suffering, Stephanos would have known. Stephanos always senses my secret moods. He always seems to know what I'm thinking, how I'm feeling."

"Beloved, I mean no disrespect, but I think the entire world can sense how you're feeling. One needn't be a seer to do so!"

Tabitha stared at Mary dubiously.

"Now don't look at me like that!" Laughing fondly, Mary squeezed Tabitha's arm. "You are a passionate woman, and I love that about you—and so does your adoring husband. One could never accuse you of hypocrisy," she added, her gray eyes sparkling with humor. "You say it like it is."

"I suppose Stephanos would agree I could be a bit less…passionate, as you have so graciously labeled it," Tabitha admitted, amused. "But concerning his father, I do wish I had been more sensitive. I'm frustratingly observant, often distracted by everything.

But apparently, I was so concerned about my own feelings, I didn't even realize my husband was hurting. I'm determined to amend that fault."

"It is a noble aspiration, Tabitha," Mary agreed kindly. "The fact that you desire to become even more sensitive to your husband's needs demonstrates your love for him."

Tabitha managed a wobbly smile as the two women resumed their stroll, arm-in-arm once again. "Thank you for listening, Mary. I'm glad Stephanos allowed me to share this with you. I know you will be praying for him."

"And this is what the body of Christ is for," Mary reminded her. "We must never forget to encourage one other, to pray for each other, to hold each other accountable. Thank you for coming to me, Tabitha."

"A strange thing has happened," Tabitha mused. "When I discovered Stephanos writing a letter to his father, the Holy Spirit brought something to my attention."

"Oh?" Mary asked, her interest piqued.

"I have an uncle in Joppa—the only living relative I know about. I vaguely remember him, but I was a very small child when we visited his estate."

"What was he like?"

Tabitha suppressed a mischievous smile. "He was a bearded man with suspicious eyes and disapproving features. He never smiled."

"Ah," Mary said, understanding. "Not the friendly sort, then?"

"Far from it," Tabitha laughed. "In fact, I was afraid of him at the time! He seemed to believe the entire world was after his money, and he jealously guarded his assets. I don't think he had any friends."

Mary nodded, saddened. "And you believe the Holy Spirit brought him to mind?"

"I think so," Tabitha confessed. "I haven't even considered him since childhood. Quite frankly, I'd forgotten he even existed. But I think I should write to him, sharing the gospel message."

"An excellent idea," Mary agreed. "This is how we preach the gospel unto all the nations."

"Last night, Simon Peter's instruction confirmed this for me. Do you remember when he said those who forsake the needs of their own families deny the faith by their actions?"

"I do," Mary consented. "It is a sobering thought."

"It certainly sobered me!" Tabitha confessed. "I never even considered my uncle's greatest need—the need for forgiveness, for acceptance of God's free gift of salvation."

"I'm proud of you, Tabitha," Mary said sincerely, her own heart warmed by her maid's desire to serve the Lord. "It's easy to sit idly by, passively waiting for opportunities to simply fall into one's lap. But you actively seek ways to bless others, heeding the Spirit's gentle prompting."

Tabitha managed a wobbly smile. "You'll never know how much I've learned by your example, my lady. Your faithfulness has been the greatest testimony to me."

"Praise God for His mercy," Mary murmured as they neared the main gate at the entrance of the large house. "Now I suppose I must return you to your husband! He's going to be wrapping up his work any moment now, and I imagine he's ready to spend a quiet evening with his wife."

Tabitha scarcely heard her. "I think I will write

that letter tonight. If I put it off too long, it's highly likely I'll talk myself out of it."

"Better yet," Mary suggested, "do it now. I'm sure your husband won't mind if you join him in the *bibliotheca*."

Tabitha's expression betrayed a moment of panic.

Chuckling softly in amusement, Mary squeezed her shoulder. "The Lord will provide the words, dear one."

Tabitha released a nervous chuckle. "I certainly hope so, because I haven't the slightest idea what to say!"

"He most certainly will, beloved," Mary promised. "And you needn't fear. God promises us His Word will not return void. Only *He* knows the harvest of blessing stemming from your obedience in this simple act of faith."

CHAPTER 5

Candace

Bending to draw steaming rounds of flatbread from her indoor clay oven, Candace nearly sent the tray clattering to the ground at the sound of a bright, unexpected voice right at her elbow.

"So what are we going to do today?"

Taking a swift moment to still her annoyance and regain her composure, Candace straightened, turning to face her exuberant young sister. Lifting the tray of loaves in a telltale manner, Candace managed a smile, attempting to match the brightness in Kelila's tone. "As you can see, I am preparing our breakfast. It should be ready shortly."

"Ah, *breakfast*." The distaste upon Kelila's lovely features was evident as her brown eyes drifted toward a pot of lentils resting upon the one small table. "Lentils and flatbread again?"

Suppressing her irritation, Candace offered another convincing smile. "I know it isn't fancy, but it's what we can afford."

"I hate lentils."

"So you've mentioned." *Several times*, Candace wished to add. "I do apologize, Kelila, but since I wasn't expecting your arrival, I didn't have time to purchase anything else. I plan to visit the market as soon as possible. Perhaps we'll find something you like there."

"I certainly do hope so," Kelila commented, further raising her sister's ire.

"Did you sleep well?" Candace asked cheerfully, dismissing her mounting irritation as she crossed back toward the oven. Reaching overhead, she secured several clay mugs from a high wooden shelf.

"How could I, rolling around in all that hay and straw? How your poor son ever managed to sleep in that miserable little loft is beyond me."

Holding her tongue with great effort, Candace resisted the urge to point out that Kelila had certainly slept in *late* for someone claiming to be so uncomfortable. The young woman slept in every morning, giving little thought to the fact that there were important chores to be done long before sunup. Not once had she offered any assistance.

Though Kelila had arrived only a few short days ago, the time had proven quite eye-opening for Candace. Despite her alluring façade of vibrant charm, Kelila was thoughtless and self-centered. She was unhappy with the accommodations. She was unhappy with the food. She was unhappy with her sister's "monotonous" lifestyle. She was unhappy with *everything*.

Sighing, Candace silently repented for allowing her thoughts to travel down the same familiar path again. At home, Kelila was accustomed to being waited upon by a slew of doting servants. Until now, her days had been spent catering to her own desires and pleasures. How could she, Candace, possibly expect an entitled young woman without the love and knowledge of Christ to conduct herself in any other way? No, it was now *her* responsibility to show Kelila a new way, the living Way. Perhaps, in time, Kelila would see there was far more to life than shallow self-indulgence, vain entertainments, and fleeting pleasures.

"So...you didn't answer my question," Kelila pointed out, interrupting Candace's thoughtful musings.

Lugging an armload of clay mugs toward the large stone jar of fresh water near the door, Candace watched as Kelila seated herself upon the plushest mat at the low table, reaching for a piece of steaming flatbread. Biting back the urge to point out that the family had not yet joined them, nor had they blessed the food, Candace forced another smile.

"I apologize," she responded again. "What question, Kelila?"

"What are we going to do today?" Kelila asked around a large bite of warm flatbread.

"Oh," Candace stammered, setting the clay mugs carefully upon the table. She was certain Kelila wasn't going to appreciate her itinerary for the day. "Well, there's the housework, of course. And I must finish stitching up several garments, as my good friend, Tabitha, plans to pick them up soon. I must also refill our fresh water supply, tend to the supper preparations, and—"

Kelila clicked her tongue chidingly, her brown eyes round with disbelief. "Work, work, work! All you ever do is *work*. How do you bear the drudgery?"

Candace stared at her sister in dismay. She had never considered her life a drudge—until now. "It's part of running a disciplined household, Kelila. Certain things must be done, and these tasks won't perform themselves."

"Why don't you have servants to do all the dull work, like Father and that rich lady you were telling me about?"

"Mary?" Candace asked blankly.

"Whatever her name is. The one who holds those secret meetings in her mansion."

"Yes, Mary," Candace affirmed. "And they are not secret meetings. Anyone who so desires can attend."

"*She* has servants. Why don't you?"

Cheeks warming at her sister's interrogation, Candace replied quietly, "We can't afford servants, Kelila." Nor would she want them even if they could. She was perfectly capable of keeping her own modest home. Besides that, she *enjoyed* housework. She enjoyed serving her husband and children, preparing delicious, healthy meals to sustain them, and keeping a neat, tidy house. She rejoiced in these important tasks the Lord had given her. She delighted in the company of her family. Since when did it become a *drudge* to love and nurture one's own family?

"Well, if you had servants, you wouldn't have to do all this work yourself. They could do the cooking, the sweeping, the sewing, and whatever else it is you do all day. Then, you would be free to do as you pleased!" Kelila announced presumptuously, her expression suggesting Candace at least consider her great wisdom.

"I *am* doing as I please," Candace responded a bit more tersely than she had intended. Placing the mugs on a low stand beside the stone jar and filling each one with fresh water, she added quickly, "It is a pleasure to serve my family."

"Spoken like a dull housewife." Kelila grinned.

"And what do *you* enjoy doing, Kelila?" Candace kept her eyes fixed upon her work, not wishing to betray her annoyance.

"Oh, anything at all, really," the young woman responded dreamily.

Anything besides being helpful, that is, Candace thought a bit snidely.

"I love the chariot races," Kelila mused, taking another bite of flatbread.

"The chariot races?" Candace repeated, alarmed.

Kelila laughed out loud at the panic crossing her sister's face. "Don't tell Father. He'd look worse than you do if he ever found out!"

"You go without his consent?"

"Oh, you wouldn't understand. You were always the obedient one, bowing and scraping at Father's every wish."

Candace arched a slender brow. Was that really what her sister thought of godly obedience?

Kelila rushed ahead, oblivious of her sister's dismay. "The races are delicious fun! I just love the rush of the flying chariots, the screams of the cheering mob. I love the excitement that sets my blood afire!"

Candace realized she was still standing near the stone jar, mugs in hand, mouth open. Promptly closing her mouth, she attempted to regain her composure. "The races are no place for an unchaperoned young woman." *Or for a woman with morals of any kind,* she added silently.

"You sound like Father," Kelila laughed merrily.

Candace wasn't surprised her father disapproved. No decent Jew or proselyte would be caught dead in a Roman arena or stadium. The Roman brand of entertainment was debauchery to its very core, glorifying violence and licentiousness of every kind, with every imaginable carnality upon full display. There was something for everyone in the Roman arenas, regardless of how base or depraved their craving might be.

"Oh, don't look so scandalized!" Kelila laughed, her amusement evident. "I doubt you'll have anything at all to worry about *here.*"

"What do you mean, here?" Candace asked, carrying several full mugs to the table.

"There's nothing to do in Jerusalem!"

"Jerusalem is a beautiful city," Candace said, feeling somewhat defensive. She didn't dare tell her sister about Herod's theater nor the Hippodrome near the Synagogue of the Freedmen.

"Beautiful, yes. But interesting? Not at all."

"I must take you to see the Temple, Kelila. It is truly breathtaking—"

"And that's just what I mean!" Kelila complained, exasperated. "That's all anyone cares about in Jerusalem—the Temple *this*, the Temple *that*. Blah, blah, blah. Who cares about a dull old building filled with gloomy priests and Pharisees sporting depressing black robes? Jerusalem is terribly stern and religious. It *is* the holy city, after all."

Candace said nothing as she brought the last few mugs of water to the table. Should she do so, her tone would surely reveal her indignation.

"I think I shall go for a walk!" Kelila popped up unexpectedly from her mat, satisfied after devouring several loaves of flatbread.

"A walk?" Candace stared at her blankly.

"I'll just die of boredom if I sit around here all day," Kelila exclaimed, rolling her eyes in an exaggerated manner.

"But...but what about breakfast?" Candace stammered, resisting the urge to point out she'd have little opportunity for boredom should she decide to make herself useful.

"I'll positively *die* if I must ingest one more despicable lentil," Kelila declared, her tone dramatic. "Besides, I'm not hungry."

I wouldn't be either, had I consumed half the bread on the table, Candace thought, miffed.

"I'll be back later." Leaning in, Kelila planted a prim kiss on Candace's cheek.

"But where will you go?"

"Who knows?" Kelila grinned, her striking features shining with anticipation. "It's a beautiful day, is it not? The possibilities are endless!"

Candace watched, dismayed, as Kelila swooped out of the quiet house like an exotic bird escaping the confines of a steel cage.

Oh, Lord, You're going to have to help me! Releasing a sigh of frustration, Candace raised soft eyes heavenward, shaking her head with a wry smile. *I imagine that girl is going to test the validity of my conversion!*

CHAPTER 6

Kelila

Tearing aside her bothersome shawl, Kelila tilted back her head, drinking in the deliciously warm rays of sunshine upon her face. She was glad her sister had remained barricaded in that tiny house of hers, doting on her solemn husband and noisy children. Had Candace accompanied her this morning, she would have surely delivered a sound lecture about the indecency of a lady removing her modest covering in public! Grinning impishly, Kelila wadded up the colorful shawl, stuffing it rather carelessly inside the elegant, gem-studded girdle accentuating her slender waist.

Glorying in her newly acquired freedom, Kelila spread her arms as if preparing to take flight. Spinning around in a wide circle, her bright eyes absorbed the splendor of her illustrious surroundings. She was completely lost in the bustle and cacophony swiftly following a Jewish festival, which is exactly what she wished for. She wanted to lose herself entirely, leaving her troubles forever behind her. She wanted to bask in the bright morning sunshine, to savor the complete and utter freedom now at her disposal! As men and women jostled past her, far too busy to wonder why a beautiful young woman spun about like a carefree child, Kelila lifted her gaze, drinking in her glorious new surroundings. The paved city streets remained swollen with pedestrians, both pilgrims and natives of Judea. Most of the traveling proselytes milling about the congested streets wouldn't return to their native lands until after Pentecost, and Kelila was dazzled by the numerous nationalities represented among the throngs, all donning the exotic traditional garb of their various homelands.

Craning her neck, Kelila drew in a sharp intake of breath at the picturesque sight that met her gaze. Just ahead, the magnificent Temple complex towered into the heavens, enclosed by myriad marble courts and seas upon seas of breathtaking Corinthian pillars, each one boasting richly colored paints and gleaming golden-topped crowns. The stunning Temple proper, crowned in glistening gold, reflected the morning sunlight like a dazzling heavenly beacon, nearly blinding the passers-by on the streets below. Enshrouded by towering walls, breathtaking stone arches, elegantly tiled, red-roofed porticoes, and layer upon layer of polished stone staircases, the complex was truly wondrous to behold. Though she'd never admit it to Candace—or anyone else, for that matter—Kelila was amazed.

I must confess, I've never seen anything quite like it, Kelila thought, nearly skipping with eagerness as she approached the vicinity of the sacred Temple.

The pedestrians going about their business, frequenting the crowded shops and vendors dotting the narrow streets below the steep walls enclosing the entire Temple complex, appeared like tiny ants in comparison with the enormity of the Jewish compound. Even the famed Temple of Zeus, the crowning jewel among the many religious shrines of Cyrene, paled in comparison, Kelila thought. Grinning, she decided that the garish house of worship dedicated to the mythological ruler of the pagan deities now seemed drab and unimpressive compared to this shining wonder of Jerusalem.

Passing beneath an impressive stone arch, Kelila meandered among brightly canopied booths and tightly clustered market stalls, browsing through the merchandise. Merchants cried out in shrill tones, hawking their wares and snagging the attention of aimless shoppers. But Kelila remained singularly unimpressed. The sea of merchandise stretching before her catered to religious Jews. *Like everything else in this prudish city,* Kelila thought, annoyed, noting the stacks upon stacks of crates imprisoning cooing doves to be purchased for sacrifice. Makeshift pens erected by greedy sellers lined the streets, in which ritually acceptable lambs and goats bleated in desperate, melancholy tones. She hadn't the slightest interest in the commerce of this Temple district.

Turning away in disgust, a booth near the end of the cluttered alleyway suddenly caught her eye. Stacked upon wooden tables, wicker baskets brimming with fresh produce glistened in the morning sunlight, both tantalizing and inviting. Stomach churning at the sight of fresh pomegranates and candied figs, Kelila drew near the booth.

Pausing before the table heavy-laden with delicious fruits, Kelila glanced discreetly about her surroundings. The seller was nowhere to be seen. Shouldn't a shopkeeper know better than to leave this delectable treasure trove unguarded?

With a prick of conscience, Kelila dared one last glance over her shoulder as she reached for a plump, scarlet-tinged pomegranate.

Firm fingers closed upon her hand, and Kelila released a sharp, frightened gasp, her gaze snapping forward. Had she been caught in the act of swiping a pomegranate from the merchant's table? What did these blamed Judeans do to thieves, anyway? Imprison them? Lash them? Chop off their hands?

Shuddering, Kelila's terrified gaze fell upon a homely, bearded young man standing across the table. His light brown eyes widened in horror at the shocking realization that he had grasped a woman's delicate hand rather than a pomegranate.

Snatching her hand away, Kelila rewarded the young man with an incriminating glare.

"Pardon me, miss," the young man stammered, clearly caught off guard. "Apparently, I was paying very little attention."

"*Apparently*," Kelila retorted even as relief flooded her entire being. "You are not the shopkeeper, then?"

"The shopkeeper?" the young man repeated blankly. Clearly thrown by this unveiled woman's dusky beauty, the stranger cleared his throat in discomfort. "Oh, no. No, I'm just looking to purchase some produce to distribute among the needy families in my district."

Kelila arched a sardonic brow. "Ah, and I now

stand in the presence of a handsome philanthropist?"

Nervously clearing his throat, the young man averted his gaze. "Um…ah, no, actually. I am simply a deacon. I serve the church located here in Jerusalem."

"The church?" Kelila repeated, tilting her head in great interest. She'd heard her sister and brother-in-law use the strange term repeatedly over the last few days. It was rather annoying. "Do tell me more about this church!"

Flustered, the deacon fleetingly met her gaze.

"If I didn't know better, I'd think you were afraid of me," Kelila teased with a hint of seemingly harmless flirtation. "You can look at me, you know. I promise I won't bite."

Blushing deeply, the young deacon lifted his gentle gaze. He hadn't wished to show any disrespect by gazing upon the stunning beauty of this bold, unveiled woman. But now she was asking questions about the church! Closing his eyes, he groaned inwardly. As uncomfortable as he felt, he knew he mustn't remain silent now.

"We meet each evening at the largest villa located near the southwest corner of the Upper City," the young man nervously explained, wondering what his fellow deacons would think if this exotic beauty should arrive at Mary's, seeking him out. "We will be meeting tonight for both prayer and worship. I know my brothers and sisters would be delighted to have you join us."

"And you?" Kelila teased, gazing up at him through thick lashes. "Would *you* be delighted if I joined you?"

The young man swallowed hard, and Kelila imagined his Adam's apple must be bobbing somewhere beneath that impressive beard of his. "It is always a pleasure to welcome new converts," he responded safely.

"Mm-hmm," Kelila mused, enjoying the way this fascinating young man colored beneath her intense scrutiny.

Though he was rather plain and unassuming, he wasn't a bad-looking sort. He was tall, with masculine shoulders and a medium build. *He has a pleasant face beneath that wild-looking beard,* she thought, her lips tipping in amusement. Despite his flyaway appearance and drab, simple dress, she imagined he would clean up rather nicely. She would enjoy the project immensely, although she knew better than to suggest such a thing to a nice Jewish boy like this one.

"I must be on my way," the deacon interrupted Kelila's mischievous thoughts, growing immensely uncomfortable beneath her bold perusal.

"But I thought you had to buy pomegranates," Kelila pointed out with a wicked grin. "You haven't purchased a single one."

"Ah, yes. Well…" the young man stuttered slightly before mustering up a rather self-conscious smile. "Another time, I suppose. Do feel free to join us this evening."

Kelila watched in fascination as the modest young deacon strode away, clearly in a hurry to escape her teasing gaze. Habited to men falling at her feet and groveling for her attention, this reserved young man's reaction was rather intriguing. As a knowing smile graced her lovely lips, Kelila reconsidered

Candace's irritating entreaties to accompany her to prayer meeting. Kelila had stoutly refused, for she hadn't the least desire to sit on a hard bench for hours listening to old men droning on and on about the strange, divisive new sect her sister had so foolishly embraced.

But now... Grinning rather impishly, Kelila made up her mind. She would attend the bizarre prayer meeting hosted by the richest lady in Jerusalem, after all.

Perhaps it would prove far more interesting than she had suspected.

***

Candace

Clearing away the breakfast table, Candace wondered what in the world her flyaway sister was up to. Where had she wandered off to, anyway? *She's probably discovered Herod's theater already,* she thought, her dark, slender brows drawing together in exasperation. *Or—heaven forbid—the stadium!*

Why, oh why, had she allowed her sister to wander off in the first place? It was a careless mistake on her part. Kelila was entirely unfamiliar with the holy city! What if she became hopelessly lost? Would she ever find her way back to the house? Assaulted by troubling thoughts, Candace hoped her sister wasn't foolish enough to pass the city gates, alone. Their stern father would never forgive her if his favorite child was abducted by highway brigands!

Oh, Lord, protect her! Why did I let her go? Why didn't I speak up? What was I thinking, Lord?

The fact was, she *hadn't* been thinking, really. She hadn't expected Kelila to even consider roaming about the city, unchaperoned. The thought hadn't even occurred to her until she was watching her sister's elegantly clad back slipping out the front door!

Glancing over her shoulder, she saw her husband seated on his mat at the table, baby Rufus on his lap. The child gurgled his delight as his father helped him stand on his own two feet. Grasping his father's strong fingers with small, eager hands, Rufus squealed with gusto, entirely unaware of his mother's distress.

Her husband, however, had taken notice. "What troubles you, beloved?"

"What do *you* think?" Candace responded with a weary smile.

"Kelila."

"Exactly." Setting aside the emptied mugs, Candace turned to face her husband at the low table. Placing hands upon slender hips, she sighed her dismay. "I shouldn't have let her go."

"She's a grown woman, Candace."

"She is my baby sister, and we are responsible for her well-being as long as she remains under our roof."

"I'm not entirely sure she would agree with you," Simon remarked, amused.

"Whether or not she agrees is beside the point." Candace sighed, swiping at the perspiration dotting her smooth forehead with the back of her hand. "But that raises an important question, Simon. How *are* we to relate to her? She isn't a child, neither is she an independent woman seeing to her own needs. Indeed, she remains entirely dependent upon us for both shelter and sustenance."

Simon nodded his understanding, assuring his wife of his full attention.

"So should she be expected to carry her share of the load around here? To help with the daily chores? To attend church meetings? Or do we simply allow her free rein, meeting all her needs without harboring the slightest expectations of her?"

Smoothing back his son's curly black ringlets, Simon appeared deep in thought. "Sometimes," he mused, "there are no easy answers. This appears to be one of those times."

"I don't even know where to begin," Candace said, shaking her head in defeat. "If we'd only had some warning before her arrival, we could have discussed these topics beforehand."

Simon nodded, watching their older son, Alexander, as he carried empty trays to his troubled mother. She accepted them with a gracious smile. "Thank you, Alexander."

"May I see to my morning chores now?" he asked respectfully, seeking to be dismissed.

"You may, dear one." Candace watched as her young son went about his assigned tasks. He was a quiet, well-mannered, responsible child, reminding her of his father. Turning her attention back to her husband, Candace's brows furrowed together in confusion. "It is unlike Father to do anything without seeing to every possible detail. I'm stunned he would send Kelila to us without even a hint of warning."

"Do you think he knows?"

Simon's practical question was a like a punch in the gut. Candace blinked several times, startled.

"Are you suggesting Kelila has run away?"

"It's unlikely, but not entirely impossible," Simon responded, swooping Rufus off his feet and planting him firmly in his lap. Candace couldn't help but smile to herself as the child squealed his delight.

"Father and Mother would be absolutely frantic if Kelila simply disappeared!" Candace groaned, distressed. "But would she do that to them, Simon? *Could* she do that to them?"

Simon's expression was solemn. "Sometimes, we neglect to consider how our choices will impact others. But we shouldn't jump to conclusions. It's fully possible Kelila is here with your father's blessing."

The more Candace considered it, the less convinced she became. Her father had scathingly expressed his disgust when she and Simon had embraced Jesus as the long-awaited Messiah. In his opinion, they were foolish and careless in their "interpretation of Messianic prophecy." Why, then, would he send his impressionable young daughter to them, possibly to be "corrupted" by their unwelcome new doctrine?

"I will write to my father," Candace decided, joining Simon at the table. Lowering herself onto a mat, she folded nervous hands in her lap. "I will do so discreetly without alerting Kelila about my intentions. I'm curious about what he will have to say about this." Silently, she thanked God that her stubborn father had insisted his daughters learn to read and write, even though it was almost unheard of for men to educate their daughters. She wanted to read her father's response with her own eyes.

"In the meantime," she added, "what should we do about Kelila? She detests rules or structure of any kind. Any expectations we may lay upon her will surely be met with resistance, possibly even rebellion."

"We must pray about this," Simon admitted, kissing the top of his son's curly head. "The Lord will show us how to navigate this tricky situation."

Candace nodded, somewhat dissatisfied. She had hoped to resolve the issue before Kelila returned, but she also recognized the danger of reacting without first consulting the Lord. Why hadn't she already done so? Her sister's shocking arrival had thrown her entirely off balance!

"Honestly, I'm most concerned about Kelila's view regarding religion," Candace said quietly, deeply troubled. "Simon, she regards godly submission as *weakness*, spiritual disciplines as useless drudgery. I've never seen one so entirely obsessed with shallow pleasures and meaningless entertainment. How can we possibly even *begin* to reach her?"

"I mean this with no disrespect," Simon said slowly, carefully choosing his words, "but Kelila—like myself—was reared in a household adhering to strict religious observances. The problem, however, is this: there was no *power* in the rules and regulations because there was no *relationship* with the One who established them. It simply became a dull routine, a meaningless bore to her, I imagine."

"And I cannot blame her for that." Candace sighed, saddened. "When rigorous religious observances do little or nothing to transform the one performing them, it often results in disillusionment and scorn—both to the religionist and to those around him."

"And how can our families possibly be transformed by the power of the Holy Spirit when they reject the Messiah who sent Him?" Simon reminded her gently. "But God is at work, Candace. He desires the salvation of our loved ones even more than we do. For now, let's simply trust Him, focusing on setting a godly example for Kelila. Perhaps, in time, she will see the miraculous power of the Holy Spirit at work; for it is the Spirit who gives the power to transform formerly dull spiritual disciplines into life-giving channels fed by the true Living Water."

CHAPTER 7

Tabitha

Nearly beside herself with nervous anticipation, Tabitha's heart had soared when a messenger arrived bearing a sealed, travel-worn scroll. When she had composed the letter to her uncle—in addition to a second letter she had discreetly failed to mention to her husband—Tabitha had known it would be months before a response, if *any*, eventually reached Jerusalem by way of a traveling caravan or a band of sojourners willing to carry a friend or relative's correspondence. How had her uncle managed a return letter so soon? He must have dispatched a personal messenger the moment he had received word from his long-lost niece!

Tearing open the seal with trembling fingers, Tabitha whipped aside a sheer scarlet tapestry, falling rather gracelessly upon the plush sleeping pallet she shared with Stephanos. Stretching out casually on her stomach, Tabitha prepared to settle in for a nice, long read. It had been over a decade since she had last seen her uncle. She imagined he must have plenty of news to share! Anxiously, she wondered how he had responded to the gospel message she had neatly and succinctly presented.

Taking a deep breath, Tabitha spread open the delicate parchment, her hazel-green eyes scanning the neat script with great interest.

What! Eyes widening in dismay, Tabitha was appalled by the letter's contents. Her uncle's curt response was a far cry from what she had expected. Not only was he *not* happy to hear from her—he all but accused her of reaching out to him simply to get his *money!*

I find it rather interesting you have not bothered to reach out until now, dear niece, after joining a bizarre sect in desperate need of financial backing... Tabitha could almost hear the scathing sarcasm in his tone, spanning the sprawling miles between Jerusalem and Joppa!

Lifting the letter for closer inspection, Tabitha's color deepened along with her mounting frustration, her eyes narrowing further as she scanned the last few lines. *In regard to your "tempting" offer to visit your home in Jerusalem; I must decline, as I detest the flattery and thinly veiled motives of "caring" relatives seeking nothing but a handout...*

The nerve, the unremitted gall of that miserable old man! Pushing herself up from the cozy bedroll, Tabitha crumpled the insufferable letter in shaking hands. Heart pounding like angry war drums, she hurled the crumpled letter across the room.

Why had she even bothered to reach out to a selfish old man, anyway? Her uncle was pompous, arrogant, and incorrigible! Let him rot in his miserable old mansion in his own foul company, for all she cared!

In her opinion, the matter was settled. She wouldn't think about the insolent old miser *ever* again!

Perturbed, Tabitha prepared to join her husband at Mary's villa for the evening service.

***

Tabitha was caught off guard when Candace hurried toward her, crossing Mary's vast reception hall with a laughing young woman in tow.

"Candace, *shalom*!" Tabitha exclaimed, noting the familiar way Candace tugged the visitor along by the hand. "Please, introduce me to your friend!" Turning her attention toward the younger woman as she drew alongside her with a rather harried Candace, Tabitha smiled in greeting. "We are so pleased to have you join us."

"Why, thank you," the young woman grinned, her entire being radiating with unharnessed zeal. "You must be the world-famous Tabitha. I hear about you *all day long*!" the girl exclaimed, dragging out the last three words with an air of annoyance and long -suffering. "Tabitha, *this*. Tabitha, *that*. Tabitha, Tabitha, Tabitha…"

Tabitha glanced at Candace, confused.

"Tabitha, meet my youngest sister, Kelila," Candace said, her tone and expression betraying her weariness.

"Your *sister*?" Tabitha repeated, stunned. As far as she had known, Candace's entire family remained in Cyrene. Doing a double take, she compared the two women and realized they shared similar features. Both possessed the beautiful, smooth, dark complexion of their heritage, with lustrous dark hair and eyes. Both were lovely to behold. Yet Candace carried herself with grace and poise, while Kelila's slender form undulated untamed curiosity paired with unbridled enthusiasm.

"She has journeyed all this way to stay with us," Candace explained, her flickering eyes promising to tell Tabitha more, later.

"That's wonderful!" Tabitha declared, wondering if her words rang true, in Candace's opinion. "For how long?"

"*Forever*, possibly!" Kelila announced, laughing merrily. "But who knows? The world is full of interesting possibilities."

"That it is," Tabitha agreed, attempting to gauge Candace's reaction. She couldn't wait to ply her friend with questions!

"My darling, you've arrived." Stephanos swooped in then, his masculine presence immediately drawing Kelila's rapt attention. Bending his head, he planted an affectionate kiss on his bride's soft cheek.

"Your husband?" Kelila purred, her dark eyes flickering over the handsome evangelist.

"Yes," Tabitha swiftly responded. She didn't appreciate the young woman's shameless perusal of her husband.

"Ah, you're a lucky woman!" Kelila teased, laughing as the color sprang to Tabitha's cheeks.

"Um...yes," Tabitha faltered. "I'm very blessed." She glanced toward Candace, begging her friend to change the subject.

But Candace appeared equally mortified as if

she'd like nothing better than to sink beneath the marble floor, landing in the vaulted storage rooms below, forever out of sight.

"Now if you'll excuse me," Kelila chirped, completely oblivious to her sister's humiliation, "I have some serious mingling to do if I'm ever to acquaint myself with all these—what do you call them, *followers? Believers?*"

Surprised by Kelila's candor, Candace, Tabitha, and Stephanos stared at her blankly, attempting to find their tongues.

"Well, whatever they are, I intend to introduce myself to every single one of them!" Kelila declared, clapping her hands delightedly. "What fun!"

Tabitha could almost feel Candace's anxiety deepen.

Grasping Candace's arm, Kelila squealed like a young girl. "I still can't believe this magnificent villa—it makes Father's look like a *shanty*! I think I shall ask your rich friend for a grand tour!" Releasing another delighted squeal, Kelila bounded off to invoke mischief elsewhere.

***

Philip

Philip's heart lurched when the exotic young woman from the fruit vendor's booth approached him, although he couldn't quite decide if his reaction was one of delightful anticipation or sheer panic.

Relieved, he noticed the young woman had donned an elaborate head covering this time. At least she'd possessed the decency to consider modesty amidst a public gathering. Watching her as she boldly approached him, Philip decided she moved like a graceful tigress, her every movement abounding with purpose and determination. Far sooner than he was prepared for, the young woman stood before him, her full beauty on display.

"Well, hello there, stranger." The flirtatious smile hidden in the lovely visitor's tone wasn't lost on Philip.

Clearing his throat rather nervously, Philip wondered who had escorted this intriguing young woman to the Upper Room. She had emerged, alone, at the top of the marble staircase with the air of a queen assessing her vast kingdom.

"*Shalom*, dear sister," he said, hoping his modest, brotherly greeting would cool her ardor...or whatever it was kindling in those dark, fathomless eyes of hers.

Looking less than pleased, she recovered quickly. "Well, here I am!" Dramatically spreading slender arms, she added, "You didn't think I would show up, did you?"

Actually, no, he thought, though he dared not voice it aloud. *Quite frankly, you are the last person I expected to set foot in a church meeting.* Instead, he said politely, "We are very glad you could join us this evening."

"*We?*" Kelila responded drolly, looking around in an exaggerated manner. "Who is this *we*, sir? The only man I see standing around here is *you*."

Philip could have argued that they were surrounded by several dozen believers—some seated on wooden benches awaiting the commencement of the service, others standing in tight clusters about the cheerfully lit chamber, deep in lively conversation.

"*You*, then, are glad to see me; are you not?" Kelila pointed out, her large brown eyes sparkling with mischief. "Is there a reason you felt compelled to hide behind this imaginary *we?*"

Glancing nervously about, Philip wondered if it was even proper to carry on this conversation. He certainly didn't wish to give this vibrant young woman the wrong idea! *Oh, Lord, please tell me she came seeking the truth rather than my company!* Even as he offered this silent prayer of distress, Philip couldn't help but sense a tweak of conscience. He couldn't deny his attraction to this laughing, teasing woman, despite the impropriety of the matter. Troubled, he returned his attention to the lovely stranger.

"I don't believe we've been properly introduced," Philip said, breezing over her impertinent question. "I am Philip—"

"Ah, Philip the philanthropist," the woman teased. "It has a nice ring to it, does it not?"

"And you are?" Philip prompted, shifting a bit uncomfortably.

"I am Kelila, Candace's youngest sister."

Philip stared at her in shock. "*You* are Candace's sister?"

"I'm afraid so," Kelila laughed, tossing a stream of lush hair over one shoulder.

Realizing his mouth was open, Philip promptly closed it. Never in a thousand years would he have guessed this fulsome young woman to be the sister of the sweet, reserved Candace!

"It's a bit of shock, no?" Kelila grinned, placing a graceful hand upon one curved hip. "We're not very much alike."

Philip acknowledged the truth of her statement with a hint of disappointment. If only this striking young woman had embraced the faith and standards of her older sister! Perhaps then, he would be free to pursue...

Catching himself in the middle of his own shocking reverie, Philip realized it was time to place some distance between himself and this enticing young woman. Forcing a polite smile, he gestured toward a group of young women huddled nearby.

"Come, allow me to introduce you to some dear friends. I know you will enjoy their company."

Kelila's confusion was evident upon her lovely features as Philip guided her toward a group of chattering young women, briefly introducing them before slipping away entirely.

***

Tabitha

Emerging at the top of the elegant stairway, Tabitha took Candace by the hand, nearly dragging her toward a vacant bench near the end of the Upper Room. As the two women seated themselves with the soft rustling of fabric and fluttering head coverings, Tabitha leaned in close. "So tell me all about your sister!" she exclaimed, eager to learn as much as possible before the service commenced.

Dark eyes flitting apprehensively toward Kelila, now standing somewhat awkwardly within a tight cluster of chatty young women, Candace felt a faint sense of relief washing over her. At least Kelila had the decency to seek the companionship of the women, rather than making a fool of herself chasing after the men!

"Well?" Tabitha demanded, fascinated by Candace's lively sister.

"She showed up on our doorstep a few days ago," Candace explained, her voice low. "As of now, I'm not even sure our father knows about it, but I've reached out to him by letter. Hopefully, we'll have some answers soon."

"Is she a believer?"

"Not yet," she admitted ruefully. Frankly, Candace was a bit surprised Tabitha even had to ask.

"Well, it looks like you have a project on your hands," Tabitha teased, squeezing her friend's slender shoulder. "How long have you been praying for the salvation of your family?"

"It seems like forever," Candace responded distractedly, wondering why she had been so surprised by Kelila's arrival. Had she simply not expected the Lord to take her up on her offer—her offer to witness to her family should the opportunity arise?

"I will pray for Kelila," Tabitha said sincerely, watching Candace's sister across the room. She appeared to be sharing a rather stilted conversation with several young women.

"Thank you, Tabitha," Candace responded earnestly. "Above anything else I might wish for Kelila, I desire her salvation the most."

"The Lord has certainly led her to the right home, then," Tabitha assured her. "You and Simon demonstrate your faith in all you do."

"I must admit," Candace confessed, "my patience has been sorely tested these last few days. It's so easy to be Christ-like when no one else is around to cramp your style or step on your toes!"

Laughing along with her, Tabitha agreed. "But the Holy Spirit will enable you to uphold your witness, Candace."

"Amen," Candace murmured softly. "Praise God for His abundant mercy, for I seem to possess none of my own!"

The women sat in companionable silence for a long moment before Candace eventually spoke up. "Now it's your turn, Tabitha. Tell me what's on your mind."

"On my mind?" Tabitha repeated elusively.

"You can't deny something is heavy on your heart tonight. I know you better than that."

"I'm a bit worried about Stephanos," Tabitha confessed, releasing a long sigh. She didn't dare bring up her uncle's letter, which was also heavy on her heart. She was still far too annoyed about the matter to speak of it. "He intends to address another gathering at the Synagogue of the Freedmen this week."

"Doesn't he always?"

"Far more often than he should."

"Stephanos is an *evangelist*, Tabitha," Candace reminded her with a faint smile. "You knew that when you married him."

"We're *all* called to evangelism," Tabitha responded a bit defensively. "That's not what bothers me. It's his *style* that concerns me. I'm afraid he merely fans the flames of the Sanhedrin's wrath."

"The Sanhedrin abhors the Way," Candace pointed out. "They despise our message regardless of its presentation."

"But if Stephanos insists upon a fiery delivery and a bold presentation, wouldn't it be wise to select times and locations less likely to attract the religious leaders' attention?"

"Tabitha," Candace replied gently, taking her friend's hand in her own, "Stephanos desires to *reach* the religious leaders, as well. That's why he preaches in their presence."

"I can't help but assume the religious leaders will perish in their stubborn unbelief. So why heap unnecessary trouble upon himself and the followers to 'reach' a worthless cause?"

Candace only smiled.

"You must think I have no faith," Tabitha said.

"I have seen your faith in action, Tabitha," Candace insisted. "We all struggle. We all face doubts and temptations."

Tabitha nodded slowly, her expression downcast.

"The goal is simply to press on," Candace reminded her, squeezing her hand. "God will honor your obedience, beloved. Trust Him, and He will sustain you."

CHAPTER 8

Philip

"I see you've met Kelila."

Philip started, unprepared for the jovial voice at his elbow. Turning his head, he managed a somewhat lopsided smile. "Ah, Stephanos. Good evening, my brother." Color deepening, Philip wondered if his fellow deacon had witnessed his entire exchange with the young woman.

"I can hardly believe she is Candace's sister," Stephanos grinned, amused. "She's quite a character, isn't she?"

"That, she is."

"It's exciting to see the Spirit of God drawing unlikely candidates unto Himself."

Philip couldn't help but smile his acknowledgement. Kelila was certainly an unlikely candidate! But would she return to their meetings after he had so swiftly dismissed her? Battling against himself, part of him hoped she would never set foot within Mary's villa again, even as another part of him feared that she wouldn't.

"It was kind of you to introduce her to the young women," Stephanos observed.

Philip did a double take. His friend's eyes were gleaming with mischief, and he groaned inwardly. Stephanos had read his warring emotions like an open book! He'd never been able to keep a secret from Stephanos.

Squeezing Philip's shoulder in affirmation, Stephanos nodded his understanding. "You are a wise man, distancing yourself from temptation. But God knows the secret longings of your heart. Entrust her to Him, my brother. In time, I believe she'll come around."

Until then, Philip knew she was entirely off limits. Even so, there was no guarantee Kelila would embrace the Way of salvation. But one thing he knew for certain—he would not disregard the Lord's clear command against marrying unbelievers. To indulge in even a seemingly innocent friendship with Kelila could fast become a slippery slope, plummeting both of them into a miry pit.

But what if the Lord brought us together for the sole purpose of her salvation? I am, after all, an evangelist. Color deepening, Philip was shaken to the core by his contrary emotions. He had known young men determined to "win" unbelieving young women to Christ. He'd also known well-meaning young women eager to "witness" to unbelieving men, no doubt praying that a proposal would swiftly follow his "conversion." The predictable outcome never ended well. Inevitably, the laws of attraction trumped the unchanging laws of God, resulting in compromise on the part of the believer.

Realizing Stephanos was still watching him intently, Philip cleared his throat, discomfited. "I've only just met her, Stephanos. I know next to nothing about her," he insisted, annoyed by the flimsiness of his own denial. "It would be sheer foolishness for me to entertain any ideas whatsoever about her."

"I wholeheartedly agree. But sometimes the heart has a mind of its own," Stephanos remarked, giving his friend a firm pat on the back. "Sometimes, our feelings forget to consult our logic."

Philip's mouth tipped in self-deprecation. There was really no point in denying his mounting interest in Kelila, for Stephanos would merely see through his shallow excuses. At least he knew his fellow deacon would present this impossible situation before the Throne Room of God, remembering him in prayer and providing godly accountability.

He was not alone in this.

Releasing a wistful sigh, Philip's gaze traveled toward Kelila's vibrant form. To him, she appeared as a lily among thorns within the tight cluster of young women. Radiant and alluring, waist-length ringlets of ebony-colored hair cascaded down her back and billowed over her shoulders. Reflecting exotic hints of green and hazel flecks, her large brown eyes were showcased beneath lush black lashes and lovely, well-shaped brows. Her full mouth was beautifully shaped, often tipping in playful or teasing expressions.

For the lips of an immoral woman drip honey, and her mouth is smoother than oil; but in the end she is bitter as wormwood, sharp as a two-edged sword... Wincing as Solomon's wise warning flooded his mind, Philip shifted a bit uncomfortably. He didn't like to think of Kelila as an *immoral woman*. He hardly knew her. Perhaps her morals were impeccable! Besides, she was far too beautiful, far too enticing, to prove dangerous.

And yet, Philip knew deep in his heart that lovely Kelila had not embraced his Savior. Even if she desired to do right, she didn't have the Holy Spirit residing within her, enabling her to honor God.

They were unequally yoked, traveling entirely different paths. While he sought the eternal, her heart was set upon temporal, earthly pleasures. Though deep physical attraction might temporarily smooth over a few bumpy, rough patches, Philip knew a union would ultimately result in heartache and frustration for both of them.

Sighing, Philip ran an anxious hand over the back of his neck. He'd always thought he would know the woman God intended for him the moment he laid eyes upon her.

Now, he wondered how he could have possibly been so wrong.

***

Kelila

"What did you think of Simon Peter's instruction?"

Drawn from her own brooding thoughts, Kelila didn't appreciate Candace's intrusion. She preferred to sulk in peace on the long walk home from Mary's resplendent villa. The magnificent home had only further aroused Kelila's angst. Why must *she* return to an ugly little hovel in the Lower City while refined women like Mary resided within grand palatial houses teeming with servants, exquisite cuisine, and fabulous furniture?

She, Kelila, belonged in a house like that! She, too, was beautiful, elegant, refined. She was made to recline upon plush couches, donning the finest of expensive imported garments, commanding the servants to perform her bidding. Why shouldn't she live like that? Mary did, and she was reputed as one of the noblest women of the city!

Hands balling into fists at her sides, Kelila's lips formed a petulant pout. Tonight, she'd learned that Mary's husband had died suddenly, leaving her with a fine villa, a fortune, and several booming businesses. And yet she, Kelila, must return to a confining stone hut in Jerusalem's poorest precinct to contemplate her great misfortune!

Some women have all the luck! Kelila thought, chagrined. *Life is unjust.*

It never even occurred to her that Mary would have gladly relinquished all worldly possessions if it could have saved her beloved husband. Nor did Kelila grasp the endless hours of discipline, dedication, and grit required to operate multiple businesses scattered throughout several provinces. But it was rather simple to covet one's situation without considering the hard work and sacrifice that had been invested to obtain—not to mention, to *maintain*—it!

"Kelila?"

Interrupted yet again amidst her silent brooding, Kelila looked at her sister askance. "What?" she asked tersely.

"Did you enjoy Simon Peter's instruction?"

How could anyone enjoy that monotonous droning? Quite truthfully, she hadn't heard much of anything the esteemed apostle, Simon Peter, had said. She had been too busy stewing over Philip's curt dismissal.

"Kelila?"

Peeved by Candace's persistent interrogation, Kelila feigned indifference. That would certainly irritate her sister, who clearly hoped against all logic that Kelila would embrace her strange new religion. "It was rather hard to follow," she responded in a careless tone.

Not if you were actually listening, Candace thought, annoyed. But remembering her Savior's endless patience, Candace took a deep breath, willing to follow His example. She couldn't possibly expect Kelila to come around overnight.

Hiding a knowing grin, Kelila strolled ahead with an air of indifference. Candace's consternation wasn't lost on her, and she felt a hint of triumph— even if the evening hadn't gone as she had planned.

"Did you understand what Peter said about Jesus' sacrifice being the ultimate atonement for our sin?" Candace persisted, glancing over her shoulder to make sure Simon and their two young sons remained a discreet distance behind them. She wanted Kelila to feel safe in this private discussion.

Sin! Kelila winced. It was such an ugly word, and one she had no desire to contemplate. Even Candace's innocent statement implied the unbending nature and rigid morality her faith required. Why should she, Kelila, seek such a faith? There were enough rules and regulations to make life perfectly dreary without adding another long list to follow! Father was staunch in his religious observances, insisting his children participate in his boring rituals, as well. And Kelila was fast learning that the apple didn't fall far from the tree. Candace, too, adhered to a ridiculously stringent moral code.

Feeling a bit guilty about her line of thought, Kelila had to admit Candace's faith was quite different from Father's. Father observed the Law to the very last letter, yet he remained cold and aloof, almost condescending. Candace, on the other hand, was warm and inviting. Though she refused to compromise her beliefs, she cast no judgment upon those of differing views. Rather than mere outward demonstrations like Father's, Candace's faith impacted everything she did, every choice she made.

Perhaps she's even worse than Father, Kelila thought, disturbed, for it seemed absurdly complicated. She had no desire to contemplate her every thought and action. How meticulous!

"I wish you could have met Jesus before He returned to Heaven." Candace sighed, seemingly unaware of her sister's silent withdrawal. "You would have loved Him, Kelila."

Setting her jaw in disgust, Kelila wondered why her sister had become so obsessed with a dead Man. It was unseemly, bordering morbid! Why, no woman of class would dare embrace such an odd sect! And yet, swiftly following her mental tirade, the poised and refined form of Mary filled Kelila's mind, shattering her entire theory. Mary was by far the most sophisticated woman she had ever met, and yet *she* believed.

Fleetingly, Kelila wished she had paid just a bit more attention to the apostle's teaching. After all, Mary—a brilliant, independent woman of means—wouldn't be easily fooled. So what was it about this stubborn faith that had drawn *her*?

"I didn't understand everything at first, either," Candace continued, her tone and expression exasperatingly patient. "Having been mired in Jewish tradition my entire life, the fact that Jesus' shed blood provided the final atonement for all my sins—past, present, and future—was nearly impossible to grasp."

Kelila said nothing, assuming there was safety in silence, almost fearing that Candace would launch into a full-fledged presentation should she betray even a hint of interest.

"If you'd ever like to talk about it, I'd be happy to answer any questions you may have," Candace said, surprising her. Then she slowed her pace, allowing her husband, with two young sons in tow, to catch up. Clearly, the subject had been dismissed—at least, for now.

Both stunned and relieved that Candace had dropped the matter so quickly, Kelila almost wished her older sister had expounded upon the disconcerting topic a bit more. After all, she'd already steeled herself for a nice, long argument. But now? Now she was left to brood over the small bits and pieces she had gleaned from Peter's message—in between alternating bouts of annoyance and self-pity.

Strolling alongside Candace's family in the gathering darkness, Kelila couldn't help but ponder some strange words Simon Peter had attributed to Jesus, the dead Rabbi they zealously followed with reckless abandon—*I have come that they may have life, and that they may have it more abundantly.*

More abundantly?

The simple statement had drawn Kelila unlike

anything else she'd overheard that evening. To experience an abundant life was all she really wanted, all she had sought so desperately. Even so, how could she possibly hope to experience an abundant life if burdened by rigid rules? Surely one experienced true bliss once free to do as one pleased, unhindered by the unreasonable expectations of one's family, religion, or society!

Still, the Teacher's promise whispered its way into Kelila's heart, filling her with a desire so sweet she found herself blinking back unwanted tears.

I have come that they may have life, and that they may have it more abundantly. The statement itself was a paradox. It defied all reason, all logic, all practicality. Perhaps the words were simply the philosophical musings of a dead Rabbi, glorified all the more after His grisly end.

As Candace and her family finally reached the old stone walls surrounding their quiet house, Kelila held back, her gaze lifting steadily toward the sea of winking, glistening stars now splashing across a dusky night sky. Gingerly wrapping slender arms about the sturdy trunk of a towering palm, Kelila fixed her gaze heavenward, attempting to dismiss the persistent promise.

To no avail.

CHAPTER 9

Tabitha

"I think you must have misplaced this, my dear."

My dear. Setting her jaw in vexation, Tabitha turned around slowly, plastering on a smile of icy sweetness. She was fast learning when her husband addressed her as such, a generous helping of good-natured ribbing was on the way. However, as she prepared their breakfast before their brief sojourn to the Synagogue of the Freedmen, she was in no mood to endure his teasing. After all, *he* was the source of her great angst! She had nearly worried herself sick contemplating all the dark possibilities likely to result from her husband's impending address.

Wearing a broad smile, Stephanos raised her uncle's crumpled letter, which she had so heedlessly tossed aside.

"What about it?" she asked shortly, having no desire to expound upon her uncle's inexcusable behavior.

"I take it you didn't appreciate what he had to

say,",'" Stephanos grinned, waving the offensive object in her direction.

Striding toward the low table where Stephanos sat upon a straw mat, Tabitha snatched up the letter.

Stephanos watched, bemused, as his wife stalked back over to her cooking station, letter in hand. Bending near the warm clay oven, she tossed the crumpled parchment into the kindling flames, her hazel-green eyes blazing in like manner.

"So when were you going to tell me the good news?" Stephanos quipped as Tabitha placed two bowls of steaming gruel on the table.

"What good news?" Tabitha huffed, seating herself upon a mat across the table from her husband.

"You received word from your uncle!"

"There was nothing *good* about that," she shot back, her nimble fingers curling around a clay mug. "It was a mistake to write him. I shouldn't have done it."

"May I ask why?" Stephanos prodded, his expression softening.

"Did you read it?" Tabitha demanded, raising flashing eyes toward her husband.

"I couldn't help myself," Stephanos grinned. "Your uncle has quite a way with words."

"He also has a way of ostracizing anyone who dares to set foot within ten miles of his miserable person."

"He sounds like a feisty old gentleman."

"Old, yes. But there's nothing *gentle* about him!"

"I see you harbor no fond memories of your estranged relative," Stephanos observed, bemused.

"None whatsoever. He is petty and intolerable."

Stephanos smiled gently, reaching across the small table to caress his wife's smooth cheek. "Don't write him off yet, Tabitha. God can still reach him."

"You think God can reach *everyone*." She sighed in dismay. Covering his hand with her own, she leaned into his touch for the briefest moment before releasing him and pulling away. "But you can't help yourself. You *are* an evangelist, after all."

"As you've pointed out so often, we're *all* called to evangelism, Tabitha. It's our sacred calling in Christ, to make disciples of all men, of all nations."

Tabitha simply stared at him, her lips curving wryly.

"Don't lose heart after one seemingly failed attempt with your uncle," Stephanos encouraged her, reaching for her hand. "He may still come around."

"You seem to forget that God grants all men free will," Tabitha reminded him, annoyed that their bowls of gruel were growing cold on the table. "And God will never force anyone—not my uncle, not that despicable Saul of Tarsus nor any of his dark-robed cronies—to receive His Son's atoning sacrifice."

"And *you* seem to forget," Stephanos replied, his dark eyes twinkling, "that our God moves in mysterious ways, masterfully orchestrating events and circumstances to draw even the worst of sinners unto Himself."

***

Kelila

Vexed, Kelila trudged alongside Candace's happily chattering family as they traversed aging streets in one of the oldest sections of the holy city. On their way to the Synagogue of the Freedmen, Kelila wasn't looking forward to enduring another unwanted sermon. How often did these overzealous "followers" meet, anyway? After last night's service, Kelila had hoped she would enjoy at least a brief reprieve from what her sister so candidly called *spiritual nourishment*. Why, these people were nearly as bad as the ultra-orthodox Jews who insisted upon participating in Temple prayers at least three times daily!

Feeling an unwelcome stab of guilt, Kelila again acknowledged that these believers were vastly unlike stringent Jews like her father. Already, she'd glimpsed many such men here in Jerusalem, donning long, trailing robes and prayer shawls, resonating with a practiced air of piosity. But those men assembled at the Temple or in the local synagogues did so to be *seen*, to make a statement. Even as a child, Kelila had recognized their sense of obligation. They went to the synagogue because that's what they were *supposed* to do, *expected* to do.

But these believers in Jerusalem? They, too, met with maddening regularity. Yet, in their case, Kelila had been unable to detect the slightest trace of grudging obligation. These believers met because they couldn't help themselves! They loved their God, they loved His Word, they loved each other. The Scriptures were something not only to *read*, but to *incorporate* in their daily existence. They grew ridiculously excited with each new discovery uncovered within those ancient pages. When they sang the old psalms, it was strikingly obvious they sang *to* the Lord, not simply *about* the Lord. Their worship was sincere. And when they prayed, they clearly believed that the Lord heard them and acted on their behalf. They reveled in the presence of God.

Kelila had tossed and turned the previous night,

contemplating these puzzling mysteries. She'd come here to escape her father's confining lifestyle, to experience the bliss and freedom she deserved! And yet she seemed to have stumbled upon an entire congregation of people who experienced the freedom and bliss she so desperately desired, without even trying! What was their secret, anyway? Most of them had nothing in common. They came from varying backgrounds, lifestyles, cultures, and family situations. Most were ancestral Jews, others were Hellenists, and some were proselytes. While some were wealthy, others were desperately poor. And yet, even the poorer families were cared for, as the wealthier members of the sect quickly noticed and met the needs. Some boasted large, thriving families, while others attended the meetings alone each week. Some were successful merchants and businessmen; others, humble fishermen and craftsmen. And yet they all possessed the same vibrant life, the same cheery countenance. These people were pleasant in every way—unlike her father and his associates, whose sour countenances conveyed their heavy burden of obligation and frustration. But the faces of the believers shone like the sun, effortlessly reflecting their deep joy, their inner peace.

Kelila wanted to experience that exultation for herself. She wanted it so badly she thought she would go mad! But she couldn't stomach the thought of resigning herself to another monotonous checklist, and the believers obeyed all the commandments without thought or question.

Sighing in grudging resignation, Kelila pushed these troubling thoughts from her mind, absorbing the unimpressive view sprawling before her as they approached the City of David nestled comfortably within the protective shadow of the Temple's southern wall just east of the Lower City. This ancient precinct wasn't nearly as palatable as the lavish, neatly paved, palm-lined avenues of the Upper City. Kelila decided she preferred the pleasant trip to Mary's villa.

"I think you will enjoy this morning's gathering, my sister," Candace divulged cheerfully, drawing Kelila's attention. "Tabitha's husband, Stephanos, plans to address the people today. He is a gifted teacher."

With great effort, Kelila resisted the urge to roll her eyes with a dramatic *harrumph*. Stephanos was dangerously good-looking, but, unfortunately, he was a married man, clearly off limits. Where was the fun in that? Fleetingly, Kelila wondered if Philip would be in attendance. She was still miffed about his strange dismissal of the night before. *Well, perhaps this day won't be a lost cause, after all,* she thought snidely. Kelila loved nothing better than a worthy challenge, and the shy deacon certainly qualified.

"Does Father still attend the local synagogue back home?" Candace asked her sister, interrupting Kelila's thoughts yet again.

"Nearly every day without fail," Kelila huffed. She'd hated how he dragged her along with him. He'd done so with each of his children, until they had married and begun families of their own. None of her siblings had resumed attendance at the synagogue after that, and she didn't blame them.

Kelila was annoyed to be reminded about a sore subject. Mother was more than happy to accompany

Father to his dull meetings, so why did he force *her* to go when she'd rather beat her head against a stone wall? A strange uneasiness curled unpleasantly in the pit of her stomach as Kelila remembered something she'd much rather forget. "Why do you still go to the synagogue?" she muttered a bit more sharply than she intended. "I thought you weren't *Jewish* anymore."

"I suppose we'll always be Jewish," Candace chuckled, hoisting Rufus a bit higher on her hip as she walked alongside Simon and Alexander. "A person doesn't stop being Jewish simply because he accepts the Way."

"Rather, a man or woman embraces the fulfillment of God's promises to His chosen people when one receives Christ as the appointed Messiah," Simon said quietly, catching Kelila off guard. He rarely engaged in conversation. "The Law and the Prophets simply foretold the coming of the Messiah, foreshadowing His great sacrifice."

Kelila wasn't following, although she had to admit she hadn't really *tried*. She'd never been particularly interested in dull religious gibberish. She was far too involved in her pursuit of adventure, excitement, and romance to bother with such tedious subjects.

"Those of us who have embraced Jesus Christ as the ultimate fulfillment of God's redemptive plan consider ourselves *completed Jews*," Simon finished with a mysterious smile.

"Well, we aren't really Jewish in the first place," Kelila pointed out, wondering how much longer she must endure this lecture before reaching the synagogue, where she would no doubt endure yet *another* boring lecture. "Our ancestors are Cyrenian, not Jewish."

"But our Cyrenian ancestors intermarried with displaced Jews during the Dispersion, hence the Jewish blood coursing through our veins," Candace reminded her, a hint of pride in her tone.

Kelila wondered what on earth her sister had to be proud about. In her opinion, Judaism was by far the most prudish religion on the face of the earth! "If we have any Jewish blood at all, it's nothing but a mere thimbleful," Kelila retorted.

Candace laughed, amused. "Perhaps," she conceded. "But I think it's an honor, nonetheless."

"It's no secret the Jews hate your new faith, even rejecting your Messiah," Kelila prodded. "So why worship in a Jewish synagogue with people who hate and disown you? Why not simply meet at Mary's house, far removed from the hatred and judgment of the religious leaders?"

"We meet at Mary's because, there, we are free to worship as we are called. But we also continue at the synagogues because the Jews are still our brothers and sisters," Candace explained, her tone patient. "We long to reach them with the blessed gospel."

"They don't want to be reached," Kelila pointed out. "They think you're crazy to believe the Messiah has come."

"But He has, nonetheless," Candace replied. "And His salvation is for all men."

"*All* men?" Kelila repeated blankly. "What would a Jewish Messiah want with a Greek? Or better yet, a Roman? Jews hate Romans."

"Many Jews do hate Romans," Candace admitted sadly, "but Jesus loves *all* men, Kelila. He died for all of us, regardless of our heritage."

"But Father always insisted the Messiah would expel the Romans. So how can He possibly love them, and why are they still here?"

"Jesus came to expel *sin*, Kelila, not the Romans," Candace explained, looking to her husband for guidance. "True, some Scriptures portray the Messiah as a mighty warrior king. But there are also many Scriptures which foretold the Messiah would be led as a lamb to the slaughter."

"Well, He can't possibly be both," Kelila put in staunchly.

Candace and Simon exchanged knowing smiles. Even young Alexander's eyes twinkled with purpose.

"Well?" Kelila demanded, annoyed by their shared secret.

"He can, indeed," Candace supplied, slowing her pace as she carefully considered her next words. "The Messiah *first* came to us as a spotless lamb, meek and lowly. He came not to condemn the world, but to save it. His shed blood upon the cross became the ultimate atonement for our sins."

"But Jesus will come again, Kelila," Simon said soberly, picking up where Candace had left off. "He has promised to do so. And when He does, it will be nothing like His first advent. At Christ's second coming, the King of kings will descend from Heaven with a shout, with the voice of an archangel, and with the trumpet of God. Those who have received atonement will be caught up to be with the Lord forever."

"And those who have rejected your Messiah?" Kelila managed, certain she wouldn't like his answer.

"Those who reject the Son of God will be cut off

from the Lord, forever banished from paradise," Simon replied solemnly.

Kelila winced.

"This is why we pursue our calling with such fervor," Simon explained gently. "The Lord doesn't desire for anyone to perish in sin. We must reach as many as possible with the message of salvation."

"You see, our people weren't prepared for Jesus when He came because they had misconstrued the timeline, interpreting the Messianic prophecies to their own liking," Candace expounded, smiling as young Rufus tightened his grip around her neck, burrowing his face in her shoulder. "The Jews wanted a powerful warrior king to banish the Roman occupation and break the chains of oppression. They didn't recognize it was their own fleshly passions which enslaved them, far more so than the Romans."

"And because they interpreted prophecy based on their own whims and fancies, they entirely missed Christ's first coming," Simon said, shaking his head. Expression sobering, he added solemnly, "My greatest fear is that God's people will make the same dreadful mistake at His second coming. When Jesus returns for His own, will we be ready? Or will we utterly miss it, blinded by our own fanciful ideas of what His coming will be?"

Discomfited, Kelila was relieved when the simple stone synagogue loomed into view, for this conversation had rendered her terribly uncomfortable. She certainly didn't relish the thought of another long sermon, but at least their arrival at the Synagogue of the Freedmen would cut short this disturbing exposition.

CHAPTER 10

Kelila

The Synagogue of the Freedmen was a conventional stone building very much like the one Kelila had known in Cyrene. The two-story, red-roofed structure boasted an adjoining building which appeared to be a guest house, of sorts, along with its own ritual baths. As the synagogue was elevated upon a raised, square pavement, Kelila noticed that people mingled freely on the great stone steps outside. She supposed this conducive outdoor space must be the location where the apostles addressed the crowds when services were not in session.

"Candace!" A beautiful, simply dressed young woman hastened down the long stone stairway, throwing her arms around Candace and a giggling baby Rufus. Kelila recognized Tabitha right away.

"*Shalom*, dear sister." Candace smiled, returning the young woman's embrace.

"*Shalom*! I see you've brought your sister." Tabitha beamed, her bright eyes conveying her pleasure.

"Kelila, thank you for joining us!"

Did I have a choice? Kelila scoffed. Forcing an overbright smile, she replied, "I've been told your husband's sermon will be a real treat."

If Tabitha noticed the biting sarcasm lurking behind Kelila's sardonic words, she chose to overlook it. Instead, she smiled warmly. "I hope you will be blessed!"

Trailing behind Candace's family and the lovely Tabitha, Kelila tuned out the women's lively chatter. It got on her nerves, and she had no desire to hear about how the Lord was "blessing" them! If the Lord was real—and she supposed He probably was—He certainly didn't seem interested in *her* plight. She had never harbored fond feelings toward a God who prized *holiness*, demanded absolute obedience, and deprived His people of the simplest pleasures.

The women fell respectfully silent after passing beneath the central of three enormous entryways gracing the front of the formidable stone building. Kelila's skin crawled as she seated herself rigidly beside her sister on a cold stone bench. Tucking Alexander beside her in a motherly fashion, Candace situated baby Rufus in her lap as her husband seated himself beside their oldest son.

Familiar, reverential yet stony silence hung so heavily in the air that Kelila felt stifled by it. Tentatively observing her surroundings, Kelila wondered if all the synagogues were this cold and impersonal. The simple, square-shaped floor plan was lined with stone benches, each row slightly raised to form a seating arrangement reminiscent of a stadium or an arena. The entire structure was upheld by plain marble pillars which sheltered the central floor.

Here, priests and congregants were permitted to address the assembly from a richly carpeted, raised platform bearing a simple pulpit. Overhead, a balcony wrapped its way around all four walls. There, listeners could peer over the wooden railing, observing the service below.

"May I sit with you?"

Kelila jerked at the unexpected request whispered near her ear. Adjusting her gaze, she saw that Tabitha had knelt beside her, her hazel green eyes reflecting both warmth and kindness.

"Of course," Kelila said, hoping she sounded polite. She liked Tabitha, even if she was insanely jealous of her situation. The young woman was gorgeous, with incredibly rare coloring and arresting hazel-green eyes. Her modest head covering did little to obscure her cascade of honey-colored curls, sharply contrasting with her startling bright eyes and bronzed complexion. Not only was Tabitha a striking beauty, but she was also married to the best-looking man in Jerusalem.

Again, Kelila was struck by a stab of burning jealousy. Tabitha had all the luck! Wrinkling her brow, she supposed Candace would say Tabitha was *blessed*, not lucky. Well, fine. Some women didn't have any idea how "blessed" they were!

Do you, beloved?

Kelila's spine straightened, stunned by the force of the startling, unexpected thought. She could have almost sworn someone had whispered the unsettling question directly in her ear!

Me, blessed? she thought, dumbfounded. How so? Her father had once adored her, doting on her as a child. But once she became a woman, he'd nearly crushed her beneath the weight of his expectations. She had no life of her own, no freedom to do as she pleased. She longed for the rush of excitement, the thrill of adventure, chafing beneath the confines of life. She wasn't privileged to dwell in a luxurious mansion like Mary, nor to have a devastatingly handsome husband like Tabitha. She had no control over her own life, whatsoever. She'd thought her circumstances would change once freed of her father's unreasonable expectations, but she remained as discontented and unhappy as she'd ever been.

She, blessed? What a joke!

Kelila hardly noticed the congregants pouring into the synagogue, so disturbed was she by her own sorry plight. Tabitha's good-looking husband appeared, smiling in greeting as he quietly seated himself beside his pretty young wife. Once the benches were full, an aging, stiffly dressed priest took his place behind the pulpit, lifting an ancient parchment scroll. Kelila was tempted to nod off as he droned on and on, reading some obscure section of Scripture. Wasn't Stephanos supposed to speak today?

Tabitha leaned in closer, seeming to sense Kelila's unasked question. "Stephanos won't address the gathering until the pulpit is opened to the congregants," she whispered so softly Kelila scarcely heard her.

Nodding stiffly, Kelila braced herself for the long reading. The priest seemed to be talking about Moses. *Go figure,* she thought. Jews were obsessed with Moses! Sometimes she wondered if they worshiped *Moses* rather than God Himself. Closing her eyes and crossing her arms stiffly over her chest, she determined to tune out anything the priest had to say. But despite her best efforts, the ancient words leaped off the scroll, penetrating her heart and mind.

According to the Torah reading, the Lord had promised to lead His chosen people into the Promised Land. The land was a living paradise, overflowing with milk and honey. But Moses insisted the promise wasn't worth having if the Lord himself didn't accompany them into the land.

Kelila wondered what Moses' problem was. If God wanted to bless His people with everything they could possibly want, what was the big deal if He didn't go with them?

What had the priest said? Closing her eyes tightly, Kelila reflected upon the words of Torah. *Then Moses said to the Lord, "See, You say to me, 'Bring up this people.' But You have not let me know whom You will send with me. Yet You have said, 'I know you by name, and you have also found grace in My sight.' Now therefore, I pray, if I have found grace in Your sight, show me Your way, that I may know You..."*

Kelila wondered about this strange passage the priest had selected. She was strangely moved by God's promise to Moses and wondered if it applied to others, as well. *I know you by name. You have found grace in My sight.*

But Moses hadn't been satisfied with this great promise. Apparently, he sought more than God's blessings and favor. He also desired God's *presence*. Moses seemed to believe that material blessings—even a living paradise on earth—meant absolutely nothing without the presence of God.

But why? If the Lord offered her all her wildest

dreams on a silver platter, she'd take it and run, no questions asked!

When the priest summoned Stephanos, allowing him to address the congregation, Kelila watched with rapt attention as the confident evangelist approached the platform with purposeful steps. A hush fell over the assembly, a hush even more deafening than the silence which previously reigned. Kelila's skin prickled in admonition, for she sensed a crackling tension growing in the air and wondered if it was simply her imagination. But no, she was certain the entire atmosphere had changed the moment Stephanos boldly took his place behind the pulpit. It was as if the entire assembly held its collective breath, awaiting an unknown yet predictable outcome.

"Greetings, my dear brothers and sisters." Stephanos smiled warmly, his strong voice carrying easily over his vast audience and resonating throughout the entire synagogue. "Peace be with you."

Peace be with you. Kelila recognized the now-familiar phrase. The believers used it often. The strangest thing about the greeting was the fact that it seemed to *work*. The believers wished each other peace, and, somehow, peace permeated their hearts.

"I have no doubt our Torah reading this morning was God-ordained," Stephanos continued, nodding toward the priest seated near the front of the gathering. "For in it, Moses asked the Lord a crucial question—one I wish to address with you today."

Many congregants visibly stiffened in their seats. Surprised, Kelila noticed Tabitha's rigid posture betrayed tension, as well. What was going on here? Glancing at her new friend's tight expression,

Kelila followed Tabitha's gaze toward the front of the gathering, where several rows were occupied by dark-robed Pharisees, their expressions severe. Suddenly comprehending Tabitha's rising tension, Kelila placed her hand over Tabitha's in a rather uncharacteristic moment of thoughtfulness.

Turning toward Kelila in surprise, Tabitha smiled sincerely, her eyes conveying her deep gratitude. She squeezed Kelila's hand before turning her attention back to her husband at the podium.

Suddenly intrigued, Kelila, too, directed her attention toward Stephanos. What could he possibly have to say that would affect this entire gathering so? She relished the Pharisees' obvious discomfort and the growing tension of the congregants, savoring the steadily building climax. This was almost as fascinating as the entertaining farces performed by skilled hypocrites in Roman theaters!

"Moses shared a relationship with our God unlike any other," Stephanos continued, and Kelila was impressed by his charismatic manner and flawless Greek. In a mixed gathering like this, in which multiple nationalities and tongues were represented, it was crucial to master Greek, a language universally recognized throughout the Roman empire. "We've learned a thing or two from that great man, have we not?"

Several people chuckled softly, and Kelila assumed they, too, were believers sympathetic toward Stephanos' cause, unlike many of the priests and Pharisees with their dark expressions.

"And what did Moses ask of the Lord?" Stephanos went on unperturbed, gripping the sides of the pulpit with strong, well-shaped hands. "He said, '*If I have found grace in Your sight, show me Your way, that I may know You."* Stephanos paused, his dark eyes bearing great compassion as his gaze traveled over his congregants. "*That I may know You,*" he repeated softly. "The Promised Land wasn't enough. To have every desire and every need met wasn't enough. To dine upon the most lavish and sumptuous fare of the land wasn't enough. No, Moses recognized that earthly pleasures mean *nothing* without the presence of God."

Kelila was unaware of her own posture as she leaned forward, aptly listening. But Candace noticed, and her lips began to move in silent petition for her sister.

"I'm sure Moses was grateful for material blessings," Stephanos expounded, leaning toward his audience in a friendly manner which set many at ease. "But Moses would have gladly traded every earthly pleasure and possession to *know God*. Moses knew this life was fleeting—how else could he have so easily denied the pleasures of Egypt to suffer with God's chosen people? Wisely, Moses recognized this life is like a vapor, here today and gone tomorrow. And Moses sought to secure *eternal life* with the God he loved—one in which pain, suffering, and death will be forever banished!"

The synagogue rippled with softly spoken *amens*, even as the Pharisees and many of the congregants eyed the bold evangelist with mounting suspicion. Where was he going with this, anyway?

Kelila couldn't help but wonder, as well. Stephanos' words tugged at her heartstrings unlike anything she'd ever heard before. She had never considered the state of her eternal soul, and it disturbed her to do so now. She certainly didn't wish to be lost, but she was nothing like the pious Moses—willing to relinquish her burning desires in exchange for knowing God. Could she bear a life of drudgery and rules, simply *hoping* the result would be eternity in paradise? Was it true? Was it even worth it? She wasn't sure.

"Moses longed to know God," Stephanos said, his strong voice filling the entire synagogue and drawing Kelila from her self-evaluation. "'*If I have found grace in Your sight, show me Your way, that I may know You.'* This was Moses' heartfelt prayer, His petition to God. And because Moses found grace in His sight, God answered him. *'Show me Your way,'* Moses pleaded, and so our God answered. To Moses, God revealed the Way—*His* Way, the *only* Way—which is why Moses could tell the people with such confidence, '*The Lord your God will raise up for you a Prophet like me from your midst, from your brethren. Him you shall hear—*'"

"And I suppose you're about to tell us this long-awaited prophet is your wretched Christ, the One you so candidly call the Son of God."

Annoyed by the ill-mannered interruption, Kelila's gaze snapped toward the uncompromising form of a Pharisee donning trailing black robes, now standing on the front row, the one whose sardonic question had dripped with unveiled disdain. Upon closer inspection, Kelila was caught off guard by the Pharisee's unlikely appearance. Despite his slight stature, he possessed the broad shoulders and muscled form of a warrior, unlike his scholarly brethren now shifting uncomfortably on the front row. His entire being exuded a dangerous and powerful energy in line with his harsh and stony features. Suppressing a shudder, Kelila was quite certain she could sense his brutality all the way across the room.

Glancing sideways toward Tabitha, Kelila saw the young bride had visibly stiffened, white-knuckled hands clenched anxiously in her lap. It was obvious she had encountered this Pharisee before. Daring a glance toward Candace, Kelila noticed her lips moving in fervent, silent prayer. This Pharisee must pose a true threat to so affect this gathering!

Even as many within the assembly blanched at the brazen confrontation, Stephanos remained undisturbed. Flashing a knowing smile, Stephanos extended a welcoming hand toward the young Pharisee. "Ah, Brother Saul. What a privilege to have you join us this morning."

"I'm not your brother, nor do I deem this sacrilege a privilege."

"A pity." Stephanos grinned, drawing a few low chuckles from his listeners. "I've always liked you, Saul."

Saul returned the deacon's good-natured humor with an icy glare, his firm jaw clenched in fury.

"I see you've been listening to my prior sermons, as you've already predicted my main point," Stephanos acknowledged with a wry smile. "You've been paying attention." More nervous chuckles echoed within the vast chamber. "Yes, I do proclaim Jesus Christ, the Son of the Living God, as *the Way* revealed to Moses long ago."

Saul's lips formed a taut, grim line. "Blasphemy."

"Not so," Stephanos responded, his bearing resonating with confidence and strength. "After His miraculous resurrection, Jesus' disciples—nearly frantic—recognized He was about to depart from this earth to join His Father. Thomas asked him, *'Lord, we do not know where You are going, and how can we know the way?'* And Jesus responded, *'I AM the way, the truth, and the life. No one comes to the Father except through Me.'* So you see, Jesus *is* the Way to the Father. Without Christ, we are utterly lost, dead in our sins. But Christ shed His blood on the cross as the ultimate and final sacrifice, our atonement! When we accept His sacrifice and free gift of salvation, our sins are banished and we are forgiven."

"Only *God* can forgive sins," Saul seethed, his countenance fearsome to behold.

"Ah, you make a valid point." Stephanos grinned, his gaze sweeping over a rapt audience. "In the words of Christ Himself, my brother, *'If you had known Me, you would have known My Father also.'*"

With bated breath, Kelila, along with the entire assembly, awaited Saul's rebuttal. The tension hung so heavily in the air that she was sure one could have easily sliced it with a knife. Would this pompous young Pharisee succeed in disproving Stephanos' grand claim?

"You still insist upon the divinity of this Jesus?" Saul nearly spat, his dark eyes burning with black hatred.

"As long as I draw breath, I will not deny the sovereignty of Christ." Stephanos' voice resounded loudly in the stone synagogue, drawing relieved *amens* from many of his brethren.

"And as long as *I* draw breath, I will refute your sacrilegious claims," Saul threatened, his dark eyes glittering with malice. "Of this you can be certain—

you will indeed be silenced, just as your so-called Christ was blotted from this life when the Romans nailed him to a wretched cross."

"Ah, but the Romans didn't know our God overcomes evil with good, dear brother. By nailing Jesus to the cross, they unwittingly participated in God's grand plan for the redemption of all mankind. And by your own stubborn resistance, you may find yourself doing that very thing."

Saul's countenance visibly darkened as Stephanos lifted his gaze to address the nervously fidgeting gathering. "Jesus *is* the Way, my friends, and He is alive, seated at the right hand of God. And because He sent the Holy Spirit to guide us, God's presence is always with us, strengthening and enabling us to follow that Way."

Pressing a hand against her chest, Kelila felt the steady pounding of her own heart. It hammered with such ferocity she wondered if the entire gathering could hear it. Leaning forward on the bench, her eyes never left the earnest face of the evangelist as he said with great conviction, "Now here is the question I must ask each and every one of you, those who now recognize the true and living Way—will you choose to walk in it?"

CHAPTER 11

Tabitha

"You've said very little this evening."

Glancing up from her mending, Tabitha released a quiet sigh. "I suppose I haven't much to say."

"A rare occurrence," Stephanos teased, watching her work from across the room. She was so beautiful, her golden head bent over her sewing, a sea of curls billowing over her shoulders, reflecting the gentle lamplight. "What troubles you, beloved?"

"We really needn't discuss it," Tabitha replied, attempting to keep the edge from her tone. How many times had they already done so? Stephanos knew how she felt about his insistence to reach stubborn Jews and religious leaders who clearly had no desire to be saved. She was exasperated with his dramatics. In her opinion, he was brash and reckless, simply asking for trouble.

Heart constricting, Tabitha remembered Saul's seething threats. She feared for her husband more than she could possibly explain to him. She couldn't bear the thought of losing him. Why couldn't he see that?

"Come here."

Lifting her gaze, Tabitha saw her husband standing across the room, arms outstretched.

Tabitha shook her head, her irritation mounting. She knew where her husband was going with this. He would take her in strong arms, insisting that everything would be all right. Then he would kiss her, gently at first, holding her close, until she could think of nothing except how fiercely she loved him, how much she wanted to be with him. It had happened enough times for her to know their disagreement would be dismissed for the evening, but there would be no lasting resolution. She'd feel just as frustrated—if not more so—the next time Stephanos engaged in heated debate with a powerful enemy.

"Come here, love." Stephanos' arms remained outstretched, his tone insistent.

Sighing in frustration, Tabitha went to him, knowing she'd hate herself for it later.

Taking her in strong arms, Stephanos held her close. "You seem to think I preach just to spite you," he whispered into her hair.

"Sometimes I wonder," she admitted, burying her face in his chest. She felt as if her heart was being torn in two—sheer exasperation battling her intense longing for him.

"I cannot refuse my calling," Stephanos said, his tone begging her to understand. "I wouldn't do this if I wasn't certain the Lord had called me to persist."

"I fear for your safety," Tabitha confessed for the umpteenth time. "The apostles have been arrested repeatedly, whipped, and beaten. By God's grace, they have survived to tell of it. But I worry for you, my husband. I worry every single day—"

"Tabitha," Stephanos interrupted her. Smiling gently, he pulled away ever so slightly so he could gaze into her anxious eyes. "*You are worried and troubled about many things. But one thing is needed.*"

Tabitha immediately recognized the familiar words of her Savior. He had spoken them to a dear saint named Martha, who resided in Bethany with her sister, Mary, and brother, Lazarus. At the time, Martha had been aflutter with resentment, frustration, and anxiety, for she was burdened with many exhausting tasks. But her sister, Mary, remained at the feet of Jesus, exulting in His teaching and glorying in His presence. When Martha had demanded why the Lord didn't force Mary to help her, Jesus had responded that Mary had chosen the better way.

One thing is needed. Sighing in resignation, Tabitha knew what that one thing was. She needn't dissolve in a puddle of frustration, fear, or resentment. Instead, she must have faith in God's perfect plan for her, for Stephanos. Ultimately, His will would be fulfilled in their lives. She must rest in Christ's love for them, His promise to never leave them or forsake them.

Raising penitent eyes to her husband's, Tabitha realized she was making the same dreadful mistake she'd made so many times before. The Lord had granted her a precious gift—this incredible man whom she loved dearly—and yet she was so concerned about the future, she couldn't possibly enjoy the sweetness of this present moment.

Draping her arms gently over her husband's wide shoulders, Tabitha intertwined her fingers at the back of his neck. "You must regret marrying a faithless woman." She sighed, her eyes bleak, her expression downcast.

"There is nothing faithless about you, beloved," Stephanos affirmed her gently, cupping her face with one strong hand. "You love me; thus, you worry for me. Can I fault you for that?"

"May the Lord forgive my doubts," Tabitha said softly.

Smiling warmly, Stephanos tucked a stray curl behind her ear. "You needn't worry, beloved. He already has."

***

Kelila

Perched high upon the cool stone steps leading to the roof, Kelila gazed up at a vast sea of glistening stars, twinkling like so many tiny gems in a soft sea of velvet. It was a delectable spring evening, with cool night breezes whispering through gently fluttering palm fronds, a silvery moon rising high overhead.

When I consider Your heavens, the work of Your fingers, the moon and the stars, which You have ordained, Kelila thought, surprised that an ancient psalm her mother had prized would return to her now. *What is man that You are mindful of him, and the son of man that You visit him?* With a rueful smile, Kelila supposed Candace would say the heavens were declaring the glory of God. But on a paradisal evening like this, Kelila admitted it was rather difficult to argue that point.

Kelila knew she should be in the house with Simon, Candace, and their children, helping clear away supper's leftovers, dishes, and cooking utensils, rather than daydreaming and soaking up the pleasant, balmy night air. Though Candace hadn't demanded Kelila pitch in and help, Kelila had sensed her silent plea. Shifting a bit uncomfortably, Kelila acknowledged her presence had indeed complicated her relatives' situation. They now had one more mouth to feed, one more back to clothe. She—virtually a stranger to them—had traipsed into their lives completely uninvited, shattering the serenity and familiarity of their comfortable routine. And yet, not once had Simon or Candace complained. They had simply accepted her, seeking to set her at ease, making her feel comfortable and welcome.

Shoving her thoughts aside, Kelila clasped anxious hands in her lap. She didn't like feeling guilty, but ever since that morning at the synagogue, guilt had become a constant, lingering presence. She couldn't remember ever feeling guilty about anything—until now. But *now*? Now she couldn't help but wonder what her father thought about her impulsive decision to leave home. She had willfully placed him in a terrible bind... Wincing, Kelila attempted to justify her nagging guilt, but her thoughts strayed toward her gentle mother. Had she wept for her youngest child when Kelila had left? Had she, Kelila, broken her mother's heart? And what of Simon and Candace? Had she placed a heavy burden upon a young couple already struggling to make ends meet? She'd never even bothered to alert them about her arrival, nor had she sought their permission to invade their sacred space. She'd simply imposed her presence upon them, all the while demanding to be pampered and spoiled.

Once again, Kelila's thoughts strayed back to Stephanos' fiery delivery before Saul, the Pharisee. For some reason unbeknownst to her, the evangelist's words resonated deep within her soul. After Stephanos' call to action, Saul had grilled him mercilessly, flinging at him dozens of recitations from the Torah combined with endless traditions of the elders, doggedly aiming to disprove the Messiahship of Christ. But Stephanos had presented astonishingly practical Scriptural rebuttals for Saul's every argument, further invoking the Pharisee's wrath.

Kelila had eventually gotten lost in the confusing semantics of the lively debate, but she didn't mind. Stephanos had already given her plenty to think about. She mulled it over even now. She knew an entire nation cried out for the Messiah's coming, but she'd never felt much need for one herself. She'd lived comfortably enough, and her father had capitalized upon the Roman system rather than resisting it. She'd never believed the Messiah's appearance would impact her on a personal level. Why should she care who ruled over Judea, a nation far removed from her own homeland? But Stephanos believed the Messiah had come to save everyone on a *personal* level. According to the evangelist, the Messiah cared about *her*. He wanted to *know* her, to *love* her! She wasn't entirely sure how she felt about that.

Kelila was beginning to understand that Stephanos' gospel was more unlike her father's than she had initially suspected. She'd never possessed the slightest interest in the dead, dry religion of her parents. Sure, they rigidly adhered to the Law, but there was no life, no joy, in either of them. Her father possessed the joviality of a darkened tomb! And her mother? She lived in fear of breaking the Law—or raising her husband's ire—Kelila wasn't quite sure which it was.

But these followers of Jerusalem? They were *alive* in every sense of the word! It was as if some mighty force overshadowed them, uniting each of them in thought and purpose. What had Stephanos said that morning? *...because He sent the Holy Spirit to guide us, God's presence is always with us, strengthening and enabling us to follow that Way.*

God's presence. The Holy Spirit. Perhaps this was the force responsible for the believers' unwavering obedience. Did adherence to the Law come easily for those who possessed this mystical Spirit?

Wrinkling her brow, Kelila gave the matter some thought. Stephanos had said the Holy Spirit enabled believers to walk in the Way. He also said Jesus *was* the Way, the truth, and the life. And *life* is what Kelila desperately longed for—a rich life brimming with wonder and whimsy, where adventure beckoned from every corner, where desires were met in pleasant pastures. But in her crazy quest to obtain her own happiness, Kelila had done nothing but further jeopardize it. Did this Jesus truly harbor the answers to discovering an abundant life? If so, perhaps this is what her parents had been missing all along. Perhaps—just perhaps—this is what she needed.

"May I join you?"

Drawing a hand to her heart, Kelila started at

her sister's unexpected intrusion. Candace stood poised at the bottom of the stairs, looking up at her. Kelila couldn't read her expression in the gathering darkness.

Feeling yet another stab of guilt, Kelila wondered if her older sister was about to lecture her for skipping out after supper and dumping all the chores on poor Alexander. Again.

"Of course, you can join me," Kelila replied, attempting to sound lighthearted. "You needn't my permission. It's *your* house, after all." Cringing inwardly, she supposed Candace must feel as if "her" house had been overrun.

Delicately lifting the hem of her robe, Candace climbed the wide stone steps, lowering herself onto the step below her sister. At first, she said nothing, and Kelila wondered what she must be thinking. Was she angry? Saddened? Exasperated?

"It's a beautiful night," Candace finally said, catching Kelila off guard. There wasn't even a hint of irritation in her tone. Her dulcet voice sounded pleasant and smooth, as if it belonged in this tranquil setting.

"Indeed," Kelila responded, resting elbows upon her knees and nervously clasping her hands.

The two sisters remained in thoughtful silence for quite some time. Kelila sensed she should say something but hadn't the slightest idea what to say. She felt agitated and out of sorts.

"Is something on your mind?" Candace inquired after another long pause.

Kelila wondered how much she dared tell her sister. Stubborn pride discouraged her tongue, even as her conscience begged for release. "I kind of barged in on your life by showing up here, didn't I?" she dared, feeling more torn than ever.

Even the growing darkness couldn't mask Candace's surprise. After a moment of stunned silence, the eldest sister chuckled softly, squeezing Kelila's knee. "It was a bit of a shock," she admitted, leaning gracefully upon the step behind her. "But, truthfully, I'm glad you're here."

Kelila blinked back unwanted tears, moved by Candace's glad acceptance. "Tell me about this Holy Spirit of yours." The moment the abrupt words had escaped her mouth, Kelila could have gladly kicked herself. Where had that even come from? She certainly hadn't intended to delve into a serious religious discussion!

"It's a fascinating concept, isn't it?" Candace remarked, not looking the least bit surprised or offended by the abrupt nature of her sister's question. "Quite frankly, the Holy Spirit is still a bit of a mystery to us, but we cannot deny the Spirit's power. First, God the Father sent us God the Son, who in turn bequeathed the Holy Spirit unto us. Now the Holy Spirit resides within each believer, leading us in the Way of life."

"Are you possessed by this Spirit?" Kelila asked innocently. "Does it control your thoughts and actions?"

"Possessed, no. *Led*, yes," Candace explained. "The Holy Spirit *nudges* us in the right direction, but our free will remains. Thus, we are free to make our own decisions."

"Then what's the point of this Spirit if it doesn't possess you?"

"The Holy Spirit is our *Helper*—He's not like the

evil spirits seeking human hosts to possess," Candace said patiently, her soft eyes conveying her great conviction. "The Lord will never *force* us to follow Him. Instead, He sent a Helper to guide us, to lead us in the right direction."

"And how does He lead?"

"It's hard to explain," Candace mused, her countenance shining with fond recollection. "Sometimes, it's nothing more than a still, small voice. One might entirely miss it if not paying close attention, looking for it, waiting for it. Then there are times when the Spirit's leading is piercingly clear, like a clarion call. When we choose to heed the Spirit's calling, we ultimately experience the sweet song of victory in our lives."

"It sounds confusing," Kelila quipped, flipping her lush dark hair with an air of nonchalance. "So if this Spirit can't *make* you obey, does it make it *easy* to obey?"

"I'm not sure it's ever *easy* to obey." Candace chuckled thoughtfully.

"Then what good is it?" Kelila demanded, impatient. Thus far, Candace's explanation hadn't suited her fancy.

"Oh, the Holy Spirit has proven invaluable to me," Candace insisted. "When I am weak, He is faithful to help me resist temptation. When I need guidance or encouragement, He brings the perfect Scriptures to mind. And when I *do* stumble in sin, He convicts me of my shortcomings."

This time, Candace's words struck closer to home. Dark eyes narrowing, Kelila attempted to sound natural as she pressed, "What do you mean, He *convicts*?"

"Have you ever felt strangely unsettled, possibly even *guilty* about anything?" Candace asked.

Was that a trick question? Instantly suspicious, Kelila wondered if Candace's Holy Spirit also enabled her to read minds! She'd felt nothing but guilt since leaving the synagogue that morning!

It must have been a rhetorical question—to Kelila's great relief—for Candace plunged on ahead. "That strange disquiet, that disturbing loss of peace, is often the Holy Spirit seeking our attention. When we sin—be it accidentally or intentionally—the Holy Spirit brings those sins to mind. This, in turn, allows us to recognize our sin, taking it before God in genuine repentance. When we confess our sins to God, He is faithful to forgive us, cleansing us from our unrighteousness."

"So if you feel guilty, your Holy Spirit is trying to tell you something?" Kelila pressed, disturbed.

"Oftentimes, yes. When prompted by the Holy Spirit, the godly sorrow one experiences over sin always leads to *repentance*. Worldly sorrow can also smite one's conscience, but rather than drawing one closer to God, it erects a self-inflicted barrier between the sinner and the Savior."

"I'm not following."

"Do you remember Simon Peter?"

"Of course." How could one forget the brassy Galilean fisherman with his fiery speech and guttural-sounding accent?

"Well, the night our Savior was arrested, Peter denied our Lord three times," Candace explained, her eyes distant as she recalled the horrors of that fateful evening. "He sinned greatly against God. But the Holy Spirit reached him, and he wept bitterly.

Peter confessed his sin, and he was forgiven. Now the Lord has granted him a place of honor among the apostles, allowing him to perform mighty wonders."

Bored, Kelila wondered where her sister was going with this.

"But that same night, another of Jesus' disciples named Judas Iscariot also denied the Savior," Candace continued sadly. "Judas betrayed Jesus, selling Him to the religious leaders for a mere thirty pieces of silver."

"That's terrible!" Kelila's eyes widened in dismay.

"Indeed," Candace agreed. "Afterward, Judas, too, experienced sorrow and deep regret. But it was a different kind of sorrow, a worldly sorrow—regret, rather than repentance. Rather than turning to God and confessing his sin, Judas allowed his guilt to fester. Crushed beneath the weight of his sin, Judas took his own life."

"That's awful," Kelila murmured, shaking her head. "So what was the difference?"

"Unlike Judas, Simon Peter allowed the Holy Spirit to draw him back to the Lord," Candace explained. "He confessed his sins to a faithful God, and he was forgiven and restored. But Judas, consumed with guilt, refused the Spirit's leading. Driven by the devil, the great accuser of men, Judas swallowed the lies the enemy fed him, believing he was beyond redemption."

"So you're saying the Holy Spirit draws men toward God and toward repentance, while the devil attempts to separate men from God, convincing sinners they are a lost cause, unworthy of God's redemption?"

Candace blinked in stark surprise. "You summed

that up quite nicely!"

"It sounds like a battlefield," Kelila remarked wryly.

"It *is* a battlefield," Candace affirmed. "The enemy of God has waged war against the Almighty and His children. The devil is relentless in his pursuit of the souls of men."

Wrinkling her brow, Kelila pondered the heaviness of this subject. It was an uncomfortable topic. She preferred carefree, breezy conversations. Still, she couldn't deviate from the subject at hand until she had confirmed her nagging question beyond any shadow of doubt. "So…then, that feeling of guilt you mentioned earlier—that's the Holy Spirit drawing you?"

"It is," Candace said, carefully masking the hope burning in her eyes. She hadn't imagined Kelila would be receptive to these teachings so soon!

"Then is it safe to say that the guiltier one feels, the harder the Holy Spirit is trying to reach him?"

"It is!" Nearly bursting with hope and thanksgiving, Candace offered her gracious Father a silent prayer of gratitude. At this very moment, He was working in her sister's heart! "It is, indeed."

Heart sinking, Kelila acknowledged that Candace must have spoken the truth. How else could she have so accurately and succinctly described the inner battle raging in her own soul?

CHAPTER 12

Kelila

The sixth day of the third month ushered in the long-awaited feast of *Shavuot*, or Pentecost, and along with it, nearly feverish festivities accompanied by pomp and ceremony unlike anything Kelila had ever witnessed in Cyrene. Almost giddy with anticipation, Kelila watched in fascination as grand processions descended upon Jerusalem, led by magnificent sacrificial bulls, their proud heads bearing lovely hand-woven wreaths of olive leaves beneath gleaming gilded horns. Flower-strewn, ox-drawn carts bearing the sacred *bikkurim* lumbered along toward the gleaming Temple complex at the eastern end of the holy city, accompanied by the lively sound of flutes borne by talented musicians.

Racing to the gate enclosing Candace's outer court, Kelila leaned against the wooden post, listening with rapt fascination as yet another procession poured down a busy Lower City street nearby, probably weaving its way through rambling, ramshackle streets toward the glorious Temple Mount rising majestically in the distance. Closing her eyes, she reveled in the song of celebration drifting down narrow, stone-paved alleyways. She longed to kick off her sandals and fly toward the great commotion for an up-close view, absorbing every fascinating detail. If only the procession would meander down the narrow road cluttered with ancient houses just outside her gate—then she could see everything! She didn't think she would ever tire of the pomp and grandness associated with these religious festivals in Jerusalem. They were certainly a far cry from the dull recitations and droning lectures echoing within the marble halls of her father's beloved synagogue.

In the past, Kelila had tuned out her father's lengthy expositions regarding this sacred time of year. But now, she found herself plying Candace with questions about the ancient feast. She'd learned of its origin on that sacred mount so long ago, when God delivered the Law to His chosen people. She'd learned of its purpose, for the agricultural festival— proclaiming the end of the spring barley harvest and ushering in the summer wheat harvest—had become a public declaration of God's grace and goodness in bringing forth faithful sustenance. She'd even discovered a few interesting new terms associated with the holiday, such as the *bikkurim*, referring to the firstfruits which were set apart and offered to God in the Temple. The *bikkurim* consisted of the seven staples of the Promised Land—wheat and barley, grapes, figs, pomegranates, olives, and dates. As the products of grapes and olives, new wine and fresh olive oil were also considered acceptable offerings.

Kelila thought it was rather fitting the Lord had

provided the Israelites with seven staple foods, since the number seven had always signified completion in the sacred texts. Candace had smiled when Kelila had divulged this interesting bit of learning.

Reluctantly turning back to the house, Kelila considered the odds of convincing Candace to visit the Temple for an up-close look at all the action. Grinning, she supposed her chances were next to nothing. Her sister preferred the security and quiet serenity of her well-kept, organized home while she, Kelila, delighted in feverish activity. Sometimes, she couldn't believe that she and Candace were actually related!

Closing the wooden door behind her with a sigh of disappointment, Kelila realized this third month of the religious year also signified her third month in Jerusalem. It had been an interesting season, marked by fascinating acquaintances, shocking new theology, and church meetings beyond number. Though she'd never admit it, Kelila acknowledged the services hosted by the apostles—whether in a stone-cold synagogue, at Mary's palatial villa, or in Candace's modest house—were far more interesting than anything she'd been forced to endure in Cyrene. She thought she was beginning to understand the Way, simply by observing the believers' conduct rather than by any particular sermon preached. It was so simple, and yet revolutionary. And she was quite certain their Holy Spirit was drawing her…

It was rather annoying. Once upon a time, she had existed in a blissful state of self-absorption, catering to her own desires without the slightest regard toward others. But now her conscience pricked the instant her thoughts became consumed with herself.

For the first time in her young life, Kelila began to notice the needs of those around her, particularly those of her new family.

And then there was Philip... The man was a maddening study in contradictions! Kelila *knew* he was attracted to her. There were times when he could scarcely pull his gaze from her graceful form. Even so, he stubbornly maintained his distance. He acknowledged her presence at each meeting with maddening politeness, carefully avoiding close contact. It was all she could do to resist marching straight up to him and demanding an explanation about his mulish resistance! True, she loved a good challenge, but this was getting ridiculous!

Pressing her back against the door, Kelila closed her eyes and released an exasperated sigh. Her heart was being tugged in far too many directions! Part of her longed to embrace this strange new sect of believers, losing herself entirely to the beauty and simplicity of the Way. And yet another part of her held back, daunted by the frightening possibilities of relinquishing her right to plan her own future, to chart her own course.

Releasing a rueful snort, Kelila admitted she hadn't proven particularly successful paving her own way thus far.

***

Saul of Tarsus

The feasting and festivities carried far into the following week, as revelers were loath to pack up their belongings and depart from the cheerful homes of hospitable relatives. The city was alive with music and camaraderie, the sound of it drifting upon the air, assaulting the senses of the rigid young Pharisee standing upon a resplendent terrace overlooking the red-roofed, marble structures of the glorious Upper City.

Saul wondered why he had allowed himself to be roped into this uncomfortable gathering—a post-Pentecost celebration, of sorts. Once, he'd felt entirely at home at this splendid Upper City villa, the house of Gamaliel, his instructor and childhood idol.

Gamaliel, the highly revered grandson of the mighty Hillel, bore many esteemed titles. *Ha-Zaqen*, the elder, signified his great wisdom. *Rabban*, or master, referenced his unrivaled authority. But it was the power-charged title of *Nasi*, prince of the great Sanhedrin, that set him apart from all the rest. Only one man, the high priest—Joseph Caiaphas— could boast a greater title. But Saul bitterly acknowledged Gamaliel wielded far more power than even Caiaphas. The Sanhedrin's pestilent ruling prohibiting the apostles' arrest proved that unwelcome fact. In his typical, mercy-saturated manner, Gamaliel had single-handedly convinced the Sanhedrin that the apostles' deranged movement would eventually fizzle and die. The respected elders, seated upon their gilded chairs, had swallowed Gamaliel's pacifist ideology hook, line, and sinker.

True, the elders—and the people—feared Caiaphas, the high priest. But they *loved* Gamaliel. Thus, Gamaliel maintained the loyalty of the masses, while Caiaphas depended solely upon their grudging obedience. Unless Gamaliel underwent a change of heart, recognizing the despicable faction as a mounting threat, nothing could be done against the blasphemous movement. Even his own hands were tied...for now.

The mindless fools! Despite their pretentious show of knowledge, the elders of the Sanhedrin were no better than dumb, lumbering oxen, poked and prodded down the path toward slaughter.

Frown lines deepening, Saul lifted his delicate, gold-rimmed goblet, taking a thoughtful sip of blood-colored wine, still brooding over the galling admission. Dark eyes burning like fiery coals, his gaze swept over the glistening city, now saturated in warm bronzed tones as a smoldering sun sank just beyond the western hills.

"Saul, my earnest student. I am honored by your presence this evening."

Stiffening, Saul's knuckles whitened around the slender stem of his goblet. Indignation mounting, he presented a stiff back to his tutor.

Appearing not to notice the slight, Gamaliel passed beneath a magnificent archway, crossing the wide balcony and drawing alongside his favored student. "You've been a stranger of late, my son."

My son. Gamaliel's fond proclamation only fanned the flames of Saul's wrath. *My son?* Not anymore. "I've been otherwise engaged."

"Ah, the destruction of the Way."

"*Someone* must do it," Saul maintained, clenching his jaw. "As Torah states, '*I am the Lord, and there is no other; there is no God besides Me.*' But this profane, polytheistic movement staunchly insists upon three gods—a Father, a Son, and a mystical Holy Spirit. You know Torah like the back of your hand, my lord. Surely this concerns you."

"Indeed, I've considered it well," Gamaliel replied in his easy manner. Resting weathered hands upon the railing before him, Gamaliel turned to evaluate his star pupil. "However, those adhering to this strange doctrine insist upon a supernatural concept of three in one—Father, Son, and Holy Spirit in perfect unity—rather than three distinct, separate gods. Regarding this tri-fold theology of the new sect—have you considered the Shema?"

Saul looked at him askance. Every Jew worth his salt knew the Shema by heart! It was engraved in his very soul!

"*Shema Yisrael, Adonai Eloheinu*," Gamaliel mused, flawlessly quoting the Hebrew rendition. "Hear O Israel, the Lord our God. *Adonai Echad*, the Lord is one. The original tongue implies the plural form of God, *Adonai Eloheinu*, even while the closing sentence, stating, *the Lord is one*—indicates the singular sense, *Adonai Echad*. Interestingly enough, the Hebrew word *Echad* often indicates a unity within diversity."

"What are you implying?" Saul contended, his eyes narrowing in distrust.

"It is a fascinating study, is it not?" Gamaliel mused, stroking his well-kept gray beard. "I find it interesting that the Shema is composed of three distinct, separate sections, forming *one* complete benediction, unrivaled in beauty and perfection. Note also that this blessing is pronounced three times each day—a rather obvious theme of three in one. So many hidden symbols—and this is but *one* ancient blessing!"

Saul opened his mouth to protest, but Gamaliel

wasn't finished yet. "And then there's the greatest and possibly the most well-known blessing of Torah, the *Birkat Kohanim*: *The Lord bless you and keep you; the Lord make His face shine upon you, and be gracious to you; the Lord lift up His countenance upon you, and give you peace.* Note the pronouncement of the sacred name three separate times—*the Lord* bless and keep you, *the Lord* make His face shine upon you and be gracious to you, *the Lord* lift up His countenance upon you and give you peace. Again we see this central theme of three in one."

"I shudder to hear you speak thus," Saul seethed, emboldened by the rage coursing through his veins. "One might almost suppose you sympathize with this blasphemous sect!"

"I am merely delving into the mysteries of the sacred Word," Gamaliel responded, unruffled by his student's unthinkable disrespect. "Is this not what we have been trained to do? The accurate interpretation of the Law is a most worthy pursuit."

"*Accurate*, remaining the key word in this instance," Saul reminded him, angrily discarding his goblet on a marble-topped stand. "Nowhere in Torah does this so-called supernatural concept exist!"

"On the contrary," Gamaliel murmured, his warm eyes roving the distant hills as if attempting to discover answers etched within the swiftly deepening shadows. "In my recent studies, I stumbled upon the account of creation, particularly the creation of man. If you will recall—"

"Please, I know what you're going to say," Saul spat out, his blood-pressure rising. "You intend to reference the verse in which God says, '*Let Us make man in Our image, according to Our likeness*,' are you not?"

"You were always my most avid pupil." Gamaliel smiled.

Saul wanted nothing more than to wipe the smile off his teacher's weathered face! "Our brilliant scholars have provided numerous practical interpretations of this clause! Some argue Adonai consulted the angelic beings before His creation of man. Others claim Adonai spoke not to a partner-god, but to the earth! The *earth* partnered with the Almighty in the creation of man! As Torah states, *the Lord God formed man of the dust of the ground, and breathed into his nostrils the breath of life; and man became a living being.*"

"The earth, you say?" Gamaliel replied, fully aware of the popular supposition. "And you suppose the Almighty required the assistance of angels—or worse—an inanimate object in the creation of man?"

"It's *poetic*," Saul argued, annoyed by the maddening logic of Gamaliel's statement. "Not to be taken literally!"

"Most often," Gamaliel mused quietly, "I find the Word of God to be quite literal. True, there are also symbolic passages. Some passages prove both literal *and* symbolic."

Clenching his jaw, Saul spoke not. He didn't trust himself to do so, as his patience was wearing thin.

"There's something I've always found troubling about this theory you've mentioned—the earth playing a role in the creation of living things. Given the surprising similarities, one might be easily persuaded to accept a pagan line of thought regarding the origins of life. The Greeks propose that the *earth* birthed living creatures and mankind—a bizarre and unlikely combination of natural elements impacted by natural forces, they say. They proclaim the world came about by chance, but we know that the world was framed by the Word of God."

"You needn't lose sleep over that concern," Saul said coldly. "I have no plans to embrace the idle musings of pagan philosophers. I fear you are more endangered than I, as you seem determined to justify and substantiate the blasphemous ideology of a dangerous religious order."

"Not *justify*, my son, but *study*, piece by piece. Line upon line. Precept by precept. We must compare every teaching to the infallible Word of God."

"Pray tell me that wretched enchantress of this bizarre, unholy cult hasn't cast her spell upon you," Saul seethed, casting caution to the wind. Should Gamaliel choose to condemn him for his honesty, so be it!

"Are you referencing Mary of Jerusalem?"

"Who else? That loathsome Jezebel has ensnared half the city with her doctrine!"

The smile conforming Gamaliel's weathered features was enigmatic. "I am somewhat amused by your terror of one poor, defenseless widow."

"Poor? Defenseless?" Saul flung back at him, outraged. "Need I remind you that woman is far from destitute? You've seen her *palace*—not to mention dozens of servants to wait upon her every whim!"

"I suppose she is a force to be reckoned with." Gamaliel chuckled, bemused by the young widow's tenacity.

"She is but a sputtering flame, and I will not rest until she is extinguished along with her hateful teachings." Dark eyes flashing, Saul stared at his instructor head-on. But the expression upon Gamaliel's face bore no judgment, only pity.

"It was a mistake to come here," Saul sneered. His old tutor was far too senile and set in his ways to see reason. Incensed, Saul turned on his heel and stalked away, passing beneath the elegantly tiled archway and into the grand house. Heart pounding like a war drum, Saul vowed never to return to the house of his former instructor.

Releasing a grievous sigh, Gamaliel turned and watched as the rigid young Pharisee disappeared from sight, clearly eager to shake the dust of this home from his expensive sandals. Turning back toward the majestic view stretching before him, Gamaliel's trembling hands tightened upon the railing. Despite the beauty of this pleasant evening, his spirit remained troubled. He feared for young Saul, his beloved student. He feared for this nation and his people.

And he feared for the followers of the Way—kind, generous people like Mary of Jerusalem, people he had known most of his life. Should they be misled in their mysterious doctrine, it was quite likely they would ultimately suffer at the hands of pontifical men like Saul, possibly even forfeiting their lives.

Lifting his troubled gaze, Gamaliel noted the first evening stars gently dusting an indigo sky. *Lord God, Creator of the stars, of time and space and all living things, reveal Yourself to me, to Saul, to this nation, to the world.*

Fleetingly, a distant memory surfaced, whirling in his mind like a hazy midnight dream. Over two decades past—on the heels of the Passover—a young Boy no older than twelve or thirteen had sat amongst the elders in the Temple. A much younger Gamaliel, leaning against a magnificent pillar of Solomon's Porch, listening in stark amazement as the Child had instructed old men with flowing robes and gray beards. The Child's understanding of the Law and the Scriptures had been exceptional, almost uncanny.

When the Boy's frantic parents had descended upon the Porch, taking the Boy aside and chiding Him for remaining in Jerusalem after they had resumed their journey home, the Child had simply looked up at them with kind, innocent eyes. Gamaliel had been utterly struck by the guilelessness of His tone. *"Did you not know that I must be about My Father's business?"*

My Father's business?

At the time, Gamaliel had been struck by the Boy's great wisdom and innocence. Chills had claimed him then, despite the afternoon's intense, unpleasant heat. Even then, Gamaliel had known there was something exceptional about the Boy called Jesus of Nazareth.

Haunted by the fading memory, Gamaliel drew his robe more tightly about his feeble form, warding off an unwelcome chill.

CHAPTER 13

Tabitha

Tabitha wasn't surprised when the now-familiar cloaked woman emerged at the top of the broad steps opening into the Upper Room. After all, it was the close of a festival season. As was her predictable custom, the woman would probably vanish after this meeting, reappearing about four months later when the Feast of Trumpets drew near.

Discomfited, Tabitha wondered about the woman's agenda for the umpteenth time. Was she trustworthy? Was she seeking the truth, or was she simply curious, entertained by the apostles' lively sermons? Or worse, had she a hidden, sinister motive in mind?

Trying to dismiss her mounting concern, Tabitha glanced toward the row of elegant, rectangular windows at the far end of the room, judging the hour by the dusky sky and swiftly retreating sun. This evening's teaching should be commencing shortly. She was glad her husband wouldn't be delivering the instruction tonight. She delighted in his teachings, but also treasured the evenings when she could sit close to him on the bench, her hand tucked safely in his, as they drank in the Word of God together.

Standing at the opposite end of the massive chamber, Tabitha's eyes roved about for her Stephanos. There he was—talking animatedly with his good friend, Philip, and several other deacons near the platform. A mere stone's throw away, Candace stood in the cheery lamplight with her children and her sister, Kelila, talking quietly with Mary. Tabitha couldn't help but notice Kelila's attention was directed toward the cluster of young deacons near the platform.

With great effort, Tabitha banished her irritation toward the brazen young woman. The girl paid far too much attention to Stephanos, a married man, *her* husband! Drawing a steadying breath, Tabitha reminded herself that she must be merciful toward Kelila. Since the girl hadn't been raised with the knowledge of Christ, she couldn't be expected to behave as a seasoned believer. Besides, Tabitha was certain she had a kind heart. Hadn't Kelila sensed her anxiety in the synagogue that day when Stephanos had addressed the gathering, covering Tabitha's hand with her own? Rather than condemning Kelila, Tabitha resolved to set an example, although she knew she would desperately need the Holy Spirit's aid to do so.

Inconspicuously, Tabitha followed Kelila's intent gaze. Puzzled, she realized Kelila's desirous brown eyes rested upon Philip rather than Stephanos. Though relieved, Tabitha certainly hadn't expected a stunning beauty like Kelila to have eyes for the quiet, homely Philip. But then again, she was jumping to quite a few conclusions. Perhaps Kelila was simply interested in the deacons' lively conversation.

Redirecting her attention, Tabitha watched as the mysterious cloaked woman floated gracefully across the vast chamber, taking her usual seat at the very back of the room. The believers had learned to grant the quiet woman her space. They offered kind, sincere greetings but honored her silent plea to leave her be.

Tabitha's eyes narrowed. Why did this woman's presence ruffle her so? She couldn't help but fixate upon the obvious fact that she attended meetings in disguise. But why? And to what purpose?

Before she could stop herself, Tabitha crossed the room, taking a seat beside the reclusive woman. "*Shalom*. Good evening."

Glancing up in surprise, the woman's large brown eyes betrayed her surprise beneath a dark, heavy cloak. "*Shalom*," she responded reluctantly.

Once again, Tabitha was struck by the woman's silky, cultured voice. She also noted that the Jewish greeting sounded rather unnatural upon her tongue. The fragrance of her expensive perfume wafted upon the air, a heady and pleasant aroma that clashed with her peasant's attire. "You are called Sarah, am I right?"

"Yes," the woman replied, attempting to mask her nervousness. "And you are Tabitha."

"Tell me about yourself, Sarah," Tabitha prodded, surprised Sarah remembered her name. They had spoken only briefly once or twice. She sensed Sarah was intelligent and observant. She posed a striking, commanding figure, even dressed in rags.

"I'm afraid there isn't much to tell," Sarah humbly

replied, annoying Tabitha to her very core.

"Did you come to Jerusalem to observe the feast?" Tabitha pried rather gracelessly. She noticed her husband watching her from across the room but quickly averted her gaze. She didn't wish to be discouraged in her mission, and Stephanos probably didn't approve of her plying this reserved woman with questions. He'd already cautioned her to allow the stranger her privacy.

Sarah seemed to consider the question carefully before responding. "I always come to Jerusalem for the feasts," she replied safely, folding smooth, manicured hands in her lap. "I am privileged to attend these meetings on such occasions."

"Do you travel with family?"

"My husband."

"Ah," Tabitha nodded. Now she was getting somewhere! "Tell me about your husband. Would I know of him?" She was certain Sarah's spouse must be ridiculously successful. Her existence was clearly one of leisure and ease. Flawless skin, carefully preened brows, smooth, manicured hands and feet, and meticulous hygiene all bespoke an aristocratic lifestyle, despite her peasant's disguise.

Is that why Sarah went to such great lengths to conceal her identity? Did she worry her husband might learn of her attendance? Was she afraid of him?

Should the church fear him as well?

Nearly jumping out of her skin, Tabitha started when Stephanos' heavy hand fell upon her shoulder unexpectedly. Glancing over her shoulder, Tabitha's countenance bloomed with contrition when she saw her husband standing behind her, his expression rueful. He knew what she was up to!

"Greetings, my husband," Tabitha managed, motioning for him to join her on the bench. "I was enjoying some conversation with Sarah here," she said lightly. "Have the two of you been formally introduced?"

"We have," Stephanos responded, sliding onto the bench beside his wife. Leaning forward, he met Sarah's hesitant gaze, his own filled with acceptance and understanding. "We are honored by your presence this evening, my lady. Thank you for joining us."

Meeting Stephanos' gaze, Sarah smiled in acknowledgment. Tabitha was struck by the warmth and dignity in that one simple gesture. It was a shame she felt the need to burrow under layers of heavy clothing, for she bore herself with the grace and poise of a queen.

With a tinge of remorse, Tabitha silently acknowledged she should be far more interested in making Sarah feel welcome and accepted—as Stephanos had—than picking apart her life story, piece by piece. Would she ever learn to accept the will of God in quietness and trust?

Clenching her hands in her lap, Tabitha supposed her interrogation had drawn to a close…for now.

***

Mary

"You never did inform me about the outcome of your letter, beloved," Mary said, seated in a straight-backed chair directly across from Tabitha in the lovely inner courtyard just beyond the stately bib-liotheca. "The one you sent to your uncle in Joppa."

Tabitha stiffened, her goblet poised halfway be-tween her mouth and the table. Sighing, she slowly lowered her goblet on the marble-topped table between them, her heart pounding at the mere thought of her uncle's galling response. She had been so mortified by his graceless accusations that she'd desperately hoped Mary would forget about the whole thing.

But she should have known better. Next to noth-ing escaped Mary's keen memory.

"It's been several months, has it not?" Mary asked innocently, delicate fingers toying with the long stem of her goblet. "Have you received any word from him?"

"He sent a letter in response," Tabitha muttered, her bright eyes flashing in indignation. "I threw it in the oven."

Biting her lower lip, Mary resisted the urge to laugh aloud at Tabitha's fiery confession. Apparently, she hadn't been pleased with her uncle's response! More curious than ever, Mary waited patiently for the young woman to elaborate upon the fascinating tale. She certainly didn't wish for Tabitha to feel interrogated or backed into a corner.

It was a balmy summer evening, and Mary cherished these rare moments when she and her former maid found respite in the breezy garden court, waiting for Tabitha's husband to wrap up his work in the bibliotheca just beyond the towering, painted marble pillars. Here, the two women shared prayer requests and little confidences, basking in the pleasant fragrance of rich summer blooms and the deliciously cool evening breezes tickling brightly colored canopies overhead.

Watching her former maid shifting uncomfortably across the table, compassion swept through Mary. Poor Tabitha. The girl had reached out to her uncle in good faith, only to receive a stinging response. Mary suspected she knew what kind of letter Tabitha had received from her distant, aloof relative.

Appearing to compose herself after a long, silent moment, Tabitha forced a self-deprecating grin. "I suppose I shouldn't have burned it," she admitted, her gaze floating distractedly over the flower-strewn court. "But he's just so...so...*exasperating*!"

"Your uncle?"

"He all but accused me of writing him to take his money to fund the church!"

Mary chuckled softly. She understood why Tabitha's wealthy uncle, an unbeliever, might assume the worst. Having run in affluent circles for years, Mary knew many ridiculously wealthy men who guarded their money more zealously than their own lives. "I suppose you wrote him back to sort things out?" she asked.

Tabitha's expression betrayed her dismay. "Why would I bother speaking to that insolent old man again? Based on his letter, he's every bit as cynical and suspicious as I remembered. Nothing I have to say will change his mind."

"Perhaps not anything you *say*." Mary smiled knowingly. "But your *actions* may prove far more impactful. Over time, he may realize you write to him because you care about him, not because you want anything from him—if you remain persistent with your letters."

"He didn't even bother to ask about my mother or father," Tabitha said dryly. "I doubt he even knows they're dead."

"You don't think word would have eventually reached him?" Mary asked, surprised.

"Why would it? My parents weren't famous or well-known. When they were murdered in cold blood, I was too young to even consider writing him. Quite frankly, I don't even recall thinking of him at the time." Unprepared for the compassion springing to Mary's eyes, Tabitha blinked back stubborn tears. "Even if I had, I would've known better than to ask him for a half-shekel, much less for a permanent home with him. I doubt it ever occurred to me."

"But God had a plan for you all along, beloved," Mary reminded her, her soft gray eyes glowing with warmth. "He brought us together for a purpose— one we may never fully know but can trust entirely."

Reaching across the table, Tabitha took Mary's hand and squeezed it. "I cannot thank you enough for all you've done for me, my lady. Had it not been for you, I would have most certainly perished."

"Had it not been for *God's* abundant mercy," Mary murmured gently. "Thank You, Father. Thank You."

The two women remained in comfortable, reflective silence for several moments. When Mary finally spoke, Tabitha was unprepared for the intensity in her tone.

"Your uncle may have responded presumptuously, Tabitha," she said, leaning forward as if disclosing an important confidence. "But don't give up on him. What if the Lord ceased to reach out to us after one snubbed attempt? No, the Holy Spirit continues to draw us, patiently wooing us. And the Father waits to welcome miserable prodigals—as all of us once were—with wide open arms."

"You sound just like Stephanos." Tabitha chuckled, folding her hands on the table in amusement. "He thinks God will save everyone."

"He would in a heartbeat if some didn't stoutly refuse Him. But God won't force salvation upon anyone."

"Which is exactly why it's a waste of time to keep reaching out to some people," Tabitha insisted, annoyed. "Stephanos refuses to accept that some people are lost causes. Like that hateful Saul of Tarsus," she steamed. "He despises Stephanos with every breath, and yet my husband continues to treat him with kindness and respect."

"Because that is our calling in Christ," Mary said gently. "He loved us while we were still sinners, Tabitha."

"And I think it's safe to say Saul is the chief of all sinners," Tabitha muttered crossly. "Just last week, he threatened me while Stephanos addressed a crowd outside the synagogue."

Mary looked concerned. "What did he say?"

"He said the day would come when our 'miserable sect' would suffer for our 'blasphemous proclamations.' He spoke to Philip, who stood beside me while Stephanos preached from the steps. But I couldn't help myself, Mary. I told Saul that *he* should be the one quaking in fear of *us*! When Jesus comes back to separate the righteous from sinners, *he'll* be the one standing in the wrong line, not us! So who is *he* to threaten us?"

"I'm not sure your response was entirely Christ-like, beloved," Mary reminded gently, holding back a smile. "And what did he say to that?"

Tabitha looked away, her color mounting. She hadn't expected Mary to ask about that.

"Well?" Mary prodded, wondering what Saul could have possibly said to elicit such a response from Tabitha.

Sheepishly, Tabitha met her former lady's gaze. "He said I was clearly the direct product of my rebellious mistress."

Mary stared at her with round eyes, stunned to silence.

Tabitha's face broke into a broad, impish grin. "I thanked him for the compliment."

"Oh, my!" Recovering from her initial surprise, Mary covered her face with her hands, laughing merrily. When Tabitha heartily joined in, the intensity of the moment waned as both women dissolved in heartfelt laughter together.

CHAPTER 14

Kelila

As the stifling summer months gently faded into the festive autumnal month of Tishri, Kelila experienced the three consecutive feasts of the seventh month unlike she ever had in her father's household. In the past, she had loathed the sacred feasts. Under the stern supervision of her father, the servants had sprung into action as the holy days approached, sending the entire household into a state of utter chaos and frenzy. The family was far too exhausted—both from Father's uncompromising demands and from the mad preparations—to enjoy the celebration once the day finally dawned. Even more than that, Kelila had been repulsed by the thought of the endless blood sacrifices the feasts required in the Temple. She wondered how one could revel in praise and thanksgiving after witnessing such bloody, gruesome displays.

But here in Jerusalem, sequestered among followers of the Way, Kelila reveled in delightful preparations and festivities associated with each feast. Rather than dwelling upon the self-imposed regulations drawn up by famous sages and elders long dead, the believers rejoiced in what they called the "symbolism" deeply ingrained within each ancient feast. According to the believers, their Messiah's mission was deeply foreshadowed in these symbolic celebrations. Though Kelila was skeptically amused by their fervor at first, she soon realized she was unable to refute their teachings. Everything they said made sense.

It was a bit unsettling.

Even so, diving headfirst into the exciting festivities, Kelila had discovered a radiant joy unlike anything she'd previously known. She couldn't help but lose herself in the wonder of the celebration.

During the Feast of Trumpets, the blast of the shofar pierced the air, reminding all of Jerusalem to heed the voice of God. It was a joyous feast intended to prepare the assembly of God for the impending Day of Atonement. While solemn Jews gathered in the local synagogues to read the Law, the believers met at Mary's villa, where the apostles joyously proclaimed the gospel of Christ. Rather than participating in the daily sacrifices, the believers declared Jesus Christ to be the end of all animal sacrifice. His shed blood now covered the sins of those who accepted His final atonement. As the trumpets blasted their joyful song, Kelila was reminded of the apostles' strong warning: Jesus Christ would soon return for His own, descending from Heaven with a shout, with the voice of an archangel, and with the trumpet of God.

The crucial question, one that now haunted Kelila's nights, was this: Did such a day truly exist? And, if so, would she be ready for it?

Directly on the heels of the Feast of Trumpets, the Day of Atonement swept in like a gathering storm. A strange, oppressive darkness enshrouded the holy city as an entire nation reflected upon the burden of their sins, committing their salvation into the hands of Joseph Caiaphas, the high priest, as he performed bloody rites within the Temple compound. Rumors abounded throughout the city, for the scarlet ribbon, symbolizing the sins of the people, had failed to turn white as freshly fallen snow. In the past, the miracle of the ribbon had signified the nation's atonement for yet another year. But this was now the third year in which the ribbon had failed to turn white.

While the religious leaders vehemently refuted such rumors, attempting to silence the troublesome truth, the people responded in panic. Jerusalem was in chaos, the hysteria scarcely contained beneath the watchful eyes of Pontius Pilate, the brutal governor of Judea, and Herod Antipas, ruler of the province.

But while the entire nation fretted and mourned, the Upper Room in Mary's villa fairly glowed with hope, brightened by the steadily burning light of dozens of lamps and the believers' shining countenances. They knew why the scarlet ribbon had failed, and they rejoiced. The ancient rite had lost its power the moment Christ shed His blood upon the cross. The believers recognized the state of their eternal souls rested not in the hands of a capricious high priest, but rather in the hands of a loving Father who sent His cherished Son to become the ultimate High Priest, interceding on behalf of those who loved Him. Together, the church praised the Almighty for sending His precious Son to bridge the gap between fallen man and holy God. Kelila marveled. She'd never known the Day of Atonement to be anything but fearsome and grim. But here in Jerusalem, the believers' jubilation was contagious!

Even so, it was the Feast of Tabernacles five days later that thoroughly captured Kelila's imagination. She was quite certain she'd never had more fun in her life than during the hours spent constructing a crude outdoor *sukkah*—a tent, of sorts—in the outer court with Simon, Candace, and their two young sons. With an excited Rufus and a somewhat cautious Alexander trailing behind her, Kelila had scavenged the area for days, collecting large palm fronds, tree boughs, branches, thick brush and foliage, and baskets of blooms and fresh flowers. She'd had to keep a sharp eye on young Rufus, now two years old and charging about happily on sturdy legs, since he found it far more entertaining to *eat* the flowers rather than stringing them carefully along bits of twine as she had instructed. Working together as a team, the family constructed an impressive sukkah, complete with sturdy wooden posts and thick boughs and palm fronds forming a formidable roof. Flickering hanging lanterns filled the three-sided structure with warmth, the cheerful glow illuminating the festive greenery and garlands of fresh flowers draping the entire structure both within and without.

For seven days, the family dwelt within the elaborate shelter. It was utterly delightful, for the weather was calm and mild. Kelila had scattered comfortable, colorful rugs upon the floor, along with plump cushions and several crude stools. A long, low table was situated at one end of the sukkah, strewn with flowers, oil lamps, and Candace's best tableware. Each evening, Candace and Kelila huddled comfortably upon straw mats with the children in the flickering lamplight, listening in wide-eyed wonder as Simon recounted sacred passages bearing the tale of the Israelites' miraculous sojourn in the wilderness. Rufus preferred to cuddle in his doting aunt's lap each evening, while Alexander sat comfortably between the two women, his mother's arms draped around his small shoulders. Heart soaring, Kelila realized she had grown to love this family—*her* family—more than she would have ever thought possible.

The eighth day of the Feast of Tabernacles ushered in the great and holy day of assembly, in which the nation commemorated this most joyous of all Israel's sacred feasts. It was a glorious day—one Kelila would not soon forget. She reveled in the trip to the Temple, carried away by the swelling tide of pilgrims traversing Jerusalem's congested streets. Upon reaching the monumental house of worship, Kelila was mesmerized by the colossal golden lampstands burning in the Temple court. Candace explained that the towering lampstands—rumored to light the entire city at dusk—symbolized the pillar of fire which had led the Israelites in their wilderness journey. It was here, Candace explained, that Jesus had declared Himself to be the Light of the world. *He who follows Me shall not walk in darkness, but have the light of life,* Jesus had said. Kelila thought she was beginning to understand. While the entire world stumbled about, blindly seeking acceptance, fulfillment, and atonement, the followers of the Way remained steadfast, their eyes fixed upon Jesus, their Savior. Daily, they weighed each decision against the teachings of Jesus, and somehow, this simplified their lives dramatically. When in doubt, they simply paused, considering the path their Savior would have taken when He walked among them. It was as if their individual paths were fully lit simply by following the Light of the World.

When the sun eventually slipped behind the western hills on the eighth and final day of celebration, Kelila's heart sank along with it, for she knew the season of the three great feasts had ended. Standing alone in the abandoned sukkah, Kelila closed her eyes, listening contentedly to the lovely night-song as the sound of chirping crickets filled the air. Cool autumn breezes rustled through the garlands and greenery, cooling and caressing Kelila's flushed face. Just beyond the canvas walls, Kelila heard her sister through the open door of the small stone house, singing to her sons as she tucked them in for the night. Her voice was lovely, low and melodic, as she sang an ancient psalm about the Israelites' wondrous journey home. "*Marvelous things He did in the sight of their fathers, in the land of Egypt, in the field of Zoan,*" Candace sang, her sweet voice carrying from the house and floating lightly upon the cool night air. "*He divided the sea and caused them to pass through; And He made the waters stand up like a heap. In the daytime also He led them with the cloud, and all the night with a light of fire...*"

A gentle breeze rustled through canvas flaps, tickling the decorative garlands and palm fronds. Wrapping her arms about her slender frame, Kelila opened her eyes, suddenly alarmed. Chills claimed her entire being. For the briefest moment, amidst the peaceful night and Candace's sacred song, Kelila had been aware of a Presence so strong it was undeniable, filling her entire heart, not to mention the small sukkah in which she stood. But just as quickly, the moment ended. Hairs standing on end, Kelila shivered, hugging her arms even closer about her frame. She knew better than to deny the Holy Spirit moving so mightily within the believers she had grown to love and cherish. Was He making His presence known to her now? And if so, *why*?

Kelila couldn't argue that her interest in the Way had grown steadily over the months, especially as she got to know the believers, particularly Mary, her sister and brother-in-law, Tabitha and Stephanos, and his best friend, the elusive Philip. She was amazed by the sincerity of their faith, the steadfastness of their convictions. Unlike the stiff religion of the Hellenized Jews in Cyrene or the flagrant immorality of the Greeks and Romans, the actions of her new friends truly mirrored their teachings, infiltrating every aspect of their lives and filling them with unmistakable, unshakable joy and peace. Their faith was not simply a religion to profess; it was a way of life!

Despite her steadily growing interest and fascination, Kelila was hesitant to accept the Way herself, for it meant inviting the Holy Spirit to reside within her. The thought both exhilarated and disturbed her. Should she do so, she knew there would be no turning back. She must be certain this was the right path for her *before* embracing a Way so radical, so all-consuming. Was she ready to relinquish the pleasures and entertainments so dear to her heart, pastimes she knew the Holy Spirit wouldn't condone? Even now, the Spirit pricked her conscience at the most annoying and unwelcome moments, and she hadn't even invited Him to do so!

Sighing, Kelila lifted delicate fingers to touch a low-hanging flower, her beautiful profile cast in the soft glow of a dozen steadily burning lamps.

It's a shame, she thought, smiling softly as her gaze swept over the simple furnishings in the humble shelter. *Soon we must disassemble this lovely sukkah, piece by piece. But I shall always cherish the memories we made here. Perhaps next year, we'll build an even better one!*

"What a lovely sight. I must confess, it steals my breath away."

Startled by the sound of the masculine voice at the open end of the sukkah, Kelila withdrew her hand from the delicate bloom, turning quickly to face the unexpected intruder. At the sight of Philip standing candidly at the sukkah's open end, Kelila's heart sprang into her throat, her pulse pounding rapidly. Philip always had this effect on her, though she couldn't possibly say why. She'd long since decided he had lost interest in her. In fact, he seemed to go to great lengths just to avoid her.

Why, then, had he sought her out?

Forcing a calm, teasing smile, Kelila straightened, her gaze beckoning. "A lovely sight, you say?"

Color deepening, Philip swallowed his obvious discomfort, though the admiration in his soft brown eyes was undeniable. "I was talking about the sukkah. It is lovely."

"Ah, and is that *all* you were talking about?"

Swallowing hard, Philip brushed aside her coy

inquiry, taking several cautious steps within the structure and clearly admiring its beauty and sturdy framework. "Simon said you designed this yourself."

"I did," Kelila grinned, proud of her work. "But the assistance of my rambunctious nephews proved invaluable. Simon and Candace helped, too."

"It's amazing."

Heart swelling with pride, Kelila feigned indifference, tossing her head with an air of nonchalance.

"I'm sorry," Philip stammered, shaking his head as if clearing jumbled thoughts. "I didn't mean to intrude upon this private moment of yours."

"You needn't apologize," Kelila purred, taking several bold steps toward him. Pausing directly in front of him, Kelila lifted dark, heavily lashed eyes to his, savoring the way his body stiffened and his color deepened at her nearness. She hadn't been this close to him since that first night in the Upper Room—so close she knew he could smell the scented oil upon her skin, see the teasing interest in her playful eyes. "I welcome this pleasant intrusion."

Expertly gauging his response, Kelila hid a knowing smile. Her hopes had been confirmed, for Philip's reaction convinced her that he was drawn to her more than he'd ever admit.

For one heady moment, Philip lowered his gaze, studying her every lovely feature with tenderness and warmth. The light of the hanging lanterns streamed down on them, casting their features in a soft, romantic glow. Fleetingly, Kelila wondered what it would be like to draw his head down and kiss him—the moment was far too perfect, as if crafted by the famous Greek dramatists and poets. But how would Philip respond should she be so bold? Would he kiss her back, or run like the wind and refuse to venture within ten miles of her ever again?

Somewhat annoyed, Kelila assumed she knew the answer.

"Philip! Thank you for coming," Simon, previously unseen, boomed from the doorway, shattering the spell between them.

Instantly self-conscious, Philip drew back, addressing Simon with an embarrassed, self-deprecating smile. Kelila could almost see the invisible wall Philip had erected between them. But why? Frustrated beyond comprehension, Kelila turned away, battling her own forward emotions. She was drawn to Philip unlike she'd been to any other man, though she couldn't possibly understand why. Philip was unlike any of her previous love interests. He was far too quiet, too settled, too disciplined. Despite his obvious desire for her, he held himself apart from her, clearly determined to squelch his own longing.

But why, Philip? Kelila's heart cried, her frustration steadily mounting. *Why?* She knew he had feelings for her! What fun it would be to take a lover, to steal the heart of a man! Why was he so determined to crush their own happiness? She sensed there was far more to his resistance than stubbornness or a shy disposition.

"My wife will be glad you've arrived, Philip," Simon was saying, drawing Kelila's brooding imaginings back to the present. "Thank you for stopping by to collect the food Candace has designated for distribution."

Color springing to her cheeks, Kelila realized her assumption about Philip's arrival had been entirely wrong. He hadn't come to see *her*—he'd come to collect a donation! When Philip's gaze flickered toward her, Kelila rewarded him with a cool glare. She certainly wouldn't give him the satisfaction of thinking she'd been fooled. Let him think she couldn't care less! Let him suffer as she did!

"Your generosity is greatly appreciated," Philip said, redirecting his focus toward Simon. "Thank you, my friend."

"You must be exhausted after this long day," Simon observed in his wise manner. "Come be seated and have some refreshments while my wife packs the items for donation."

Philip didn't argue when Simon guided him beyond the sturdy sukkah, intending to welcome him into his small stone house beyond.

Simon glanced over his shoulder then to address his sister-in-law, almost an afterthought. "Kelila? Will you join us?"

With a stubborn set to her jaw, Kelila ignored Philip's beseeching gaze. "There's much work to do if this sukkah is to be deconstructed properly. Do pardon my absence, Simon."

"As you wish," Simon responded, his eyes clearly betraying his confusion.

Presenting a rigid back toward the two men, Kelila reached over her head to remove a low-hanging lantern. It wasn't until the sounds of the men's sandals slapping against the flagstones ceased that Kelila turned, casting a soulful glance over her shoulder.

For some reason unbeknownst to her, snubbing the kind young deacon hadn't provided the satisfaction she had desired.

CHAPTER 15

Candace

Pleasantly brisk weather arrived with the wintry month of Kislev, along with the patriotic Feast of Dedication, also called the Feast of Lights. This feast commemorating the bravery of the famed Maccabees was rather like the Feast of Purim honoring Queen Esther's courage, risking her life for the sake of her people. Though neither celebration was divinely ordained like the other feasts, Candace eagerly anticipated the holiday festivities, thankful for the opportunity to reflect upon the mighty works God had accomplished throughout history.

Smiling to herself, Candace went about lighting candles, breathing in the tantalizing aroma of fresh baked goods wafting through the house. Pausing after lighting the last candle, Candace glanced anxiously out the latticed window. She hoped her sister would return soon. Though sunset would tarry for at least another hour, the streets were already darkening beneath a wintry, cloud-filled sky.

Kelila had eagerly volunteered to tote a heavy basket of hand-sewn garments to Tabitha's house over an hour ago. Chuckling to herself, Candace supposed the poor girl had been desperate for distraction. Kelila wasn't fond of baking, and Candace had spent the entire afternoon concocting delectable pastries and sweet treats for family and friends. Kelila hadn't been too interested in rolling up the sleeves of her delicate tunic to knead and shape sticky, messy dough. When Candace had casually mentioned the garments prepared for the orphans and widows of the district, Kelila had jumped at the opportunity to escape the domestic scene, offering to deliver the basket herself.

Smiling indulgently while rearranging the brightly burning candles upon the low table, Candace savored the inner peace springing up within her. Almost a year had passed since Kelila had arrived on her doorstep, rocking her safe, comfortable world. But in His abundant mercy, the Lord had paved the way, smoothing the path and granting Candace the inexplicable privilege of ministering to her youngest sister. Candace was certain Kelila now tottered on the brink of accepting Christ. Daily, her prayers of intercession intensified for her laughing, dancing, teasing sister. How she had grown to love her!

Wiping flour-dusted hands upon her apron, Candace turned to inspect the aromatic sweet bread cooling near the clay oven. She was quite certain nothing could disrupt her joy and inner peace today!

"Abba! Abba!" Alexander and Rufus erupted in frenzied excitement as their father entered the small abode now glowing with the light of a dozen lovely candles.

Simon scooped up squirming sons in strong arms, planting a kiss on each of their foreheads.

Satisfied her loaves had browned so nicely, Candace crossed the room, stepping gracefully down the single stone step near the entry. Her husband towered over her, both sons clinging to his neck as they giggled in delight. Rufus reached for Simon's bearded face, cupping his father's prominent cheekbones in chubby hands.

Somewhat surprised, Candace noticed her husband clutched a parchment scroll, careful not to crush it beneath the weight of his children. A strange sense of foreboding settled over her, though she attempted to dismiss it.

Sensing Candace's curiosity, Simon gently lowered the children to the ground. Giggling, they scampered off like eager little mice in search of crumbs. Straightening to his full height, Simon offered his wife the parchment scroll. "A letter," he explained, his eyes conveying his support and understanding. "From Cyrene."

Candace's heart nearly stopped. Had her parents finally responded to her inquiries about Kelila? She'd nearly forgotten about writing them, it had been so long! Now, she wondered if she should even open it. Life had fallen into a familiar and happy routine. Would the tidings of this letter merely confirm her joy or shatter her peace?

Hesitantly accepting the letter, Candace wondered why her fingers trembled.

"I'll spend some time with the boys," Simon said, his tone laced with understanding. "Take your time with the letter, beloved." Bending to plant a kiss on his wife's cheek, Simon went to his happily chattering sons.

Releasing a somewhat shaky sigh, Candace pulled her warm shawl tighter about her shoulders, suddenly aware of the unusual chill. Determined not to borrow trouble, she bravely returned to her kitchen space, settling down on a low wooden stool by the hearth. Lifting the letter for inspection, Candace broke her father's stately seal. Then, with trembling fingers, she unrolled the parchment letter, uttering a silent prayer as her gaze fell upon her father's bold, familiar script.

***

Kelila

Kelila knew she should hurry back. After all, Candace would worry. The poor woman was a *mother* through in through!

Even so, Kelila couldn't resist the temptation to meander along the way, reveling in the cheerful lights burning gloriously in the windows and on the rooftops. Joyful singing filled the streets, spilling out of the simple, well-lit houses of the Lower City. A sense of excitement and celebration filled the air, and not even the heavy storm clouds rolling overhead dampened Kelila's sense of wonder. Filling her lungs with fresh air, Kelila threw back her head, her covering slipping back and pooling about her shoulders. Closing her eyes, she basked in the wonder of the rare wintry season. She loved the coolness upon her flushed face, the feel of the steady wind teasing her flowing, colorful garments! She loved everything about this festive season! For the briefest moment, she felt the urge to break out in heartfelt prayer or song, as she had witnessed the believers do on many occasions. She felt as if her entire world was *right*. She was in the right place, at the right time. Something new and exciting beckoned her forth, though she couldn't quite name what it was. Candace would say it was the Holy Spirit, drawing her toward salvation.

Maybe it was. Maybe it wasn't. Either way, she was content in this perfect moment.

"Kelila?"

Instantly recognizing the male voice, Kelila hid a knowing smile. Just when she thought this day couldn't possibly get any better!

Gracefully turning her head, Kelila's lips formed a look of surprise. "Philip? What are you doing here?"

"I'm on my way to the house of Stephanos and Tabitha. They have invited me to dine with them this evening."

Instantly envious, Kelila imagined Tabitha sharing a meal with *two* handsome young men! She already had the most good-looking man in Jerusalem all to herself! Must she dominate Philip's attentions, as well?

It wasn't fair.

With great effort, Kelila swallowed her envy, forcing a dazzling smile in its place. "You are a lucky man."

"Blessed, not lucky," Philip reminded her merrily.

"Well, of course," Kelila agreed, a bit peeved. Why did he have to smile at her like that? He had such a nice smile, transforming his plain features into something wonderful. It was unsettling!

Closing the distance between them, Philip looked

around as if expecting to see someone else. "Did you travel alone?" he finally asked, the shock evident in his tone.

"I'd hardly call a quick trip to Tabitha's house worthy of the term *travel*," she responded snidely. "We've run into each other because you were *going* as I was *leaving*. I delivered Candace's garments for the poor."

"I see," Philip said, although his tone was laced with concern rather than understanding. Nearby, a group of rowdy young men loitering by a decrepit stone wall erupted in raucous laughter, several of them openly leering at the beautiful, unveiled Kelila. A few doors down, a disheveled drunk man crouched in the doorway, cup still in hand.

Nervously, Philip ran a hand over the back of his neck. It was a shame some people used the festival season as an excuse to indulge in revelry and drunkenness. He felt terribly uncomfortable dismissing Kelila now, knowing the eye-catching young woman could fall easy prey to any number of degenerates carousing in the streets. But was it proper to walk her home? What if he gave her the wrong impression by offering to do so?

Despite his initial misgivings, Philip decided her safety must trump his own discomfort. *Lord God,* he prayed silently after a brief, inward struggle, *lead me not into temptation.* Fortunately, the house of Simon and Candace was only a few short blocks away, and the road was crowded with celebrators, providing plenty of accountability for them. For that, he was quite grateful.

"May I walk you home, Kelila?" Philip dared, cringing inwardly at the hope springing into those gorgeous brown eyes.

"Ah, has the shy Philip finally found his nerve?" she teased, reaching out as if to take his arm.

Philip forced a smile he was far from feeling, though he didn't offer his arm. Instead, he gestured toward the road before them with a sweeping hand. "Shall we?"

"We shall, kind sir." Kelila grinned, batting her long lashes playfully.

"Let's be on our way then." *The sooner we reach Simon's house, the better,* Philip thought, attempting to suppress his mounting nervousness.

Swooping in unexpectedly, Kelila grasped his arm, clearly determined to stroll along arm-in-arm. Flustered, Philip wondered what he should do about that. But Kelila was already speaking long before his befuddled mind had pieced together a decent escape route.

"I just love the Feast of Dedication," she gushed, a contagious spring in her step. "The lights, the singing, the cheerful songs of celebration! Don't you love this time of year?"

Bracing himself for an eventful stroll, Philip decided to dismiss the troublesome fact that Kelila still clung to his arm like a lifeline. He hadn't the slightest idea how to politely address the issue, and he certainly didn't wish to squelch her enthusiasm for the celebration. When one embraced the feasts wholeheartedly, he or she couldn't help but recognize the hand of God in their lives. He prayed that would be the case for this beautiful woman.

"I've always enjoyed the Feast of Dedication," Philip agreed staidly.

Though his gait appeared casual enough, his alert

brown eyes scanned the way ahead of them, on the lookout for danger or threats of any kind. When the streets were this swollen with revelers and celebrators, explosive arguments and violence could erupt without warning.

Pausing in the middle of the street, Kelila's gaze swept across a city enshrouded in dark clouds yet afire with the light of a million candles, glowing bravely from every windowsill, ledge, and rooftop. "The lights are stunning," she breathed, shaking her head in wonder. "Have you ever seen anything so beautiful?"

I have, indeed, Philip thought, his heart lurching at the sight of the dark-haired young woman clinging to his arm, her cheeks ruddy and flushed, her eyes bright with wonder. Clearing his throat, he decided he'd best steer his thoughts to safer ground. "Do you know why we burn candles during the eight days of this feast?"

"Something about the menorah in the Temple," Kelila said rather heedlessly. "I've never been too interested in ancient history."

"Ancient history?" Philip chuckled, amused. "These events transpired less than two hundred years ago!"

"Too long ago to interest me," Kelila grinned.

"Even so, you're right about the seven-branched candlestick," Philip smiled, sensing an opportunity buried within their seemingly casual conversation. "The eternal flame in the Temple represented the presence of God. After the Maccabees cleansed the Temple of pagan influence, they needed to light the menorah. But they had oil enough for only one night. In faith, they lit the lamp, asking God's blessing upon it. And miraculously, the lamp burned for eight days without fail, until a fresh supply of oil was obtained."

"Ah, so that's why we light candles for the eight days of the feast—to commemorate that miracle," Kelila mused, fascinated in spite of herself.

"Yes," Philip supplied, glad for her enthusiasm. "Without the presence of God, all our rites and rituals are empty, futile. The steadily burning lamp within the Temple has always symbolized God's presence and blessing upon His people. Knowing this, you can see why the priests have been so concerned in recent years."

"Concerned?" Kelila repeated, glancing at him sideways. "What do you mean?"

"Well, the priests persistently light the lamp, yet it continues to go out—swiftly, without explanation. And this began on the day of Christ's atoning sacrifice."

"Wait," Kelila cut in, confused. "If the light representing God's presence has gone out in the Temple, wouldn't that indicate His presence no longer resides in it?"

"You are very perceptive." Philip looked at her then, his brown eyes approving. "The Spirit of God now dwells in the *heart* of each believer, not in a building shaped by the hands of men. As the body of Christ, the church has now become the Temple of the Holy Spirit. He resides in us when we *believe*, accepting Christ's atoning sacrifice."

"It's an interesting concept," Kelila mused, disappointed they'd already reached the tall stone gate encircling her sister's house. She didn't want this moment to end. She felt *alive* in every sense of the

SEEKING THE TRUTH | 155

word, with the wind teasing her hair and cooling her face, the chill breeze whispering its way through candlelit streets, this wonderful, steadfast man beside her...

"It's more than just a concept," Philip reminded her, feeling somewhat bereaved when she released his arm. "It is truth."

"If I didn't know any better," Kelila teased, her dark eyes sparkling with mischief, "I'd think you were trying to make a believer out of me, Philip."

"Only the Spirit can draw you," Philip told her, his soft brown eyes filling with warmth. "I see Him doing so, even now. Lean into God's love for you, dear one, and do not resist Him."

You will seek Me and find Me, when you search for Me with all your heart... Kelila blinked several times, startled by the clarity of the ancient promise springing unexpectedly to mind.

"Good evening, Kelila," Philip said, jarring a stunned Kelila back to the present moment. "May you find the happiness you seek in the will of God. He has good plans for you, if you will but accept them—walking in the Way, seeking the truth, and then embracing the abundant life God has in store for you."

CHAPTER 16

Candace

Kelila swept into the house like a whirlwind, her countenance aglow. Candace couldn't help but wonder what had transpired to deepen the rosy color in her sister's cheeks, intensifying the shine of her eyes.

After closing the creaky door behind her, Kelila pressed her back up against it, her features stretching into a dreamy smile.

Seated rigidly upon the stool near the hearth, letter in hand, Candace wondered how long her sister planned to stand there, fancifully gazing into the dreamy ethers of nothingness. After nearly a minute had passed, Candace cleared her throat a bit more loudly than necessary, her eyes upon her sister.

"Candace!" Kelila nearly jumped out of her skin at the unexpected sound. "You startled me!"

"Just as these unhappy tidings startled me, I'm afraid," Candace said, waving the letter with a hint of both sadness and frustration.

Kelila's eyes widened in a combination of both suspicion and apprehension. Blowing it off, she glanced curiously about the candlelit house. "Where are my crazy nephews?" she asked lightly, forcing a cheerfulness she was far from feeling.

"Simon took the boys for a walk."

Oh dear. Candace had sent the others away. This *must* be serious! Squirming like a cornered child, Kelila bit her lower lip. What in the world could possibly be hidden in that letter to so alter her sister's typically shining countenance?

"Come sit with me, Kelila."

Feeling a sudden surge of rebellion, Kelila reluctantly performed her sister's bidding, seating herself on the wooden bench across from Candace. She didn't like being told what to do. After all, she was a grown woman—not a child! But something in her sister's expression warned her she must tread carefully.

"I received word from Father."

Good Lord, have mercy! Kelila knew she was about to go through the wringer.

"Kelila," Candace said slowly, clearly struggling to keep her tone even, "you told me Father approved of your journey here."

"I never actually said those words, exactly," Kelila reminded her in her most charming, persuasive tone. "I just never said otherwise."

"You deceived me," Candace said quietly, her softly spoken words like a punch in the gut.

Kelila straightened on the bench, defensive. "I *had* to!" she declared vehemently. "Aren't you glad I came? You *said* you were!"

"And I *am*," Candace admitted, closing her eyes and massaging her forehead with delicate fingertips. "You're my sister, and I love you, Kelila. But this… this is unthinkable! Father and Mother have been worried sick about you. They had no idea you were here or even safe."

"Oh, please. They don't care about me at all," Kelila declared stoutly, crossing her arms in defiance. "Why should they care if I'm safe or not?"

"They're our *parents!*"

"They hate me, both of them!" Kelila insisted, shaking her head forcefully. "I know they do. I shouldn't have to stay with them."

"You fled an arranged marriage, Kelila!" Candace exclaimed, desperately trying to remain calm. "How could you?"

"I couldn't possibly marry that old bore!" Kelila cried fiercely, propelling herself to her feet and pacing about the small kitchen space like a caged tigress. "He was dull beyond imagining! He'd put me to sleep on my feet!"

"He was the man Father chose for you, Kelila, and you were legally and morally bound to marry him."

"Never!" Kelila cried, stamping an elegantly sandaled foot in emphasis. "I'll never marry that man! Even if Father came after me himself, dragging me back to Cyrene kicking and screaming, I'd find another way out!"

"Kelila—"

"If I *ever* decide to wed, I shall marry someone of my own choosing—not Father's! I refuse to be chained to a dreary old man the rest of my life."

Candace drew a calming breath, silently beseeching God for answers. What was she to do now? She knew she must remain calm, for her witness before Kelila was at stake. She mustn't respond in anger or retaliation. But before she could speak, Kelila erupted with yet another raging outburst.

"I won't go back!" Kelila nearly shouted, crossing

her arms over her chest. "I won't! No one can make me—not you, nor Father, nor anyone else!"

"You needn't worry about that, Kelila," Candace said quietly, feeling sick.

"Oh?" Kelila asked haughtily, arching a slender brow. "And why not?"

"According to this letter, you are no longer welcome to return."

Kelila stared at her sister, the color draining from her face as the air left her lungs.

"Father says you have shamed the family. In your long absence, your betrothed has wed another bride of his choosing."

Kelila could only stare, so stunned was she by this sudden turn of events.

"Father has disowned you, Kelila," Candace said, her soft eyes reflecting a sheen of tears. "He doesn't want you back."

"What?" Kelila snatched up the letter, her eyes widening in disbelief as she reviewed her father's curt dismissal. Before fleeing Cyrene, she hadn't considered she might go too far, pushing her father past his limit. "How could Father do this? How could he disown me?"

"You shamed and humiliated him, Kelila," Candace said gently, rising and taking the letter from her sister. "Father is a proud man. Your actions disgraced him."

Kelila stared at her sister in shock, weighing the consequences of her hasty decision for the very first time. "But how could he do this to me? He worships the ground I walk on! Father *loves* me. How could he disown me?"

Candace could have pointed out that, only moments earlier, Kelila had accused their father of *hating* her. Kelila's accusations were deeply rooted in vacillating emotions rather than logic. So how was one to reason with someone determined *not* to see reason?

Sighing dismally, Candace folded the parchment scroll, placing it on a high shelf. She didn't wish to look at it any longer. It only emphasized the terrible predicament in which Kelila had unwittingly placed her. She would need to think and pray about the best course of action to take. How could they possibly make amends? Her father, proud and unbending, would be unlikely to accept an apology from either of them, even a sincere one. Somehow, she, too, had been drawn into Kelila's web of deceit, for Father now considered Candace an accomplice, aiding and abetting his willful daughter's rebellious scheme. According to his letter, she should have sent Kelila back to him immediately, without qualm or question.

Perhaps she should have. Perhaps she had been naïve to assume the best about her sister. But had she done as Father suggested, Kelila would have returned to Cyrene without the knowledge of Christ. Perhaps the Lord was indeed at work, despite Kelila's selfish motives. He was the Master at working all things together for good, and even *this* was not beyond His reach.

Sighing, Candace lowered herself onto her stool again. Though she strongly disagreed with her father's harsh treatment, she knew Kelila's willful defiance had humiliated him, possibly even ruined him. His word could no longer be trusted among his peers. Kelila had, indeed, placed him in a terrible bind.

Despite his stern, controlling nature, Father had

doted on Kelila since the moment she had uttered her first frail, infant cry. *Kelila always had her way with him,* Candace thought sadly. But this time, Kelila had gone too far. This time, her selfish display had backfired.

"I only meant to teach Father a lesson," Kelila murmured, interrupting Candace's solemn train of thought. Limply, Kelila lowered herself onto the bench across from Candace. "I'll never see Mother again, will I?" she breathed, lifting tear-filled eyes to her sister. The impact of her grave misdeed was beginning to sink in. "Oh, Candace, I'm so happy here in Jerusalem with you and Simon. But I never intended to cut myself off from Mother and Father *forever.* You know I didn't mean to do that."

"I know," Candace assured her, her tone etched with sympathy. "Sometimes we make decisions we later regret. But God is merciful, always willing to forgive—"

"I don't need *God's* forgiveness," Kelila snapped, gripping the edges of her bench with white-knuckled hands. "I need *Father's!*" Kelila looked away, troubled by the alarm springing into Candace's eyes. Why must Candace make everything a religious issue, anyway? She had enough to worry about without bothering with silly religious rites of repentance!

Biting her lower lip, Kelila weighed her options. None of them were particularly appealing. She could return to Cyrene, begging Father's forgiveness. She needn't fear her betrothed, for he'd already taken another unfortunate woman to be his wife! Perhaps if she groveled and begged, Father would forgive her. Perhaps, in time, he'd see reason!

Wincing, Kelila recalled gruesome tales of disowned children executed by their father's own hand.

But no, Father would never do such a thing! He would never hurt her! Shuddering, Kelila realized she certainly hadn't expected him to disown her, either. Perhaps returning to Father's estate wasn't a good idea, after all.

"Candace, what am I going to do?" Kelila groaned, raising hopeless eyes toward her sister.

Candace met her gaze, her own filled with sorrow.

Kelila knew what Candace was thinking. Why had she even bothered asking her opinion, anyway? *If you tell me to repent, so help me...* Kelila thought, miffed. She didn't need to waste her precious time reciting pious prayers—no, what she needed was a course of *action*, and fast!

It was a long time before Candace eventually spoke. When she finally did, her tone was numb, almost devoid of feeling. "We must pray long and hard about this," she said, her graceful countenance inexplicably grieved. "Somehow, we must make amends."

"And how exactly are we supposed to *make amends* if I'm forbidden to set foot within ten miles of Father's estate?" Kelila grumped, annoyed.

"I'm not sure," Candace admitted, shaking her head as if to scatter jumbled thoughts. "But Father doesn't know Christ, so we can hardly expect him to extend mercy, at this point. He's reacting the only way he knows how."

"Like a tyrant?" Kelila muttered, perturbed.

"Let's pray about this, Kelila," Candace said, graciously overlooking her sister's snide comment. "God is faithful. He will grant us wisdom in this matter."

Biting back a sharp retort, Kelila resisted the urge

to roll her eyes in contempt. It was an easy thing for *Candace* to pray for guidance, but what about *her*? She didn't have a special relationship with God, unlike her *perfect* sister, Saint Candace! In fact, Kelila was quite certain that, at this point, God wanted nothing to do with her. Why would He? She had willfully destroyed her own father, carelessly broken her mother's heart, and then deceived her trusting older sister! God listened to His *chosen ones*, the devout followers of the Way—not sinners like her. The believers were of a different sort, and she doubted any of them had *ever* behaved in such a manner. No, the chances of a so-called "holy" God answering her prayers was next to nothing.

Those who are well have no need of a physician, but those who are sick. Startled, Kelila wondered where such an odd thought had originated. Especially amidst her own tirade of frustration and self-loathing. *I did not come to call the righteous, but sinners, to repentance...*

Hairs prickling on the back of her neck, Kelila's heart pounded wildly in her chest. Perhaps it was Candace's Christ speaking to her heart. Disturbed, Kelila shook her head, convinced such thoughts must be the product of her own desperate imagination. Releasing a sigh of frustration, she covered her face with trembling hands. This time, she had gone too far.

Forgiveness was entirely out of reach.

CHAPTER 17

Tabitha

"Stephanos! Where have you been? I've been worried sick!"

Closing the door behind him, Stephanos turned to address his wife with a rueful smile. "I think it's adorable how you worry over me."

Tabitha rewarded him with a glare of challenge. "You said you would return before sunset. That was hours ago!"

"I did say that, didn't I?" Crossing the candlelit room, Stephanos paused in front of his wife, cupping her flushed cheek in a strong hand. She had lit dozens of candles to commemorate the Feast of Dedication, and the small house glowed with cheerfulness and warmth. "I'm sorry, beloved. I should have said I would return before sunset *if* the Lord permitted. Sometimes His plans contradict our own."

"What happened?" Tabitha demanded, unable to shake the strange sense of foreboding clawing at her heart.

"I got held up on the way back from Solomon's Porch," Stephanos admitted, clearly attempting to brush off the matter. "Supper smells wonderful, by the way."

"It smells far better than it tastes, no doubt," Tabitha said tersely. "It's been congealing in the pot over the fire for several hours now. And don't change the subject, Stephanos!"

"Everything is fine, beloved," Stephanos assured her, tiredly removing his outer tunic.

Sensing her husband's great weariness, Tabitha softened slightly. He'd had a long, trying day, and here she was—grilling him with unwanted questions. Taking his tunic from him, she draped it dutifully over her forearm, attempting to soften her tone. "I want to know what happened, Stephanos. What do you mean, you got 'held up'?"

"The temple guards detained me briefly—*very* briefly," he added when Tabitha blanched in horror. "Apparently, some Pharisees thought I was disturbing the peace."

"You were *arrested*?" Tabitha gasped, heart constricting.

"Not arrested—detained," Stephanos quickly amended. "You needn't worry, beloved. The guards didn't even lock me up. They simply asked me a few questions and ordered me not to cause any further disturbances."

"And by that, they mean don't preach the gospel again," Tabitha huffed, miffed. "Stephanos, this is getting dangerous."

"Not nearly as dangerous as ignoring God's clear command," Stephanos reminded her gently.

"Who instigated this? By whose authority were you *detained?*"

Stephanos' wry smile told Tabitha everything she needed to know.

"It was Saul, wasn't it?" she snapped, hot anger coursing through her veins.

"It doesn't matter, dear one," Stephanos assured her. "Everything is fine now."

"And I assume you plan to preach again tomorrow?"

"Unless the Lord directs me otherwise."

"Stephanos! This is absurd. You can't keep doing this!"

"I can do all things through Christ, Tabitha, as can you."

"I can't deal with this...this constant stress!" Tabitha insisted, backing away when Stephanos reached for her. "I can't keep doing this, Stephanos."

"Yes, you can," Stephanos responded gently, ignoring her resistance and drawing her into his strong arms. "You can do anything and everything God asks of you."

Nettled, Tabitha looked away. She couldn't bear to meet her husband's burning gaze, to face the passionate fire swirling in his dark eyes. Surely her lack of faith was disappointing to a Spirit-filled man like Stephanos, but she just couldn't bear to lose him!

"Something must be done about Saul," she finally said, relaxing ever so slightly in her husband's arms. "He hates you, Stephanos. He hates you with a burning passion."

"But you forget—the *Lord* loves me with an everlasting love," Stephanos reminded her, kissing the top of Tabitha's head as she buried her face in his shoulder. "We must trust His will to prevail."

"Why the Lord continues providing breath for that wretched man is beyond me," Tabitha huffed, pulling away in frustration.

"God loves Saul, too, Tabitha."

"Well, Saul certainly doesn't love *Him*."

"But don't you see? Saul believes that he *does*, Tabitha. He is zealous for the Law, zealous for what he believes to be the will of God. As difficult as it is to understand, Saul truly believes he is serving God by challenging us."

"That doesn't make any sense."

"Saul is deceived by a cunning adversary," Stephanos explained, his eyes pleading with Tabitha to understand. "And I am convinced that God must have a powerful purpose in mind for Saul."

"Oh, come now!" Tabitha exclaimed. "You can't be serious!" She couldn't help but hope that plan involved a long walk off a short pier.

"No, it's true," Stephanos insisted, taking his wife's hands in his. "Why else would the enemy attack Saul with such calculated fury?"

Tabitha stared at her husband, strangely unsettled by his observation.

"For some reason unbeknownst to us, our enemy is engaged in a relentless battle for the soul of that man," Stephanos spoke calmly and with great conviction.

"Well, the enemy can have his soul, for all I care," Tabitha retorted sharply, her anger returning full force. Stephanos believed the best about everyone, but *she* certainly had no intention of justifying Saul's unspeakable offenses!

Stephanos looked at her then, his kind eyes filling

with sympathy. "I pray you will have a change of heart, beloved," he said softly, tenderly stroking her flushed cheek. "But as for me, I refuse to surrender our brother, Saul, without a fight."

***

Mary

"My lady, you have a visitor."

Sequestered within the quiet bibliotheca, Mary glanced up from her massive desk, alerted by the slight tremor of excitement hidden in her pretty little maid's announcement.

"Good morning, Rhoda," Mary smiled, gladly setting aside her stylus. She'd been busily reviewing ledgers all morning. A brief reprieve was more than welcome!

"May I send in your guest?" ten-year-old Rhoda asked shyly, her large brown eyes dancing with secret happiness.

"May I ask who it is?" Mary responded, her curiosity piqued.

"He wished to surprise you, my lady," Rhoda replied, her eyes silently pleading with Mary not to press any further.

"All right, then," Mary agreed, her curiosity further aroused. "Send him in."

"Yes, my lady." Bowing her head respectfully, Rhoda hurried away, an eager spring to her step.

Mary watched her go, intrigued. Whoever this mysterious visitor was, her maidservant was clearly excited to introduce him!

A moment later, Rhoda reappeared at the pillared

entrance, her eyes dancing with merriment. "Your guest, my lady," she said with a grand sweep of her small arm.

Mary sprang to her feet, releasing a short gasp when her brother, Barnabas, strode in, smiling broadly with arms outstretched to her.

"Barnabas!" Mary cried, rushing around the large desk to meet her brother halfway across the vast, stately chamber.

"*Shalom*, Mary!" Taking his sister in strong arms, Barnabas nearly lifted her off her elegantly sandaled feet, holding her close for a long moment before releasing her. When he did, there were tears in Mary's eyes.

"Barnabas! How I've missed you, my brother!" Mary exclaimed, suddenly remembering her blithe maid waiting at the entrance. "Rhoda, what a wonderful surprise!" she smiled, and the servant girl beamed with appreciation.

Having received Mary's polite nod of dismissal, Rhoda turned away with a little smile, pleased to have witnessed her lady's happy surprise.

Watching as the contended young maid walked gracefully across the inner court, disappearing beneath a courtly archway, Mary turned back to her brother, her eyes brimming with happy tears. "Rhoda was nearly bursting with excitement when she informed me about your arrival," she told him.

"I shall never forget the day you rescued that sweet little one from ruthless slavers," Barnabas mused, shaking his curly head in amazement.

"The Lord is gracious," Mary declared, her slender brows drawing together at the distant memory. "As always, He led us to the right place at the right time."

"Thanks be to God. She is a kind little soul."

"She is."

"And still smitten with John Mark, I imagine?" Barnabas teased, lifting a knowing brow.

"I believe half the young ladies of this city are smitten with him. I can only pray the attention won't go to his head," Mary remarked drolly.

Barnabas laughed in hearty acknowledgment. The familiar sound was wonderful to Mary's ears.

"You didn't send word about returning from Cyprus!" she exclaimed, taking his arm and leading him toward two gilded chairs before her desk.

"I thought it would be more fun to surprise you," Barnabas grinned, obediently seating himself on one of the elegant, straight-backed chairs. "Was I right?"

"You're always right." Rather than taking a seat behind her impressive desk, Mary lowered herself gracefully onto the matching chair beside her brother. "How are your business holdings in Cyprus, Brother?"

"Fine, just fine," Barnabas responded in his easy manner. "Though I must admit, I spent more time sharing the Good News than overseeing my assets."

"Good for you," Mary smiled, reaching out to pat his hand in approval. "Has the gospel fallen upon fertile ground in our homeland?"

"Occasionally," Barnabas acknowledged with a self-deprecating smile. "But the Jews of the community remain set in their ways, mired in centuries of religious tradition, while the Gentiles cannot possibly comprehend a faith like ours. I must admit, my preaching has garnered little interest, thus far."

"Don't lose heart," Mary encouraged him, sensing his hidden discouragement. "In time, the seeds you are planting will take root, reaping an abundant harvest."

"Amen. May it be so," Barnabas said warmly, squeezing his sister's hand. "Your faith is precious, dear one."

Mary acknowledged her brother's praise with a genuine smile. Basking in his pleasant company, Mary took a moment to study her beloved Barnabas. She didn't see him nearly enough these days, so involved was he in the Lord's blessed work! His kind face—framed by a sea of curly, light brown hair and an equally wavy beard—was incredibly endearing. His soft eyes betrayed both compassion and warmth. Despite his powerful status, Barnabas dressed simply and presentably, his easy manner instantly setting others at ease. He possessed the special ability to relate to just about *anyone*, regardless of their age, background, religion, or social status. A wealthy man with a generous spirit, Barnabas was constantly on the lookout for those in need. And as a frequent traveler, he knew his way around a ship like a practiced sailor, the roadways of the empire like the back of his hand. This unique gifting allowed him to minister to those far beyond the apostles' reach.

Mary was proud of her brother. He'd risen to a prominent position within the church, busily engaged in preaching the gospel and meeting needs. She knew Barnabas dreamed of planting a thriving church in their homeland of Cyprus, as well, but it was indeed a daunting task for one man. Perhaps, in time, the Lord would send workers who shared his passion, men eager to assist him in his mission.

"Your new name truly suits you," Mary observed candidly, her heart bursting with love and pride for her older brother. "I hardly think to call you Joses anymore, so fitting is the name Barnabas. Truly, Brother, you are the kindest, most encouraging person I've ever known."

"You honor me, Sister." Chuckling lightly, Barnabas, lovingly dubbed *son of encouragement* by the apostles, waved aside her glowing praise. "Now tell me, where's that young rascal, John Mark?"

Mary couldn't help but smile at the thought of her handsome, carefree son. At nearly fifteen years of age, he was fast becoming a man. She knew her brother cherished his friendship with the lad. "John Mark is studying with his private tutor. He will be thrilled about your arrival and disappointed I spotted you first," she added, bemused.

"And how does the boy fare with his studies?"

"He endures them with good humor," Mary admitted, somewhat troubled by her son's delightful—yet sometimes *exasperating*—boyish nature and casual attitude. At times, she worried John Mark didn't take his studies seriously enough. He was far too busy relishing every moment life had to offer.

"Ah, good for him," Barnabas chuckled, shaking his head in amusement. "That boy is so full of life and energy, it's no small wonder you've managed to cram so much learning into that whimsical head of his."

"I suppose I should be grateful he endures, but I wish I knew how to excite his interest," Mary confided. "Sometimes, I fear the Scriptures are little more than dull words upon a page to him."

"Ah, you needn't worry, Mary," Barnabas assured her. "John Mark is a grounded young man. He loves the Lord, and there's no doubt about that. He's simply eager to experience everything life has to offer."

"Well, hopefully not *everything* life has to offer," Mary amended with a wry smile. "But all the good things."

"Amen," Barnabas agreed.

"Will you stay for tonight's service, Barnabas?" Mary asked hopefully, changing the subject. Fleetingly, she wondered if there was time enough to convince him to deliver the instruction that evening. Wouldn't the others be thrilled to see him?

"You couldn't persuade me otherwise," Barnabas teased. "Of course, I'll stay."

"The others will be overjoyed to see you again, my brother!"

"Perhaps, although I noticed your doorkeeper wasn't particularly thrilled to see me," Barnabas chuckled good-naturedly. "I often pray for that man, Mary. His countenance grows darker with every visit. I suppose it's safe to assume he hasn't yet joined our ranks?"

Zev. Mary shifted in her seat uncomfortably. She'd been bold enough to ask Barnabas to pray for Zev's salvation but hadn't dared to disclose the guard's impossible feelings for her. Many nights, she'd lain awake wondering what to do about Zev, and yet the Lord had remained strangely silent. She'd learned it was best to wait on the Lord during these silent matters, though she'd feel far better dismissing Zev from her employ. Mary was a staunch, courageous woman, but Zev's burning gaze unsettled her.

"Mary?" Barnabas was watching her closely, sensing her inward struggle.

Embarrassed, Mary forced her thoughts back to their conversation. "Sadly, you are correct in your assessment," she said. "Zev remains combative toward the faith."

"As you've just reminded me, Mary, don't lose heart. A harvest of blessing may be right around the corner."

Unlikely, Mary thought, but refrained from voicing her opinion.

"Now, I want you to tell me all that has transpired during my absence," Barnabas said personably, settling comfortably in his chair as if readying himself for a nice, long chat. "Tell me what's happened, Mary. Tell me everything."

Mary was more than happy to oblige, for the church had experienced an unlikely season of peace following Gamaliel's shocking edict to leave them be, flourishing amidst sound doctrine and instruction, welcoming thousands of eager converts. Bound by the faith and camaraderie they shared, brother and sister talked late into the afternoon, both strengthened and encouraged by the other's faith-filled presence.

CHAPTER 18

Kelila

Seated on a hard bench in the Upper Room, Kelila wondered why she'd bothered to attend the service at Mary's house this evening. Candace had remained home with the boys, both of whom were suffering winter colds. Alexander and Rufus had been miserable for several days now, and Kelila was thankful she'd managed to escape catching the unpleasant malady. Poor Rufus was crying inconsolably when Kelila had left the house, and his harried mother had looked sorely tempted to throw up her hands and follow suit.

I should have stayed home with Candace, helping her care for the boys, Kelila thought, peeved. But then again, why should she? She never did the right thing, anyway. Why start now? Having been restless and frustrated for days, Kelila had jumped at the chance to accompany Simon to the church service that evening. At least the meeting should offer some distraction, even if she didn't belong with all these "righteous" people.

It had been over a month since she'd been disowned by her father, and his harsh proclamation weighed upon her heart and mind more heavily than she'd thought possible. *Unworthy. You are unworthy,* was the constant refrain now pounding at the door of her mind. *You are a failure. It's too late.*

Squeezing her eyes shut, Kelila bowed her head, massaging her aching temples. She tried to focus on the words of the speaker on the platform, but then wondered why she even bothered listening. It's not like the words were for *her,* after all. Unlike the others, she was not righteous. She was not one of them. No, she was a selfish, willful woman, unlike these kind, wonderful people surrounding her. Despite the warmth of the magnificent chamber and the gracious worshipers on all sides, Kelila had never felt more isolated, more alone.

Lifting dull, hopeless eyes, Kelila watched the Apostle John upon the platform, disinterested. John was one of the "special" followers. He often called himself the disciple whom Jesus loved, much to Simon Peter's obvious annoyance.

Cringing inwardly, Kelila supposed she didn't wish to know what Jesus would have to say about *her.* She was no faithful disciple, and certainly not a cherished follower like the lovable John. John's unwavering love for God shone through everything he did. Oftentimes, his eyes glistened with tears as other apostles spoke of precious memories shared with the Savior.

Kelila directed her gaze back toward John's energetic and boyish form, forcing herself to pay attention to the sermon. He was telling a story, a parable of his beloved Jesus.

"*A certain man had two sons,*" John was saying, standing behind a simple wooden pulpit, his kind eyes traveling over the audience. "*And the younger of them said to his father, 'Father, give me the portion of goods that falls to me.' So he divided to them his livelihood. And not many days after, the younger son gathered all together, journeyed to a far country, and there wasted his possessions with prodigal living...*"

Kelila straightened upon the bench, for the apostle now had her attention. She couldn't help but recognize the similarities between this parable and her own impossible situation. She, too, was the youngest child of a prosperous man. And she, too, had forsaken her father's house, traveling to a distant country to find happiness.

John expounded upon the story, and Kelila was spellbound as he described the younger son's endless quest for pleasure and happiness, finally freed from his father's watchful eye. Recklessly blowing through his inheritance, the young man soon became penniless. To make matters worse, a famine arose in the land. The prodigal found himself in dire straits. Kelila shivered in disgust when John said that the young man eventually found work feeding filthy swine. Apparently, he became so desperate he even considered filling his belly with the swine's stale pods.

"Eventually, the prodigal admitted his folly," John was saying, and Kelila found herself hanging upon his every word. "*When he came to himself, he said, 'How many of my father's hired servants have bread enough and to spare, and I perish with hunger! I will arise and go to my father."*

Ha, good luck with that, Kelila thought bitterly, resisting the urge to release a loud *harrumph.* Most likely, his father had disowned him, too! And frankly, she wouldn't blame him even if he did. The greedy prodigal had absconded with his father's fortune, blowing it on wine, women, and all manner of wickedness. Had he even bothered to tell his father he was leaving, or had he simply vanished in the night, as she had? Shifting a bit uncomfortably, Kelila recalled pilfering her father's coins to book passage on a ship. She remembered slipping out of her warm bed and stealing down a long torchlit corridor, escaping the confines of Father's magnificent house in the dark of night. Sighing, her thoughts returned to the prodigal son. He, too, had defiled himself with shallow, immoral living, eventually wallowing in the mud with filthy swine. And now he expected his father to take him back?

It would never happen.

But then John was speaking again, plunging ahead with the tale depicting a prodigal's tragic plight. Kelila leaned forward, listening intently.

"Now this, my friends, is the most beautiful part of the parable," John said, his kind eyes alight.

Jarred by John's unexpected statement, Kelila cocked her head in confusion. She couldn't imagine what could possibly come next. Something beautiful, as John suggested? Surely not.

"The prodigal son prepared his speech, hardly daring to hope that his father would accept his apology," John continued, leaning forward and gripping the sides of his wooden stand. "*'Father,'* he planned to say, *'I have sinned against heaven and before you, and I am no longer worthy to be called your son."*

Tears burning her eyes, Kelila looked away. She was no longer worthy of being called a daughter, either.

"But rather than asking his father to restore his sonship," John continued, his voice swelling with sympathy, "the prodigal decided to simply petition his father for employment. If his father permitted, he would become a hired servant at his father's estate. After all, the prodigal wouldn't dare ask his father to take him back as a beloved son, for that was unthinkable. He'd sinned too greatly against him," John said, his kind eyes flickering with pity. "This time, he'd gone too far."

Too far. Blinking back hot tears, Kelila's heart constricted. She, too, had gone too far. Plagued by burning fear, deep regret, and paralyzing grief, she wondered how long she must endure it. Obviously, the prodigal hadn't been able to bear the pain, either, for he planned to return to his father. But she had more sense than the prodigal son, for she knew better than to seek her father's forgiveness! The son should have known better, too. He should have saved himself the trouble.

"Now here's the most amazing part of this parable," John said indulgently, leaning over his pulpit.

Kelila's brow furrowed in confusion as the entire assembly resounded with enthusiastic *amens.*

"The son journeyed toward his father, practicing his pitiful little speech the entire way. What he didn't know was that his father was already waiting for him, scanning the distant horizon, his father's heart aching with love for his lost child. And while the son was still far off, the father spotted him. Now what do you suppose the father did?" John asked, his eyes sparkling merrily. "Did he run back to the house and bolt the door? Did he call the authorities to arrest the young delinquent?"

Already sensing what came next, the congregation chuckled softly. Puzzled, Kelila leaned forward on the bench, her heart beating wildly in her chest, salty tears stinging her eyes.

"The father did none of these things—all things which we, in our corrupt and fallen state, might consider," John explained. "Instead, the father *ran*—not *away* from the miserable offender, but directly *to* him! And taking his child in strong arms, the father held him close, welcoming him home."

Kelila raised her head in disbelief. The son was *welcomed* after all he'd done? After all his unthinkable misdeeds?

"Stunned, the prodigal began reciting his practiced apology," John continued with a knowing smile, "but his father interrupted him long before he finished his speech, commanding the servants to bring out the best robe for him, a ring for his hand, and sandals for his feet. He then ordered a feast to commence in his son's honor, no doubt weeping as he proclaimed, *'This my son was dead and is alive again; he was lost and is found.'*"

Kelila couldn't fathom the ending of this unlikely tale. The father had simply *forgiven* the prodigal, without question or condemnation? He hadn't presented a list of his son's faults nor railed about how much he had suffered due to the prodigal's willful, selfish actions? He hadn't placed conditions upon his son's return, nor had he assumed his son would fail again?

Bowing her head in shame, Kelila envied the prodigal son. Like him, she'd taken her father's money to board a ship and escape his reach. But unlike the prodigal, *her* father refused to take her back. Her father refused to forgive her.

"We've all sinned against God, dear ones. And we've all sinned against those we love," John continued, his voice laced with deep compassion. "Some of us have been forgiven by those loved ones. Others have not."

Kelila's eyes narrowed in disbelief. Candace had told no one of their father's disownment, nor had she spoken a word of Kelila's deception. And yet John's example spoke directly to Kelila's circumstances, directly to her heart!

"But what does our heavenly Father promise us?" John smiled, his eyes drifting lovingly over those gathered before him. "*When my father and my mother forsake me, then the Lord will take care of me.* This, dear friends, is a promise. Sinful man may or may not grant their forgiveness, but like the father in the parable, our heavenly Father waits for us to return to Him, scanning the horizon with each new sunrise, longing to lavish His tender mercies upon us, for they are new every morning. And when we seek Him, our merciful Father welcomes us with open arms. He, too, drapes His robe of righteousness over our bent, sagging shoulders. He places His ring like a seal upon our hands. He shods our feet with the preparation of His blessed gospel of peace."

Wrapping slender arms tightly about herself, Kelila bent her head and wept softly. Did she dare believe John's blessed proclamation? Could she, too, be forgiven and welcomed by God? She wanted to believe it. She wanted to believe it desperately. But she knew she was a wretched sinner. She hadn't cared about her own family, nor had she lived to please God. Instead, she'd spent her time chasing shallow pleasures and pursuing foul entertainment. She wasn't worthy to be called the daughter of God.

"When Jesus was with us," John said, interrupting Kelila's train of thought, "He said, *'I did not come to call the righteous, but sinners, to repentance.'* Brothers and sisters, you are not beyond the Lord's reach. You are not beyond His grace. His love for you is infinite, His mercy without bounds. Repent, and submit yourself to Him. Like the father of the prodigal son, He, too, waits for His beloved children to return to Him."

I did not come to call the righteous, but sinners, to repentance. Weeping softly, Kelila realized she certainly qualified. She was, indeed, a miserable sinner! For the first time in her life, Kelila felt crushed beneath the weight of selfish, petty sins. And she realized that the Way wasn't simply a *lifestyle* that may or may not suit her fancy—it was the *only* Way to find peace and fulfillment, the *only* Way to live!

I need Jesus, she thought, her heart constricting in her chest. *I need His mercy. I need His forgiveness. I can't keep living this way, mired in sin and selfishness.* In that moment, it all became startlingly clear. Kelila realized she'd once loathed religion because, in her father's household, there was no life, no *love*, in it. The religion her father practiced was one of ritual and obligation. But here in Jerusalem, God had shown her what it really meant to *follow Him*.

Lovingly, mercifully, undeservedly, God had shown her the Way.

A woman actively engaged in serving God, busily meeting the needs of those around her, hasn't time to feel bored or dissatisfied, Candace had once explained. And for the first time in her life, Kelila was beginning to grasp this shocking concept.

And not only that, Kelila thought, her anxious heart nearly bursting within her, *my future is safe in God's hands.* God was not like her fallible earthly father, dominating and controlling others to gain his own desired end. The Lord's plans were truly best, and she could trust Him, gladly surrendering her will to Him. She no longer needed to fight and claw, desperately trying to build the maddeningly elusive future she desired. What a relief to lay aside that burden! No, every moment, every step, could become an unpredictable and exciting adventure if she allowed God to direct her path!

Cheeks warming in embarrassment, Kelila suddenly realized the entire sea of believers surrounding her had bowed their heads, for John was uttering the closing prayer! Quickly following suit, Kelila bowed her head, squeezing her eyes tightly shut. Even so, warm tears slipped down her cheeks, falling into her lap. When John breathed the last *amen,* Kelila lifted her head.

To her great amazement, Mary was standing before her, hand outstretched.

Heart leaping, Kelila raised sheepish, tear-filled eyes. How had Mary known she was ready?

"*Shalom,* dear one," Mary said warmly, taking Kelila's hand.

"*Shalom,* Mary." Allowing the beautiful widow to raise her up, Kelila forced a wobbly smile. Surely Mary would know how to lead her in a prayer of repentance! Bursting with genuine hope for the first time in her entire life, Kelila spoke through a stream of liberating tears. "Can we talk?"

Ethereal eyes sparkling, Mary's lips curved into a knowing smile.

***

Walking home alongside her smiling brother-in-law, Kelila felt lighter than air. With Mary's gentle guidance, she had prayed a heartfelt prayer of repentance, confessing a lifetime of selfishness and sin, accepting Christ's atoning sacrifice, and receiving the blessed promise of the Holy Spirit's everlasting guidance and presence.

That glorious moment would remain forever etched in her heart. Clasping Mary's hand like a lifeline, Kelila had lifted her head after a tremorous, whispered *amen*. Then Mary had raised Kelila's hand high overhead, drawing the girl to her feet and announcing through happy tears, "Everyone, welcome our newest little sister in Christ!"

The Upper Room had exploded with shouts of joy and triumphant applause. Smiling believers had flocked toward the blushing Kelila, all eager to congratulate her, excitedly welcoming her into the church family.

And then Kelila had seen Philip standing across the room, beaming with emotion, his tender brown eyes conveying his approval.

Heart springing into her throat, Kelila had met his gaze, her dark eyes shimmering with tears of happiness. And Philip had offered her one sure nod, a promise burning in his warm brown eyes that nearly stole her breath away.

Kelila shivered in recollection, wondering what the future held for them.

Oh, my! So lost in delightful thought was she, Kelila hadn't noticed they had reached the small stone house. She could hardly wait to tell Candace about her decision! How her sister would rejoice! She was certain Candace had spent many hours each day praying for her wayward little sister. And the seeds Candace had sown in tears had been reaped in overwhelming joy!

Candace must have heard Simon opening the creaky gate outside, for the door swung open as the pair crossed the small outer court.

"You're back," Candace smiled, her delicate features glowing in the court's dancing torchlight.

Exchanging a knowing look with Simon, Kelila turned to smile at her older sister, her entire face alight with joy and peace.

Candace took one look at her sister's shining countenance and knew.

"Praise God!" Candace cried, flying out the door and wrapping her arms around Kelila in a tight embrace.

Bathed in the healing presence of the Holy Spirit, the two sisters held each other close, faith and family fully restored.

CHAPTER 19

Tabitha

A.D. 34

The first month of the new year swept into Jerusalem, bringing unexpected news to the house of Tabitha and Stephanos.

"Stephanos!" Tabitha stared, openmouthed, at the letter she held between trembling hands. "Stephanos, come see this!"

Concerned, Stephanos dropped the distribution ledgers he'd been busily reviewing, rushing to his wife's side. "Tabitha, what is it, my love?"

"I've received word from your mother!" Tabitha exclaimed, stunned to her very core.

"My mother?" Stephanos repeated blankly, reaching for the parchment letter. "I'm afraid not, Tabitha. My mother cannot read or write."

"No, but the salutation states it was penned for her by someone named Dorian." Tabitha stared at her husband in accusation. "Does your mother own slaves?"

"I hope not. This letter was probably penned by a hired hand," Stephanos replied with a wry smile. Taking the letter from her, he held it up for examination. "Ah, good old Dorian! How could I forget? He is a trusted manservant in my father's household. I remember him drilling me on my lessons as a boy. I even recognize his script, though it's a bit shakier now."

Tabitha's face drained of color as the tidings of the letter hit her full force.

Lowering the parchment page, Stephanos touched her pale cheek in concern. "Tabitha? What is it, love?"

"Your father and mother…" she managed, shaking her head to clear the sudden fog. "They are coming to stay with us!"

"What?" Stephanos raised the letter once again, his eyes furiously scanning the meticulous script. "My mother has addressed you by name," he exclaimed, puzzled. "But my father has returned every letter I've sent, unopened. How does my mother know your name?"

Further unsettled, Tabitha cleared her throat nervously. "She knows my name because…well, because I wrote her a letter."

"When?" Stephanos blinked at his wife in bewilderment.

"So long ago, I'd forgotten all about it," Tabitha admitted, shaking her head in dismay. "I sent it when I wrote to my uncle in Joppa at least a year ago!"

Stephanos stared at his wife in utter disbelief.

"I'm sorry, Stephanos," Tabitha plunged ahead, pacing like a nervous child. "I should have told you.

But I didn't want you to be disappointed should she return the letter unopened or respond unfavorably, as my uncle did."

Stephanos only studied her, his expression strangely veiled.

"I'm sorry, Stephanos," Tabitha groaned, burying her face in her hands. "Truly, I am. I should have told you before asking them to stay with us—"

"No, beloved."

Lowering trembling hands, Tabitha met her husband's tender gaze. Swept by confusion, she saw his eyes, wet with tears. "My love?"

Taking her by the shoulders, Stephanos drew her close. "This may be the kindest thing anyone has ever done for me," he said hoarsely, bending to kiss the top of her golden head.

"Then...then you're not angry?" Tabitha dared, wrapping her arms around his trim waist.

"Angry?" Perplexed, Stephanos tightened his grip around his wife. "How could I be angry, beloved? Somehow, you've reached my family when I was unable to do so. I wonder what my mother must have done to convince my father to acquiesce."

Tabitha allowed her husband a moment to process all that had so suddenly transpired. Shaking his head, he smiled broadly, looking into her hazel-green eyes. "They're coming, Tabitha."

"They're actually coming!" Tabitha nearly shouted her glee, her bright eyes dancing with exuberance. "Good heavens! There's so much to do to prepare for their arrival! Do you think they will arrive before Passover?"

"Based on the time they plan to set sail, I can't imagine they will arrive before Passover or even

Pentecost," Stephanos said, deep in thought. "My father never leaves in a hurry, nor does he do anything hastily. But perhaps it is better that way. Festivals can prove stressful for someone like my father. He prefers quiet routine and solitude."

"You must tell me everything about your father and mother, Stephanos!" Tabitha declared, her eyes roving about their modest little home. Where on earth would she *put* them? Would they even *fit*? "What do they like to do? What do they like to eat? How can we best make them feel welcome?"

"There will be time enough to make plans, beloved," Stephanos laughed, amused by the way she fluttered frantically around the house. "You look like a busy little butterfly," he grinned.

"I can't believe they're coming all the way from Athens!" Tabitha squealed, inspecting the dry goods stacked on the shelves. She would need to restock her supply before their arrival.

"Thanks to *you*, beloved," Stephanos said, smiling broadly.

"Thanks to *God*," Tabitha reminded him, crossing the distance between them and planting a kiss on his clean-shaven cheek. "The Holy Spirit must be at work, Stephanos. Perhaps, this time, your parents will be receptive to the gospel."

"We must pray for that without ceasing," Stephanos agreed, considering his father's disapproving scowl and glowering countenance. His gentle mother would be far easier to reach, he imagined. But he refused to give up on his father, either. Perhaps this time would be different. Perhaps he had softened a bit. After all, his mother had convinced him to visit, hadn't she? That was, indeed, a good sign!

"I can't explain how much this means to me, Tabitha," Stephanos said with a wobbly smile. Taking her in his arms, he looked deeply into her eyes. How he loved those eyes—at times, so sweet and tender, though sometimes flashing fire! "To be given this unspeakable privilege of sharing Christ with my father and mother before—" halting abruptly, Stephanos looked away, his dark eyes clouded with something Tabitha couldn't quite comprehend.

"Before *what*, Stephanos?" Tabitha demanded, a hard knot twisting in the pit of her stomach. Something about the way her husband spoke filled her entire being with a dreadful premonition.

"These are uncertain times, that's all," Stephanos replied, wearily rubbing his neck. "Even if we weren't living in this tumultuous age, none of us are guaranteed another day. Praise God, for in His abundant mercy, He has sent my father and mother while there is still time to reach them."

"Still time for them, or time for *you*?" Tabitha demanded, strangely unsettled. "You'd best not plan to depart from this life anytime soon, Stephanos. I couldn't bear it."

"Love bears all things," Stephanos pointed out, smiling softly. "Do you not remember my last sermon at the Synagogue of the Freedmen when the Holy Spirit revealed so much about the love of God, the love we must have for one another?"

"How could I forget?" Tabitha huffed. "That insufferable Saul glowered through the entire thing."

"The Spirit must be convicting him, then," Stephanos grinned. "You mustn't forget, we often behave the worst when experiencing unwanted conviction."

"Ah, and is that Saul's problem?" Tabitha scoffed.

"A guilty conscience?"

"We can only hope—and pray."

Tabitha resisted the unladylike urge to snort in derision.

Taking his wife's hands firmly in his own, Stephanos stared into her eyes, his own burning with the fiery heat of white-hot coals. "I want you to promise me something, Tabitha," he said, the intensity of his gaze startling her to her very core. "If anything happens to me—today, tomorrow, or even eighty years from now—you must promise to carry on the Lord's work, Tabitha. Can you do that?"

Licking dry lips, Tabitha wondered if her pounding heart would come crashing through her chest. "You're scaring me, Stephanos."

"You needn't fear, beloved," Stephanos said tenderly, holding her cold hands captive in his own, "even if the earth be removed and the mountains be carried into the midst of the sea. No, we needn't fear, but we must prepare."

"Prepare for what?" Tabitha demanded, anxiously searching his dark eyes.

"Jesus said we will be hated by all nations for His name's sake, and the love of many will grow cold. A time will come, beloved, when men will imprison, torture, and kill followers of the Way, believing they are serving God by doing so. We don't know exactly when these things will come to pass, but we must be ready."

"Are you forgetting Gamaliel's edict?" Tabitha huffed, her stomach twisting in fearful knots. "He forbade the Council to arrest the apostles, remember?"

"For now. And praise God for this blessed season

of peace," Stephanos assured her, pulling her close. "Even so, we must brace ourselves for what will surely come. Jesus Himself warned us to be ready, and ready we must be."

Burying her face in her husband's firm chest, Tabitha closed her eyes, listening to the steady beating of his heart—and what a heart this man possessed, so full of love for God and mercy toward men. Would she ever possess a heart like his?

Releasing a tremorous sigh, Tabitha sensed that something weighed heavily upon her husband, something he wasn't yet ready to share. Perhaps he didn't even fully comprehend it.

"I love you, Stephanos," Tabitha whispered hoarsely, comforted by his steady heartbeat, for it conveyed hope and life—precious, God-given life. *His* life. The life she cherished far more than her own. "I love you so much more than words can tell."

"I know, beloved," Stephanos said tenderly. "And you needn't search for words. Your love for me shines through all you do."

Tabitha closed her eyes, content in his embrace.

"And I love you, my bride. More than you'll ever know."

"I won't let anything happen to you, Stephanos," Tabitha insisted stoutly, breathing in his wonderful scent. "And Heaven help the man who dares come against you."

Stephanos hid a knowing smile. "Vengeance is the Lord's, dear one. May His will prevail, not ours."

Having nothing positive to say, Tabitha held her tongue.

"Now, how about that promise?" Stephanos smiled, tipping Tabitha's chin and forcing her to look into his eyes. "If anything happens to me—"

"I told you, I won't let anything happen to you!"

"But if it does," Stephanos implored, gazing deeply into her eyes. "Promise me you won't lose faith, beloved. Promise me you will carry on the Lord's blessed work."

Releasing a long sigh of frustration, Tabitha shook her head in dismay.

"Beloved?"

"Fine," Tabitha snapped, suppressing her annoyance for the sake of the one she loved so fiercely. "I promise." How could she deny this wonderful man anything, much less her word? She could only hope—and pray—that God would preserve her husband, despite fierce opposition and the mounting odds against him.

"That's all I ask, dear one." Noticeably relieved, Stephanos pulled her even closer, resting his chin on the top of her head. "May God grant us the strength to endure."

CHAPTER 20

Kelila

Simon and Candace had been acting strangely all day.

Puzzled, Kelila wondered what was afoot. She'd seen her sister and brother-in-law exchanging secret glances all afternoon, as if waiting to unveil a delightful surprise for Alexander and Rufus. Kelila knew they were up to something. In the past, she had always been privy to such secrets involving her nephews. If Simon and Candace were planning an exciting surprise for the boys, why hadn't they asked for her assistance? She was the queen of fun and adventure, after all. She couldn't help but feel a bit left out.

"Kelila, would you mind making a quick trip to the market for me?" Candace asked, innocently adding insult to injury. "I'd like to purchase some pomegranates for the daily food distribution."

Chancing a glance out the latticed window, Kelila noted the position of a rapidly retreating sun. Had

Candace gone mad, sending her out to return home after dark, unchaperoned? Typically, Candace was overly cautious, mothering Kelila like an overprotective hen. And while Kelila always chafed at her sister's constant fussing, she couldn't help but wish Candace had assumed her role as Mother Hen today. She wasn't looking forward to a long trip to the market, nor an even longer walk home in the dark! And what if Simon and Candace surprised the boys with their "secret" before she returned? She would surely miss out on all the fun!

"Kelila?" Candace repeated, drawing her sister's attention. "Did you hear me?"

"I heard you," Kelila acknowledged, feeling a bit put out. "Can it wait until tomorrow? It will soon be dark."

"Oh, it won't be dark for quite some time," Candace countered with a cheerful smile, expertly kneading dough at the low table. "I could really use your help."

Annoyed, Kelila swallowed any further protests. After all, Candace served her constantly, day and night. As a new believer in Christ, Kelila knew it was now her responsibility to serve others, as well. If Candace needed her help, so be it. She would help and do it gladly.

"Pomegranates, you said?" Kelila clarified, reaching for her warm wool shawl hanging from a peg near the door.

"No, not that one," Candace interrupted, eyeing the worn shawl with disapproval. "You should wear your lovely maroon one—the one with the golden embroidery."

Kelila stared at her sister in protest. "To go to the

market?"

Appearing as if she'd caught herself in a terrible blunder, Candace quickly amended, "There's a bit of a chill in the air, and the other shawl is a bit longer, is it not? It will keep you warm."

Quite certain that the cozy wool shawl would be far warmer than her gauzy maroon headdress, Kelila decided not to argue. She didn't wish to waste any more time, after all.

Climbing the wooden ladder to her loft, Kelila retrieved the shawl and a matching gold-studded belt before clambering back down the rickety old ladder. Strapping the belt around her slender waist, she fitted the headdress on top of her lush, raven-colored waves just as Candace crossed the room, wiping floury hands on her apron.

"You look lovely," Candace said approvingly, pressing several coins into Kelila's hand.

"What else would you like me to purchase at the market besides pomegranates?" Kelila asked, wondering if she'd simply made herself a more appealing target by donning finer garments.

"Oh, just the pomegranates will do."

"Just pomegranates?" Kelila repeated, arching an incredulous brow.

"The fresh fruit will be a wonderful treat for the orphans and widows, will it not?" Candace asked, her eyes begging Kelila not to press any further.

Mystified, Kelila slipped the coins into the elegant girdle attached to her belt.

"Now go on," Candace prodded, steering Kelila toward the door. "No need to hurry home, Sister. We shall see you when you return."

No need to hurry home? Now Kelila was even

more confused. If only Simon hadn't taken the boys out on an afternoon stroll! She felt a bit uncomfortable leaving Candace alone in her present state. She wasn't acting at all like herself!

Sensing Kelila's hesitation, Candace swung open the front door, ushering her out as one might hurry along a pesky fly. Before Kelila could even offer a casual goodbye, Candace had shut the door behind her with a loud *thud.*

Good heavens! Kelila thought, blinking in surprise. Had Candace tired of her company? Did she *want* to get rid of her little sister for a few hours? Resisting the urge to demand an explanation for Candace's odd behavior, Kelila recognized a familiar sensation sweeping over her: self-pity. Steeling herself against it, Kelila determined to walk in the Spirit rather than catering to her own weak flesh. She was a child of God, bought and paid for with the precious blood of Christ! She would not allow the enemy to use her own fragile emotions against her. Her days of self-pity were far behind her now!

With a small smile, Kelila hastened across the outer court, slipping past the creaky old gate. Perhaps if she hurried, she would beat the rapidly setting sun.

The cobblestone streets of the Lower City remained congested as people hurried to accomplish their tasks before sunset. Young women with baskets on their arms and babies on their hips returned from the market while shopkeepers meticulously swept their booths and secured their canopies. Hawkers vied for the attention of the passersby, loudly advertising their many wares. Kelila stiffened at the sight of several intimidating Roman shoulders standing near a tax collector's booth, their callused hands resting almost casually upon the hilts of their gladiuses. One looked her way, his dark eyes glistening beneath his silver helmet.

Kelila hurried past them, becoming more aware of the threat such men posed against those she loved.

As the majestic Temple façade towered into view, Kelila caught her breath in awe. She had resided in Jerusalem for over a year now, and yet the city's crowning jewel never failed to steal her breath away. How differently she viewed the impressive structure now. Before, it had been wondrous to behold, but nothing more. Now, as a new believer, the Temple symbolized everything the Lord Jesus had finished upon the cross. No longer must sinful man appear before a fallible human high priest, seeking intercession. No longer must one sacrifice frightened, bleating beasts upon a bloody altar to receive a fleeting, temporary form of atonement. Now, Jesus' shed blood provided the final atonement for all who were willing to receive it. Now, by the power of the Holy Spirit, all believers communed freely with Almighty God. He wasn't imprisoned within the marble walls of an ancient temple. No, He was enthroned within the hearts of His children!

Considering the powerful God she now loved, Kelila wondered why man had ever thought it possible to confine His all-consuming presence upon a single mountaintop. He was the Creator of the universe, of time and space, of the sun and the moon, the glittering stars, and spectacular galaxies. The gentle rivers and the billowing seas were His, the gently rolling hills and snow-capped mountains clothed in majesty were spoken into existence by His own mouth. He crafted every single human on the face of the earth, lovingly shaping and forming them in the womb! Surely mortal man hadn't thought to harness or confine that power!

Approaching the bustling market within the Temple district, Kelila fondly contemplated all that had transpired since her arrival in Jerusalem. She had belonged to the Lord Jesus for over three months now, and what a time it had been! Every moment presented an opportunity to learn, to grow in faith, love, patience, and understanding! Shortly after her conversion and baptism, Kelila had experienced the Passover and the Pentecost unlike ever before, trembling inside as she had celebrated the Lord's finished work upon the cross and His miraculous resurrection. His blood had paid her ransom. His supernatural resurrection guaranteed her own someday. And now her entire life stretched before her, untarnished by the sins of her past, brimming with exciting possibilities!

What marvelous things did God have in store for her? She had begun to pray unceasingly, asking the Lord to direct her path, to guide her life as He saw fit. She suddenly understood why the believers desired to remain in the will of God, for it was the safest place to be.

Nearing the fruit vendor's booth, Kelila's thoughts strayed toward the patient young deacon who had stolen her heart. How he'd done so, she often wondered about. Perhaps she'd never know. It was a mystery to her, why her own wild heart was so drawn to a tame, quiet man like Philip! But her love for him had grown slowly, steadily, over time, almost catching her unawares. At first, he'd merely proven a fascinating distraction to occupy empty thoughts and spare time. But as she'd watched him for over a year, her heart had been drawn to him unlike any other. She loved his warm brown eyes, his gentle smile, his willingness to help those in need. She loved the way he cherished the Word of God, longing to see others embrace the truth. She loved the subtle bursts of humor he released at the most unexpected times, instantly easing the tension in the room. Truly, Philip was a peacemaker in every sense of the word.

Oftentimes, Kelila sensed that Philip was studying her from afar. More times than she cared to admit, her gaze had traveled toward him during church meetings, only to find him watching her, his brown eyes intent.

What exactly were his intentions toward her? Had he any feelings for her, and if so, would he *ever* make them known? Much to her exasperation, Philip related to Kelila as he did to everyone else—with courtesy, kindness, and respect. He certainly didn't single her out from the rest, lavishing his attention and affection upon her! No, at times, she wondered if she was merely another sister in Christ to him. Secretly, she'd hoped to see him swoon like the amorous lovers of famous Greek literature, sweeping her off her feet and carrying her into the sunset, all while mounted upon a golden steed!

Kelila couldn't help but smile at that ridiculous thought. She imagined the shy young man would sooner sprout wings and fly before making such a melodramatic display! Even so, she couldn't help but harbor the hope that Philip would eventually profess his love for her—if he had any, that is. At this point, it was becoming dreadfully challenging to stay focused on the apostles' sermons when her heart's desire was seated just a few short rows away!

Finally reaching the booth laden with fresh spring produce, Kelila forced her thoughts back to the task at hand. She wouldn't think about Philip right now. She would leave him right where he belonged—in God's hands. No doubt, the Lord knew far better than she what was best for her—and for Philip.

Inspecting the luscious pomegranates piled high in a wooden crate, Kelila reached for the prettiest one, gasping when a masculine hand firmly clasped her own.

"Do you remember how we met?"

Lifting her eyes in shock, Kelila saw that *Philip* stood behind the vendor's table, the large box of pomegranates between them. Had he been hiding behind the stacks of crates, waiting for her? Surely not!

"How could I forget?" Recovering with a bit of effort, Kelila's gaze rested upon her hand, now captive in her beloved's. Blushing, she forced a wobbly smile. "You were every bit as presumptuous then as you are now, taking a lady's hand without permission!"

"Ah, forgive me, my lady." Brown eyes dancing, Philip held her gaze, slowly releasing her hand. "Please, do permit me to amend that grave mistake."

"Go on," Kelila teased, her dark eyes dancing.

"All right, then. Kelila, may I have your hand?"

"You may," she laughed, shaking her head in amusement.

"No, I think you misunderstand me," Philip said, very much in control of the situation. Kelila had never seen him more commanding nor surer of his mission. "I am asking you, beautiful Kelila, may I,

Philip, *have your hand*...in marriage?"

Kelila stared at him in utter shock, her heart pounding furiously within her chest. Never in a million years had she expected this! But suddenly, it all made sense...Candace and Simon's secret smiles exchanged throughout the day, Candace's sudden desire for pomegranates and her insistence about the lovelier shawl, a trip to the market at this late hour...

"Kelila, may I?" Philip asked again, his tone surprisingly confident.

For the briefest moment, Kelila's eyes flickered with doubt. It was all so sudden, so unexpected...

Lord God, what should I do?

Philip stood before her, tall and confident. Gently, he held out his hand to her.

Gazing into the eyes of the man she loved, the peace of God—surpassing all understanding—instantly flooded Kelila's heart and mind. For in His kindness and great mercy, the Lord had brought them together. Philip was a good man, a godly man. The *only* man for her.

How could she have possibly doubted this perfect match?

Taking his hand in her own, Kelila raised tear-filled eyes to his, trembling with deep inner joy. "Philip," she breathed, glorying in this sacred moment ordained by God Himself, "I would be honored to become your wife."

"Praise God," Philip breathed, releasing a sigh of relief.

Kelila's heart hammered in her chest as his grip tightened about her hand. This certainly wasn't anything like the soppy, melodramatic proposals she had witnessed on the stage, but it was *perfect*— perfect in every way, perfect for *them*.

"I have one more request of you, my love," Philip said, his brown eyes never leaving hers.

Tingling at his nearness and his blessed endearment, *my love*, Kelila smiled through her tears. "Anything, Philip," she said, and she meant it with all her heart.

"Will you take a walk with me? In your absence, Candace has prepared a special supper in our honor, and Simon has obtained the documentation to officiate our betrothal."

Ah, Simon and Candace. Her wonderful, sneaky family! How she loved them!

"I would be delighted!" Kelila laughed as Philip came around the table. Taking his arm, Kelila could hardly believe this wonderful man was her betrothed! *Her betrothed!*

"Wait!" Kelila exclaimed, suddenly remembering Candace's request. "I really must purchase some pomegranates this time!"

"Already done," Philip grinned, turning to face his bride-to-be. "The pomegranates are being delivered to the orphans and widows of Stephanos' region even as we speak."

"Philip the Philanthropist—just as I predicted when we first met," Kelila teased, her dark eyes playful.

"I think you've always seen the best in me," Philip smiled.

"And, sadly, you've seen the worst in me," Kelila admitted, looking away in shame.

"No." Tenderly cupping Kelila's face in one strong hand, Philip looked deeply into her eyes. "What I have seen is a breathtakingly beautiful young woman, seeking the truth with all her heart. Once she found it, she embraced it with her entire being—heart, mind, and soul. And my love for you has only grown, Kelila, as I've watched your faith flourishing day after day."

Melting inside, Kelila leaned into his touch, praising God for His goodness and abundant mercy.

"I love you, Kelila," Philip said, lowering his head until his face was only inches from hers. "I love you with all my strength. You are a gift from God, beloved, and I promise to cherish you as long as God grants me breath."

"I love you, too, Philip," Kelila managed, tears tracing slender lines down her cheeks. "I always have, from the moment we met—even if I didn't know it, yet."

Tenderly, Philip swiped away her tears with his thumbs, and Kelila wondered how quickly the wedding could be officiated. Smiling to herself, she realized she'd gladly marry Philip right then and there, amidst the piles of crates, fruit stands, and harried pedestrians, should she be permitted to do so!

CHAPTER 21

Tabitha

Taking a step back, Tabitha admired her work. She'd dusted, swept, and scrubbed every inch of her small house until it gleamed. The items on her shelves were neatly stacked and arranged, her pantry replenished, and large stone jars filled to the brims with fresh water. Oil lamps burned invitingly from the low table and windowsills, and she'd strategically placed several hanging lanterns to provide additional light in the house, enhancing the cheery glow within.

She was certain Stephanos' parents would arrive any day now. She'd corresponded with Dorian, the trusty manservant, several times since receiving his first letter. She had agonized upon receiving his second letter, when he had regretfully informed her their trip had been delayed. But once she finally received word that they had set sail in the first month of summer, she knew her guests would arrive shortly. She wanted them to feel right at home in the cozy little house Stephanos had so lovingly provided for her. And quite frankly, she couldn't imagine anyone *not* settling comfortably into her cherished home. In her eyes, it was perfect.

Traveling around the gauzy partition sectioning off the makeshift bedchamber from the rest of the one-room house, Tabitha surveyed the soft blankets and plush cushions she'd artfully scattered over a thin sleeping pallet. Cheeks warming, she thought of the many nights she had spent here, wrapped in her husband's arms. It felt a bit odd, offering this sacred space to his parents during their stay. But she couldn't possibly ask them to sleep on the roof! No, that was unthinkable!

She would happily offer this cozy space to Stephanos' father and mother if it granted her the opportunity to share the love of Christ with them. Reluctantly, she had constructed a temporary bedroom for herself and Stephanos, utilizing the flat, walled-in roof by setting up large canopies to shield them from the elements—and prying eyes. She hadn't slept under the stars since she was a lonely, orphaned child. Shaking her head in awe, Tabitha marveled at how far the Lord had brought her in a few short years. Now, the thought of sleeping outside didn't disturb her in the least. She knew she would be safe, sheltered within her husband's strong embrace. Tabitha knew she would gladly sacrifice all she had if it meant sharing her life with the man she adored.

Allowing herself one final inspection of her work, Tabitha released a contented sigh. Everything seemed to be in order. Now all she had left to do was *wait.*

Tapping a sandaled foot impatiently, Tabitha supposed the waiting would be the hardest part.

"Tabitha, beloved."

Jarred from her silent musings, Tabitha was surprised to see her husband peeking his handsome head in the front door.

"Stephanos! Have you come home early from working at Mary's?"

"I have," Stephanos nodded, slipping inside and discreetly shutting the door behind him. "Can we talk a moment?"

Alarmed by his unusual manner, Tabitha cocked her head, confused. "Are you hiding from someone?"

Stephanos stared at her blankly, then released a hearty laugh. "Not yet," he grinned, taking her by the shoulders and bending to kiss her gently.

"What do you mean, *not yet?*"

"My parents have arrived."

"What?" Tabitha exclaimed, instantly befuddled. "How do you know? Where are they?"

"They're right outside."

"*Outside?* In the outer court?" she gasped.

"Yes," Stephanos said, tickled by her reaction. "I didn't wish to surprise you by barging in with them in tow."

Lifting a hand to her pale forehead, Tabitha forced herself to breathe. *This is what I've been praying for, preparing for, waiting for,* she reminded herself, drawing a calming breath. *Everything is in order. We are ready to welcome them.*

"May I escort them in?" Stephanos dared, his dark eyes gleaming with hope. "Are you ready to meet them?"

"I do hope so," Tabitha breathed, suddenly far

more nervous than she'd ever thought possible.

"Don't worry, beloved. They're going to *love* you," Stephanos assured her, cupping her face and kissing her deeply. Pulling away, he smiled broadly. "How could they not?"

Catching her breath, Tabitha was about to argue with her husband's candid assumption when he released her, swinging open the front door.

Oh, my! Tabitha hoped she wouldn't appear too disheveled. In his excitement, Stephanos had already reached the outer court to usher in their guests. Pausing before the small, gilded mirror near the door—an expensive wedding gift from Mary—Tabitha reached for her nearest head covering, delicately placing it over her long, honey-colored braid. Hastily removing her apron, she flung it onto its designated peg, smoothing down the front of her simple tunic.

"Just look who I stumbled upon on the main thoroughfare, headed our direction?" Stephanos announced, emerging at the front door and leading a string of well-dressed people behind him.

Swallowing her nerves, Tabitha produced her brightest, most winning smile, stretching forth her arms as a grim-faced older man entered the house behind Stephanos, grousing. "Of all things, making us stand in the outer court rather than simply escorting us inside!"

"You must be Father!" Tabitha exclaimed warmly, delighted. "What great joy it is to finally meet you!"

The older man paused by the door, followed by a lovely older woman and a stern-faced Greek manservant. After a cursory inspection of the small house, the man's eyes landed rather scornfully upon the radiant Tabitha. "I am called Amal, and you may address me as such," he said curtly, ignoring her outstretched arms.

Tabitha blinked in surprise, caught off guard by the unexpected slight. Even her typically composed Stephanos appeared stunned and speechless. But the moment of lingering, awkward silence was interrupted when the woman stepped forward, taking Tabitha's hands in her own. "My name is Daphne," she said kindly. "But you may certainly call me *Mother*."

Instantly drawn to the gentle woman, Tabitha returned Daphne's smile, respecting her graciousness. Studying the attractive woman before her, Tabitha saw from whom Stephanos had inherited his charisma and good looks. Daphne carried herself with humility and simple grace despite the expensive Greco-Roman apparel fitted about her trim frame. She wore her dark hair in an elaborate Roman style with a sheer veil pinned carefully in place. Elegant amphora earrings dangled from pierced ears, matching the lovely golden pendant gracing her slender throat.

"Mother," Tabitha smiled, happily squeezing Daphne's smooth, delicate hands before releasing them. "It is a pleasure to meet you."

"Likewise," Daphne responded, her tone pleasant. "Thank you, dear Tabitha, for your gracious invitation."

"It is a pleasure to serve you, Mother," Tabitha beamed.

Daphne. Tabitha thought it was a lovely name, though stringent Jews would no doubt scorn its origin. Less conservative Jews would more likely accept a woman bearing the name of an idolized, mythological Greek figure, emphasizing instead the literal translation of the name: *laurel*.

Tabitha thought the name was particularly fitting, since Daphne's son bore the name Stephanos, meaning *wreath* or *crown*, alluding to the laurel crowns placed upon the heads of triumphant victors.

Precious Lord, help us minister to these dear people, Tabitha pleaded silently. *Open their eyes to Your truth and grant them Your unfading crown of righteousness.*

Tabitha's train of thought was interrupted as Stephanos addressed his family, spreading his arms wide in acceptance. "We are honored and delighted by your presence here," he said, his eyes conveying the truth of his statement.

Tabitha nodded her agreement, relieved that Stephanos had wisely ignored his father's insult.

"And Dorian, my friend!" Stephanos exclaimed, surprising the tall, stoic-looking manservant at Daphne's elbow with an unexpected embrace. Dorian remained taut, arms stiffening at his sides. Tabitha bit back a chuckle of amusement at the sheer relief crossing the servant's features when Stephanos finally released him. "How glad I am to see you! When I set sail from Athens, I hadn't dared hope we'd meet again."

Tabitha noticed Amal's deepening scowl, his piercing eyes narrowing in disapproval. Glancing nervously toward the startled manservant, she noticed Dorian's eyes flicker in dismay. Tabitha was certain he must sense Amal's glowering disapproval.

Forcing another smile, Tabitha turned lovely hazel-green eyes toward the stoic Dorian, hoping to set him at ease—despite his master's deepening scowl. "We are overjoyed to welcome you to our home, Dorian," she said warmly.

Dorian was a lean, solemn-looking man, sporting rather fine attire for a manservant. Tabitha supposed Amal's father must compensate him well. Though he appeared thoroughly Roman with a close-cropped haircut, a clean-shaven face, prominent cheekbones, and elaborate apparel, Tabitha suspected Dorian was Greek. His unblinking stare—completely devoid of emotion—caused her to wonder what must be going on in that solemn-looking head of his.

"Surely you wouldn't expect us to travel without proper help," Amal said coldly, rewarding his son with a withering stare. "A manservant is needed to assist in our travels."

"Then you have the right man under your employ," Stephanos acknowledged, unfazed by his father's animosity. "Dorian has always been a capable associate."

Amal's closed expression indicated he strongly disagreed with Stephanos' use of the term *associate*. In his opinion, a hired hand graced the bottom rung of the social ladder, equivalent to slaves or beasts of labor. Clearly, he didn't appreciate his son's perspective.

Having been a servant herself, Tabitha sympathized with Dorian. Though she'd been blessed to serve in a godly home, she'd known others far less fortunate. Turning questioning eyes toward Amal, she allowed herself a moment to study the father of her beloved Stephanos.

Unfortunately, Amal wasn't anything like she'd imagined. Though his coloring was much lighter than his son's, his glowering countenance proved exceedingly darker. He wasn't a bad-looking sort, but his rigid posture and hardened features were somewhat repellant. His form radiated with restless energy and poorly masked frustration. Both his expression and his stance betrayed an unreasonable, uncompromising nature. Even his strident voice hinted at his belligerence.

Like most Jewish men, Amal sported a beard, although his was neatly trimmed and meticulously kept. Showy, imported garments and stacks of gold rings hinted at his high station. He and his wife were Hellenists—Greek-speaking Jews embracing many elements of Greek culture. Tabitha had known many Hellenists. Some rigidly adhered to Jewish customs, while others considered strict religious observances both radical and prudish. Tabitha assumed Amal must possess a more traditional background than Daphne. It certainly appeared so, for he had disinherited Stephanos the moment he'd learned of his son's "defection." Tabitha was certain an extremely liberal, secularized Jew wouldn't have taken Stephanos' conversion so personally.

"So this is the best an itinerant evangelist has to offer?" Amal observed coldly, his gaze sweeping over the small house with an air of disdain. "A crumbling, ancient hovel in the eastern slums?"

Tabitha stared at Amal in disbelief. How could the father of her wonderful husband prove so cruel, so dastardly? What was his problem, anyway? They had shown him nothing but kindness, extending a completely undeserved olive branch! Was Amal's sole purpose in coming to mock and humiliate his only son?

Thankfully, Daphne spoke before Tabitha had the chance to retort. "I think this is a lovely house," she said, smiling at Tabitha. "You have made this place a cozy home, my dear. You should be proud."

"And you should be mortified," Amal retorted, his gaze landing condescendingly upon Stephanos. "Why take a wife when this is the best you have to offer?"

"I would have married your son had he offered me an empty barrel to live in," Tabitha spoke up, lifting her chin. "He is the godliest man I've ever known, and I'm proud to be his wife."

"And he is blessed to call you his own," Daphne asserted, touching Tabitha's shoulder. "*He who finds a wife finds a good thing, and obtains favor from the Lord.*"

"Ah, Solomon's wisest proverb," Tabitha laughed, drawing an approving smile from her mother-in-law and easing the crackling tension in the room. "Now the three of you must be famished," Tabitha remarked, turning warm eyes toward Stephanos. "I'll prepare supper straightaway. Would you be willing to bring in their bags so we can help them get settled in?"

"That won't be necessary," Amal interrupted gruffly. "We haven't any luggage with us."

"No luggage?" Tabitha repeated blankly.

"Surely you didn't expect us to lodge *here*?" Amal declared incredulously. "I've made our own arrangements."

"What kind of arrangements, Father?" Stephanos inquired patiently, sensing his wife's disappointment.

"A prestigious friend of mine has offered the use

of his Upper City villa—not that it's any of your concern," Amal responded haughtily. "He makes a fortune renting his estate to affluent travelers for the pilgrimage feasts."

"I see," Stephanos responded slowly.

"Our belongings have been sent ahead of us and are awaiting our arrival," Amal stated, his tone daring his son to argue with him.

"Well, then," Tabitha said brightly, recovering with a bit of effort, "you shall join us for supper once you've had the chance to freshen up. We'll send a litter for you," she added, receiving a questioning glance from her husband. Suppressing a smile, she felt a brief sense of satisfaction when Amal's expression flickered in confusion. He no doubt wondered how his "poverty-stricken" son could afford to send a litter! He needn't know that Mary had kindly volunteered such services during their stay.

"We'd love to join you—"

"That won't be necessary," Amal cut in, interrupting his wife. "We'll send Dorian to the local market. He can oversee the preparation of fine cuisine during our stay."

Tabitha stared at her father-in-law, perplexed. If he didn't intend to stay with them nor to share meals with them, when did he expect to find time for fellowship?

"You may join us for supper the hour before sunset, if you wish," Amal said curtly.

Annoyed, Tabitha realized Amal was making it plain he would fellowship on his own terms—not theirs. *Lord God, You've called me to love this man, but he is making it so difficult! How can I, Lord? I already love Daphne, but Amal? How can I possibly love him, Lord?*

Love one another as I have loved you, beloved.

Taking a deep breath, Tabitha reached for her husband's hand. Intertwining her fingers in his, she accepted his silent strength, offering her own support.

"We would be honored to join you for dinner," Stephanos assured his father, his tone filled with warmth. "Thank you for extending the invitation."

The expression crossing Amal's tightened features conveyed his bewilderment. Clearly, he had expected—possibly even anticipated—an argument. Saddened, Tabitha recognized that this was a man who knew absolutely nothing about the peace of God.

Noting the relief on Daphne's placid face, Tabitha mustered a genuine smile. If the enemy had his way, Amal, Daphne, and their loyal manservant would eventually depart from Jerusalem no better than they had arrived—without the Savior's blessed atonement, without the comfort of His unfailing love.

Suddenly enlightened, Tabitha wondered why she had expected this mission to be *easy*. Had she expected the great deceiver to simply lay aside his weapons of strife, inviting her to shatter his own dark purposes?

Bracing herself for the spiritual war at hand, Tabitha prepared her heart for battle. There was far too much at stake to allow petty grievances and her own stubborn pride to interfere with her mission.

Smiling wanly, she allowed her gaze to sweep over Stephanos' dear family—his imperious father, gentle mother, and their stone-faced servant—and her heart surged with a deep sense of protectiveness, for their very souls were at stake. The war had been waged, the battle plans drawn up.

Tabitha resolved that the enemy wouldn't have his way with these loved ones—not now, not ever. Not on her watch.

Squaring her shoulders in deep resolve, Tabitha imagined the games were about to begin.

CHAPTER 22

Tabitha

"Thank you, beloved, for agreeing to meet on Father's terms this evening."

Tabitha leaned in as her husband bent to kiss her cheek. Her stomach was aflutter with nerves as they prepared to dine with Amal and Daphne in their rented Upper City villa. Though she was no stranger to lavish estates, having dwelt happily in Mary's palatial villa for years and visiting a dozen others while tending to her mistress, she sensed this time would be different. This time, she would be an unwanted guest. Tolerated, perhaps, but not welcomed.

"We must remember what's important," Tabitha reminded Stephanos, though she spoke more to herself than to him. "Your family must be won. This may be our only chance to reach them."

"You amaze me, beloved." Standing behind his wife, Stephanos gave her shoulders a comforting squeeze. "I'm so sorry their visit hasn't gone as planned."

"Does anything ever go as planned?" Tabitha responded with a wry smile, watching him through the small oval mirror in front of them.

"I'm afraid not," Stephanos laughed in amusement. "The Lord must find it entertaining when we make our own plans, often without consulting Him."

"*A man's heart plans his way, but the Lord directs his steps*," Tabitha said. "I suppose we must simply trust He knows what He's doing." If Amal was accustomed to luxurious living and fine dining, perhaps being forced to stay in her small, modest house would further strain a volatile and tenuous relationship. Perhaps he would prove far more receptive to the gospel in his natural environment.

"You look beautiful, my bride," Stephanos said, nuzzling her neck as she critically studied her own reflection in the polished glass.

Frowning at her inspection, Tabitha adjusted the most elegant head covering she owned. Even her finest garments paled in comparison to the attire of Stephanos' family, and she was quite certain they wouldn't be the least bit impressed with her apparel.

"Stop worrying," Stephanos grinned, tweaking her shoulder. "You look lovely."

Tabitha didn't argue. What was the point? Besides, all the jewels and finery in the world couldn't win a person to Christ. No, that was accomplished by the Holy Spirit of God moving through the obedience of a fully surrendered believer. Sighing in resignation, she determined to remember that important fact.

"Was it difficult for your father to arrange passage by ship?" Tabitha inquired as Stephanos slipped away to change.

"I imagine not," he responded wanly, "since he traveled on his own ship."

Tabitha froze in surprise. "Your father owns a ship?"

"A fleet of ships."

"*What?*" Countenance paling, Tabitha surveyed her own modest home. She had known Stephanos' father was a wealthy, powerful man, but she'd never imagined... "I thought your father was a scholar!"

"Among other things." Coming around the partition sectioning off their bedchamber, Stephanos belted the clasp around his waist with a wry smile.

"Your father is a sea trader?"

"And a scholar, and an investor. He also dabbles in real estate every now and then."

"Is there anything he *doesn't* do?"

"Oh, there are plenty of things my father doesn't do," Stephanos teased. "Manual labor, for example. Or anything else he considers beneath him."

Tabitha knew her husband well enough to know his jest was one of endearment, not of criticism. "I suppose I should brush up on my geography," Tabitha remarked a bit snidely. "I didn't even know Athens was a port city."

"The largest harbor in the ancient port of Piraeus is reserved for commercial use," Stephanos explained.

Fleetingly, Tabitha wondered if Amal had ever encountered her uncle, a powerful sea trader in Joppa.

"I can't help but ask..." Tabitha ventured, turning from her own startled reflection. "If your father has established such a powerful commercial empire in

Athens, why did you ever leave?"

"Quite frankly, I never planned to remain in Jerusalem," Stephanos admitted, seating himself on a low stool and securing the thongs of his sandals around muscled calves. "My father never kept the pilgrimage feasts. He did observe them in his own way—when convenience allowed. But he refused to leave his operations in Athens three times each year to go to Jerusalem."

"I see," Tabitha supplied, fascinated by this unknown piece of her husband's family history. "His work must have meant everything to him."

"It still does, I'm afraid." Stephanos sighed, securing his last sandal strap. "Quite frankly, I'm astounded he left Athens to come here now. Especially given the circumstances—our estrangement of recent years."

Tabitha nodded, reaching for the pot of warm lentils she planned to contribute toward supper.

"The feasts had always intrigued me, particularly Passover and Shavuot. So, eventually, I decided to observe them. I booked passage on one of Father's ships and set sail. When I finally arrived in Jerusalem for Passover, the city abounded with rumors about a traveling Rabbi reputed to heal the sick and work mighty miracles."

Tabitha studied her husband, enthralled. Why hadn't she thought to ask about this sooner?

"Naturally, I had to meet Him," Stephanos grinned. "I did, and the rest is history. But the moment I met the Lord Jesus, I knew I'd found my purpose in life. I couldn't refute His teachings, even with all the fancy learning Father's philosophers and tutors had crammed into my head. His words kindled like a fire in my heart. I knew Jesus spoke the truth. He *is* truth!"

"Amen," Tabitha murmured, proud of her husband's unwavering dedication to Christ's message.

"I became one of the Seventy sent out to proclaim the gospel message, readying each city and village for Jesus' arrival," Stephanos continued, his eyes fondly distant. "Philip and I were paired to teach and travel together."

Tabitha smiled, thinking of Stephanos' best friend, humble, quiet Philip, and his recently betrothed, the vibrant, whimsical Kelila. In her opinion, they were a perfect match.

"Once Jesus appointed me for evangelism, I knew there'd be no turning back. This was my mission now. This was my calling. I had to walk in obedience, even knowing my father and mother would disagree."

"How did you tell you them?" Tabitha dared, intrigued.

"I wrote a letter, praying their eyes would be opened to the truth. Father responded with a scathing letter of his own then promptly disinherited me."

"I'm so sorry, my husband," Tabitha whispered, aching for him.

"Jesus said, *'He who loves his father or mother more than Me is not worthy of Me.'* As much as I crave my father's love and approval, I cannot relinquish my faith in Christ."

"But we have a Heavenly Father who will never leave us nor forsake us," Tabitha said gently. Having lost her own father and mother, she understood her husband's pain. "His love is everlasting, eternal. And His approval isn't based on anything *we've* done.

We have been forever justified in His sight by the precious blood of Jesus."

"Amen," Stephanos said, smiling softly. "Thank you, beloved."

"What happened after Amal disinherited you?"

"I wrote him again, pleading with him. But as you know, every letter since then has been returned to me, the seal unbroken... until now. Until *you*, Tabitha."

Blinking back tears, Tabitha smiled tenderly as Stephanos rose, taking her in his arms. They laughed together when the large pot of warm lentils between them prevented further contact.

"Somehow, someway, your message got through to my mother," Stephanos said, his hand landing upon her shoulder and then tracing the length of her slender arm.

"Only by the grace of God," Tabitha reminded him gently.

"My mother must have had the wisdom to ask Dorian to read it to her, rather than taking it straight to my father."

"Sometimes the Holy Spirit moves in our lives in mysterious ways, even before we are aware of His presence. Perhaps this is what happened with Daphne."

"It wouldn't surprise me," Stephanos agreed. "I don't think my mother is entirely closed to the truth."

"Neither do I," Tabitha exclaimed, her tone tinged with excitement. "She is a kind, gentle woman."

"Like the woman I married," Stephanos grinned.

"On occasion," Tabitha teased, laughing merrily. "But I do try."

"You are pleasing in every way, beloved."

"I suppose we should depart for the Upper City." Tabitha sighed, her stomach fluttering anew. "I don't think your father would take kindly to us arriving late for supper."

"You don't think he'd wait for us?" Stephanos teased, his dark eyes sparking with mischief.

"He might save us a few crumbs if he's feeling especially generous."

"Unlikely." Chuckling, Stephanos offered his wife his arm.

CHAPTER 23

Tabitha

Supper was strained, to say the least.

The rented estate was a mere stone's throw from Mary's resplendent villa, and Tabitha was sorely tempted to turn aside and flee to the house of her beloved mistress as she walked tentatively alongside her husband, the warm pot of lentils in hand.

As they approached the main gate, Tabitha noted a stern-looking guard positioned at the entrance. Wondering where he'd come from, Tabitha trailed behind her husband as he approached the guard, attempting to reflect Stephanos' confidence since she bore none of her own.

"I am Stephanos, son of Amal, and this is my lovely wife, Tabitha."

The guard appeared singularly unimpressed.

"The master of the house is expecting us," Stephanos clarified, wondering if they were about to be turned away.

Reluctantly, the guard stepped aside, grudgingly

granting them entrance.

Crossing the vast outer court and approaching a towering entrance framed by enormous bronzed double doors, Tabitha's observant eyes noted the intricate mosaics swirling underfoot and the gleaming, palm-lined walls enclosing the elegant courtyard. Seasonal flowers spilled over graceful vats and filled Grecian urns, suggesting that the owner of the house hired servants to tend the estate year-round. Without proper care, the plants would have most certainly wilted in the summer heat.

Naturally, she thought a bit snidely. *Amal wouldn't dare rent lodging without a slew of servants to wait on him hand and foot.* Recognizing the fruitlessness of her recalcitrant thoughts, Tabitha quickly dismissed them and focused her attention upon her surroundings. Surprised, she noted the villa boasted an expensive roof paved in red tiles, unlike many of the more practical, flat-roofed dwellings in the city and surrounding areas.

As if on cue, the double doors yawned wide open at their approach, and they were met by the solemn-faced Dorian, donning a fresh toga and new sandals. He looked so thoroughly Roman, Tabitha almost expected to see a wreath of olive leaves gracing his head.

"Dorian, my friend! We are delighted to sup with you this evening," Stephanos exclaimed, receiving a look of confusion from the manservant.

Tabitha supposed a haughty merchant prince like Amal wouldn't dare permit a servant to share his table, hence Dorian's look of utter perplexity.

Recovering from his initial surprise, Dorian's gaze fell questionably upon the earthen pot Tabitha clutched in both hands. He spoke not a word but raised inquisitive hazel-tinged eyes to hers.

"Oh, I've brought some lentils roasted with fresh onion and garlic to accompany the meal," she explained, lifting the pot in question.

Dorian's dark brows lifted in puzzlement—or was it amusement? She couldn't be sure.

"This way," the manservant directed in a crisp, even tone, and Tabitha realized the simple order constituted the first and only words he'd spoken to them since his arrival.

Gripping Stephanos' hand like a lifeline, Tabitha cradled the cookpot close to her chest as they followed Dorian through a brightly frescoed vestibule.

Unlike Mary's, this villa boasted only two levels and was considerably smaller. And though it wasn't nearly as grand as her former mistress's abode, Tabitha had to admit it was stunning. She couldn't help but notice that the owner of the stately home had spared no expense to "Romanize" the place. Even the inner court had been transformed, resembling a Roman *atrium* complete with a fountain, a shimmering blue pool, and painted marble pillars. Tabitha half expected to spot the forbidden marble forms of Roman idols with their disquieting, unblinking stares, tucked away in a household *lararium*. Following Dorian into the lavishly overdone *triclinium*, or dining hall, she was relieved to note the absence of such.

"Welcome, Stephanos, my son! And Tabitha, my lovely daughter, welcome."

As Daphne swept into the room, Tabitha felt sheer relief course through her. The hostess appeared sincere in her welcome, genuinely happy to see them.

Tabitha also noted that Daphne seemed perfectly at home in the lavish rental, causing Tabitha to ponder what her *real* home—Stephanos's childhood home— must be like. For the first time, she was beginning to comprehend the unspeakable sacrifice her husband had made to honor Jesus' appointment as a traveling evangelist, and later, as a deacon in the Jerusalem church.

My wonderful, selfless Stephanos, Tabitha thought, suddenly blinking back tears. *Like Moses, choosing rather to suffer affliction with the people of God than to enjoy the passing pleasures of sin, esteeming the reproach of Christ greater than the treasures of Egypt.* What a man she had married! What a gift from God!

"You've arrived." Donning resplendent garments graced with gold and sparkling gems, Amal entered the triclinium with the air of a prince, his hands pressed together and almost resembling the posture of prayer. "Please, be seated."

Tabitha watched as Amal lowered himself onto the upholstered *lectus* situated before the table at the place of honor. Obediently, Daphne took her place beside him.

When Stephanos nearly selected the lowliest position at the farthest end of the three-sided tri- clinium-style table arrangement, Tabitha quickly swept in front of him, taking the place herself. She would not allow Amal to glower smugly at his son across the table all night.

Smiling to himself as he sensed his wife's hidden ire, Stephanos seated himself beside Tabitha, shar- ing the luxuriant couch-like lectus with her.

"We are delighted to partake of this meal with

you," Daphne spoke, softening the tense atmosphere in the room. Her bright eyes watched approvingly as servants rushed back and forth, depositing steaming trays of food upon the long, rectangular wooden table. "And what's that you have there, Tabitha?" she asked, her eyes shining with interest.

Suddenly remembering the warm cookpot still clutched to her breast, Tabitha quickly placed it upon the table. "I have brought some lentils roasted with fresh onion and garlic to compliment this lovely spread," she explained, hoping she sounded at least *somewhat* refined. It suddenly occurred to her that she'd never seen anyone contribute anything to the rich banquets hosted at Mary's. Had she made a blundering fool of herself? If so, it was too late now.

"How thoughtful," Daphne replied artfully.

"Lentils, eh?" Amal remarked sardonically.

Cheeks flaming, Tabitha bit back a sharp retort. She refused to be baited by his scathing sarcasm. With great effort, she reminded herself that her witness far outweighed her pride.

"Tabitha is a wonderful cook," Stephanos said proudly, placing an arm around her shoulders and attempting to lighten the mood.

Tabitha smiled wanly, further embarrassed, as Amal—who probably possessed fleets of professional chefs, the pompous lout!—appeared less than impressed.

"I wish I had learned to cook," Daphne commented earnestly, ignoring her husband's pointed look. "Tabitha, perhaps you can teach me a few basic lessons during our stay."

"I'd be honored, Mother," Tabitha said with great feeling, warmed by Daphne's humility. Lowering her head, she uttered a silent prayer of thanks. Already, God was opening doors for them! Sensing Tabitha's triumph, Stephanos squeezed her hand, sharing her secret joy.

Once the entirety of the meal had been festively presented by dutiful servants, Amal stood, lifting a large, rounded loaf of plump leavened bread in one hand. Sensing the benediction was on the way, Tabitha bowed her head.

"Baruch Atah Adonai Eloheinu Melech ha'olam ha'motzi lechem min ha'aretz," Amal proclaimed, taking Tabitha by surprise as he flawlessly recited the traditional Hebrew prayer in a booming voice: *Blessed are You, Lord our God, Ruler of the universe, who brings forth bread from the earth.*

As Daphne and Stephanos echoed softly spoken *amens*, Tabitha raised her head in question, watching as their host lowered himself back onto the couch. In her opinion, Amal presented quite a study in contrasts. A Hellenized Jew living in Athens, he refused to keep the required feasts and yet uttered traditional Jewish prayers in flawlessly spoken Hebrew, though Greek was clearly his language of preference. He'd married a woman bearing the name of a pagan minor goddess, yet disinherited his son for embracing a "questionable" religious sect. The very fact that he chose to dwell in Athens—a land of shrines and idols—indicated a spirit of tolerance, for men commonly jested there were far more "gods" than men to be found in Athens. And yet, Amal was the most obstinate, opinionated man she'd ever met.

Frankly, she couldn't help but wonder why he bothered with religion at all. Clearly, his pursuit of power and prestige occupied the bulk of his time.

Perhaps he merely observed the aspects of the Jewish religion that suited him. She was fast learning that Amal wasn't one to be dictated to or inconvenienced. Tabitha decided that must be the case. In his great arrogance, Amal had fashioned his own brand of religion.

Turning her thoughts from the troublesome Amal, Tabitha considered the lovely Daphne. Stephanos' mother was an attentive, gracious hostess. She encouraged Tabitha and Stephanos to freely partake of the extravagant delicacies gracing the table, smiling cordially and expertly commanding the servants as they came and went. Tabitha decided the aristocratic woman must spend quite a bit of time entertaining "important" people.

And then there was the faithful Dorian. With his dignified stance, aristocratic features, prominent cheekbones, neatly styled hair graying at the temples, and his penetrating gaze, she decided he must have been very handsome as a younger man. She could only guess at his age now—perhaps his late forties or early fifties, but she couldn't be sure. He served his masters efficiently, without argument or question. Despite his servant's status, he bore a solemn air of authority, suggesting he was accustomed to supervising the entire staff and household affairs. Stationed in the doorway, he oversaw the current gathering with watchful eyes. On several occasions, he beckoned the servants to him, speaking to them in hushed tones. Tabitha wondered if they were being reprimanded or simply instructed.

Despite Daphne's benevolent overtures, the supper conversation remained somewhat awkward and stilted, as Amal brushed aside anything his son or daughter-in-law had to say as ignorant or inconsequential. If Tabitha learned anything at all, it was that Amal enjoyed discussing one topic, and one topic only: matters of business.

Glancing across the table at Daphne, Tabitha saw how she endured her husband's arrogant droning with a pained smile. Amused, Tabitha folded her hands in her lap. She knew she must be patient. Perhaps if they graciously endured his lectures, Amal would eventually return the favor, opening his heart to the love of Christ. Tabitha and Stephanos had already agreed not to plunge headfirst into a detailed exposition of the gospel message. After all, Stephanos had already outlined it in his first letter—and Amal had promptly rejected it.

Attempting to muster interest as Amal droned on about a recent business acquisition, Tabitha hoped and prayed for the strength to *demonstrate* the gospel message rather than simply *stating* it.

We're going to need Your help, Lord, Tabitha prayed, somewhat thankful Amal had dominated the evening conversation. She hadn't the slightest idea what to say, anyway. She was thankful Stephanos handled himself so well, conversing easily, as he was familiar with his father's various enterprises.

When Amal finally stood, reciting the traditional blessing at the close of the evening meal, Tabitha breathed an inward sigh of relief.

Once the expected pleasantries had been exchanged and farewells had been said, Dorian dutifully escorted them out of the impressive house, dismissing them at the guarded gate. "Thank you for your assistance, my friend," Stephanos said, refraining from offering a hearty embrace. It was obvious such displays of affection rendered the manservant terribly uncomfortable.

With a deep nod, Dorian turned and left them without a word.

Watching him go, Tabitha reached for her husband's hand. Her head was still spinning from Amal's dull conversation and the overwhelming, cloying scent of the incense burning in the triclinium.

Disheartened, Tabitha couldn't help but wonder how many more such evenings they must endure. And would it really make any kind of difference in the lives of her husband's family?

She could only hope and pray it would.

CHAPTER 24

Kelila

"Oh, it's divine!" Catching her breath in awe, Kelila reached out to touch the gauzy white veil Candace had lifted for her inspection. "Oh, but I couldn't wear this, Candace! This was your wedding veil!"

"Don't be silly!" Candace insisted, lifting the intricate veil and arranging it around her sister's head and shoulders. "Ah, this soft white contrasts beautifully with your smooth, dark skin tone, Kelila. You are breathtaking."

Lovingly fingering the graceful folds, Kelila closed her eyes, savoring the wonder of this moment. She could hardly comprehend that she would soon marry the man of her dreams—in a stunning bridal gown! Candace had insisted Kelila wear the bridal attire she herself had worn when she married her dear Simon, and Kelila couldn't be more pleased. The handmade gown was a family heirloom of sorts, as their mother had pieced together the entire ensemble with the help of a dozen maidservants for her own wedding. Every golden stitch, every elegant seam, was utterly flawless. In Kelila's opinion, the graceful gown, with its fitted bodice, flowing sleeves, and billowing train, paired with the delicate, snowy white veil, was absolute perfection.

"Once Simon heads to the synagogue, I'll send the boys outside to tidy the courtyard so you can try on the gown," Candace said, her own excitement mounting as she set aside the veil.

Smiling fondly, Kelila glanced over her shoulder toward her beloved nephews at the door, both saying reluctant goodbyes as their father prepared to leave.

"We may have to make a few alterations," Candace observed, always practical.

"I think it will fit perfectly," Kelila responded with a casual wave. "Don't you dare start cutting up that beautiful gown!"

"Tabitha has already volunteered her services should any alterations be necessary," Candace reminded her, laughing. "You know she's a remarkable seamstress."

"The best," Kelila agreed, swooping across the room and planting herself on a soft mat before the low table, where Candace's gown was lovingly spread. "But we're almost the same size. I'm sure it'll fit."

Arching a brow, Candace studied Kelila's lithe, slender form. Kelila was a few inches taller than she was, with longer legs and torso. Candace also had a few pounds on her younger sister, though she supposed she'd been about ten pounds lighter on her wedding day, before birthing two children! Since Kelila's curves weren't quite as rounded as hers, Candace assumed the dress would need to be altered slightly to flatter her sister's slightly more athletic-looking frame.

Even so, the adjustments should certainly prove to be minor—hardly a challenge for the skillful Tabitha!

"Oh, if only my bridegroom would arrive today!" Scooping up the gown and clutching it to her heart, Kelila squealed her delight.

Laughing, Candace lowered herself onto the mat beside her sister. "If he did, you'd have no gown to wear. I'm certain this one will need to be slightly adjusted."

"It would do just the way it is," Kelila teased, burying her face in the soft folds. "Honestly, sister, I'd marry Philip in a burlap sack if it meant beginning our life together sooner!"

"Judging by the way he looks at you, Philip wouldn't even notice the burlap," Candace chuckled. "That man adores you, Kelila."

"Not half as much as I adore him," Kelila insisted, inwardly praising God for His goodness. It had been nearly three months since their official betrothal. Philip had purchased a modest dwelling for them just a few houses down from Candace and Simon's. He'd obtained it at bargain price, but it was sorely in need of repairs. Kelila thought she would burst waiting for him to ready their new home.

"Mary spoke with the priest who officiated Tabitha and Stephanos' wedding," Candace informed her, her eyes sparkling happily. "He said he would be happy to perform the ceremony when the time comes."

"If I don't die of impatience before then!" Kelila moaned, dropping the gown in her lap. "When, oh when, will Philip come for me?"

"You know the bride never knows the day or the hour her bridegroom will return for her," Candace reminded her, playfully poking her shoulder. "The bride must be ready for her bridegroom's appearance at all times—even when least expected."

"I'd best prepare that burlap sack then, just in case!" Kelila teased, her dark eyes sparkling with fun and mischief.

Affectionately clasping hands, the two sisters dissolved in mirthful laughter.

***

Tabitha

"You look troubled, beloved."

Glancing up in surprise, Tabitha realized she'd merely been pushing around her roasted lentils with a cold piece of pita. The bread had been warm from the oven when she'd begun breakfasting with Stephanos. How long had she simply sat there, brooding? Had she taken a single bite?

"I'm fine," Tabitha assured her husband, forcing a smile she was far from feeling. "It's just...well, I thought Amal and Daphne would be sharing this meal with us. I never expected them to lodge elsewhere."

"We've already promised to sup with them this evening," Stephanos reminded her. Reaching across the low table, he squeezed her hand, offering his encouragement.

"I know." Tabitha sighed. Should she be entirely honest, she dreaded another evening breaking bread beneath Amal's condescending gaze. She could still see him draped indolently upon his gilded lectus, fingering the stem of an elegant goblet, dark eyes inspecting them over the wide rim. "This has just been so different than I'd imagined, that's all. Your father and mother, and even Dorian, well, they seem so—"

"Distant?" Stephanos finished for her, his gentle tone conveying his understanding. "My father and mother are formal to a fault. Aloofness comes with the territory, I suppose."

"Do you think we've made any kind of impact, Stephanos?"

"We've shared but one supper with them, my darling. These things take time."

But how much time? Tabitha wanted to groan. She wasn't sure she could stomach many more of these "formal" dinners with Stephanos' imperious father. How was she supposed to demonstrate the love of Christ when the man irked her on every possible level? The way he stared at her with those cold, unblinking eyes…she was certain he could read her every thought! And frankly, most of them were rather unlovely. Thus far, she feared her witness had proven less than stellar.

Lowering her eyes in shame, Tabitha released another long sigh.

"Put your trust in God, beloved," Stephanos reminded her with a knowing smile. "He longs to welcome my family into His kingdom even more than we do."

"Why does your father loathe you so?" Tabitha dared after a long, uneasy pause. "He himself isn't a devout Jew, so it's strange to me that he's so upset you've embraced the Way."

"You have always been astute," Stephanos acknowledged with a wry smile. "It's not so much my faith in Christ that disturbs him, but the fact that my faith interferes with his wishes."

"And what does your father wish?"

"I'm his only son," Stephanos replied easily, as if that explained everything.

"So?" Tabitha prodded, not following.

"Father has long desired for me to work alongside him in the family business. And I did, for several years—before the Lord led me to Jerusalem. But when his time on earth is done, my father desires for me to take over his enterprises."

"Why couldn't you?" Tabitha asked around a bite of cold, soggy flatbread. Crinkling her nose, she pushed it aside.

"I most certainly could—and quite frankly, I'd be happy to—had Father not placed one stringent condition upon my inheritance."

"What condition?"

"That I renounce my faith in Christ."

Tabitha stared at her husband, speechless. How could Amal do such a thing, placing manipulative, unreasonable conditions upon his own son? Why, it was unthinkable! Eyes flashing, Tabitha attempted to conceal her steadily mounting anger.

"Be still, beloved," Stephanos soothed, coming around the table and lowering himself beside her. "Father doesn't know Christ; therefore, he knows not what he does."

"But how could he ask you to renounce your faith?" Tabitha snapped, wondering if the steam had begun coming out of her ears yet. "You would oversee his enterprises with diligence and integrity *because* of your faith!"

"My father has given his life to matters of business, establishing a booming commercial empire with his own two hands," Stephanos explained, tucking a wayward golden strand behind Tabitha's ear. "He's simply afraid, beloved—afraid all he's worked so hard for will fall into the hands of someone eager to donate his hard-earned capital to an unpopular, hunted sect located in the farthest reaches of a remote Roman province."

"He should know you wouldn't give away his precious money," Tabitha huffed. "But even if you did, it would be far more noble than what *he's* doing with it!"

"But now you see Father's dilemma—he has no heir to oversee his life's work."

"He has no heir by his own choice!" Tabitha pointed out, miffed.

"I love your protective nature," Stephanos teased, leaning in to kiss her firmly. "But, please, don't take offense for my sake. I am right where I belong—in the center of God's will. Had it been the Lord's will for me to oversee Father's affairs, I would be doing so now. But *this* is where He has placed me—here in Jerusalem, serving in the church, employed by the most generous businesswoman in the province, and married to the loveliest woman on earth. And, truly, I couldn't be happier, my love."

"Well, how can I argue with that?" Tabitha bantered playfully, somewhat pacified as Stephanos reached for her, pulling her onto his lap. Draping her arms over his broad shoulders and clasping them behind his neck, Tabitha ventured curiously, "Why didn't your parents have more children?"

"That's an odd question," Stephanos commented, placing his hands on her hips to steady her. "Why do you ask?"

"Knowing your father, he would have intentionally produced multiple heirs to ensure the welfare of his business ventures—had the decision been his," Tabitha mused.

"Ah, I see," Stephanos nodded slowly. "My parents did desire a large family. Sadly, my mother lost three children during her childbearing years."

"Oh no," Tabitha breathed, her eyes softening sympathetically. "Poor Daphne."

"An infant daughter died of an unknown fever before I was born. After my birth, my mother suffered two miscarriages."

Tabitha's heart went out to Daphne, for she, too, knew the sting of bereavement.

"I could be wrong," Stephanos ventured quietly, his dark eyes distant, "but I believe my father lost faith after my sister died. Mother said she was a sweet, beautiful child, and she had my father wrapped around her little finger. I think her death was more than he could bear. I've always wondered if he didn't throw himself into his work simply for distraction, to numb the pain. Eventually, it just became a habit."

"I suppose I've been a bit harsh about your father," Tabitha admitted, lowering her gaze in shame. "I didn't know about the losses he's suffered."

"We all bear hidden scars," Stephanos said. "Sometimes it's difficult to see past a person's crusty, unpleasant exterior to truly understand them, to recognize why they are the way they are. But we must strive to do so, nonetheless."

And that's why you *are the evangelist instead of me!* Tabitha thought with a twinge of conscience. Stephanos took the time to get to know people, sympathizing with their weaknesses rather than condemning them. Offering a silent prayer of repentance, Tabitha resolved to bear more patiently with Amal—even if it killed her!

"But what about your mother, Stephanos?" Tabitha suggested after a moment of thoughtful silence. "If Amal doesn't trust *you* to oversee his enterprises after he's gone, couldn't Daphne resume his work? That's what Mary did when her husband, Mark, died."

"You forget, my mother can neither read nor write."

"But surely your father could teach her!"

"He'd never have it," Stephanos concluded. "Father can't stomach the thought of a woman telling him how to run his business. That alone will keep him from training her."

"He'd prevent Daphne from receiving an education just to maintain control?" Tabitha exclaimed, bristling.

"It's been my experience," Stephanos said very slowly, very thoughtfully, "that some of the most demanding, controlling people in the world are also the most *fearful*. That's why they seek to control others, Tabitha—because they're afraid of what might happen should they relinquish the illusion of control. But these are the ones in desperate need of our prayers. Only the perfect love of Christ can cast out fear, releasing them from their self-inflicted prison of torment."

For some reason unbeknownst to her, Tabitha thought of Saul—the arrogant young Pharisee consumed with hatred and bitterness. Biting her lower lip, Tabitha swiftly shoved him aside, for she hadn't the slightest desire to entertain the fearsome scholar—not even in her thoughts.

For now, she had far more important things to consider—first and foremost, the salvation of her husband's loved ones. Today, she would focus on the matter at hand.

She'd worry about the bothersome Pharisee later.

CHAPTER 25

Tabitha

"I hope it was a wise idea to invite your parents to synagogue," Tabitha breathed, standing before the mirror and expertly twisting her honey-colored tresses with nimble fingers.

"You worry too much," Stephanos teased, swooping in to kiss his wife's rosy cheek. "It'll be fine."

"Please, Stephanos," Tabitha pleaded, turning around to face him, "if Saul or any of the others attempt to engage you in debate this morning, let it go." Immediately catching the stubborn set of his firm jaw, Tabitha rolled her eyes in frustration. "Just this once, Stephanos! Do you want to scare off your parents for good?"

"If the opportunity to share the gospel is presented, I cannot ignore it, beloved. You know that."

Releasing a sigh of frustration, Tabitha reached for her nicest shawl. Today was the Sabbath Day, and she would honor the Lord by looking her best.

"Don't be upset, beloved," Stephanos soothed,

helping her adjust the elegantly embroidered shawl over her head and shoulders. "Everything is in God's hands. He will guide this day."

"I'm just asking you not to cause a scene," Tabitha emphasized as Stephanos opened the door for her.

"Who, me?" Stephanos teased, ushering her out the door. If they didn't hurry, they would be late.

Stepping into the outer court, Tabitha was nearly blinded by the brilliant sunlight. Clearly, there was no use arguing with her husband. Squaring her shoulders, she resolved to hold her peace. She didn't wish to become like the contentious woman described by Solomon, although Stephanos was making it nearly impossible to resist a quarrel!

Accepting his proffered arm, Tabitha decided to pray rather than worry. That's what she was supposed to do, after all.

***

Upon reaching the Synagogue of the Freedmen, Tabitha was momentarily distracted from her angst when a wave of dear friends converged upon them on the stone steps, all eager to meet Amal and Daphne.

Candace and Simon were there along with their two young sons and a beaming Kelila, happily leaning on her Philip's arm. Even Mary and her handsome son, John Mark, along with her smiling brother, Barnabas, had forsaken their synagogue of choice to welcome Stephanos' family.

When Amal and Daphne finally arrived with their silent manservant, Dorian, awaiting their beck and call, Stephanos made formal introductions.

Daphne was warm and gracious while Amal held himself aloof, just as Tabitha had expected. Even so, his grudging respect and admiration for Mary and Barnabas was obvious once he learned of their thriving businesses.

Suppressing a slight smile, Tabitha reminded herself to thank Mary when they had a moment alone. Hers might be the only testimony Amal would willingly accept. In his opinion, the savvy businesswoman was a credible source. Why hadn't she thought of introducing Amal and Daphne to Mary and Barnabas sooner?

Tabitha breathed a sigh of relief once the group finally trickled its way into the cold stone synagogue. The cool air within was a blessed relief from the penetrating summer heat. Taking a seat on the cold stone bench between her husband and Daphne, Tabitha marveled that the sixth month was nearly upon them. She'd scarcely noticed the winter's chill before the season's swift retreat, ushering in a bright, hopeful spring followed by the stifling summer months. How quickly time slipped by!

To Tabitha's great surprise and relief, the morning progressed smoothly. She even found herself relaxing slightly on the bench as the Torah was read from the platform. Allowing her gaze to sweep over her loved ones clustered nearby, Tabitha praised God for the presence of these dear friends. The believers had gone out of their way to make Amal, Daphne, and Dorian feel welcomed.

Yes, she was truly blessed!

Heart pounding in her chest, Tabitha stiffened as a strange premonition suddenly claimed her. Puzzled, her gaze swept over the congregants. There, at his usual spot nearest the platform, stood Saul. He appeared so rigid, so still, Tabitha smugly supposed one might mistake him for one of the many pillars upholding the simple stone structure. Instantly sobering, Tabitha realized in alarm that Saul's fiery gaze rested not upon the speaker behind the podium; instead, his loathing eyes were fixed upon her husband.

Saul's burning hatred was like a tangible presence in the room, sending cold shivers of fear skittering up and down Tabitha's spine. Unable to tear her gaze away, she reminded herself that Saul was but one man under the authority of Gamaliel and the Sanhedrin. He could do nothing of his own volition. But even this solid fact brought Tabitha little comfort. Something dark, something sinister, lurked behind those dangerous eyes. Clenching her fists in her lap, Tabitha battled against the dread claiming her entire being.

Something wasn't right. Danger was at hand.

With great effort, Tabitha tore her gaze from Saul. Reaching protectively for her husband's hand, she bowed her head, praying with such fervency her entire body trembled.

***

Saul of Tarsus

The synagogue was dim, dank, and cold, perfectly suiting Saul's current mood. Even the smoldering candles and elegantly latticed hanging lanterns could not dispel the chill in his heart nor the darkness enshrouding his soul.

A dark-robed Pharisee sporting a heavily tas-seled *tallith* and an impressive-looking phylactery strapped to his forehead stood upon the elevated platform in the center of the synagogue, droning on and on in a low, mesmerizing tone, squinting slightly as he scanned the ancient lines upon the weathered scroll spread before him.

Swallowing the bile rising in his throat, Saul smirked at the sight of so many cursed "believers" polluting his synagogue. This was the first time Mary of Jerusalem had frequented the Synagogue of the Freedmen—he deducted she must consider its humble origins "beneath" her high class. Why had she bothered with attendance today?

The tranquil man seated beside Mary was no stranger to Saul—Joses, whom everyone now re-ferred to as *Barnabas*. Saul's scowl deepened as he decided the apostle should have kept his given name.

Barnabas, *son of encouragement*. Now there was a title to strike fear in the hearts of his enemies! What a laugh.

Even so, the name fit the man like a glove. Saul had known Barnabas when they were both students, excelling under Gamaliel's tutelage. Both had mas-tered the art of debate, though Saul wondered why Barnabas had wasted his time learning the famously Jewish craft. While Saul verbally assaulted his oppo-nents with the force of a battering ram, tearing their arguments apart limb by limb, Barnabas had simply listened to his opponent's perspective before calmly expounding upon any point he wished to make.

Shaking his head in disgust, Saul decided Barna-bas was far too harmless to pose any kind of threat. Why, his younger sister—a *woman*, for heaven's sake—had proven more threatening than him, thus far!

As his stormy gaze traveled over the serene faces of those now dubbed the "believers," scarcely harnessed rage kindled inside of Saul. It had begun as a tiny spark, but as it festered and kindled within his heart, the spark had grown steadily over time, consuming his thoughts, plaguing his nights, threatening to set his entire world ablaze.

Fixing his gaze upon the rogue evangelist called Stephanos, Saul clenched his jaw along with his fists. Unlike the mild, unassuming Barnabas, Stephanos had bewitched the entire city with his doctrine of demons. Having been educated by the most brilliant minds of the empire, Stephanos was a skilled speaker and debater. He possessed an uncanny knowledge of the Scriptures and ancient prophecy, along with an impressive understanding of the various religions of the empire, resulting in the ability to systematically tear down any argument presented against his sacrilegious doctrine. Worse, Saul couldn't deny that Stephanos was fueled by something beyond himself. The evangelist called it a *holy* Spirit, but Saul was certain it was demonic in nature. The signs and wonders the young man performed must be driven by the devil himself, for Stephanos' message contradicted everything Saul had firmly believed since childhood.

Unlike the ignorant and uneducated masses, Saul refused to be swept away by Stephanos' compelling arguments, for he knew certain things to be true: God had no son but Israel, and yet Stephanos unwaveringly hailed a dead rebel as the Son of God. The proclamation was so utterly blasphemous Saul tasted bitterness in his mouth at the mere thought of it. Adding insult to injury, Stephanos promulgated yet another filthy sacrilege—a concept of *three* gods forming one distinct Being, casually calling it the godhead. But the Torah clearly stated *the Lord is one*. Saul couldn't understand why the religious leaders turned a blind eye to these dangerous teachings. Soon, the entire nation would be swept away by Stephanos' dynamic preaching. Soon, their entire race would be polluted, a stink in God's nostrils!

Saul had fasted and prayed unceasingly, demanding that God crush the mounting threat against the religion and traditions of His people. And yet the Almighty had remained strangely, maddeningly silent. Why hadn't He intervened? Shouldn't He care that His reputation had been tainted, tarnished by ignorant, careless men?

Saul's eyes narrowed in disdain, forming two uncompromising slits. He knew something must be done to crush this movement, for it continued to gain momentum at an alarming rate. The leadership of this blasphemous sect must be annihilated, crushed without mercy. The Sanhedrin should have already made an example of the wretched apostles, for a violent demonstration against the church leadership would fill the people with such fear and dread they would shy away from the mere mention of the Way. But the Twelve were untouchable, revered by the masses and shielded by Gamaliel's cursed ruling.

Instantly, unexpectedly, an idea took shape in Saul's mind, hitting him with the force of a battering ram. The sensation of triumph was so powerful, so strong, he was nearly knocked off his feet. Steadying himself with a bit of effort, Saul realized he had discovered a loophole, one not even Gamaliel would suspect...

From the distant platform, the Pharisee's ceaseless droning suddenly faded in the background as Saul could think of nothing but his masterful plan. Even his surroundings dimmed, and Saul felt as if he stood alone in the stone chamber...alone, and yet subtly aware of another dark, unsettling presence...

Quickly brushing aside his superstitious premonition, Saul reevaluated his idea. A slow, predatory smile crept about the corners of his hard mouth as his thoughts began to take shape. Not only would he utterly crush the morale of every believer in the city, but his masterful plan could also convince the high priest—possibly even Gamaliel—that this pestilent sect must be crushed, uprooted, and destroyed. He would prove once and for all that the Way was a threat to the peace of Jerusalem, capable of provoking violence and uprisings in the holy city and beyond, tempting the Romans to intervene.

Drawing a ragged breath, Saul recognized he must move quickly. Should he act now, he'd have plenty of time to plant his seeds of dissension and strife, plenty of time to watch them take root and grow. *I will need allies,* Saul thought grimly. *No more than two or three.*

Fortunately, allies could be *bought.*

And just as suddenly as the plan had possessed him, Saul relaxed. He became sharply aware of his surroundings once again—the cold, stone walls, the sturdy pillars, the musty smell lingering in the air, the toneless droning of the aging Pharisee.

Suddenly recognizing the familiar passage of Scripture being proclaimed from the podium, Saul realized the droning Pharisee spoke of Abraham and Sarah. God had promised them a son in their old age, and yet they remained barren after years of desperate prayer. Since the Almighty had failed to bring about their desired end, Abraham and Sarah had taken matters into their hands.

Pain and hardship followed their rash act, for Abraham took an Egyptian maid to wife, producing a child through her. This, in turn, resulted in endless bloodshed and strife, as the descendants of Sarah and the descendants of Hagar battled to the bitter death.

A bloody rivalry existing to this very day, Saul thought, a strange twinge of conscience catching him unaware.

Abraham had failed to wait on God. Instead, he had taken matters into his own hands. Flinching inwardly, Saul couldn't help but wonder if he was about to do the same. Gamaliel had commanded the Council to leave the troublesome sect, the Way, in God's hands. In time, Gamaliel had insisted, Adonai would provide the solution, whatever that might be.

Setting his jaw in derision, Saul crushed the still, small voice vying for his attention. For soon he, Saul of Tarsus, would be hailed as the man who had demolished the Way, silencing the gospel of Jesus Christ forever.

CHAPTER 26

Tabitha

Going about her household chores, Tabitha agonized inwardly over her seeming inability to reach Stephanos' family. They had resided in Jerusalem for over a month, and yet she and Stephanos had seen very little of them. They'd shared a handful of formal meals at Amal's rented villa, and though Tabitha had extended countless supper invitations, Amal obstinately refused her kind overtures. Apparently, he found it distasteful to dine in their small "hovel," partaking of peasants' fare.

Stephanos, too, had extended multiple invitations for his parents to join them at the synagogue for Sabbath worship, to no avail. Amal had been quite vocal about his keen distaste for Stephanos' beloved Synagogue of the Freedmen, grousing about the "inferior" architecture, the musty smell lingering in the air, the "tedious" Scripture readings, and the "dull, inept" speakers.

Surprisingly, Amal was eager to accept invitations to the church services hosted at Mary's villa, though Tabitha had promptly discovered his attendance had nothing whatsoever to do with interest in the Way. She had been mortified when Amal approached Mary at the service's end, drilling her with intrusive questions about her various business holdings. But Mary had responded with poise and ease, candidly answering his audacious inquiries. Tabitha had apologized to Mary for the shameless presumption of her father-in-law shortly after, her cheeks stained with humiliation.

"Why should you apologize, dear one?" Mary had asked in her gracious way. "Possessing a common interest with someone can become the gateway to sharing the message of Christ with them. I am happy to discuss matters of business with Amal and Daphne if such conversations will result in their reception of the gospel."

Taking comfort in the familiar *swish*, *swish*, *swish* of her broom, Tabitha wished she possessed half the graciousness and poise of her former mistress. Mary handled the challenging Amal as easily as a gifted teacher might manage an obstinate child!

Praying silently while she worked, Tabitha sought the Lord's guidance concerning her in-laws. She so desperately wanted to reach them—for her husband's sake as much as for their own, she realized. She knew how longingly Stephanos desired to welcome them into God's everlasting kingdom.

I suppose I'm rushing things a bit, Lord, Tabitha admitted as she swept. *It's hardly been one month, and yet here I am, brooding that Amal and Daphne haven't yet accepted You!* Sighing wistfully, Tabitha paused her sweeping, leaning ponderously upon the long wooden broom. If only she had more time! If Amal and Daphne lived nearby, her mission wouldn't feel nearly as urgent. But what if her in-laws returned to Greece without accepting Christ's atoning sacrifice for them? For all she knew, Amal could pack up his wife and his belongings tomorrow, setting sail for his native Athens! How much time did she have left to make an impact?

But then again, I suppose none of us really knows how much time we have left with anyone, Tabitha thought, reluctantly resuming her gentle sweeping. *We should do everything in our power to reach the lost while we can—while there's still time.*

Attempting to focus her thoughts on prayer, Tabitha tried to dismiss the contrary emotions vying for her attention. She couldn't help but wonder if Amal had *really* journeyed to Jerusalem to visit his son, or if he'd simply traversed the sparkling Mediterranean Sea to enjoy several leisurely months vacationing in a lavish villa in the holy city!

Peeved, Tabitha swept more ferociously, taking her frustrations out on the fine dust that had settled upon the hard-packed earthen floor. She had been so certain Daphne would come around. Had she been wrong about Stephanos' gentle mother? Perhaps so, or perhaps the poor woman was too afraid of her husband to even consider such things. But as of now, it appeared Daphne remained neutral toward her son's faith. She was polite and understanding—enduring the apostles' long sermons with a gracious smile—but nothing more. Amal, however, remained downright belligerent in his disgust toward followers of the Way, excepting Mary and Barnabas, of course. And then there was Dorian...

The mere thought of Amal's right-hand man made Tabitha want to throw up her hands in defeat. Dorian's perspective—rather like the servant himself—remained a complete mystery to her. How was she supposed to know what he—with his somber expression and fathomless eyes—was thinking?

Propping her broom against the wall, Tabitha was about to move on to the next task when an unexpected *tap, tap, tap* at the door made her jump.

Now who could that be? Tabitha thought, glancing down at her dusty apron in dismay. It certainly wasn't Stephanos—he wouldn't be returning from his work at Mary's for several hours yet, nor would he have knocked at his own front door!

Taking a deep breath to compose herself, Tabitha smoothed her mussed tresses, reached for a convenient shawl, and draped it over her head in one fluid motion. Swinging open the front door, her eyes grew round at the sight of an unexpected visitor.

"Dorian?"

"My lady."

"What a...what a pleasant surprise," Tabitha stammered, confused. Had he come to see Stephanos? If so, she would have to redirect him to Mary's villa.

"The Lady Daphne wishes to see you," Dorian explained in his crisp, even tone.

The Lady Daphne? Tabitha thought, heart racing. Standing on tiptoes, Tabitha attempted to look over the tall servant's broad shoulder.

She needn't have bothered, for at Dorian's announcement, Daphne stepped into view, smiling rather shyly. Tabitha was instantly impressed, for the woman had wisely chosen to wear plain, inconspicuous garments for her trip into the Lower City. She had also removed her expensive jewelry, to Tabitha's great relief. It certainly wouldn't do for the poor woman to get mugged on her way home!

"I do apologize for arriving unannounced," Daphne said sincerely, interrupting Tabitha's silent tangent. "But the opportunity presented itself, and I asked Dorian to escort me. I hope that's all right."

"Oh, you needn't apologize." Snapping out of her initial stupor, Tabitha swung the door open even wider, happily gesturing for them to come inside. "I am delighted you came, Mother!"

"Dorian won't be staying," Daphne spoke up, dismissing her manservant with a polite nod of her graceful head. "He has other matters to attend to."

"Oh?" Tabitha watched as Dorian turned smartly on his heels, strolling through the outer court, and disappearing through the gate without a word.

"He shall return for me at the proper time," Daphne explained, sensing Tabitha's confusion.

"Of course," Tabitha said quickly. "Please, do come in!"

Daphne did so, appearing somewhat anxious.

Curious about her typically composed in-law's nervous demeanor, Tabitha quickly decided to prop open the front door rather than closing it behind her guest. It was a stiflingly hot summer day, and the afternoon breezes would be more than welcomed. "Now, to what do I owe the pleasure of your company, Mother?" Tabitha asked, suddenly nervous. She knew she must look an absolute mess after several hours of grueling chores!

"It appears I've caught you in the middle of house-cleaning," Daphne observed apologetically, noting the broom still propped in the corner.

"Oh, think nothing of it! I'm so happy you're here," Tabitha insisted, guiding Daphne toward the sturdiest bench in the house. Never had she been more aware of the absence of luxurious furnishings in her cozy little home, for Daphne was accustomed to reclining on plush couches, a goblet of the finest wine in hand. Chagrined, Tabitha realized all she had to offer by way of refreshment was some cold flatbread, dried fruit, cool water recently drawn from the well, or goat's milk. Cringing inside, she wondered what a woman accustomed to feasting upon the finest hors d'oeuvres would think of her simple fare!

To Tabitha's great relief, Daphne lowered herself upon the low wooden bench near the hearth without complaint.

"Allow me to prepare some refreshments," Tabitha offered, turning toward her wooden shelves stacked with cooking pots, utensils, and dried goods.

"Oh, no. That won't be necessary," Daphne insisted, lifting a delicate hand. "We may not have much time. And if you don't mind, I'd like to ask a few questions."

Instantly alerted by the urgency in Daphne's tone, Tabitha released a string of emergency prayers heavenward. What could Daphne possibly wish to discuss with her? Attempting to appear at ease, Tabitha pulled up a stool across from her mother-in-law and sat down.

"What do you wish to discuss?" Tabitha asked, nervously clasping her hands in her lap.

"You needn't look frightened, my dear," Daphne said quickly, reaching out to touch her knee in a motherly fashion. "I have a few questions, that's all."

"Ask away," Tabitha smiled, attempting to squelch her unease.

"As I'm sure you've guessed, nothing would make my husband happier than to know his life's work rests in capable hands," Daphne explained, folding manicured hands in her lap. "Amal has long desired to bequeath his enterprises to Stephanos, but something has held him back for quite some time now."

"Stephanos' faith," Tabitha supplied, praying desperately for wisdom in this conversation. She sensed the Lord was opening a door for her, one she didn't wish to slam shut by her own lack of thought.

"Yes," Daphne admitted, her color deepening.

"I can understand that." Leaning forward, Tabitha reached for Daphne's hand. "Your husband has given his life to his work. It's only natural he would be protective of his enterprises."

"You're not angry?" Daphne stared at Tabitha in disbelief.

"Of course not," Tabitha explained, praying silently as she spoke. "Amal's enterprises are his own. Why should we assume we have any right to them?"

"Stephanos is his only son. It stands to reason he should inherit his father's assets."

"But ultimately, that is Amal's decision to make," Tabitha smiled, amazed at the peace now flooding her entire being. "Not ours."

"Amal knows how devoted Stephanos is to the orphans and widows of this region," Daphne admitted, her color mounting.

"And he fears Stephanos would donate all the profits to assist those in need—even in Athens," Tabitha finished for her, her tone compassionate rather than condemning.

"Yes," Daphne confessed, lowering her gaze in shame. "I must admit, I used my husband's suspicions to my own advantage, for I have long desired to see my son. Amal agreed to come here because he wanted to see for himself if Stephanos' faith was clouding his better judgment."

"And what has he decided?" Tabitha asked pointedly, suppressing the white-hot offense searing through her and rearing its ugly head. She had long suspected Amal's motives for this journey were self-driven. But to hear Daphne confirming her suspicions filled her entire being with indignation!

"Amal remains conflicted." Daphne sighed, her hands twisting nervously in her lap. "He cannot deny our son's strength of character, for it resonates with his every word, his every deed. But Amal is still concerned that Stephanos' desire to spread his gospel message might tempt him to utilize company funds to do so."

"For what it's worth," Tabitha said evenly, "I can give you my word that Stephanos wouldn't touch a half-shekel that didn't belong to him."

"I believe that," Daphne said with great feeling. "I'm just not sure my husband will be so trusting."

Oh, the love of money, Tabitha thought, deeply saddened. *It truly is the root of all kinds of evil.* Couldn't Amal see that his obsession with wealth and luxury was destroying his life? He had everything a man could possibly desire, and yet he was possibly the most miserable, suspicious person she had ever met. His entire existence amounted to jealously guarding his wealth.

"May I ask you an honest question?" Daphne

ventured quietly, shaking Tabitha from her silent reverie.

"Of course, Mother," Tabitha agreed, wondering where this conversation was headed.

"Do you think...well, do you suppose that Stephanos would...do you think he would renounce his faith in order to work alongside his father and eventually inherit his estate and life's work?"

"No," Tabitha responded with great conviction. "No, Mother. Stephanos would never do that."

"But why not?" Daphne asked, raising eyes full of questions. "He would cling to this new faith even at great personal loss? You would inherit great richest, financial stability and security."

"Stephanos would relinquish his *life* before denying our Lord," Tabitha said gently, sensing Daphne's desperate confusion.

"But...but why?"

"Because this life is fleeting, Mother. It's temporal. Stephanos knows that no measure of treasures accumulated on this earth can supply lasting happiness or security. What does it truly matter if a man gains the whole world, but forfeits his soul?"

Biting her lower lip, Daphne looked away.

"You see, God loved us so much that He sent His Son to redeem us from eternal death," Tabitha went on, her heart going out to Daphne, for she sensed her deep inner turmoil. "We will all die once, hence the fleeting nature of this life. But when we accept Jesus' finished work on the cross, we will be spared the second death. We will dwell in paradise with God for all eternity. And *that* is true security, true happiness and bliss."

"But how is one to know if the afterlife really

does exist?" Daphne ventured, her large brown eyes hesitant and full of questions. "Even our religious leaders remain conflicted on this matter. The Pharisees insist on resurrection after death, even as the Sadducees stoutly refuse to accept their doctrine. According to the Sadducees, there is nothing beyond this life—we must eat, drink, and be merry, for tomorrow we die." Expression clouding, Daphne added, "My husband favors that line of thought."

I can see why, Tabitha thought, miffed. Such thinking justified his greed and materialism. *Oh, Lord, what can I say to convince her?*

And then the answer came, filling Tabitha's entire being with confidence.

"I know the resurrection exists," Tabitha declared, her hazel-green eyes alight with wonder, "because I have seen it."

"You have seen the resurrection? What do you mean?" Daphne asked, cocking her head.

"After Jesus suffered a tortuous death upon a Roman cross, my friends anointed His body and wrapped Him in graveclothes. Do you remember meeting Joseph of Arimathea at Mary's house?"

"Indeed. My husband was quite impressed with him."

"Well, Jesus' body was laid to rest in Joseph's immaculate tomb. There are countless witnesses to attest to this fact."

Daphne studied her daughter-in-law as if in a trance.

"But Jesus rose from the dead, Mother. And I know this because I saw Him—I saw Him with my own eyes!"

"You saw Him yourself?" Daphne repeated,

stunned.

"In the Upper Room, where we still gather to worship."

"Tabitha, I know you wouldn't lie to me," Daphne murmured, shaking her head in confusion. "During our stay, you have proven yourself innocent and good and pure. But is it possible you were deceived?"

"Absolutely not. Over five hundred witnesses saw our resurrected Lord. I will take you to see them, every single one of them, if that will set your mind at ease."

"I thought the resurrection of your Christ was but a rumor..." Daphne mused, visibly shaken. "I had no idea there were viable witnesses involved."

"The resurrection is *real*, Mother," Tabitha said, leaning forward to take Daphne's trembling hands in her own. "Jesus was but the firstfruits of those who will be raised from the dead."

"But what does this mean for us? For the world?"

"One day, we shall all stand before Almighty God," Tabitha explained, her tone urgent. "But because all have sinned, none of us shall be deemed worthy of His eternal kingdom—unless we have accepted Christ's atonement, His shed blood."

"But how?"

"Just as the apostles have instructed: *If you confess with your mouth the Lord Jesus and believe in your heart that God raised Him from the dead, you will be saved.* For in His mercy, God sent His Son to take our punishment upon Himself, to cancel the debt we could never pay."

"Some have argued that one sinless Man couldn't pay another's ransom," Daphne remarked thoughtfully. "But I disagree."

Tabitha stared at her mother-in-law, stunned.

"A brash young employee of ours once found himself indebted to my husband. The poor man owed Amal an exorbitant sum—a sum he couldn't possibly pay, based on the salary he received."

Tabitha's eyes softened as Daphne's own shimmered with unshed tears.

"As I'm sure you've noticed, Tabitha, my husband isn't a merciful man. He threatened this employee, insisting he would turn him in to the authorities if he failed to repay him. This would have undoubtedly led to the young man's arrest. And how could he possibly repay his debt, chained in a Roman cell?"

"I see," Tabitha said quietly, her eyes conveying her deep sympathy.

"Well, the boy's father learned of his sad plight and found my husband. He brought enough to pay even more than his son's debt required," Daphne continued. "Amal accepted the father's payment, immediately canceling the son's debt. So you see, I understand how one man can pay the price for another. I have witnessed a father's love for his erring child. And if it isn't too bold to say, I believe…I believe God's love is like that."

Tabitha could only nod her wholehearted agreement, for her throat had entirely closed.

"Is that why God sent His Son to cover our sins, Tabitha? To cancel a debt we could never pay?"

"Yes, Mother," Tabitha said, rising from her stool and placing a hand on Daphne's shoulder. "I couldn't have said it better myself."

"I understand," Daphne whispered, releasing a long, quavering sigh. "But Amal will never accept this."

"He may in time," Tabitha encouraged her. "Don't lose hope. Nothing is impossible with God."

"But don't you see?" Daphne asked, her dark eyes bleak. "My husband will never permit me to join the Way, Tabitha. I shudder to think of what he might do."

"Nothing can separate you from the love of Christ, Mother," Tabitha said firmly, her anger kindling against Amal. "Not even your husband's wrath."

"I have lost my father, my mother, and three children throughout the course of my life, and my heart still breaks for each of them." As Daphne closed her eyes, tears slipped beneath her thick lashes, tracing slender lines down her cheeks. "To know with absolute certainty that I would see them again...well, that would be worth living for."

Tabitha's heart sprang into her throat, for she knew this dear woman stood upon the threshold of Heaven. She was so close, so very close to making the most important decision she would ever make, the only decision that truly mattered—

Rap, rap, rap!

Both women started at Dorian's persisting knocking on the front door.

Why, God? Tabitha could have screamed out her frustration. *Daphne was so close, so close to receiving You! Why must Dorian return now?*

Rising anxiously, Daphne took Tabitha by the shoulders, her desperate gaze boring into her daughter-in-law's. "Please, speak of this meeting to no one except my son. Not even my husband."

"You have my word," Tabitha said, heart breaking.

Dabbing at her tears with the corner of her shawl,

Daphne quickly mustered a brave smile as Tabitha opened the door.

Dorian stood there, still as stone.

"Shall we be on our way, Dorian?" Daphne asked a bit too brightly.

"As you wish, my lady." Dorian's eyes flickered slightly, detecting that something was amiss.

As Daphne stepped over the threshold, Tabitha took hold of her and whispered into her ear, "Promise me you will consider all I've told you."

"I will," Daphne assured her, returning her embrace.

Heart pounding in her chest, Tabitha watched as Daphne slipped out the door. Having crossed the outer court, Dorian opened the gate for her mother-in-law, promptly closing it behind them. As they ventured out onto the street, Tabitha leaned against her doorframe, consumed with heartfelt prayer.

Precious Lord, water the seeds You have so graciously allowed me to plant today. May they take root and grow, reaping an abundant harvest of everlasting life!

CHAPTER 27

Mary

Mary's spirit was strangely unsettled as darkness enshrouded the holy city.

Stealing down a lamplit corridor, Mary emerged beneath a towering stone archway, crossing the inner court with its burning torches casting writhing shadows upon the colorful awnings flapping smartly in the rustling night breezes.

Having reached the impressive office library, Mary sank onto the throne-like chair behind her massive desk, gripping the armrests like a lifeline.

She had experienced this deep sense of disquiet, this troubling unrest, before—the night Jesus had been arrested and tried before the Sanhedrin. The night her husband, Mark, had perished in her arms. The night Ananias and Sapphira had conspired against the Holy Spirit, only to be struck dead in her villa the following day.

She sensed it even *now.* Dark forces were at work, swirling in the chill night air, eager to perform the bidding of a cruel master.

Shuddering, Mary raised cool fingertips to touch her aching forehead. Perhaps she should awaken Tobias, her faithful overseer and fellow believer. She knew he would humbly join her in prayer without demanding an explanation for the strange premonition she was experiencing.

Oh, how I wish my dear Tabitha was still in residence! How often had her spunky maidservant stumbled upon her in this very chamber, somehow aware of Mary's need! Undoubtedly, Tabitha would have sensed the danger, too. Perhaps she sensed it even now. Perhaps she lay awake at this very moment, offering prayers to God on behalf of His saints in Jerusalem and beyond.

The subtle treading of stealthy footfalls shook Mary from her poignant musings. Swiftly raising her head, Mary's sharp eyes scanned the inner court sequestered just beyond the rows of painted marble pillars gracing the office entrance.

An unfamiliar shadow flickered past the stone court, teasing several marble pillars.

Instantly alert, Mary rose slowly from her chair, her heart pounding, her gray eyes scanning her desk for any object that might possibly serve for self-defense. A heavy gilded paperweight caught her eye, glittering in the golden lamplight. Reaching for the sculpted paperweight, Mary's slender fingers slowly closed around the cool metal object.

A dark specter clothed in a hooded, flowing black robe emerged from the tall pillars, his gait dangerously purposeful as he closed in on Mary's desk.

Planting her bare feet firmly on the cold tiles beneath her, Mary lifted her weapon high overhead.

"Don't scream."

Mary froze, instantly recognizing the deeply masculine voice.

The specter threw back his hood, grinning broadly and revealing a dangerously handsome face, obsidian eyes, and a swarthy complexion.

"Alexander!" Mary gasped, feeling weak as relief coursed through her entire being.

"Surprised?" Alexander grinned, closing the distance between himself and Mary's wide desk.

"Nearly surprised to death," Mary admitted ruefully, falling onto her chair.

"I thought I'd find you in here," Alexander quipped, helping himself to the straight-backed chair across from Mary's desk. "I do apologize about the manner of this meeting, but I was denied entrance by that bullheaded cretin guarding your gate."

"How did you sneak in?" Mary asked, suddenly feeling very insecure.

"Don't look so pale," Alexander laughed, settling comfortably on the chair. "I work for the high priest, remember? I've become quite the expert at alluding armed guards at various checkpoints."

Mary couldn't help but wonder about more dangerous men possessing Alexander's rare talent. Perhaps she should reinforce her household guard...

"I'm delighted to see you, Mary," Alexander confessed. "And my wife, Mara, sends her love."

"Send her mine, as well," Mary said, warmed by the thought of Alexander's courageous young wife. "And I'm glad to see you too, Alexander, though I daresay your presence indicates trouble is afoot."

"Ah, yes," Alexander quipped, his dark eyes dancing in amusement. "Regrettably, I've somehow become known as the bearer of bad news."

Mary couldn't help but smile at Alexander's zeal and gusto. The young man had proven himself invaluable, serving as an undercover agent, of sorts, in Caiaphas' palace. Anytime the tide turned against the Way, Alexander slipped out of the lion's den, unseen, to update Mary, his informant, about the goings-on within the high priest's household.

"Was it difficult to slip away, unnoticed, so soon after the Day of Atonement?"

"I find the feasts and festivals are actually the best times to do so," Alexander indulged, relishing the danger and intrigue. "The chaos and the noise create rather useful diversions."

Mary hadn't thought of that.

"Are you aware of a young Pharisee called Saul of Tarsus?"

Jarred back to the present moment by Alexander's odd inquiry, Mary's lips tipped in thinly veiled amusement.

"Ah, so you have heard of him," Alexander grinned, assessing her reaction. "A rather interesting character, isn't he?"

"Indeed," Mary agreed, refraining from voicing any negative thoughts regarding the zealous student of the Law.

"Well, he's up to something," Alexander announced, leaning forward in his chair. "Of what, I haven't the slightest idea. But he's frequenting Caiaphas' office with maddening regularity. He seems to be gathering allies, picking up momentum for...*something*." Alexander paused long enough to allow the information to sink in before plunging ahead with the remainder of his message. "Whatever it is, he's keeping it close to the vest. But here's what we *do* know: Saul hates the Way with a single-minded determination bordering complete and utter madness. I believe he's simply waiting for the chance to strike."

"Do you think he intends to harm the apostles despite Gamaliel's edict?" Mary asked. She certainly wouldn't put it past the ruthless Pharisee.

"It's certainly plausible," Alexander mused. "But how can we really know? He would have to procure the Sanhedrin's consent, and given Gamaliel's stance on the subject, that would prove tricky enough, even for a slick one like Saul."

"So we will just have to wait and see what he's up to," Mary murmured, deeply troubled. "In the meantime, have you any suggestions for us?"

"Pray," Alexander declared with great conviction. "Pray for protection, fervently, without ceasing."

Mary nodded, a familiar knot tightening in the pit of her stomach. She had known something wasn't right, and now it seemed her worst fears had been confirmed.

"And always be vigilant, ever watchful," Alexander reminded her, rising from the gilded chair. "Our adversaries are masters of manipulation and deceit. We must remain on guard."

"I will tell the others," Mary promised, pushing back her chair and rising to her feet. "Thank you, Alexander, for risking so much to warn us."

"I am at your service," Alexander assured her with an exaggerated, over-chivalrous bow. "You know that."

"May God bless you and keep you, Alexander."

"And you, as well."

Mary smiled warmly, wondering when—or if—she would see Alexander or his wife, Mara, again.

"Now if you don't mind, I'll see myself out the same way I sneaked in." Flashing her a knowing grin, Alexander raised his hood over his head, veiling his flashing dark eyes and charismatic features. Turning sharply on his heels, he slipped past the rows of marble pillars, vanishing into the inky darkness of the outer court.

"God be with you," Mary whispered, lifting her eyes toward Heaven. "Merciful Father, protect us all."

***

Tabitha

After a long night of restless tossing and turning, Tabitha wearily lifted herself from her sleeping pallet, rising long before the sun.

Careful not to awaken her slumbering husband, Tabitha lit an additional oil lamp. Gingerly lifting the small lamp and shielding its faint, flickering glow with one hand, she crossed the room, moving toward the intricately latticed window.

Pushing open the rough wooden lattice, Tabitha placed her lamp upon the windowsill, gazing wistfully at a velvety pre-dawn sky still sprinkled with glittering stars.

Her spirit was deeply troubled. Was she simply imagining it, or was this oppressive darkness before dawn far heavier than usual? Tabitha felt as if she was being smothered in it.

How Tabitha longed to awaken her husband

and slip into his arms, burying her face in his chest and pouring out her anxieties and concerns! She knew he would listen with understanding, but she just couldn't bring herself to disturb him. Stephanos had been working relentlessly managing the food distribution for the orphans and widows, overseeing donations, and organizing complicated ledgers—not to mention, continuing his day job at Mary's and preaching in the Temple courts and local synagogues. His ministry in Jerusalem had exploded as the Holy Spirit enabled him to perform signs, wonders, and healings. And though Stephanos had not uttered a single complaint, Tabitha knew the long, grueling hours were taking their toll.

He desperately needed rest, and she would not disturb him.

Glancing over her shoulder, Tabitha discerned the still form of her beloved husband behind the gauzy scarlet tapestry sectioning off their bedchamber. Listening to his gentle breathing, a fierce protectiveness welled up inside her.

She'd seen the way the religious leaders watched him with vipers' eyes. As the flaming jealousy of the Pharisees, Sadducees, scribes, and elders increased, the hostility of many devout Jews rapidly escalated. But even the unbearable tension crackling in the air couldn't keep Stephanos from his mission, nor could it mar the steadfast love he harbored for his people. Though most Jews and proselytes attending the local synagogues refused to accept the Messiah, clinging rigidly to the traditions of their Jewish fathers, Stephanos continued to reach out to them.

Why couldn't he see that they didn't want to be reached?

Releasing a ragged sigh, Tabitha returned her gaze to the glistening stars overhead. How could they look so tranquil, so serene, amidst her own burning inner turmoil?

The mounting animosity of the Jews and religious leaders was not her only concern, though Tabitha was certain that alone was enough to drive her mad. There was also the matter of Amal and Daphne and their trusty manservant, Dorian. Many weeks had elapsed since Tabitha's private conversation with Daphne. She had only seen the couple a handful of times since then, and only at their rental estate.

Tabitha couldn't help but wonder if Amal suspected that his wife was seeking. He had clearly tightened the reins of Daphne's already limited freedom, refusing to leave her alone with Tabitha and Stephanos for even a moment. And he had completely forsaken the services at Mary's villa. Even as the long-awaited month of Tishri arrived, ushering in the most sacred festival season of the year, Amal had remained barricaded within his luxuriant Greco-Roman mansion in the Upper City, completely disregarding the Feast of Trumpets and the sobering Day of Atonement.

Tabitha had agonized over Amal's stubborn refusal to observe the holy days. How she had longed to unveil the deep mysteries hidden within the feasts, each one pointing directly to Jesus Christ! How her husband's family would have benefited from the special sermons hosted at Mary's villa, commemorating the holy days!

Tabitha already knew there was no point in extending an invitation for Stephanos' family to join them in celebration of the fast-approaching Feast of Tabernacles. First, she would have to pry Amal out of his plush habitat with a crowbar. And even if she succeeded, he'd die before resigning himself to living in a tent, exposed to the elements, for an entire week.

Lord, Amal stands like a stumbling block between his wife and Your salvation, Tabitha complained, attempting to suppress her mounting frustration. *If he's determined to perish in his own sins, so be it! But why must he drag Daphne down with him?*

Closing her eyes, Tabitha waited for something— anything—from the Lord.

Her lamentation was met by thunderous silence.

Sighing in resignation, Tabitha lifted her lamp and shut the lattice. Turning from the window, she crossed the room, pausing before the ornamental mirror near the door. Raising the lamp a bit higher, Tabitha studied her own troubled reflection now cast in writhing bronzed shadows.

She was struck by her unusual pallor and the large, haunted eyes staring back at her.

The devil has asked to sift you as wheat.

The shocking revelation came as clearly as if someone stood behind her, whispering in her ear. Stunned, Tabitha dropped her lamp. It clattered noisily to the ground, strewing olive oil across the hard-packed earth, extinguishing the tiny flame.

Tabitha stood alone in the inky darkness, still as stone.

Hands balling into fists, she closed her eyes, drawing short, ragged breaths, struggling against the panic rising in her chest. From across the room, the sound of her husband's quiet, steady breathing reached her, filling her with a sense of relief.

Somehow, she hadn't awakened him.

But *she* had been awakened to a dreadful possibility. Would she, too, be sifted—as Simon Peter, the night he denied his Lord? What dark portents must loom dangerously in her future? She knew the devil roamed about like a roaring lion, seeking someone to devour, someone to utterly destroy.

Well, he can't have me, she thought fiercely, her eyes flashing in the dark. *He's not going to win this one. Not now, not ever.*

Frightful memories surfaced, unbidden. Tabitha remembered watching as the apostles were bound, led away by ruthless men intent on their destruction. She saw the hatred burning in the eyes of the high priest, the oozing gashes slashed into the apostles' bleeding backs…

Taking a deep, steadying breath, Tabitha's eyes hardened in firm resolve. She had been warned. No matter what, she would remain on guard. And she would stand firm, regardless of the horrors that might lie ahead.

CHAPTER 28

Saul of Tarsus

The Day of Atonement came and went, shrouding Jerusalem with an air of apprehension and solemnity.

Standing upon a high Temple wall overlooking the Kidron Valley cast in early morning shadows, Saul's eyes were fixed upon the steadily rising sun, a smoldering ball of flame, its golden light teasing the flourishing groves gracing the Mount of Olives.

The believers claimed their Christ had wept there, pleading with God to remove His cup of suffering.

Saul's countenance hardened. The bloody crucifixion was testament enough—the cup of suffering had not been removed.

Why had a simple, uneducated street Preacher expected the Almighty to intervene or hear His prayers? Not only had the One called Jesus belittled the Law of Moses, but He had defied the powers of Rome. And then His followers mourned and wailed when He was nailed to a Roman cross. What had they expected? A different outcome?

Rome always had her way.

And now the same cursed followers continued spreading their poison, polluting the Holy City, the bride of Almighty God. They had no right to defile this sacred place, the guardian city of the holy Temple.

Somehow, Saul curbed his outrage, his dark eyes glittering in disdain. The iniquitous followers of the dead Rabbi had brought this calamity upon themselves. *They* had set his hand against them.

He had no choice but to extinguish this rising threat.

Then they will deliver you up to tribulation and kill you, and you will be hated by all nations for My name's sake...

On the Temple steps just a few days before, that cursed evangelist had proclaimed these troubling words of His Christ, urging his fellow believers to stand firm.

And when these things come to pass—when they are arrested and tormented and utterly silenced— the same ones will insist the words of their Christ have been fulfilled, Saul thought, a muscle jerking in his tightening jaw. No doubt, they would hail *him* as the fulfillment of their self-proclaimed Messiah's prophecy.

How ironic.

Saul knew it was time to make his move, amidst the feasting and revelry, while Jerusalem's borders remained swollen with pilgrims and celebrators awaiting the Feast of Tabernacles—when their strict Roman wardens expected a bit of noise and commotion. Allies had been procured. A plan was in motion.

Now was the opportune time.

Steeling himself for what must be done, Saul turned sharply on his heels and departed.

***

Tabitha

Tabitha was cleaning up from breakfast when Stephanos re-entered the house bearing a regal-looking scroll. Her curiosity was instantly piqued since he had already kissed her goodbye and set out for Mary's villa.

Why had he turned right back around?

"What's that?" she asked, her eyes fixed upon the suspicious scroll in his hand.

"A messenger just met me at our gate," Stephanos explained, breaking the seal and unfurling the letter with little ceremony. "It's from Mary."

"Why would she send word knowing you'd be seeing her within the hour?"

"It must be urgent," Stephanos guessed, smiling at his wife's avid curiosity.

Coming around the low table, Tabitha took her husband's arm. Peering around him, her sharp eyes scanned the open letter's contents.

"Stephanos!" Tabitha gasped, snatching the parchment from his hands. "Mary says trouble is at hand."

"Isn't it always?" Stephanos teased, calmly retrieving the letter from his anxious wife.

"You know Mary isn't one to overreact," Tabitha insisted, watching in dismay as Stephanos folded the letter, nonchalantly placing it inside his leather satchel. "Alexander must have learned something."

"Ah, her informant," Stephanos agreed candidly. "You must be right."

"What do you suppose is amiss?" Tabitha asked, irked that Stephanos appeared to be taking Mary's caution so lightly.

"It could be any number of things," Stephanos answered honestly. "Besides," he grinned, "we're not exactly on the best of terms with the Jews *or* the Romans, which isn't ideal given the fact that we live among Jews in a Roman province."

Tabitha was not amused.

"Please, my darling, try not to worry about tomorrow." Taking her by the shoulders, Stephanos kissed her firmly. "*Sufficient for the day is its own trouble.*"

"Glibly quoting the words of Jesus is hardly addressing the issue," Tabitha argued, stiffening at his touch.

"His words are truth, beloved. We would do well to live by them."

"You mean *I* would do well to live by them," Tabitha huffed.

"Well, yes. That, too." Another dashing smile.

"Stephanos, I'm genuinely concerned you're not taking this seriously. Mary is a steadfast, courageous believer. She isn't given to idle gossip, nor does she blow matters out of proportion. If she thinks trouble is at hand, I believe her."

"As do I," Stephanos assured his anxious wife, gently stroking her cheek. "But we also know that worrying is futile. Didn't Jesus say, '*Which of you by worrying can add one cubit to his stature?*'"

"We don't need to add any cubits to your stature, Stephanos. We need to keep you safe!"

"Am I safe anywhere apart from the will of God?"

"So I assume you'll be preaching again after work today?" Tabitha ground out, crossing her arms in defiance.

"Unless the Lord directs me otherwise," Stephanos replied, unperturbed.

Fleetingly, Tabitha considered sharing the startling revelation she had received while standing before the gilded mirror in the wee morning hours, but she knew it would do little good. Stephanos was entirely given to the Holy Spirit's leading. Nothing could shake him from his course, not even an angry wife.

"I'd best be off," Stephanos noted, clearly dismissing the issue. When he stooped to kiss her forehead, Tabitha drew back, peeved.

"Stephanos, please," she argued. "We need more information. We need to find out who's in danger!"

"I imagine we all are," Stephanos replied lightly. "But those in leadership always face a higher risk."

"Those in leadership—like *you?*" Tabitha demanded, hands planted firmly on her hips.

"Possibly," Stephanos supplied, "although the Sanhedrin has always targeted the Twelve first."

"I just want you to be safe, Stephanos," Tabitha insisted, her volume escalating in her exasperation. "Is that too much to ask?"

"Of course not," Stephanos assured her, sensing her deep inner struggle. "But, Tabitha, you seem to forget we've placed ourselves in God's hands. That means we've given Him permission to do as He sees fit."

"Meaning?" Tabitha demanded curtly, her nerves worn thin.

"Meaning His will may contradict our own, at times," Stephanos gently reminded her. "But no matter how bad things look, no matter how hard it gets, God is still in control."

"So what, then?" Tabitha snapped, her blood boiling. "Do we take no precautions whatsoever, intentionally placing ourselves in harm's way and casting caution to the wind just because *God is in control?*"

"I never said that," Stephanos said quietly, both his tone and expression etched with weariness. "I intend to speak with Mary as soon as I arrive at work because I agree—we *do* need to know what we're up against. And based on what I learn today, I *do* intend to take proper precautions."

"But you still insist on teaching at the Temple and the synagogue!"

"I do," Stephanos acknowledged quietly. "Unless the Lord has other plans."

"And what if I told you not to go?" Tabitha stared at her husband long and hard, her eyes flashing in challenge, daring him to argue with her. "What then?"

"Then I would humbly ask you not to put me in the position of having to choose between my wife and my God." Turning from her with a pained expression, Stephanos slipped out the front door without another word, quietly closing it behind him.

Trembling in anger, Tabitha stared at the closed door, wide-eyed and openmouthed. Had Stephanos seriously walked out in the middle of their discussion? And had he really accused her of making him choose between her and God?

But didn't you, beloved?

Instantly recognizing the still, small voice within—not condemning, but gently entreating—Tabitha's shoulders crumpled in defeat. She knew the gnawing fear within her heart threatened to tear her marriage apart. And wouldn't the enemy be pleased if she allowed such fears free rein! How could she have been so foolish?

Today, she had hurt her husband deeply, drawing a line in the sand and forcing him to decide. Would she ever forget the raw grief on his weary face, the sorrow in his eyes?

How could he possibly forgive her? Would he?

Should he?

Shuddering in horror, Tabitha saw herself as her husband must have seen her—proud, contentious, faithless, mean.

Covering her face with her hands, Tabitha wept as if her heart would break.

CHAPTER 29

Mary

"Stephanos! Do come in," Mary invited warmly, shuffling through the paperwork on her desk before setting it aside in a neat, orderly stack. The sun had already begun its steady retreat just beyond the western horizon, casting slanting beams of golden light across the marble pillars and tile floor of the bibliotheca. Soon, the servants would begin lighting the lamps.

Early that morning, Stephanos had requested a private meeting with her. Mary assumed it must be serious to keep him away from his pretty young wife even a moment longer than necessary.

"May I have a word with you?" Entering the office library, the handsome evangelist paused before Mary's resplendent desk, his dark eyes flickering slightly, betraying his carefully concealed distress.

An odd little pang claimed Mary's heart, for this quiet meeting was poignantly reminiscent of another time, a happier season—the night this dear man had approached her in this very room, respectfully requesting Tabitha's hand in marriage.

At the time, there had been a sparkle in his dark eyes, a spring in his step, his charismatic features shining with hope and promise.

Tonight, he appeared purposeful and resigned, possibly even sorrowful.

"I'm listening, dear one," Mary said gently, steeling herself for…something.

"May I ask a favor of you, Mary? It is of the utmost importance."

"Anything," Mary said, and she meant it. With all her heart.

Without a word, Stephanos retrieved a sealed parchment scroll from his leather satchel. Locking eyes with his benevolent employer, he held the scroll out to her, willing her to take it.

Instantly, Mary understood. Fighting back tears, she accepted his offering.

***

Tabitha

With trembling fingers, Tabitha lit the last candle before turning around to inspect her work.

The small house glowed with the light of dozens of steadily burning candles. She had spent the evening placing them strategically about the house, obtaining the perfect rosy glow she desired. The table was spread with glistening trays boasting a delectable feast; the very best her limited budget could boast. Underfoot, flower petals were strewn about, reminiscent of her wedding night.

Crossing her arms over her chest, Tabitha nodded her approval. Everything was ready. The table was set, the food prepared, the candles lit. She knew she looked more beautiful than she ever had. She had bathed, anointed herself with fragrant oil, and weaved her golden tresses into a lovely, becoming style. Anxiously fingering the linen sash at her waist, Tabitha smoothed her flowing white gown—the gown she had worn on her wedding day.

Precious Lord, this morning I behaved like a selfish, willful child, she prayed, hot tears stinging her eyes. *Please forgive me. May this display of love for my husband touch his heart and soothe his hurt.*

Dusk had settled when the front door finally creaked open, groaning on ancient hinges. Standing near the low table, Tabitha's heart thumped a nervous rhythm in her chest. What would Stephanos think of this display? Would he take her in his arms, accepting her apology and smothering her with kisses, or would he want nothing to do with her?

She wouldn't blame him if he didn't.

Stephanos entered the house with his head down, his shoulders bent with weariness. He looked utterly consumed with exhaustion.

Aching inside, Tabitha went to him.

"Tabitha?" Suddenly aware of the soft candlelight and the decadent feast spread upon the table, Stephanos lowered his leather satchel to the ground, blinking in confusion.

"I must ask your forgiveness, my husband," Tabitha managed, her voice catching. Taking his strong hands, Tabitha looked into his eyes. "This morning, I behaved like a quarrelsome, contentious woman. What's worse, I hurt you, Stephanos. Please forgive me, my husband. I love you and I never want to hurt you again."

"Oh, beloved." Raising her hands to his lips, he kissed them. "If only we could promise not to hurt each other again, but we're sinners, aren't we? But praise God, He is ready to forgive, and abundant in mercy to all those who call upon Him. And by the power of His Holy Spirit, we can learn to be like Him."

"I'm so sorry, Stephanos. So very, very sorry." Blinking back tears, Tabitha went into his arms.

"It's forgiven," Stephanos whispered into her hair, cradling her like a hurting child. "I love you."

Weeping, Tabitha buried her face in his chest.

Stephanos let her cry. In time, he gently lifted her chin, gazing deeply into her eyes. "You are precious to me, beloved, my bride. More precious than you'll ever know."

"My role as a believer and as a wife is to demonstrate my love through service, Stephanos," Tabitha managed with a wobbly smile. "Today, I failed miserably. But tonight, I humbly ask that you allow me a second chance."

Stephanos watched her intently, sensing something hidden in her words, something mysterious.

Taking his hand, Tabitha led her husband toward a bench beneath a window ledge graced with brightly burning candles. "Please, be seated Tabitha smiled.

Intrigued, Stephanos did as she requested.

"The night our Lord was crucified," Tabitha explained, untying her linen sash and setting it aside, "He rose from supper, laid aside his garments, took a towel, and girded Himself. *After that, He poured*

*water into a basin and began to wash the disciples'
feet, and to wipe them with the towel with which
He was girded."*

Taking a worn towel hanging from a peg, Tabitha
wrapped it securely around her slender waist. Stephanos watched her, spellbound, as she slid a basin
of water from beneath the bench. Then, kneeling
before him, she began to unstrap his sandals.

"Tabitha," Stephanos protested, touched. "This is
a beautiful gesture, my love, but it isn't necessary—"

"But it *is*," Tabitha insisted, setting aside his travel-worn sandals. "Jesus said, *'If I then, your Lord
and Teacher, have washed your feet, you also ought
to wash one another's feet. For I have given you an
example, that you should do as I have done for you.'*
Tenderly, she placed her husband's feet in the warm
water. "My desire is to serve you, Stephanos. I am
called to be one with you; not only one in body, but
one in thought, deed, and purpose."

"I know my calling hasn't made it particularly
easy, dear one," Stephanos admitted, gazing down
at her, his eyes filled with love.

"God has called you to mighty things, Stephanos,
but I have hindered rather than strengthened your
mission," Tabitha confessed, producing a small flask
of fragrant oil. Anointing his aching feet, Tabitha
massaged the oil into his skin. "I cannot promise I
will serve perfectly, but with God's help, my desire
is to encourage you in your calling, beloved. Please
forgive my fears and my doubts."

Leaning forward, Stephanos caressed her cheek
with a strong hand. Tabitha leaned into his touch for
but a moment, then returned to the humble task of
washing his feet, nervous beneath his penetrating

gaze. Lifting his foot from the water, Tabitha gently dried it with the towel about her waist. After drying his other foot, Tabitha pushed the basin back under the bench.

"Thank you, my bride," Stephanos smiled, his expression tender. "I am indeed a blessed man."

Seated with her knees drawn beneath her, Tabitha clasped her husband's strong calves, gently massaging tight muscles. "I love you, Stephanos. From this point forward, I vow to demonstrate my love through action."

"You are being too hard on yourself," Stephanos told her, lightly touching her golden hair. "Your love for me shines in all you do."

Tabitha smiled through her tears.

"Come here," Stephanos said hoarsely, reaching for her.

Tabitha went into his strong arms. Returning his tender kisses, the steaming feast upon the table was soon forgotten.

CHAPTER 30

Tabitha

Stirring, Tabitha squinted against the slight trickle of early morning light wafting through the lattice-work above her sleeping pallet.

It was no small wonder she had overslept after enjoying half the night in her husband's arms, talking, laughing, sharing, and delighting in each other's presence.

What a gift from God!

Turning on her side, Tabitha's lips formed a tiny smile, taking in the sight of her sleeping husband. As his chest rose and fell along with his steady breathing, Tabitha's heart swelled with love for him. He was so handsome, but it was his character, his heart, that she truly treasured. His obedience to God was unwavering; his love for her, steadfast; his willingness to reach others with the blessed truth, boundless.

Crinkling her honey-colored brows, Tabitha wondered what had aroused her. The house remained perfectly quiet, utterly still—

And then she heard it again. A small, plaintive cry, rather like that of a tiny, injured animal... What could it be?

Sitting up, Tabitha listened intently, her soft blanket slipping off her shoulders and pooling about her lap.

There it was again!

Slipping out of bed, Tabitha reached for the robe at her bedside. Slipping it over her thin nightgown, she tiptoed to the front door, opening it slowly, painstakingly, so as not to awaken her slumbering husband. It was a trying task, given the creaky nature of the protesting old hinges!

Once the door was finally open, Tabitha's sharp eyes scanned the perimeter of the outer court, the aging white stones bathed in soft, golden sunlight. All was calm and perfectly quiet. A sparrow lit on the iron gate, studying her with tiny, curious eyes before spreading its wings and taking flight.

The mewling cry sounded again.

Startled, Tabitha's gaze fell upon a small child curled in a tight little ball, hugging the doorpost at her feet.

Oh my!

"Stephanos!" Tabitha shouted, giving the poor child a terrible fright. "Stephanos, come quickly!"

Bleary-eyed, Stephanos stumbled out the door a moment later, shrugging into his robe amidst his frantic dash. "Tabitha! What is it, love?"

"Look," Tabitha exclaimed, gesturing toward the frightened child cowering near the post.

Recovering from his rude awakening, Stephanos' dark eyes filled with pity. "Well, I'll be. Is she alone?"

"I don't know." Stooping near the little girl, Tabitha touched her shoulder.

The frightened little thing jerked away from her touch.

"Hello, little one," Tabitha coaxed gently, glancing nervously toward Stephanos. "Where is your mother?"

Pushing herself up on shaky legs, the little girl tottered across the courtyard, plopping down a safe distance away and burying her face in the stone wall.

Tabitha and Stephanos exchanged looks of concern.

"Could she have wandered away from home?" Straightening, Tabitha crossed her arms and shook her head in perplexity.

"The gate is closed," Stephanos pointed out. "She's far too small to have opened and closed it back herself."

"Are you suggesting that someone left her here?" Tabitha asked, appalled.

"I think it's very possible."

"But *why?*" Tabitha gasped, her heart skipping frantically in her chest.

"For any number of reasons," Stephanos replied sadly. "Perhaps her family couldn't afford her care. Everyone knows about our ministry to the poor."

"You truly believe a mother would just *dump* her child on someone's doorstep?" Tabitha declared in disbelief.

"I've seen it happen far too many times," Stephanos replied sadly, his eyes filled with sympathy. "But we can't possibly begin to guess this one's situation unless we can locate her family."

"And how on earth will we do that?"

"It won't be easy," Stephanos admitted, watching as the toddler dared an anxious glance over her shoulder.

"Perhaps if we gain her trust, she will tell us about her family," Tabitha suggested hopefully.

"This little one is no more than two years old," Stephanos observed. "She won't be able to tell us much, I'm afraid."

"Candace's little Rufus can talk up a storm."

"Yes, but he's over three years old now. A child's vocabulary increases extensively between the ages of two and three."

Well, naturally.

The little girl glanced at them again, tears streaking through the dirt caked on her tiny face. Despite her unhealthy pallor and puffy red eyes framed with dark circles, she was a beautiful child. Soft wispy curls matched the girl's wide brown eyes. Observing her bare feet, soiled, threadbare garment, and dirt-smeared arms and legs, Tabitha's heart went out to the child, for she knew what it was like to be alone on the streets, frightened and hungry.

"She's far too thin," Tabitha said, shaking her head in dismay. "She must be hungry."

"We have plenty of leftovers from last night's supper," Stephanos reminded her.

"Let's see what we can do," Tabitha resolved, marching purposefully toward the child. Kneeling beside her, Tabitha held out her hand. "Hello there, little one. Would you like something to eat?"

The little girl turned her face away.

"You must be hungry. We have lots of good things to eat," Tabitha coaxed in her most persuasive tone. "Will you come inside with us?"

Her request was met with stony silence.

Raising rueful eyes toward Stephanos, Tabitha shrugged her shoulders.

"Perhaps if we brought the bread to her?" Stephanos suggested.

"We'll try it." Trekking into the house, Tabitha emerged a moment later with a flat loaf of unleavened bread.

Lowering herself on the ground beside the reticent toddler, Tabitha held out the bread to her. "Here is some bread," she said brightly. "You can have it. I brought it for you!"

Glancing over her shoulder at Tabitha, the little girl's thin brows furrowed together in dismay. Pushing herself up on her feet, she toddled across the courtyard, plopping down heavily on the opposite side and presenting a rigid back to her rescuer.

"I don't think she approves of your cooking," Stephanos laughed.

"Stephanos, it isn't funny," Tabitha huffed, glaring at the toddler's rigid back. "She needs to eat!"

"Perhaps she isn't hungry."

"Look at her! She's skin and bones."

"It may take some time to gain her trust," Stephanos pointed out with maddening logic.

"Well, let's hope we gain her trust before she withers away and blows off with the slightest puff of wind," Tabitha grumped, rising to her feet and approaching her husband.

"Perhaps we should try to locate her family," Stephanos mused. "If they need help caring for her, then we as the body of Christ have plenty of resources available."

"But where would we even begin?" Tabitha asked.

"We can't possibly knock on every single door in this big city, asking if the child belongs to them!" How long would it take to track down this little one's family? What kind of selfish person dumped their child on another's doorstep, anyway?

"Let's start with Mary," Stephanos suggested. "She knows everyone. Perhaps she will recognize the girl and help us find her family."

"Well, I wouldn't say she knows *everyone*," Tabitha protested, miffed.

"All right, she knows *almost* everyone," Stephanos grinned. "We should talk to her first."

"But how? You promised to speak at the synagogue this morning. Shall we take her with us, then visit Mary afterward?"

"I'm not sure it would be wise to take her with us," Stephanos mused, watching as the little girl forlornly studied her own bare toes. "Tensions and emotions are running high at the synagogue. The hostile environment might prove a bit too stressful for her in her already fragile state."

No kidding, Tabitha thought. It was stressful for *her,* too!

"Why don't you take her to Mary's rather than accompanying me to the synagogue this morning?" Stephanos proposed. "She must be anxious and frightened being separated from her family. Finding them would be in her best interest, I imagine."

"Perhaps you could postpone your teaching and come with me," Tabitha offered, alarmed at the prospect of tending the child alone.

"I wish I could, love," Stephanos said sincerely. "But several young men requested a specific teaching about the Temple and the sacrificial system in light of Christ's atonement on the cross, and I promised to answer their questions today."

"That sounds like a rather explosive topic given your audience," Tabitha commented, concerned.

"It is," Stephanos admitted. "But these men are seeking the truth, and they're afraid to join us for meetings at Mary's villa."

"Why is that?"

"Naturally, they're nervous about attending our church meetings. To do so would alienate them from their Jewish friends and relatives who haven't yet received the gospel."

Sighing, Tabitha refrained from arguing with him. She had promised to support him in his mission from now on, inwardly vowing to do so even if it killed her!

Which it very well might, she thought rather glibly.

"Take a moment to dress and freshen up, dear one," Stephanos suggested, stooping to kiss her cheek. "Then you can take the little one to Mary's while I instruct the young men at the synagogue."

"I'd prefer to go with you, Stephanos."

"As my wife or as my bodyguard?" Stephanos teased.

"Whichever is most needed," she smiled.

"I am in God's hands, remember?" he replied, smoothing back her wayward tresses. "We needn't fear even the worst in this life. Even men's greatest fear, the sting of death, is but a gateway to everlasting life and joy for us believers."

"Nevertheless, I'd prefer to prolong the inevitable as long as possible," Tabitha quipped dryly.

"Freshen up," Stephanos instructed, kissing her

firmly. "I'll wait here with the little one until you are ready."

Reluctantly, Tabitha slipped into the house to perform her husband's bidding.

When Tabitha emerged from the house a few minutes later, Stephanos was kneeling on the ground across from the toddler. The little girl held a half-eaten loaf of unleavened bread between grubby fingers, appearing perfectly at ease.

"Well!" Tabitha declared, looking back and forth between the two of them. "I see you had far better luck than I."

"She's been a perfect angel," Stephanos announced, receiving a shy smile in response from the child.

"Perhaps *you* should take her to Mary's and *I* should instruct the young men," Tabitha laughed.

"I wouldn't want you to scare them," Stephanos grinned.

Tabitha rolled her eyes.

Casually resting an elbow on his knees, Stephanos leaned in toward the small girl. "You have been a very good girl," he smiled, his tone laced with pride. "Now do you see my lovely wife over there? Her name is Tabitha, and she is going to take you to meet our good friend, Mary."

Instantly, the little girl's demeanor changed. Eyes widening in fear, she clutched the unleavened bread with trembling fingers.

"You're going to like Mary," Stephanos promised. "She's a very nice lady."

Rising slowly, Stephanos dropped a hand on Tabitha's shoulder. "Are you ready for this?"

"Absolutely not," Tabitha grimaced. "But we'll see

how it goes."

"I have confidence in you, beloved."

"Did she happen to disclose her name to you?"

"She hasn't spoken a word."

Extending her hand toward the cowering child, Tabitha mustered her biggest, brightest smile. "Hello there. Will you come with me to see my friend?"

The child turned her face away, whimpering softly.

"You will love Mary's house!" Tabitha exclaimed, hoping to entice the little girl. "It's a big, beautiful mansion with tall pillars and pretty flowers and a marvelous stone fountain! Shall we go see it now?"

The child acknowledged her entreaty with a stubborn frown.

Peeved, Tabitha swooped down to scoop up the child. Her arms had scarcely closed about the tiny frame when the toddler released a series of shrill, ear-splitting screams capable of waking the dead. Nearly dropping her, Tabitha drew back in shock as the child clambered to her feet, shrieking like a wild banshee.

"My goodness!" Tabitha exclaimed, covering her ears in dismay. "How does such a big sound come from such a tiny child?"

"I must admit, it's quite impressive." Chuckling, Stephanos shook his head in amusement.

"Well, what should we do? How do we stop her from screeching?" Tabitha shouted over the child's deafening screams, at her wit's end.

Calmly going to the child, Stephanos knelt before her once again. Taking the little girl's hands, he spoke to her gently. "It's all right, little one. It's all right. We're not going to hurt you. I promise."

The child's hair-raising shrieks gave way to short, sniffling sobs.

"There, there," Stephanos smiled, squeezing her tiny hands. "That's better, isn't it?"

Quieting, the child bowed her head, sniffing softly.

Lifting her gently in his arms, Stephanos carried the toddler to his wife. Stroking her back, he murmured words of comfort as he passed her to a very reluctant Tabitha.

Accepting the hiccupping bundle, Tabitha stood still as stone. She hardly dared to breathe for fear of setting off another chorus of ear-piercing screams.

"There now," Stephanos smiled, stroking the toddler's fluffy brown curls. "Be still, dear one. Even in our darkest hour, God is with us. By His grace, we can overcome."

Balancing the weeping child on her hip, Tabitha looked to her husband in near panic as the girl buried her face in her shoulder, dampening her garment with salty tears.

"You will do just fine, my darling," Stephanos assured Tabitha, leaning in to kiss her gently. "I entrust her into your care."

"But for how long?" Tabitha quipped rather drolly.

"You'll have to consult the Lord about that," Stephanos teased, stepping back.

"I shall be praying for your instruction at the synagogue this morning," Tabitha assured her husband, reaching for his hand. "I wish you'd let me go with you."

"This is best," Stephanos assured her, accepting her loving squeeze. "And, yes, please do pray, beloved. Pray without ceasing—for God's will to prevail."

"I will," Tabitha promised, strangely unsettled by his request.

"I love you, Tabitha," Stephanos said, cupping her face in a strong hand and searching her eyes intently. "You mean the world to me."

"I love you, Stephanos." Taking her husband's tunic, Tabitha drew him in and kissed him firmly, eliciting a whimper of protest from the toddler in her arms.

Drawing apart, they shared a knowing smile.

"I suppose it's time to be off." Tabitha sighed, steeling herself for the long trek into the Upper City.

Opening the gate for his wife, Stephanos ushered her through the opening with an overly chivalrous bow, relishing the musical sound of her resulting laughter. Latching the gate behind her, he watched as Tabitha strolled gracefully down the cobblestone way, a protesting bundle upon her hip.

Stephanos smiled, entrusting them into the hands of a faithful God. By His grace, the two of them should arrive at Mary's villa in one piece!

CHAPTER 31

Tabitha

It was a grueling trek to Mary's house with the petulant child in tow. Tabitha had fallen for it the first time the child writhed out of her arms, making it perfectly clear she wished to plod along on her own two feet. But the moment the child's two little bare feet had hit the ground, she'd streaked off like an athlete in Herod's stadium, giggling like a little imp, having outsmarted her captor.

Gritting her teeth, Tabitha had sprung after her, snatching her up just before the child reached a bustling intersection. The moment Tabitha's arms had encircled the defiant toddler, the girl had released an earth-shattering scream, alerting the attention of everyone within a three-mile radius, Tabitha was quite sure. What must her fellow pedestrians think? The silly child sounded as if she was being flayed!

Furious, Tabitha had tucked the girl on one hip, ignoring her shrill screams as she plunged ahead, unwilling to be deterred this time.

Once she finally reached Mary's estate, Tabitha

couldn't decide who was more exhausted—her, or the screaming child. As she approached the gate with a bleary-eyed, hiccupping toddler in tow, the captain of Mary's guard approached her, a scowl hardening his firm jawline. "My lady is not expecting you today."

"Then I'm sure this will be a pleasant surprise for her," Tabitha huffed, in no mood to deal with Zev's antagonism. Suppressing a grin, she recalled the first time she had encountered Mary's crusty guard at this very gate. She had been recently orphaned, seeking solace from the kind couple who once rescued her from a drunken attacker. When Zev had refused her entreaties that day, she had clambered up a tall palm near the gate, refusing to come down until she'd seen Mary.

Had it been up to Zev, she would have been promptly dismissed that day, turned away at the gate. How differently her life would have turned out! How merciful her Lord had been to her then!

The Lord was still merciful, even now.

Blinking back tears, Tabitha glanced at the little one on her hip. She supposed they had a lot in common.

Well, Zev hadn't had his way with *her* as an orphaned child. He wouldn't have his way with this one, either, even if she had to clamber right back up the palm again. She could only imagine his trepidation should she do so!

"Well? What do you want?" Zev demanded gruffly, rudely interrupting her visit down memory lane.

"As you can see, I've stumbled upon a lost child," Tabitha said coolly, adjusting the heavy bundle on her hip. "I'm hoping Mary can identify her."

"Go away. You will only trouble my lady."

"You know as well as I that Mary would want to help!"

"She has enough on her plate as it is," Zev snapped, glancing over his shoulder as if concerned his lady might overhear the exchange."

"I need to see her," Tabitha insisted.

"Another time."

Arching a brow in challenge, Tabitha leaned in just enough to discomfit the surly guard. "Shall I make a scene, Zev?"

"Tabitha! I thought I heard you out here!" Little Rhoda appeared on the other side of the imposing gate, broom in hand. "I was sweeping the outer court and heard voices."

"See what you've done?" Zev hissed, his face inches away from Tabitha's. Rhoda—the self-righteous little traitor—would most certainly alert Mary about Tabitha. If he denied her entrance now, he'd surely hear about it from Mary!

"A word of advice," Tabitha said to Zev with icy sweetness, "avoid such close proximity after consuming leeks and garlic, my friend." Stepping around the guard, Tabitha met Rhoda at the gate. "Rhoda! How good it is to see you!"

"And you, as well!" Rhoda said brightly, her large brown eyes alight with happiness. "How I have missed you."

"And I, you," Tabitha assured her, reaching through the grate to take Rhoda's small hand in hers.

At eleven years old, Rhoda was blossoming into a lovely young lady with large brown eyes and dark hair framing a gentle face, prettily contrasting with her soft, creamy complexion. She was still timid, but her innocence and gentle nature was sweet and endearing.

Fascinated by Rhoda's dulcet tone, the toddler lifted her head, daring a shy glance at the maidservant.

Rhoda was delighted. "What a sweet, beautiful child!"

"She's a handful," Tabitha confessed, shifting the child's weight on her hip. "And heavy!"

"A perfect angel!" Rhoda declared, delightedly clasping her hands together.

Just wait, Tabitha thought snidely.

"Wherever did you find her?"

"She was left on our doorstep this morning," Tabitha explained, and Rhoda's soft eyes filled with pity. "I'm hoping Mary can help locate her family."

"You have come to the right place," Rhoda asserted with confidence.

"Well, shall we open the gate?" Tabitha asked Zev over her shoulder, her eyes sparkling with mischief.

"I will tell my lady you've arrived!" Rhoda giggled, skipping off with broom in hand.

Grumbling under his breath, Zev opened the gate.

Just like old times, Tabitha thought, amused. Triumphant, she strolled past the guard, relishing his consternation.

***

"My, what a darling child," Mary crooned, reaching out to take the exhausted toddler from her former maid.

Yes, that seems to be the general consensus, Tabitha thought, wondering if Mary would feel the same had she endured the girl's defiant screams the entire way over.

"She doesn't like being transferred from one person to another," Tabitha apologized, bracing herself for another bout of angry tirades.

Amazingly, the toddler simply gazed up at Mary, mesmerized by her exotic gray eyes and the elegant amphora earrings dangling from her ears.

"She's doing just fine," Mary smiled, cuddling her close.

"She must have worn herself out on the way over here," Tabitha decided, relieved. A tantrum would be unbearable in this vast reception hall, the volume magnified a hundredfold by echoing and bouncing off the glistening mosaic floors and frescoed walls.

"Rhoda," Mary said, tenderly stroking the child's wispy curls, "this little one will need to be washed. She will also need a change of clothes. Will you please fetch a basin of warm water and washcloths, along with a suitable garment for her from our stash in the storage vault?"

"Of course, my lady!" Beaming, Rhoda hurried away to perform Mary's bidding, excited to select an outfit from the chests stored in the cool vaults below the mansion.

"I should have thought of that before heading over here," Tabitha confessed, cheeks flaming in embarrassment. "Thank you, Mary."

"Oh, I can't imagine the shock you must have experienced stumbling upon this little one on your doorstep," Mary said in her gracious way. "But you had the presence of mind to feed her and begin the search for her family. You have nothing to be ashamed of."

Tabitha wasn't convinced.

"Rhoda will probably select one of the little garments you have sewn, Tabitha," Mary smiled. "I'm quite certain over half the clothing and blankets in storage for distribution are *your* contribution. You must work furiously producing all those lovely things for those in need."

"It's truly the least I can do," Tabitha said, feeling terribly inadequate.

"Our Lord is pleased when we utilize the talents He has given us to further His kingdom by helping those in need," Mary assured her. "This is what you are doing, dear one."

Rhoda returned shortly, carefully balancing a basin of warm water, several linen cloths, and a tiny little garment draped over her forearm.

"Thank you, Rhoda," Mary said appreciatively, lowering herself onto a straight-backed chair and adjusting the toddler in her lap. "You may set the basin on this stand."

Obediently, Rhoda placed the basin on the elegant marble-topped stand beside Mary's chair. At the sight of the basin and washcloths, the toddler's eyes narrowed in suspicion.

Groaning inwardly, Tabitha braced herself for yet another noisy ordeal.

"Look at this sweet little outfit," Rhoda beamed, lifting it up for Mary and Tabitha's inspection. "This shade of blue will look charming with her fair skin, dark hair, and brown eyes!"

"She has your coloring, Rhoda," Mary commented fondly, accepting the small garment and setting it aside. "This gown is an excellent choice."

Tabitha immediately recognized the miniature blue gown with white trim. She remembered selecting the soft blue fabric, her excitement mounting as the piece took shape in her skillful hands. As with all the pieces she designed, Tabitha had prayed a special blessing over this one—and over the child who would eventually wear it.

"Would it not be better to take her to your baths?" Tabitha asked innocently. The child was in desperate need of a thorough washing. She suspected the little girl required more than a simple wipe-down with a damp cloth.

"I'm not sure she's ready to be submerged in the baths," Mary replied, always practical. "We might frighten the poor thing to death. For now, a quick touch-up will have to do."

Tabitha hadn't thought of that, but she was glad Mary had. She had no desire to endure the fallout that would undoubtedly follow a proper washing in the luxuriant underground *mikveh*.

The child whimpered softly when Mary fingered her soiled garment, gently lifting it over her head. The moment the garment was removed, the little girl screamed her outrage, snatching it from Mary's hand and clutching it possessively to her heart.

"Don't worry, dear one," Mary said soothingly. "We will wash and mend your little robe and it will be better than new." Reaching for a washcloth, Mary dipped it in the warm water, wringing it out before placing it upon the child's skin.

The little girl screamed in angry protest at the apparent indignity, furiously attempting to writhe out of Mary's lap.

"Shhhh," Mary soothed, gently wiping the child's dirt-stained face. "It's all right, little one."

Tabitha was tempted to cover her ears as the

child's shrill cries rang through the reception hall. She exchanged an apologetic look with Rhoda, whose entire countenance had paled. Clearly, she'd never heard anything like it, either.

Undaunted, Mary carried on with her task, humming softly as if completely oblivious to the child's tantrum. Holding the toddler firmly in her lap with one practiced hand, Mary bathed her dirt-encrusted arms and legs with the other. "There, there," she said gently, wringing out the dirty cloth and setting it aside. "All finished. That wasn't so bad, was it?"

Enraged, the child writhed and flailed, screaming out her fury at the top of her lungs.

"She's a headstrong little thing, isn't she?" Mary observed with a knowing smile, lifting the girl enough to resettle her in her lap.

"Is...is she all right?" Rhoda dared, her face as white as a sheet. "Is she hurt?"

"She's perfectly fine," Mary assured her young maidservant, slipping the new garment over the protesting child's head. "Most children abhor bath time. As a youngster, my John Mark used to put up quite a fight, as well!"

Rhoda's cheeks warmed at the casual mention of Mary's handsome son. "Shall I take her soiled garment to wash?" Rhoda asked, tactfully changing the subject.

"I don't believe she's ready to part with it yet," Mary observed with a faint smile, for the child still clung to the filthy garment like a lifeline, angry tears streaming down her cheeks. "I do wish we knew her name. A child should be addressed by name."

"We know absolutely nothing about her." *Except that she boasts the finest set of lungs in Jerusalem,* she amended silently. "Do you recognize her, Mary? Have you seen her before?"

"Not that I can recall," Mary confessed, turning the child around in her lap. "What is your name, little one?"

The child stared up at her with puffy, red-rimmed eyes, entranced. Reaching forth, she gingerly touched one of Mary's dangling earrings, intrigued.

"She hasn't spoken a word since we found her," Tabitha said, exasperated.

"Perhaps she cannot speak," Rhoda suggested, her tone saturated with sympathy for the poor child.

"Based on her capacity to throw a screaming tantrum, I think that's highly unlikely," Mary chuckled in amusement. "But she was abandoned by her mother, and who knows what horrors she experienced prior to that? Her refusal to speak may pertain to the trauma she has endured."

And what of the trauma she has inflicted? Tabitha thought, annoyed. She knew she should feel more pity for the deserted child, but at the moment, her heart remained maddeningly conflicted. *Forgive me, Lord, but I feel terribly uncomfortable about this whole ordeal. I should be at the synagogue with Stephanos—not trying to track down the incompetent mother of an obstinate child!*

Chagrined, a discomfiting parable of Jesus flashed through her mind, igniting her conscience and filling her with remorse. She remembered the priest and Levite of Jesus' famous parable, *The Good Samaritan*. Both religious leaders had ignored a dying man lying by the road. Given their status, they were probably on their way to serve at the Temple or the synagogue, unwilling to be deterred from their "worship" even after encountering the needy soul! Sighing, Tabitha acknowledged that the priest and the Levite would have honored God far more by incorporating the lessons they had learned at the synagogue rather than being so determined to arrive in time for the commencement of yet another sermon. Conscience burning, Tabitha acknowledged she had done the right thing by saving this little one, despite its many challenges.

As her gaze fell upon the sniffing child, Tabitha couldn't help but wonder what would happen if they were unable to locate her mother. Obviously, *someone* would have to take the child in. Would the apostles take the matter into consideration, assigning the task to one of the believing families?

Oh, Lord God, what if they choose me*?* Panic coursed through Tabitha, filling her entire being with trepidation. *What if they ask me and Stephanos to care for her?* They hadn't yet been blessed with their *own* little ones! Tabitha desperately wanted a family, but she longed to bear her own children – *Stephanos'* children. How would this impact her own plans about family and motherhood? Peeved, Tabitha knew Stephanos would receive the child into their home without a second thought.

Tabitha's attention was brought back to reality when the child accidentally dropped her little garment, throwing back her head and howling her displeasure.

Pierced to the heart by the child's cries, Rhoda quickly retrieved the garment, offering it to the child. As she did so, a tattered slip of parchment dislodged from a tiny pocket, fluttering to the ground.

Once the child had protectively snatched up

the garment, burying her freshly washed face in the soiled folds, Rhoda bent to retrieve the slip of parchment. Lifting it for inspection, she squinted as she studied the fading print.

"What is that, Rhoda?" Mary asked, rocking the child on her lap.

"Tabitha," Rhoda said hopefully, "can you cipher this faded script?"

Accepting the tattered parchment, Tabitha studied the splotchy symbols, her heart pounding furiously in her chest.

"Tabitha?" Mary prompted gently. "What does it say?"

"*Don't look for me,*'" Tabitha read, her voice catching slightly. "*Spent all my money on medical treatments. Cannot feed her. Too weak to care for her. I will die soon. Please love her.*'" Raising full eyes to Mary, Tabitha whispered, "There is no signature. Nor has the mother disclosed the name of her child." Cheeks flaming, Tabitha had never felt so ashamed.

"Oh, my lady," Rhoda whispered, tears slipping down her pale face. "What can we do? How can we help that poor woman?"

"It sounds like we have very little time to find her," Mary said, grieved.

"It would seem she can *write*," Tabitha pointed out. "That should narrow it down considerably."

"I'm afraid *anyone* could have written that note for her," Mary said. "But it's possible. I want to consult Luke, the physician. He treats some of the most hopeless cases. Perhaps he will know about this woman and recognize her child."

"That's an excellent idea," Rhoda agreed, her tender heart breaking for mother and child.

"But is he here in Jerusalem?" Tabitha asked, doubtful. "I thought he established his practice in Antioch."

"He should be," Mary replied. "He still travels to Jerusalem for many of the feasts and holy days."

Bowing her head, Tabitha prayed it would be so.

"Rhoda," Mary said, snapping into action, "please find Tobias. Ask him to visit Luke's favored inn to inquire of his whereabouts. Please instruct Tobias to do everything in his power to locate the physician."

"Yes, my lady." Dipping her head in submission, Rhoda hastened away, her lips moving in fervent, silent prayer.

Tabitha watched her go, her heart racing as a thousand contrary emotions vied for her attention. She supposed she should volunteer to receive the child until the mother could be located. After all, a dying mother had entrusted the girl to her care.

But why? How had the mother even known about her, about Stephanos? Had she, too, been affected by Stephanos' preaching?

Sighing, Tabitha lifted anxious eyes toward Heaven. *Father God, what would You have me do?* Turning from Mary and the child, Tabitha paced the vast reception hall, feeling absolutely *nothing* in response to her heartfelt plea.

She didn't wish to contemplate that perhaps the Lord remained silent because He had already given her an answer.

CHAPTER 32

Saul of Tarsus

The Synagogue of the Freedmen was dim, cast in the eerie shadows of flickering lamps and torchlight despite the cheerful early morning sunshine beyond its thick, aging stone walls. Though the service would not commence for nearly an hour, the stone structure was already swarming with people, all of whom had gathered to hear the fiery evangelist's controversial preaching. Some came out of sincerity; others were merely curious, adventurers and thrill-seekers chasing their next diversion.

Saul was sickened by the shocking turnout. Had a respectable Jewish scholar announced an exhaustive discourse upon the unchanging and holy Law of Moses, the turnout would be next to nothing. But a rogue preacher grossly misinterpreting the Scriptures and promulgating the teachings of a dead revolutionary garnered a sea of hundreds, sometimes thousands!

As his steely gaze swept furtively over the dank,

smoky chamber, Saul assessed that all seemed to be in order. His vantage point amidst the tall pillars behind the speaker's platform confirmed that his "witnesses" were already in place. One of them—an earnest-looking young Jewish man—sat at Stephanos' feet with several avid listeners, appearing utterly enthralled by the evangelist's teaching. His role was the most important, for he would voice the question that would set the entire assembly ablaze, fanning their wrath against the self-righteous, self-proclaimed teacher. There were also ruffians dispersed among the gatherers, hired to goad on the crowd and provide additional brute force, if needed.

He'd thought of everything.

Hands folded behind his back in a sober, pious manner, Saul closed his eyes. Hazy streaks of smoke from dozens of lamps and smoldering torches hung heavily in the air, stinging his eyes and nostrils. The cloying, overpowering scent of burning incense nauseated him. Steeling himself, he offered silent prayers to Adonai, seeking His favor for the mission at hand. Surely his masterful plan pleased the Lord! He, Saul, had taken action against a rapidly growing cult even while his colleagues had shrunk away in fear or had fallen prey to a paralyzing apathy. But *he* had taken a firm stand against the apostasy infiltrating the holy city.

A righteous man who falters before the wicked Is like a murky spring and a polluted well, Saul remonstrated coldly, annoyed by his own weak misgivings. He knew the Word of the Lord. He knew he served a jealous God, One who would share His sovereign title with no other. To instruct Adonai's chosen people to acknowledge a dead rebel or a mystical, invisible spirit as equals of the Almighty was unthinkable, and yet this is precisely what the evangelist's sect encouraged. Shaking his head in disgust, Saul steeled his nerves against creeping doubts. Without his intervention, the entire nation risked God's wrathful judgment, having been deceived by pretty words and fanciful tales of careless, uneducated men.

Saul vowed he would die before allowing the apostles' dangerous charade to carry on any further. Today, the counterfeit message of a self-proclaimed Messiah would perish. Today, this sacrilege would end.

Your Word, Lord, says this: Give them according to their deeds, and according to the wickedness of their endeavors; give them according to the work of their hands; render to them what they deserve. Releasing a steadying sigh, Saul lifted his head in determination. *Today, I honor Your Word.*

My Word also says, Do not strive with a man without cause, if he has done you no harm.

No harm? Saul protested, outraged. The evangelist had misled an entire nation! *The soul who sins shall die!* he vowed inwardly, resisting the urge to pump his fist in emphasis.

All have sinned and fall short of the glory of God.

All? He, Saul, was most righteous among his peers! He embodied the Law of God with his every thought, his every breath. Surely he had nothing to fear—unlike the brazen evangelist manipulating the Law to his own advantage.

And to what advantage is that?

Jarred from his fuming thoughts, Saul became

suddenly, disturbingly aware of his silent dialogue with...*what?* Himself? Surely not the Lord?

Proudly raising his chin, Saul banished his concerns. He was honorable above all men, perfect in speech, blameless in thought and deed, excelling in his studies far beyond his peers.

These six things the Lord hates, yes, seven are an abomination to Him: A proud look...

Saul stiffened.

A lying tongue...

Stroking his neatly cropped beard, Saul promptly justified the lies he had spread within this house of worship.

Hands that shed innocent blood...

Innocent? There is nothing innocent about this sect! They all deserve to die!

A heart that devises wicked schemes...

Bowing his head, Saul contemplated what he was about to do, the deception his heart had devised.

Feet that are swift in running to evil...

Soon, dozens, if not hundreds, of sandaled feet would pound against the earth, past the gates of the city, beyond the Roman's sharp supervision. And he, Saul, would lead the way.

A false witness who speaks lies...

Heart pounding like a war drum, Saul's gaze landed upon a false witness—a man he himself had hired—gracing the feet of the evangelist.

And one who sows discord among brethren.

Discord? The tension in the synagogue was heavy and unmistakable, growing thicker by the minute. Saul himself had fanned the flames of discord, nurturing the hatred and animosity his fellow traditionalists bore against followers of the Way.

But can't You see, Lord? My intentions, my motives, are righteous! Someone must defend Your holy name!

Ask Me who I AM, Saul.

Saul froze, suddenly oblivious to everything except that still small voice within.

Ask me who I AM.

I know who you are! Saul's heart cried. *I know! Can't you see? It is Your very nature, Your essence, I am seeking to preserve!*

Silence. Deep, thunderous silence followed Saul's railing justification.

Shaken, Saul drew his tallith about his rigid frame, wondering if he was losing his nerve—or worse, his mind.

Steeling himself against assailing doubts, Saul strengthened himself in his mission.

***

Kelila

Seated on a stone bench in the synagogue beside Philip and surrounded by family who loved her, Kelila was certain she couldn't possibly be any more blessed. She was betrothed to the most amazing man in the world, and she loved him deeply. They planned to be wed after the Feast of Tabernacles, which meant she would be his wife before the month was over! She could hardly fathom this wonderful bit of news!

In addition to that, her relationship with her family continued to flourish. She adored her two young nephews, treasured the friendship she shared with Candace, and truly respected and admired her brother-in-law, Simon. The Lord had blessed her with a precious family, and she vowed to never take them for granted. She would treasure them as long as God gave her breath to do so.

Most importantly, her faith continued to blossom, driving her even closer to the Lord. To share sweet fellowship with the Creator of the universe was nearly incomprehensible! Her spirits soared at the mere thought of it!

All is well, Kelila reminded herself, forcing herself to relax on the bench between Candace and Philip. *Everything is wonderful. God has been gracious to all of us...*

So why, then, this heaviness of spirit? Why this deep sense of dread?

Earlier that morning, Kelila had been surprised and delighted when Simon suggested they journey to the synagogue to hear Stephanos' address, since it was unusual for the entire family to attend services at the synagogue unless it was the Sabbath Day. But Kelila had happily agreed. Stephanos' powerful sermons always bolstered her faith, and it was exciting to witness many men and women accepting Jesus Christ as their Lord and Savior at the service's end. She never tired of watching the evangelist lead beaming new converts in prayers of repentance.

Wondering at her own discouragement, Kelila's gaze swept over the crowded synagogue. Stephanos stood on the platform, patiently answering the questions of a group of young Jewish men clustered tightly around him. It was a rather casual meeting this morning, more like a question-and-answer session than an actual sermon. Since the synagogue's official service wouldn't commence for another hour, Stephanos had plenty of time to address the people's questions.

Every available seat was taken, and still many flooded the doorways, standing in tight clusters on all four sides of the platform. There were many new faces amidst the audience today, and Kelila noted with some alarm that several of them looked extremely rough around the edges. She couldn't help but wonder if they had daggers strapped to the belts beneath their robes.

Gazing casually at her sister's family, Kelila attempted to read their expressions. Were they, too, troubled in spirit? Candace sat beside Kelila, Rufus in her lap. Her arms encircled the small boy somewhat protectively as she listened to Stephanos' lecture. Alexander sat on the other side of her sister, in between his mother and father. They didn't *seem* disturbed. At least, not visibly.

Perhaps she was simply borrowing trouble. Maybe everything was fine.

Sensing his betrothed's distress, Philip took Kelila's hand, offering a consoling squeeze. Kelila smiled up at him, hoping to convey her deepest gratitude. He was such a wonderful man, often sensing her anxiety before she was even aware of it.

Shifting in her seat, Kelila forced her attention back to Stephanos, still addressing the gathering from the platform. The young men at his feet were asking many questions, and Stephanos answered them humbly and readily, his sincere love for them reflected in his eyes.

Tilting her head, Kelila attempted to tune in to their conversation. Whatever issue Stephanos was addressing, the listeners were visibly tense.

"But didn't your Christ say He would *destroy* the Temple?" a rapt young man seated at Stephanos' feet on the edge of the platform demanded. Those seated near him visibly shrank back from the student, troubled and disturbed by his suggestion.

"Ah, I'm glad you asked about this," Stephanos assured the young man, his gaze traveling fondly over his audience. "This is important for us to understand."

"Did He say it or not?" the impertinent young man demanded, eliciting an angry response from the crowd. Several others chimed in, demanding that the evangelist answer the question.

"I am happy to answer your query," Stephanos responded calmly, unruffled by the audience's gathering animosity. "When Jesus said, 'Destroy this Temple, and in three days I will raise it up,' He was referring to—"

"BLASPHEMER!"

The shrill cry rang out over the synagogue from somewhere amidst the crowd, resonating off the stone walls like a piercing battle cry.

Stephanos' dark eyes scanned the crowd in search of his accuser, his expression conveying both understanding and sympathy. "Allow me to explain—"

"You've said enough!"

"This Stephanos speaks blasphemes as freely as his dead Messiah!"

"He says the Temple should be *destroyed*!"

"Blasphemy! He utters blasphemies!"

The entire synagogue erupted with shouts of alarm and cries of disapproval, shaking their fists, hissing, and shouting curses upon the evangelist.

The unholy cacophony reverberated and echoed off the stone walls, filling the stale air like the roar of a savage beast.

Kelila had never seen or heard anything like it. It was as if a malevolent force rippled through the crowd, fanning the flames of hatred and jealousy. Heart pounding, Kelila looked to Philip in question, her eyes wide with fear. "What is happening?"

"Hasn't Stephanos addressed this topic before?" Candace shouted over the din, stunned by the assembly's ominous reaction.

"Someone is stirring the pot," Simon said grimly, exchanging knowing looks with Philip. "That young man near Stephanos voiced a very pointed question, and someone in the crowd knew it was coming."

"Where is Gamaliel?" Candace gasped, her dark eyes frantically searching the tumultuous crowd. Surely the wise leader would reprimand the mob, soothing their madness.

"Service won't commence for another hour yet," Simon pointed out. "Gamaliel is not here."

"Oh no," Candace breathed, rising from the bench to shield her sons from the furious crowd now jostling them on all sides.

"Seize him!" The heart-stopping command rang out over the vast mob, issued by Saul of Tarsus, propped almost indifferently against a towering pillar behind the platform, arms crossed, expression enigmatic. "If the man speaks blasphemies, he must be tried."

"What?" Philip gasped, dumbfounded. "Someone needs to stop this!"

"We will do everything in our power to halt this madness." Gripping his wife's shoulders, Simon's gaze bore into his wife's. "Candace, take the boys home. Now."

"But, Simon—"

"Do it now," Simon commanded, his tone boding no argument. His mind was filled with gruesome images of another innocent Man and another jaded crowd, resulting in a swift, unlawful trial and a violent death on Golgotha's hill. He could still feel the rough wood of the cross tearing the flesh upon his back as he bore it up the hill alongside his stumbling, bloodied Maker, hearing the blow of the hammer upon the nails, the screams of terror and pain, and the shouts of derision from a possessed mob.

He would not allow his wife and children to be caught in the middle of this.

"I will go," Candace agreed reluctantly, her dark eyes filling with tears as she lifted Rufus onto her hip, grasping Alexander's hand. "Simon, you must stop this. But, please, be careful."

Simon nodded solemnly, kissing her and his two sons.

"Kelila, go with them," Philip instructed firmly, helping her rise from the bench amidst the jostling crowd.

"I won't leave you!" Kelila declared hotly, frightened for him.

"God will protect me," Philip insisted. "Now go, help your sister direct the boys to safety."

Reluctantly, Kelila acquiesced.

Pushing through the raging mob proved nearly impossible. Grasping hands, Candace, Kelila, and Alexander formed a human chain, a wide-eyed Rufus latched firmly onto his mother's hip. Kelila yelped when someone's elbow jammed into her ribcage just as they reached one of the towering exits. Pausing beneath the crowded stone archway, Kelila watched in horror as a sea of dark-robed Pharisees descended upon Stephanos like a flock of hungry carrion birds.

"Oh, Candace!" Kelila wept, her feet nailed in place.

"Kelila, we must go *now*!"

"They're taking him!"

"Pray for him, Kelila, and pray for our men, too," Candace shouted over the din, weeping. "God, protect them. Grant them wisdom!"

Turning after her sister, Kelila knew the expression on Stephanos' face would be forever etched in her memory—as if he had known and had seen this coming, perhaps for a very long time. When his ruthless captors slammed his body into an uncompromising stone pillar, binding his hands tightly behind his back, he did not resist. But his lips were moving in fervent, silent prayer, his eyes filled with empathy and compassion toward the raging crowd.

Somehow, Kelila knew the evangelist prayed not for his own safety, but for the salvation of his accusers.

CHAPTER 33

Tabitha

"She's finally asleep," Mary said softly, gently lowering the child onto her own large canopy bed.

Tabitha watched anxiously as Mary drew the plush blankets over the sleeping child, tenderly tucking her in before bending to kiss the small, pale forehead. The child stirred briefly before curling up into a tight little ball, her tiny ribcage rising and falling along with her rapid breathing.

"I've asked the servants to ready some refreshments and send them up here directly," Mary informed Tabitha, settling into an upholstered chair in a comfortable sitting area across from the massive bed. "I think it's best not to leave the child alone. It's never pleasant to awaken in a strange, unfamiliar environment, and she may be frightened."

Tabitha assumed the girl would awaken with shrill screams, regardless of whether they remained in the beautiful bedchamber. Nonetheless, she kept such thoughts to herself.

"It's been quite a while since I've visited this room," Tabitha said instead, taking the elegant chair across from Mary. Everything appeared as it had the day Tabitha departed on the arm of her new husband. The canopy bed still dominated the chamber like a slumbering beast, boasting decadent Egyptian sheets and luxe Babylonian tapestries that fluttered in the welcome breezes slipping through elegantly latticed windows. The furniture was richly upholstered and expertly arranged. Plush Persian rugs scattered tastefully across the swirling mosaics underfoot invited one to sink bare toes into the thick, lush carpeting. Tabitha had always admired the gilded vanity beside the bed, complete with a matching throne-like chair and a shimmering mirror.

"Rhoda is responsible for this chamber's upkeep now," Mary stated matter-of-factly.

"She does a lovely job maintaining it," Tabitha commented, remembering the days when Rhoda was her shy little shadow in this palatial home. Truthfully, she missed the girl's sweet companionship.

"Well, she learned from the best," Mary smiled, knowing full well Tabitha had taken Rhoda under her wing the day she arrived from Cyprus.

"I have brought refreshments, my lady," Rhoda announced from the doorway, bearing a large tray of tantalizing delicacies.

"Excellent," Mary smiled, gesturing for Rhoda to enter. "Do join us, Rhoda." She didn't have to instruct the girl to speak in hushed tones to avoid waking the sleeping toddler. Rhoda was naturally soft-spoken.

"Thank you, my lady," Rhoda beamed, setting the tray on the marble-topped table between Mary and Tabitha.

"Please, be seated," Mary said generously, gesturing toward an empty chair across from Tabitha.

"Yes, my lady." Gracefully, Rhoda lowered herself onto the upholstered chair, happily folding her hands in her lap.

Tabitha couldn't help but notice that Rhoda was becoming very grown-up. She carried herself with feminine grace far beyond her eleven years.

"How is she doing?" Rhoda whispered, her eyes traveling toward the sleeping child.

"Better than can be expected, I suppose." Mary sighed, her gray eyes welling with sympathy. "Has Tobias set off to find Luke?"

"Immediately upon your request several hours ago," Rhoda assured her.

"I do hope Tobias locates the physician quickly."

You and me both, Tabitha thought, inexplicably troubled by the sound of the child's erratic breathing. She ached to depart for the Synagogue of the Freedmen to be with her husband, but she knew Stephanos wouldn't approve of her thrusting the child upon Mary, and he'd made it perfectly clear the toddler shouldn't be brought to the synagogue.

Sighing, Tabitha hoped the doctor would not only arrive speedily but would also identify the abandoned child.

"What troubles you, beloved?"

Glancing up in surprise, Tabitha saw that Mary's concerned gaze was upon her. "Oh, I'm fine," Tabitha assured her, though her flat tone did little to convince the discerning widow.

"You don't look fine," Mary observed, taking a delicate sip from a slender-stemmed goblet.

"I'm...worried. That's all."

"About Stephanos?"

"Yes," Tabitha blinked, surprised. "How did you know?"

"He said my letter of caution disturbed you."

"I wasn't *disturbed*," Tabitha protested, annoyed by her husband's choice of words. This fearless woman must think her a coward! "I just can't help but wonder what Saul is up to. He can't be trusted."

"I agree," Mary said. "Have you yet begun to pray for him?"

Tabitha was caught off guard by Mary's question. She stared blankly at her former mistress, clearly skeptical.

"I'll assume that's a *no*," Mary chuckled, amused.

"Saul doesn't want to be *prayed for*," Tabitha put in stoutly.

"Isn't it amusing that the people we least desire to pray for are often in most desperate need of intercession?"

Rhoda stared back and forth between her mistress and her friend, fascinated by their rapid conversation.

After a long stint of somewhat awkward silence, Mary asked tactfully, "What topic is Stephanos addressing at the Synagogue of the Freedmen this morning, Tabitha?"

Tight-lipped, Tabitha attempted to dismiss her irritation...and her guilt. How long had Mary been counseling her to pray for her enemies? Only the light of the gospel could transform stony hearts. And yet she stubbornly refused to pray for those most desperately in need of God's transformational truths.

"Tabitha?" Mary prodded gently, her concern growing.

"Some young men have posed difficult questions regarding the Temple, the sacrificial system, and the Law of Moses," Tabitha responded mechanically, clearly distracted.

"What kind of difficult questions?" Rhoda dared, cautiously entering the conversation.

"I'm not entirely sure, but it's an explosive subject," Tabitha said. "For devout Jews, both Moses and the Temple are considered as sacred as God Himself. And they accuse *us* of blasphemy," she huffed, further peeved.

"And who are these young men seeking truth about these hard questions?" Mary inquired, uneasy.

"Again, I'm not sure." Something about the way Mary voiced the question gave Tabitha pause. "They began attending meetings several weeks ago. If I didn't know better, I'd think they were purposely trying to stir up trouble with all their pointed questions..." Tabitha froze, her voice trailing off as a thought—a dreadful, horrid thought—hit her like a ton of bricks. Gripping her chair's armrests like a vice, Tabitha's entire countenance paled.

"Tabitha," Mary said slowly, exchanging a look of concern with young Rhoda. "Are you all right?"

"Alexander believes Saul has been planning something..." Tabitha murmured, her face entirely draining of color as the pieces began falling into place for her. "What does Saul want more than anything, Mary?"

"To abolish the Way, I'd imagine," Mary said,

following Tabitha's line of thought.

"But Gamaliel forbid Saul to touch the twelve apostles," Tabitha slowly contemplated, her heart pounding so furiously she wondered if it would come crashing through her chest. "Mary, Rhoda, if Saul can't destroy the apostles, he'll go after *someone else*... A public figure, but not public enough to draw the attention of Rome...someone important and influential in the church...someone whose destruction would shatter our confidence and decimate our morale..." Breathing rapidly, Tabitha's eyes widened in awful realization. "Someone like Stephanos!"

"We should have seen this coming," Mary declared, slamming down her goblet.

"Stay with the girl." Springing into action, Tabitha propelled herself to her feet with such force her chair toppled over behind her, rudely arousing the sleeping toddler who promptly released a chorus of terror-ridden screams.

"Tabitha, wait," Mary exclaimed, rising in alarm. "I believe your safety is at risk."

"The only one at risk right now is *Saul*," Tabitha flung over her shoulder fiercely. Her own safety was the last thing on her mind as she hastened to rescue the man she loved.

CHAPTER 34

Tabitha

Flying across the city congested with revelers eager to usher in the Feast of Tabernacles, Tabitha realized Saul had utilized the time span bridging two esteemed holy days to his own advantage. The noisome throngs of early celebrators created a natural diversion, numbing the Romans to any further disruptions. Had Saul waited to act until after the Feast of Tabernacles, the ensuing quietude would surely draw attention to a rowdy dispute.

Tabitha clung to the faintest hope that perhaps it was unlawful for the Sanhedrin to convene during this brief stint between the Day of Atonement and the Feast of Tabernacles. Even so, the religious leaders had completely disregarded sacred protocol when they arrested the Lord, calling an emergency council amidst the festival season. Why should they behave any differently this time?

Saul was shrewd, but she had always known that. *Why, oh why, did I underestimate him this time?*

Tabitha could only pray her mistake hadn't proven fatal.

Hardly winded despite the intense heat soaking through her garments, Tabitha's heart dropped as she approached the Synagogue of the Freedmen.

Something wasn't right.

The simple stone structure appeared utterly lifeless. Flashing up the broad stone steps two at a time, Tabitha burst into the vacant synagogue, her heart nearly stopping in her chest. The gathering place was eerily, strangely silent, wholly deserted. A few lone lanterns flickered forlornly, faintly illuminating the aftermath of a terrible stampede.

The typically orderly synagogue was in shambles. Articles of clothing and several stray sandals were strewn across the stone tiles, clearly lost by panicking congregants fleeing the scene. Catching her breath in horror, Tabitha's gaze fell upon the platform. The wooden podium where her husband so often stood had suffered a terrible blow. Several parchment scrolls were scattered, forgotten, across the vacant platform.

Struggling to suppress her rising panic, Tabitha's gaze shot toward a soft clattering sound echoing at the opposite end of the deserted meeting hall.

A troubled young Pharisee emerged from beneath a row of stone pillars, his countenance clouded as he kicked aside shards of broken pottery. The long, braided tassels dangling from his tallith quivered as he shook his covered head, surveying the damage with open displeasure.

"You, there!"

The Pharisee lifted his gaze, jarred by the presence of the disheveled young woman and her curt address.

"Tell me what happened here! Where is my husband?"

"Your husband?" The Pharisee repeated, puzzled.

"I have no time for games." Closing the distance between them with alarming speed, Tabitha snatched the front of the Pharisee's garment. "Where is he?"

"Who is your husband?" the Pharisee asked, blinking in surprise.

"His name is Stephanos," Tabitha ground out, easing her grip on his collar. She suspected the mild Pharisee was being forthright with her. "He spoke to the congregation early this morning."

"The evangelist?"

"Yes! Where is he?"

The Pharisee averted his gaze, inexplicably troubled.

"Where is he?" Tabitha demanded, tightening her grip on his collar.

Swallowing hard, the Pharisee's Adam's apple bobbed beneath his neatly trimmed beard.

"*Tell me!*"

"They took him away," the Pharisee faltered, unable to meet the young woman's fiery gaze.

"Where did they take him?" Tabitha demanded, certain her heart had stopped beating.

"The religious leaders disagreed with his teaching." Reluctantly, the Pharisee raised eyes full of sorrow. "They accused him of blasphemy and took him to be tried before the Sanhedrin."

Releasing the Pharisee's expensive garment, Tabitha turned sharply on her heels, making a mad dash for the wide double doors.

"I remained here because I disagreed with their haste."

Tabitha froze, pierced by the young Pharisee's shocking confession. She dared a cautious glance over her shoulder.

The Pharisee stood rooted in place amidst the wreckage and debris, his countenance clouded with concern.

Turning from him without a word, Tabitha pushed open the heavy double doors, breaking out into the sunlight. Choking on her own sobs, she fled toward the Temple compound, her sandaled feet pounding against the earth in rhythm with her frantically beating heart.

***

The imposing Temple façade loomed heavenward like a cold, uncaring beacon, its resplendent golden crown glistening in the early afternoon sunlight.

Pounding up a broad flight of marble steps, Tabitha approached two modestly dressed older women descending the gleaming steps.

"Excuse me," Tabitha gasped, eliciting looks of surprise from the two women. "Do you know if the Sanhedrin is in session?"

Exchanging fearful glances, the eldest of the two spoke first. "There was a trial this morning, but I was told it didn't end well."

Eyes welling with tears, Tabitha managed brokenly, "What happened?"

"We were told a heretic was tried and condemned," the second woman inserted sympathetically, sensing Tabitha's mounting distress. Reaching out, she touched the distraught young woman's arm. "Are you all right, dear?"

"A man was condemned by the *Sanhedrin*?" Tabitha clarified, striving for calm. "Do you know if he was imprisoned? And if so, where?"

"If the rumors can be trusted, the Council hadn't opportunity to condemn him," the older woman said, her tone laced with pity. "The crowd condemned his speech. The session was disrupted when the heretic was seized by the mob."

"The mob?" Tabitha swayed dangerously, the blood draining from her face. Surely God would not have allowed her husband to fall prey to the violence of a despotic mob!

The older woman caught her arm. "Do you need help, child?"

"Which way did they go? Where did they take him?" Tabitha demanded, feeling faint. Her heart sank as the two women exchanged looks of concern. "*Where did they take him?*" Tabitha ground out, desperate.

"We were told the heretic was dragged outside the city gates," the older woman responded apologetically.

Tabitha needn't have asked which gate. Visions of her Lord's excruciating path to Golgotha beyond the city gates danced in her mind.

"No!" With a heart-rending cry, Tabitha exploded into action, pounding down the broad steps with such force startled pilgrims and worshipers leaped out of her path.

Consumed with terror and dread, Tabitha drew upon every ounce of athletic ability she possessed to reach her destination in time. As her blistered, sandaled feet pounded against the earth, Tabitha's strong legs ate up the distance between the glistening city and the dusty, barren wasteland beyond.

***

Standing before a scattered sea of blood-stained, jagged rocks and stones, Tabitha's hands clenched into fists at her sides, her fingernails biting into her palms' tender flesh until they bled. Gazing upon the broad scarlet stain soaking through ancient, crumbling pavement and wetting the dry earth beneath, Tabitha's entire being cried out against the perversity, the injustice, committed against the love of her life.

How could they do this to him? How could they stone him in cold blood? Tabitha thought, a dull pain coursing through her body with every throbbing heartbeat. *All he wanted was to serve them, to love them. That's all he ever wanted, all he ever did.*

The unholy, rasping *caw-caw* of a crow soaring high overhead rang out above the barren wasteland, his melancholy song drifting across dusty plains, tearing at Tabitha's bleeding heart.

"Tabitha. Oh, dear sister."

Numbed to her very core, Tabitha raised hazel-green eyes as lifeless as her barren surroundings.

Stephanos' best friend, Philip, approached alongside Candace's husband, Simon. She'd never seen either powerful man so limp, so utterly dejected. With faces and garments smudged in dust and soil, Tabitha knew from whence they had come.

Simon and Philip—possibly others, as well—had buried her beloved husband.

"How did you know, Tabitha?" Simon spoke as the men drew alongside her, each draping comforting arms around her stiff shoulders.

"I just knew." Swallowing salty tears, Tabitha cursed her decision to assist the abandoned child that morning. She should have been with her husband. She should have perished with him.

"Where is he now?" she asked flatly. It didn't occur to her to ask what had happened. All she knew was that she needed to be with him.

The men exchanged expressions of deep concern.

"We buried him, my sister," Philip said gently, aching for his best friend's grieving wife.

"Take me to him."

"Beloved—" Simon countered gently.

"*Take me!*"

CHAPTER 35

Tabitha

Blinking back tears, Tabitha stood before a freshly dug mound. She could hardly grasp that her powerful, charismatic, devastatingly attractive husband had been committed to the earth.

Stephanos was a force to be reckoned with, a powerhouse for the furtherance of the gospel. None had been able to refute his arguments. None had successfully come against him.

Until now.

God, where are You? How could You allow this?

Crumbling, Tabitha collapsed on her husband's grave, watering the mound with relentless tears, trembling fingers twisting and digging into the moist earth. Choking on her own heartrending sobs, Tabitha cried out her anguish.

"Oh, Stephanos. My beloved Stephanos, what will I do without you? How can I go on without you, my love?"

Standing a respectful distance away, Simon and

Philip waited helplessly, aching for their bereaved sister.

"What can we do for her?" Philip breathed, his heart breaking in his chest.

"We can be here for her," Simon replied without hesitation. "We can allow her time to grieve, extending mercy and grace when needed. We can see her through this."

"But how can she recover from this, Simon?"

"She can't," Simon responded soberly. "Not by her own strength."

"Only by the grace of God," Philip agreed softly.

Standing vigilant guard, the men waited grimly, willing to grant her as much time as she needed. Even if it meant waiting all night.

***

Facedown in the soil, Tabitha breathed deeply of the musty, earthy scent. How long had she lain here, her body crumpled like a child's decrepit rag doll, her face streaked with mud and tears? It could have been minutes or possibly hours—she didn't know. She wondered if time had stood still, for her entire world remained suspended in a dreadful state of pain and uncertainty.

Even as her ears absorbed the chorus of chirping birdsongs and the faint clatter of wagons and horses' hooves within the distant city gates, Tabitha's brain failed to register or acknowledge any of it. She was too numb, too exhausted, to comprehend what her mind was telling her. Closing her eyes, Tabitha floated upon a sea of nothingness, longing for comfort, wondering if there was any to be found...

"Oh, my precious girl."

Mary! Pushing herself up on trembling forearms, Tabitha lifted her dirt-and-tear-streaked face, glancing anxiously toward the sound of the beloved voice.

"Oh, my Tabitha, my poor darling." With a soft rustling of expensive fabric, Mary swept into Tabitha's field of vision, kneeling in the soil and paying little mind to her elegant sandals or luxurious gown as she gathered the weeping young woman in her arms. "Shhh, shhh. I'm here, beloved. I'm not going anywhere."

Gasping for breath, Tabitha buried her face in Mary's elegant bodice. Here was someone who understood. Here was someone who had experienced the same unspeakable loss and *survived.*

Relief coursed through Tabitha's shuddering frame, for she knew Mary would not bombard her with questions or flowery sentiments. No, Mary would simply *be there* amidst her great pain, and that blessed knowledge provided the slightest shade of solace.

For the longest time, neither spoke. Mary held her former maid, allowing Tabitha's tears free rein; for she, too, understood the sting of sudden loss.

She also knew that nothing she said or did could ease Tabitha's all-consuming pain, not yet. In time, that would change. But it would, indeed, take time. Perhaps, lots of it.

Raising full eyes toward Heaven, Mary offered silent intercession on behalf of her grieving friend, pouring out her heart to the God who still healed the brokenhearted, binding up their wounds.

Relieved to their very core by Mary's soothing

presence, Philip and Simon exchanged knowing looks from their faithful post. The wealthy widow's disheveled appearance, tousled hair, and the sweat glistening upon her delicate brow wasn't lost on them.

"Has she been searching for Tabitha all this time?" Philip asked, amazed.

For the first time since tragedy struck, Simon's lips curved in the faintest hint of a smile. "Knowing our Mary, she has probably torn the entire city apart, brick by brick, in search of her grieving sister."

CHAPTER 36

Mary

The Feast of Tabernacles dawned at sunset on the fifteenth day of the seventh month, mere days after the martyrdom of the fearless deacon. As the entire nation indulged in feasting and revelry, the believers quietly mourned the loss of their beloved brother, Stephanos.

Standing upon her own sprawling rooftop, Mary's sharp gray eyes swept over a city cluttered with crudely constructed booths as the sun began its swift descent beyond the western hills. Here, on the roof of the mansion's highest level, the servants had faithfully fashioned a resplendent tabernacle adorned with branches, palm fronds, and wreaths of fresh, aromatic flowers. Mary had considered relieving them of the monumental task, but swiftly decided against it. It would be good for them to tackle an important project—something to busy their hands and minds, distracting them from their intense grief.

Disheartened, Mary acknowledged that Saul had

seemingly accomplished his purpose by orchestrating Stephanos' cruel death. She had never seen her fellow believers so fearful and apprehensive, so completely demoralized.

The unspoken question rippling through the entire congregation seemed to be *Who will be targeted next?*

Emboldened by the unlawful execution of the famous evangelist, enemies of the Way had become increasingly brazen in demonstrating their hostility toward the believers, hurling insults, rocks, and handfuls of dust and dung on the streets. Disturbing rumors swirled in the air about Saul of Tarsus and the high priest. If such rumors could be trusted, the relentless Pharisee had finally persuaded the Sanhedrin and the high priest against protecting members of the Way. According to Saul, the "random" riot and ensuing mob violence "instigated" by Stephanos' final address was proof of the dangerous and inflammatory nature of their sect.

As tensions mounted on all sides, Mary feared it was only a matter of time before the Romans intervened.

"I would bid you *good* evening, but..."

"But it isn't a very good evening, is it?" Mary didn't react when her cloaked informant drew alongside her, seemingly materializing out of nowhere. She had been expecting him. "Greetings, Alexander."

"Nice sukkah," Alexander commented, referencing the elaborate structure behind them.

"It is."

The solemn pair stood upon the walled rooftop in reverential silence for several long moments, gazing upon the deceptive beauty of a hostile city.

"How is she?" Alexander finally spoke, his deep

voice shattering the somber silence.

"As can be expected, I suppose." Mary needn't have asked whom Alexander referenced. "Tabitha is grieving the loss of her dear husband. There is little comfort to offer her right now, I'm afraid."

"Ah." Alexander swallowed hard, clearly struggling to mask his grief. "You know what that's like."

"I do." Mary despised this dull ache in her chest, the heavy shroud of sorrow hanging over their heads. She had walked this path before. It wasn't an easy one, not for anyone—least of all, her dear Tabitha.

Thinking of the distraught young woman sent a sharp pang through Mary's compassionate heart. How she wished she could have convinced Tabitha to return to the villa with her! There, Tabitha would be loved, comforted, and consoled. But the young woman had stoutly insisted upon staying in her own house, the home she had shared with her Stephanos.

Mary understood, though she had been relieved when Tabitha hesitantly allowed her to stay that first night. Lovingly, Mary had tucked Tabitha into bed, blinded by her own tears as her former maid wept inconsolably, burying her face in one of her husband's tunics. It was a difficult, sleepless night for both of them. When morning finally dawned, Tabitha had numbly requested time alone.

Mary had been deeply unsettled by Tabitha's request. Somehow, overnight, Tabitha's grief had been replaced by something else, something far more destructive and dangerous. The hardness around her jaw, the darkness lurking in her eyes, warned Mary that bitterness and rage had crept into her heart, uninvited.

Reluctantly, Mary had honored Tabitha's request.

But that certainly wouldn't stop her from visiting every single day.

"She will get through this," Alexander said, interrupting Mary's train of thought.

"By the grace of God, she will," Mary agreed quietly.

"I imagine you've heard rumors about Saul of Tarsus and the high priest?"

Mary offered a subtle nod.

"Unfortunately, they're true."

"I suspected so," Mary replied calmly, drawing upon God for strength. "Tell me more."

"Saul has obtained permission to arrest anyone sympathizing with or belonging to the 'dangerous sect' called the Way."

"Permission from the high priest?"

"And the Sanhedrin."

Fleetingly, Mary wondered about Gamaliel's involvement. Had the respected teacher finally cast his vote against them?

"Fortunately," Alexander continued with a sarcastic edge, "at this point, an arrest cannot be enforced without 'sufficient cause'—for example, breaking the law or disrupting the peace. But this is only the beginning, Mary. In time, our brothers and sisters will be arrested simply for bearing the name of Christ."

"Women are also at risk?" Mary asked, her slender brows lifting in surprise.

"Remarkably, yes. The religious leaders are clearly petrified if they are threatened by our women," Alexander said dryly. Glancing at the formidable woman standing calmly at his elbow, he flashed a sardonic smile. "On second thought, I'd imagine their concerns are justified."

Mary acknowledged his statement with a dry smile of her own.

"This is only going to get worse," Alexander observed after another long pause, his dark eyes smoldering like the rapidly setting sun. "And despite the Sanhedrin's ruling to refrain from making an arrest unless the believer has broken the law or disrupted the public peace, we are still at risk. As I'm sure you've noticed, Jerusalem is swarming with false witnesses looking for a payday. Our loved ones will be sold for a mere pittance."

"We will get through this," Mary replied, firm in her resolve. "We all knew this was coming."

"In the meantime," Alexander inserted, his tone deadly serious, "I would caution every believer to remain alert, more cautious than ever. We can't afford to lower our guard, not for a moment."

"I understand."

The daring manservant hesitated, clearly wrestling with his own thoughts.

"What is it, Alexander?"

"I'm wondering if we should urge our families with young children to relocate, even if it's in the rural places just beyond our borders."

Though her initial inclination was to disagree, Mary allowed herself a moment to contemplate Alexander's unexpected proposal.

"Some families might hesitate to leave, for fear of being considered disloyal or cowardly," Alexander expounded. "But I am considering their little ones. In my opinion, it isn't cowardly to prioritize the safety of one's children."

"I agree," Mary conceded. "I suppose each family must seek the Lord individually and heed His calling for them. Some may be called to relocate, carrying the message of the gospel to new lands; while others, like Stephanos, are called to danger here in Jerusalem, possibly even death."

Alexander nodded slowly, recognizing her wisdom.

"The important part is allowing God to lead each believing family," Mary maintained, walking gracefully to the ledge and folding her hands upon the stone enclosure encircling the perimeter. "Surely some will be called to leave; others, to stay. It would be terribly easy to fall into judgment, condemning those who are led differently than we are. But we must remain united, standing together and refusing to be critical of others—even if their calling appears quite unlike our own."

Joining her at the wall, Alexander nodded his consent.

The two remained in respectful, companionable silence for many moments, watching the rapidly diminishing sun retreating beyond the distant hills.

How swiftly the light is extinguished, Mary thought, *enshrouding the entire city in darkness. But praise God, the promise of another sunrise is something even the deepest darkness cannot dispel.*

"*Blessed are you when men hate you,*" Alexander reminisced, his powerful voice drifting upon the still evening air like a hopeful beacon. "*And when they exclude you, and revile you, and cast out your name as evil, for the Son of Man's sake...*"

"*Rejoice in that day and leap for joy,*" Mary smiled faintly, resuming the recitation where Alexander had left off. "*For indeed—*"

"*—your reward is great in Heaven,*" they concluded together.

CHAPTER 37

Tabitha

It all happened so fast.

One moment, her wonderful Stephanos was *there*, strong and vital and full of life, taking her in his arms, whispering sweet nothings in her ear, making her feel like the most treasured, beautiful woman alive. Then the next, he was *gone*, a blameless victim of a senseless, hate-driven mob, violently stripped from her life in one cruel instant.

It felt so...surreal. Like a nightmare that would eventually end. Perhaps she would soon awaken to the wonderful realization that it was just a bad dream.

Reaching for her husband's favorite robe, Tabitha slipped into it before rolling off the sleeping pallet. Rising on wobbly legs, she gathered the robe closely about her slender frame, breathing in her husband's beloved scent. How long would it linger upon his garment?

What would she do once it faded?

Tabitha stood as one rooted in place, her mind

muddled with confusion. Bleary-eyed and exhausted, she observed her familiar surroundings. Nothing was out of place. Everything appeared exactly as it always had. So much so, she half expected her husband to walk through the door, his leather satchel slung over one shoulder, after a long day's work. How often had she seen him do just that? How often had she happily crossed the room to greet him, standing on tiptoe to plant a firm kiss on his mouth?

Pushing such thoughts aside, Tabitha supposed she should be praying for strength. But since she had returned from her husband's grave, she had not uttered a single prayer. Why should she? The Lord had turned His face from her.

Hadn't she begged Him to save her husband? How much grief did He expect her to bear? First her father and mother, and now Stephanos! Did the Lord wish for her to be utterly alone in this world?

You are not alone, beloved.

Angrily, Tabitha crossed the room. For the very first time, she found no comfort in that still, small voice. She didn't wish to hear it.

Lo, I AM with you always, even to the end of the age.

Are You, Lord? Tabitha thought angrily, dashing at her tears. *You cannot sit at the table with me, sharing breakfast each morning. You cannot take me in strong arms when I am troubled or afraid. You cannot share my bed tonight, loving me as my husband does...or rather, did.*

Your Maker is your husband, the Lord of hosts is His name.

Tabitha didn't dare express it, but at that moment, the unseen presence of God seemed to her a very poor substitute.

Though Tabitha had known many people who denied the existence of God in the face of great suffering and oppression, she was not among them. She didn't doubt the existence of God, even amidst this great trial. She *knew* that God existed. Her great question was, *Why?* Why had He allowed a faithful man to endure cruel torture and indignity? Hadn't He delivered the apostles from certain death? Was it too much to ask the same for her Stephanos?

Frustrated beyond comprehension, Tabitha wondered why she had bothered to get out of bed. She didn't know what time it was, nor did she care. Warm sunbeams slanted through the latticed windows, casting long beams of light upon the earthen floor. Based on the intensity of those rays, she guessed it to be mid-afternoon, possibly even later. She knew she should be hungry, but the thought of consuming anything made her want to vomit.

Parched, she lifted the ladle hanging on the stone rim of the water jar by the door, helping herself to a long, unladylike swig. Carelessly dropping the ladle in the wide mouth of the stone jar, Tabitha ignored the ensuing *splash*. The dumb thing probably sank all the way to the bottom of the jar.

Pausing briefly before the gilded mirror, Tabitha's heart constricted at the sight of the ghostly stranger staring back at her.

What had happened to her? She had never seen such pallor, such dark circles framing vacant, hollow eyes. With tousled hair, smudged cheeks, and unkempt, wrinkled garments, she looked more like a wraith than her usual vibrant self.

Would she ever look the same—or *be* the same—again?

I am a widow, Tabitha realized, taken aback by

the sudden thought.

Closing her eyes tightly, she nearly drowned in a surge of unwanted guilt. She knew she wasn't the only one suffering. She thought of Amal and Daphne in mourning, sequestered behind the impenetrable walls of a luxurious villa. She knew she should be with them, comforting them, sharing the light and love of Christ amid their consuming grief. But how could she? She had no comfort to give them. They must think her a fool and a coward, for she hadn't possessed the strength to inform them of their son's brutal passing. Courageous Mary had offered to carry out the unpleasant task, paying them a visit the following day and gently breaking the news to them.

Thoughts of selfless Mary only further intensified Tabitha's feelings of guilt, for she couldn't help but think of the abandoned little girl she had thrust upon the busy woman. As Zev had aptly stated, his lady already had enough on her plate.

I entrust her to your care, Stephanos had said that fateful morning in the outer court, placing the whimpering child in her arms—the last conversation she would ever share with him. She knew Stephanos would want her to care for the lost little one. And yet Tabitha just couldn't bring herself to retrieve the small child. How could she take in the toddler when she couldn't even bear to look at her? To do so only reminded Tabitha that she hadn't been there for Stephanos in his darkest hour, his hour of need. Had she been there, she could have done something to save him!

Slowly opening her eyes, Tabitha gazed into the mirror. Here she had stood, only days earlier, in the balmy predawn hours. Here, she had felt an inexplicable impression: *The devil has asked to sift you as wheat.*

Clenching her fists at her sides, Tabitha supposed she was, indeed, being "sifted," for the most precious thing in her world had been violently stripped from her life. Hazel-green eyes narrowing dangerously, Tabitha clenched her jaw in fury.

Saul of Tarsus would pay for this.

The world would be a far better place, a safer place, without the presence of one foul, self-righteous, blood-lusting Pharisee. If Saul had his way, the believers would be hunted down and destroyed, one by one. He was a hindrance to the gospel message, a barrier to all that was good.

Mary had suggested she pray for Saul. *Pray* for him? Ha! She'd pray for him, all right—she'd pray a maelstrom of curses upon his head! She'd pray he would suffer a fate far worse, far more humiliating, than his innocent victim. She'd pray every foul disease would overtake him and consume him. She'd pray for *vengeance.*

Saul is deceived by a cruel adversary... Standing before the mirror, Stephanos' bold pronouncement filled Tabitha's senses with such resounding clarity she nearly stumbled. Recalling the fire burning in his dark eyes, the conviction of his tone that day, Tabitha's heart pounded steadily against her ribcage. *I am convinced that God must have a powerful purpose in mind for Saul,* Stephanos had insisted.

At the time, Tabitha had strongly refuted her husband's claim, but Stephanos had been prepared with a ready argument: *Why else would the enemy attack Saul with such calculated fury?*

To think that Stephanos had been concerned for the *soul* of that wretched man! During the course of their conversation, Tabitha had sharply commented that the enemy could have Saul's soul, for all she cared. Now, she'd gladly hand it over to the devil on a silver platter!

For some reason unbeknownst to us, our enemy is engaged in a relentless battle for the soul of that man... Stephanos' earnest words pounded through her brain along with her rapidly beating pulse. She should have fought harder, arguing against her husband's madness. She should have dissuaded him from placing himself in the line of fire, sacrificing himself for a rabid mob craving innocent blood.

Turning harshly from her own reflection, Tabitha stalked away, her entire being filled with rage.

Stephanos was wrong about Saul. He should have listened to reason.

He should have listened to *her*!

Grasping her head in her hands, Tabitha paced about the small house, grappling with fierce emotions. What was happening to her? Had years of training in the ways of Christ merely evaporated overnight? Had her faith crumbled beyond repair?

Mary had lost her husband, and yet the brave widow had carried on with strength, dignity, and conviction. But she, Tabitha, was not like Mary. Her faith in God's "perfect" plan was shaken to the very core.

Groaning in anguish, Tabitha sank to the ground, defeated. She had promised Stephanos she would carry on the Lord's work if anything happened to him.

Now, she wondered if doing so would be a screaming farce.

CHAPTER 38

Kelila

Perched on the highest step of the crumbling stone staircase leading to the roof, Kelila gazed upon the commencement of another breathtaking sunset. Across the city, locals and pilgrims alike worked tirelessly deconstructing their elaborate shelters, for the Feast of Tabernacles had drawn to a close.

Recalling last year's celebration was bittersweet. Kelila had gloried in the festivities, discovering the hand of God upon the sacred feasts for the first time in her life. She hadn't known it at the time, but the Holy Spirit was gently, patiently wooing her, drawing her unto Himself, making straight the path toward everlasting life. What a wondrous season that had been!

This year, Kelila's heart was heavy. A dark cloud of apprehension had settled over the church after the brutal loss of a respected leader, which had shaken them to the core. Kelila ached for her new friend, Tabitha, unable to imagine what the young widow must be going through.

With a slight shudder, Kelila contemplated another disturbing thought. How would she ever cope if something happened to Philip? It was entirely possible, given their current circumstances. Every believer now risked imprisonment, torture, or worse…

Lord God, we need Your strength and protection more than ever.

Glancing up in surprise, Kelila's gaze drifted toward the gate now creaking open on rusty hinges.

"Philip!" Her heart constricted at the sight of her beloved.

Closing the gate behind him, Philip approached her with a weary smile. Climbing the steep stairway, he lowered himself onto the step below Kelila.

"This is a pleasant surprise."

"I needed to see you," Philip answered, gazing up at her with the brown eyes she adored.

Blushing, Kelila slipped her shawl over her head. Lost in silent musings beneath a pastel-colored sky, she hadn't noticed when her covering had slipped off her head, pooling about her shoulders.

"You are a sight for sore eyes," Philip admitted, tweaking her knee.

"Does something trouble you?" Kelila asked, tenderly brushing his hair back. His eyes were deeply shadowed, his shoulders slightly bent.

"I just keep thinking about him," Philip said quietly.

"You miss him, don't you?"

Philip nodded, swiftly dropping his gaze and appearing to study his own sandals.

Kelila's heart wrenched, for she saw that her

betrothed was blinking back tears. "You needn't be strong for my sake, Philip," she whispered, stroking his hair as a mother might console her grieving child. "I know Stephanos was your dearest friend. You can grieve, my love."

Shaking his head, Philip forced an uncomfortable chuckle. "He wouldn't want that."

"He wouldn't want you shoving it all inside either, allowing it to fester and seethe."

"I know what he would want because he *told* me," Philip said, meeting her gaze.

Kelila stared at him in surprise. "What do you mean, he told you?"

"He said if anything ever happened to him, he wanted me to carry on the Lord's work without him."

"Philip," Kelila asked slowly, feeling somewhat guilty for voicing her niggling question. "If the Lord chose the two of you to serve together, why do you think He allowed Stephanos to die?"

"I wondered about that, at first," Philip confessed, clearing his throat a bit gruffly. "But then the Lord reminded me that *to everything there is a season.*"

"And your season of working with Stephanos has drawn to a close." Kelila lowered her gaze, deeply saddened for him.

"Jesus granted us the unspeakable privilege of working together for many years. And it was the most exciting time of my life," Philip continued, a slight tremor in his deep voice. "In the process, God also blessed us with a beautiful friendship. Though it's tempting to demand an explanation for this great loss, instead I will praise the Lord for the sweet fellowship He allowed us to share in that special season. I will treasure those memories for the rest of my life."

"I know you will," Kelila responded wholeheartedly.

"It was a bit daunting at first, the thought of continuing without him," Philip admitted, gazing up at her with honest eyes. "But then it hit me, Kelila—how gracious our God really is. See, He already knows the future, the end from the beginning. And knowing it was time to call my brother home, the Lord provided a completely undeserved, unexpected blessing—another worthy partner to engage in the Lord's work with me."

"Philip, that's wonderful!" Kelila exclaimed, her eyes welling with hope. "But, who?"

"*You*, beloved."

Kelila stared at her betrothed, openmouthed. "*Me*?"

"Yes, you," Philip laughed, tenderly cupping her face in his hand. "And I couldn't imagine a worthier, more capable partner, Kelila. Your passion for the Lord is contagious, life-giving, and pure. Others are drawn to the light you bear."

Moved, Kelila took his wrist, leaning into his touch.

"Stephanos saw it before I did, which is nothing new," Philip mused, his eyes smiling fondly in remembrance of his brilliant companion. "I think he tried to tell me, in so many words. But I was too dense to comprehend it...until now. After days of wrestling with God in prayer."

"I cannot wait to begin our life together," Kelila breathed. "What do you think the Lord wants us to do, Philip? How shall we carry on His work?"

"We must earnestly seek the Lord in this matter," Philip told her, his tone etched with great conviction. "In the meantime, Kelila, there's something important we need to talk about."

"Our wedding plans," Kelila responded. "I know what you're going to say, Philip, and I agree with you."

"With this tragedy hanging over our heads and the heavy sorrow enshrouding our community, it just doesn't seem appropriate to host a wedding celebration," Philip said bleakly.

"What should we do, Philip?" Kelila asked earnestly. "I desperately want to marry you, but I certainly wouldn't want to be insensitive to our grieving brothers and sisters."

"I think we have several options," Philip stated in his practical way. "We could forgo the wedding celebration and festivities, marrying quietly before a priest and appointed witnesses. Or we could postpone the wedding, allowing our friends and family time to grieve."

"I trust your judgment about this, Philip," Kelila said, taking his hand with a gentle squeeze. There'd been a time in her life when she wouldn't have dreamed of sacrificing her perfect wedding for the sake of others. But now, especially in light of their recent loss, Kelila recognized what was truly important. A fancy wedding was certainly not at the top of that list—at least, not for *her*.

"Shall we seek the Lord's guidance in this matter?" Philip asked in his quiet way.

"Absolutely," Kelila responded without hesitation. "He knows best, after all."

Playfully sliding down a step, Kelila drew alongside her betrothed, taking his arm and gently resting her head on his firm shoulder, smiling when he kissed the top of her covered head.

She didn't know how long they lingered in companionable silence, watching the first evening stars dusting the distant horizon. But she *did* know she would treasure these cherished moments with Philip for the rest of her life.

CHAPTER 39

Saul of Tarsus

These six things the Lord hates, yes, seven are an abomination to Him...

Tossing and turning violently, drenched in cold sweat, Saul lay upon his bed, struggling against a fitful state of both slumber and wakefulness.

These six things the Lord hates, yes, seven are an abomination to Him...

Saul groaned, thrusting aside his sweat-soaked covering, resisting consciousness even as his troubled soul craved it.

A proud look, a lying tongue...

Even in his sleep, Saul was plagued by unpleasant memories. He saw the evangelist cast violently to the ground before the throne of Caiaphas, the high priest. The sorrow upon the face of Gamaliel, his childhood idol, would forever haunt Saul's tortured mind.

Despite all his elaborate planning, Gamaliel had known Saul's intentions all along.

Panting, Saul turned over in bed, burying his head in the pillow as if attempting to smother the harbingers haunting sleepless nights.

Hands that shed innocent blood...

Images of the evangelist, his body crumpled and broken, warm blood seeping beneath the jagged stones, filled his mind, searing Saul's entire body with inexplicable pain.

He, too, bore the weight of those stones. He'd borne it since that fateful moment his false witness had cast the very first one.

A heart that devises wicked schemes...

Saul cried out in his sleep, slamming aside his pillow, his mentor's tragic expression filling his frame of vision.

Feet that are swift in running to evil...

The rumble of a thousand sandals pounding against the dry earth resonated in Saul's mind, pounding with the intensity of heavy hammer blows. With the savage roar of a rabid mob ringing in his ears, Saul cringed as the sound of ruthless stones pummeling the body of a dying man filled his senses.

A false witness who speaks lies, and one who sows discord among brethren.

With a savage cry, Saul shot up like a lightning bolt, his head in his hands, his entire body trembling, drenched in slick, cold sweat. Tugging at the thin tunic plastered around his tense, damp body, Saul's breath came in short, powerful huffs as his eyes roved about the darkness closing in on his bedchamber.

Everything appeared as it should. Silver moonlight slanted through the open window framed by gently fluttering curtains, bathing the entire chamber in an ethereal, heavenly glow. Sighing in relief, Saul wondered what he had expected to find. A dark specter crouched in the corner, seeking to capture his tortured soul, sending it catapulting to Hades? Shaking his head in disdain, Saul banished his concerns.

Clearly, all was well.

Releasing his troubled breath, Saul slowly eased his body onto the comfortable bed. Clamping his eyes shut, he beseeched the Almighty for blissful, dreamless sleep.

Scarcely had he begun to doze when the dreadful chorus began anew, ringing shrilly in his ears, pounding in time with the excruciating pain of yet another unbearable migraine.

These six things the Lord hates, yes, seven are an abomination to Him...

Propelling himself from his bed with the force of a charging beast, Saul clenched his fists and bellowed out his rage.

***

Tabitha

Knock, knock.

Jerking awake, Tabitha moaned, cradling her aching head in her hands.

Knock, knock, knock.

Groaning in dismay, Tabitha covered her head with her husband's soft tunic, loath to rise from her pallet to answer the door. She was in no mood for company—not now, not ever. She preferred to fret, stew, and rage in peace.

Knock, knock. Knock, knock, knock!

Growling her displeasure, Tabitha hurled aside her covering, slipping into her husband's tunic. Stumbling to the door, she assumed the mere sight of her would scare off the instigator of such persistent knocking. She hadn't bathed nor changed clothes since her husband's death. Nor had she bothered to comb her tangled tresses or wash her face. Briefly, she considered pausing for a cursory glance in the mirror before confronting the person behind the door but decided against it.

She didn't want to know what she looked like.

Swinging the door open, Tabitha supposed she shouldn't be surprised to see Mary standing on the threshold, a basket brimming with tasty provisions balanced delicately on one arm. Her former mistress had called on her every single day, without fail, since Stephanos' tragic death.

"Tabitha," Mary said warmly, mindful of her full basket as she gathered the grieving young widow in her arms.

Softening slightly, Tabitha leaned into Mary's embrace, blinking back tears. She hadn't realized how much she needed Mary until she was in her arms.

"I've brought you some warm broth and fresh bread," Mary informed her gently, graciously over-looking Tabitha's frightful appearance.

Tabitha's stomach turned at the thought of eating. Pulling away, she opened her mouth to protest.

"Now don't give me that look." Entering the small house, Mary deposited her large basket on the low table.

Tabitha trailed behind her, annoyed.

"It's been over a week since our dear Stephanos' passing," Mary said, her tone gentle but firm. "You have scarcely touched a thing since then, dear one, but you need sustenance to keep up your strength."

What strength? Tabitha thought, peeved. "The thought of eating sickens me," she said stubbornly.

"But your body requires nourishment even if it's just a little bit here and there."

Seeing that Mary didn't appear in any hurry to depart, Tabitha decided she'd best shut the door. Crossing the room, she slammed it a bit harder than necessary.

"Come," Mary said invitingly, gesturing toward the impressive spread on the table. "You must take nourishment."

"I'm not hungry."

Straightening to her full, impressive height, Mary's arresting gray eyes pinned Tabitha in place. "My dearest Tabitha, you may come take sustenance of your own accord, or I will take you into my lap and spoon-feed you like a small child. Which would you prefer?"

Tabitha stared at her former mistress, blinking in surprise.

"Well," Mary prodded, a hand propped on her graceful hip. "Which will it be?"

Peeved, Tabitha crossed the room without a word, lowering herself onto her mat and tearing off a hunk of bread.

"Ah, that's better," Mary acknowledged with a knowing smile. "And you'll feel much better after a decent meal."

I'll never feel better, Tabitha thought, her anger

steadily kindling. Since Mary's gaze remained upon her, she dipped her bread in the steaming broth and grudgingly popped it in her mouth.

Gracefully lowering herself onto the mat across from Tabitha, Mary reached over the table to take her hand. "I know this is so hard—excruciating. But, Tabitha, you know as well as I, death is not the end. Rather, it's just the beginning. You will be reunited with your dear Stephanos, just as I, too, will be re-united with my beloved Mark."

Tabitha knew she should take comfort in Mary's words, for they were true enough. But she found no solace in them. Yes, she would join her beloved *someday*. But what about *now*? Was she to muddle through the next forty, fifty, possibly even sixty years without him? How *could* she? She wasn't strong enough.

She wanted him back. She couldn't bear this hateful silence, this consuming pain. For the umpteenth time, she wondered why the God she had served so faithfully hadn't intervened on her behalf.

Mary's tenacious presence only intensified Tabitha's feelings of guilt and frustration, sharpening her awareness of her own glaring weaknesses and shortcomings.

Like her, Mary had lost her husband in the blink of an eye. But *unlike* her, Mary had carried on with steadfast faith and unwavering trust in the will of God. Within hours of losing Mark, Mary had resolved to set her face like a flint to do the will of God, and so she had. Boldly resuming her husband's enterprises, Mary not only supervised half a dozen thriving businesses, but also became a pillar of strength in the infant church.

But me? Tabitha thought, further chagrined by her own glaring weakness. *I haven't the faith to utter a single prayer, much less take charge of my husband's thriving ministry or carry on without him.*

Sensing that Mary awaited a response, Tabitha lowered her eyes, ashamed to meet her gaze. "I'm not like you, Mary. I can't just keep going as if nothing has happened."

"I wouldn't expect you to, dear one; nor did I, when I lost Mark."

"Please, Mary. You rolled up your sleeves and dove headfirst into both business and outreach the moment your husband was laid to rest," Tabitha pointed out, miffed.

"Frankly, the outrageous amount of work demanding my attention kept my hands and mind occupied, Tabitha," Mary said honestly. "Looking back, I see the Lord was merciful to me—He kept me so busy meeting the needs of others, I had little time to sit around feeling sorry for myself."

"Like me?" Tabitha challenged, arching a brow in question.

"I understand your grief, dear one," Mary assured her, squeezing her hand. "And I will be here to help you through it."

Tabitha looked away, blinking back another stubborn sheen of tears.

"Beloved," Mary said, her heart going out to the wounded young woman, "the evening you came to me as an orphaned child, you said something that impacted me greatly. In fact, I thought of it many times after losing Mark."

Tabitha looked at her, puzzled.

"You had endured so much, Tabitha, but you were such a brave little girl. With clear, honest eyes, you looked at me and said, 'My father taught me to make the most of what you've been given. That's the best I can do.' Do you remember that?"

She remembered it well. Swallowing hard, Tabitha's gaze dropped to her lap.

"Since then," Mary ventured softly, "you have learned something even more valuable—you've learned to trust your *heavenly* Father, making the most of what has—or has not—been given."

"Or *taken*?" Tabitha dared, her hazel-green eyes flashing angry fire.

"Yes," Mary said, very gently. "That, too."

Vehemently, Tabitha shook her head.

"My precious girl," Mary said, reaching across the table to take her hand once again, "where is that fighting spirit now?"

Raising flashing eyes, Tabitha said coldly, "It must have died with my husband."

"You know, we do serve the great God of the miraculous resurrection," Mary reminded her with a small smile. "He can rekindle that spirit of valor, beloved."

"Well then, perhaps He will resurrect Stephanos, too, while He's at it," Tabitha responded, a hard edge to her tone.

Surprisingly, Mary did not condemn her for her biting cynicism. Tabitha almost wished she had, for then perhaps her self-appointed guardian would leave her in peace. With a sympathetic smile, Mary offered Tabitha's hand a final squeeze before rising gracefully and busying herself about the small house.

Tabitha watched dully as Mary straightened the shelves, inspecting the dry goods supply. No doubt, Mary had already made a mental note about which provisions to replenish. A moment later, Mary retrieved a linen cloth and ladled fresh water into a basin, carrying it to the low table. Kneeling before Tabitha, she dipped the cloth in the basin, wringing out the excess water. Without a word, she then pressed the damp cloth to Tabitha's forehead, gently washing the girl's grimy face.

Cheeks burning in humiliation and shame, Tabitha wondered if this was how the disciples had felt when Jesus washed their feet. She knew her recent behavior toward Mary was childish, ungrateful, and petty, and yet Mary continued to serve her patiently, lovingly, without faltering.

Closing her eyes, Tabitha savored the coolness of the damp cloth against her flushed skin. It felt wonderful, though she was unable to voice it around the lump of tears forming in her throat.

"There," Mary said, pleased with her work. "Much better." Swishing the soiled cloth in the basin, she wrung it out once more before rising, emptying the basin in the slop bucket, and draping the cloth over a fraying rope line to dry.

A moment later, Mary returned with Tabitha's comb. Settling comfortably behind the younger widow, Mary separated Tabitha's thick tresses, smoothing them carefully and locating angry snarls with deft fingers.

Wincing, Tabitha bit her lower lip, determined not to yelp as Mary wielded the comb, expertly working through the tangles. Mary hummed quietly as she worked, a hymn Tabitha recognized from prayer services. After what felt like hours, the difficult task was finally completed.

"Ah, there now," Mary announced, setting aside the comb, satisfied with her accomplishment. With nimble fingers she tied Tabitha's thick honey-gold tresses into a practical braid. "How is that, dear one?"

"Thank you," Tabitha murmured quietly, embarrassed.

Gently squeezing Tabitha's tight shoulders, Mary rose with a soft rustling of fabric, disappearing behind the crimson curtain sectioning off the bedchamber. She returned a moment later with one of Tabitha's garments draped over her forearm.

"What is that for?" Tabitha asked, her eyes narrowing in suspicion.

"I've selected something for you to wear to the prayer service this evening," Mary stated matter-of-factly.

The prayer service? Tabitha nearly choked on a piece of bread. "What are you talking about, Mary?"

"Once you've finished your supper, I'd like you to accompany me to this evening's prayer service, Tabitha."

Tabitha stared at Mary in alarm.

"We have tried to grant you time and space to mourn, my dear girl," Mary said. "But it's not good for you to remain holed up in this dark house, all alone. The church is a place of healing, Tabitha. Please, don't shut your heart against those who love you and wish to help you."

"I'm not leaving this house," Tabitha protested stoutly, heedlessly tossing aside the rest of her bread.

"Yes, you are."

"No, I'm not."

Slowly lowering herself before her former maid, Mary took Tabitha by the shoulders, her gray eyes conveying her deep concern. "Tabitha, dear one, when is the last time you prayed?"

Stubbornly setting her jaw, Tabitha looked away.

"Tabitha, please listen to me," Mary implored, her gray eyes pleading. "I know what you're feeling right now—longing to drown out the entire world and simply retreat within yourself. But right now, Tabitha, you are being sifted."

Tabitha froze, her heart pounding madly in her chest.

You are being sifted.

Tabitha had told no one of the profound impression she experienced before her husband's death. Despite her deep inner struggle, Tabitha knew she must confess that Mary's choice of words was no accident, no mere coincidence.

You are being sifted.

"Please, come with me, dear one," Mary was saying, drawing Tabitha from her silent stupor. "Philip will be speaking this evening. He asked specifically for you."

Tabitha raised her head. Her husband's dearest friend had requested her presence? Why?

"Philip shares your grief, Tabitha, and he believes the Lord has a word of comfort for you tonight."

Pulse pounding heavily in her ears, Tabitha released a long, tremorous sigh. Composing herself with great effort, she met Mary's intense gaze and nodded her consent.

CHAPTER 40

Tabitha

Emerging at the top of a broad marble staircase, Tabitha's gaze swept furtively over the Upper Room, her heart constricting sharply in her chest. Everything looked so familiar and yet...different. Despite throngs of believers speaking in hushed, reverent tones, the vast, lamplit chamber felt empty, bereft, without Stephanos' assuring, powerful presence.

The first unexpected wave of agonizing sorrow hit Tabitha with the force of a tidal wave, with successive waves billowing over the young widow, threatening to overtake her. Placing her hand against a frescoed wall to steady herself, Tabitha closed her eyes, battling against intense grief.

I can't do this.

She just wasn't ready. How often had she entered this room on the arm of her beloved, so proud to be his wife? How often had she sat contentedly beside him on those benches, soaking up the wisdom of the apostles? Or watched with shining eyes, beaming, as her husband delivered an inspiring sermon from the platform?

"You're not alone, Tabitha." Drawing alongside her, Mary took Tabitha' arm, sensing her inner struggle. "I'm here for you, as are your brothers and sisters in Christ. Even more importantly, the Lord is here. He walks beside you everywhere you go, even when you are unaware."

Tabitha was about to turn and bolt down the stairs when a familiar voice called out to her.

"Tabitha, our dear sister. Thank God, you're here."

Reluctantly opening her eyes, Tabitha saw Philip approaching her with his lovely betrothed leaning on his arm. Releasing Philip's arm, Kelila hastened toward her friend, throwing her arms around her.

"Oh, Tabitha, how we've prayed for you! And how we've missed you, sister."

Blinking back tears, Tabitha woodenly accepted Kelila's exuberant embrace.

Pulling away, Kelila looked into Tabitha's clouded eyes. "How are you, Tabitha? How are you *really*?"

Staring at her own sandaled feet, Tabitha fought for composure. She knew these people loved her. Their sincere concern for her was touching, as well as a bit overwhelming. She wasn't quite sure how to respond.

"Thank you so much for coming, dear sister," Philip said warmly, joining Mary, Tabitha, and Kelila near the top of the stairs. "I'm so glad you're here. We've been worried for you."

"Tabitha!"

Spotting Tabitha, Candace emerged from a group of nearby women, enshrouding the young widow in an embrace only slightly less exuberant than her sister's. When Candace finally pulled away, her smooth cheeks were wet with tears.

"Praise God, it's an answer to prayer seeing your beautiful face here this evening," Candace crooned, tucking a wayward tress behind Tabitha's ear in a motherly fashion. "We've all been worried sick."

Tabitha couldn't speak. She didn't trust her own voice, for the pain welling up inside her chest greatly hindered her ability to do so.

"Shall we find a comfortable place to sit?" Mary suggested, sensing Tabitha's mounting anxiety.

"Of course," Candace said softly, her tone and features etched with understanding.

"We shall speak after service," Philip promised as Kelila nodded her wholehearted agreement.

Tabitha allowed Mary and Candace to guide her toward a bench near the platform, wishing they had chosen a seat on one of the back rows. As throngs of well-meaning believers approached her, offering their prayers and sincerest condolences, Tabitha somehow managed to nod in appreciation. At least, she thought she did. She felt strangely trapped in time, as if everything around her moved in syrupy slow motion while her own world stood still, having been driven to a violent, screeching halt.

Tabitha was deeply relieved when Philip finally approached the platform. Now the believers would have to remain seated. She appreciated their concern but hadn't the strength to conduct herself as they probably expected her to. Even forcing a smile felt like the greatest of hypocrisies, bordering on downright sacrilege. How could she possibly smile now, knowing that her husband had been cruelly ripped from this life? Never again would his masculine form emerge at the top of that staircase. Never again would he stand behind the pulpit, proclaiming the word of God with passion and charisma. Never again would he take her hand as the apostles led them in prayer, his head bowed toward her, their foreheads touching.

At least, not in this life. But even the promise of eternity felt hollow. Empty. So very far away.

Woodenly, Tabitha bowed her head as Philip offered the opening prayer, but her thoughts were elsewhere. Somehow, she managed to endure several hymns, her heart aching at the glaring absence of her husband's lusty baritone.

Despite the cheerful nature of the robust hymns, Tabitha sensed an almost tangible apprehension hovering over the gathering. Stephanos' untimely death had left a gaping hole not only in the leadership but also in the heart of the church.

It was evident the believers were utterly shaken.

When Philip began his address, Mary reached for Tabitha's hand. Accepting the strength Mary offered, Tabitha released a shaky breath, resigning herself to endure a lengthy, undesired sermon. Despite her lack of interest, Tabitha couldn't help but notice something entirely changed about Philip. The shy deacon's presence was both eye-catching and powerful, his countenance shining and utterly transformed. She was instantly reminded of the apostles' transformation after they had encountered the risen Jesus. The death of their beloved Rabbi had rendered them confused, cowardly, and utterly defeated. But their apprehension had vanished the moment their risen Lord appeared to them, and in its place, courage, strength, and determination prevailed.

What could have possibly affected Philip so dramatically, especially amidst this dark hour of the infant church's history? What had prompted such devout inner strength and stirring confidence?

As Philip offered a brief introduction, it became increasingly evident that he intended to speak about Stephanos' final moments.

Heart wrenching in her chest, Tabitha mentally calculated the distance from her current location on the bench to the nearest exit. Should she make a break for it, could she escape before a throng of concerned believers converged on her?

"I can't imagine how many of you must be feeling right now," Philip was saying, his soft brown eyes welling with genuine compassion. "Especially you, our beloved Tabitha," he added, his sympathetic gaze landing upon the young widow.

Chagrined, Tabitha's fists clenched instinctively at her sides. She felt more than saw the entire congregation's tender gaze upon her. Gritting her teeth, she attempted to nod in acknowledgment of Philip's kindness.

"I would be dishonest if I said I didn't struggle with this, at first," Philip confessed. Tabitha released her breath, thoroughly relieved when his unsettling gaze lifted from her, moving back over the assembly. "And it's obvious a spirit of fear and apprehension has settled over our congregation. But may I humbly point out that Stephanos, my best friend and close colleague, wouldn't want that. What's more—the Lord Himself doesn't want that. Has He given us a spirit of fear? No, our God has granted us a spirit of power and love and a sound mind—the same spirit possessed by our beloved brother Stephanos."

Brows furrowed, Tabitha's troubled gaze fell to her lap. She couldn't deny Philip's assessment about Stephanos. She knew beyond any doubt that he would urge them all to carry on with faith and confidence. Had he been able, he would have warned them against fear and doubt, reminding them to stand guard against the enemy's calculated advances.

Philip's exhortation was true enough; she couldn't argue with that. Perhaps those within the church would take courage, strengthened by Philip's address.

Tabitha, however, knew it was not courage which she lacked. No, she hadn't known a moment of fear since her husband's violent death. But had she known a steadily growing fury, beginning as a spark of anger that kindled, sputtered, and burned within her chest, now threatening to burst into raging flames.

A bit snidely, she wondered what Philip would have to say about that. He probably thought she was far too sweet, far too innocent and Christ-like, to harbor burning hatred against her husband's accusers. At times, even *she* was surprised by the direction her dark thoughts were taking.

Clenching her fists, Tabitha knew better than to express them before this gentle, pious gathering.

"The death of our dear brother seems cruel and unjust," Philip was saying, briefly capturing the brooding widow's attention. "But the Lord has shown me that our Stephanos was but the first of us to gain the greatest victory, the ultimate triumph. He has received the crown of everlasting life, and

Jesus Himself ushered him into His kingdom."

Tabitha glanced around, on edge, as the assembly resonated with softly spoken *amens*, accompanied by sniffles and quiet weeping.

"Before he was condemned, Stephanos delivered a powerful speech," Philip explained, his pained expression conveying the difficulty of his message. "Every listener was cut to the heart. But rather than acknowledging the error of their ways, both the mob and the Sanhedrin became dangerously hostile, rushing him and attempting to drag him out of the city."

Stiffening, Tabitha longed to plug her ears, drowning out the gory details regarding her husband's demise. She didn't want to hear this. And yet, some small part of her gently urged her to listen, to stay. Perhaps it was that still, small voice within— the one she had been squelching all week—pleading with her.

"The moment the mob laid hands on him, something happened—something that shook the mob so fiercely, many of them staggered back." Philip paused, blinking back tears as he attempted to swallow his grief.

Tabitha lifted her head, watching, spellbound, as Philip struggled to compose himself.

What happened? Whatever it was, it had deeply impacted the young deacon.

"Something like an invisible shock wave pounded through the gathering. That's the best way I know how to describe it," Philip managed, his eyes wet with tears. "But the power of it resonated through the marble hall, filling the entire assembly with dread. And then the Lord—yes, I said *the Lord*—

appeared to Stephanos!"

Tabitha gasped, unaware that her hand had flown to her mouth.

Stephanos had seen the resurrected Lord? There, in the Royal Stoa? Before the entire Sanhedrin? Before the very men desperate to end his life?

"Simon of Cyrene was with me when this happened and can also testify to these things," Philip continued in his practical way, nodding toward Simon, who was seated quietly beside his wife. "No doubt, he can describe it far better than I. And though none of us could see the Lord, there was absolutely no denying His presence. It was like a raging storm brewing over the heads of the great Sanhedrin."

The congregation rippled with murmurs of awe and amazement. Tabitha couldn't help but marvel, as well. If only she had been there. If only she, too, could have strengthened her husband in that fateful moment...

"Undaunted by the ferocity of the mob, Stephanos raised his arms heavenward, his gaze fixed overhead," Philip continued, lost in his own powerful narrative. "*'Look!'* he cried out, his entire countenance transformed like the shining face of Moses when he beheld God's awesome glory. *'I see the heavens opened and the Son of Man standing at the right hand of God!'* In that moment, friends, our brother *knew.* He knew our Lord Jesus had risen from His throne, arms outstretched to welcome His beloved saint, ushering him into His everlasting kingdom. Now shall we who remain weep and mourn because he was perfected before us?"

Lowering her head, Tabitha's tears fell onto her

lap. She felt Mary's strong arms around her but couldn't respond around the lump forming in her throat.

She could hardly believe that Jesus Himself had welcomed her husband, rising to usher him in with open arms and nail-scarred hands. What an unspeakable honor! Every believer knew that Jesus was seated at the right hand of God. That was no great revelation, for Jesus Himself had said it would be so. But their Savior had *stood* for Stephanos, rising from his magnificent throne—ready to *fight* for Stephanos, to *aid* him in his final mission, and—ultimately—to *receive* him into glory.

"And this, my dear brothers and sisters," Philip remonstrated, his earnest gaze traveling over the awestruck congregation, "is how each of us will also be received, if we stand firm and do not lose heart. Remember, Jesus warned us that *perilous times will come*. But He also said that *he who endures to the end shall be saved.*"

More quiet weeping, echoed by gently spoken, heartfelt *amens*, followed Philip's exhortation.

"Later, I found myself pondering the meaning of Stephanos' final address. Frankly, I was a bit perplexed," Philip admitted, absentmindedly stroking his beard. "His speech seemed to me a rather concise summary of the history of our people, but the Jews already know that subject by heart. Why had he chosen to expound upon a past they were already so familiar with? Only later did I recognize our brother's wisdom, for his powerful recounting bore a common theme, one we all must heed: *The righteous have long been persecuted by the wicked.* First, Stephanos spoke of Abraham and the trials he endured. From there, he mentioned righteous Joseph—sold into slavery by his own jealous brothers. He then touched on the captivity our ancestors endured in Egypt at the hand of a Pharaoh who'd forgotten all that Joseph had done for the Egyptian nation. Last, Stephanos reminded his audience of Moses, chosen by God but oft rejected by his own people. Now, do you see the theme woven throughout these various stories?"

Philip paused, allowing the magnitude of his discovery to impact the congregation.

"The righteous ones chosen by God are oft rejected and persecuted by wicked men," Philip declared, shaking his head in amazement. "It's no secret; we've seen it happen since the beginning of time. And not without cause, for the great deceiver has always sought to suppress and annihilate the truth, and this point in history is surely no exception."

A quiet murmur rippled through the congregation as the gravity of Philip's words sank in. Tabitha, too, was startled by the power of the deacon's instruction. She couldn't deny his logic, despite the stubborn rage lodged within her heart.

But Philip wasn't finished yet.

"As our brother, Stephanos, boldly proclaimed before the Sanhedrin: *'Which of the prophets did your fathers not persecute? And they killed those who foretold the coming of the Just One, of whom you now have become the betrayers and murderers, who have received the law by the direction of angels and have not kept it.'* This is when the people became outraged. Rather than accepting Stephanos' valid reproof and forsaking their stubborn unbelief, the people turned against our brother." Lowering his head, Philip allowed himself a moment to wrestle against memories he surely longed to forget. Once he had composed himself, he spoke with a sense of urgency. "Our dear brother, Stephanos, was not afraid, not for a moment. He went boldly to his death, his faith on full display. He walked in the footsteps of our Savior, laying down his life for the sake of the world. When the end had come, he said, *'Lord Jesus, receive my spirit.'* But his final words I will never forget: *'Lord, do not charge them with this sin.'*"

Oh, Stephanos. Tabitha's heart constricted in her chest. He didn't deserve to die. But the bodies of the blood-lusting mob should be scattered in the wasteland, rotting beneath a pile of dusty stones. Her entire being cried out against the injustice of it all.

"Stephanos' dying words, my brothers and sisters, are indeed words to live by," Philip continued softly. "Even in this, our brother emulated the life of our Savior, who willingly forgave His betrayers and murderers while still on the cross. And I can say with great assurance that our brother's unspeakable sacrifice will reap a harvest of blessings, for how can even the meanest of souls *not* be impacted by such pure, unrelenting love?"

Lifting her head, Tabitha glanced around in surprise, for the heavy shroud of fear and apprehension had visibly lifted. Was it simply her imagination, or did the candles and lamps burn just a bit brighter, rather like the countenances of those basking in the presence of God, finally comprehending Philip's profound spiritual teaching?

Perfect love casts out fear, the Apostle John

often proclaimed. Now, Tabitha couldn't help but agree with him. It was obvious Stephanos' undying love—which so vividly reflected their Savior's—had banished the gnawing fear tearing at the believers' hearts.

"In closing," Philip said, his eyes shining with hope as he gazed upon the courageous men and women seated before him, "I'd like to leave each of you with a powerful reminder. These are indeed dark days for the church as Satan comes against us with great wrath and fury, knowing he has little time. But what happens when you light a candle in a very dark room?" he asked candidly. "I'll tell you. Your eye is automatically drawn to that light. It stands out like a powerful beacon, appearing far brighter than it would in the daylight. So, too, shall our faith shine in this present darkness."

The assembly agreed softly with Philip, offering quiet *amens* and firm nods of encouragement.

"Even now, we must stand firm, shining brightly in this dark world. Brothers and sisters, let us now pray, asking the Lord to guide us in this holy endeavor."

Bowing her head along with the rest, Tabitha woodenly accepted Mary's hand on her right and Candace's on her left. She could almost feel their faith and strength flowing into her. The entire atmosphere of the Upper Room had shifted, for Philip's faith and confidence had bolstered their own.

Clenching her eyes tightly shut, Tabitha knew she should take heart, heeding Philip's powerful instruction, but how could she? How could she burn brightly amidst a dark and broken world when she had no light to give?

CHAPTER 41

Tabitha

"Have you considered my offer, Tabitha?"

Soul-weary, Tabitha managed to acknowledge Mary's question with a tired nod. Her mind felt like a muddle of confusion, and the sea of chattering believers buzzing about the Upper Room after the service only compounded her anxiety. Feeling angry and overwhelmed, she just wanted to go home.

I want Stephanos, she thought, sensing his absence more keenly than ever. *I want my husband.*

How strange it would be to leave this church meeting without him. She kept expecting him to emerge from the gathering, offering his arm as he flashed that broad smile she adored. But, no. That would never happen again. Not in this life.

From now on, she would travel home alone.

That is, *if* she continued attending. She hadn't made up her mind about that yet. Right now, these meetings were far too painful—merely an excruciating reminder that her beloved Stephanos was dead.

"And?" Mary prodded, very gently. "What have you decided?"

"I cannot leave my home, Mary," Tabitha responded more tersely than she intended. "But thank you for asking me to reside with you. That was very kind."

"I worry for you, Tabitha," Mary responded frankly. "I'm not sure it's wise for you to be alone right now."

"I'm fine."

"*Are* you?" Mary asked, gazing intently into her eyes.

Tabitha looked away. She felt as if Mary's perceptive gray eyes bore into her very soul.

"Tabitha?"

"I can't leave him, Mary."

"Do you speak of Stephanos?" Mary asked, her expression troubled.

"Yes," Tabitha responded curtly. "Who else?"

"Oh, beloved." Taking Tabitha's hands in her own, Mary studied the young widow intently. "Stephanos isn't in that house, Tabitha."

"But the memories I made with him are there," Tabitha replied stoutly. "His essence is there. His belongings are there. It's the home he made for us. I cannot leave."

"I understand," Mary assured her, deeply saddened. "But if you change your mind at any time, you know you have a home here with us, Tabitha."

"Thank you, Mary, but I won't be needing it. I'll be fine."

A cloaked figure slipped past them, gliding gracefully down the broad staircase.

With her husband's ruthless martyrdom fresh on

her mind, Tabitha made a swift decision, one she hoped she wouldn't regret. "I must go."

"Please, let me walk you home. It's getting late—"

"I'll be fine."

"Tabitha, please. If you must leave right now, allow me to send one of my guards to—"

"Mary, I said I'll be fine."

Mary studied the hurting young woman, inexplicably grieved. Tabitha had lost so much in her young life—mother, father, husband. Though Tabitha's anger was justified, it was not productive or helpful. In fact, if not properly dealt with, it had the frightening potential to destroy her—and her faith.

"We will talk later," Tabitha promised, sensing Mary's mounting concerns. "Please, don't worry about me."

Aggrieved, Mary watched as Tabitha slipped past her, disappearing into the depths as she descended the dim, lamplit stairway.

***

Brow furrowing in suspicion, Tabitha followed the cloaked woman down a confusing maze of backstreets and alleys. Dusk had settled over the ancient city, making it increasingly difficult to keep her eye on her target, who clearly didn't wish to be seen or known.

For far too long, the enigmatic stranger who called herself *Sarah* had been attending church meetings, cloaked in mystery and a telling silence. The brethren hadn't pried into the woman's life, background, or personal affairs, believing she would reveal herself—or her true motives—in time.

Now, after the brutal passing of her beloved husband, Tabitha's mercy and understanding toward the suspicious figure evaporated like the morning mist. Something wasn't right about Sarah, and Tabitha was determined to find out what it was. It was entirely possible the woman housed dangerous secrets—secrets capable of destroying more believers.

Tabitha refused to stand passively by. She refused to allow anyone to pose a threat against her loved ones, and she was prepared to take drastic measures to ensure the safety of her brothers and sisters.

The cloaked stranger reached the mouth of a dim alleyway just as the first glittering stars brushed across the evening sky. Tabitha suppressed a gasp as the woman gingerly approached an elaborate, heavily curtained litter bearing a royal crest. Standing at the edge of a paved road, four richly clad, brawny menservants awaited her arrival, daggers strapped on the belts at their waists.

As one of the men assisted the mysterious woman by taking her hand and helping her into the litter, she lowered the hood of her cloak, revealing an elaborate Greco-Roman hairstyle woven with sparkling gems.

Anger welled inside Tabitha, filling her with a reckless boldness. Stepping forth, Tabitha threw back her shoulders and shouted at the woman's graceful back before the men had opportunity to hoist the litter upon strong shoulders.

"That's a fancy litter for a lowly peasant woman."

The woman froze, halfway into the litter.

"Get out." Tabitha's tone mirrored the hard, uncompromising set of her jaw.

The menservant's hands instinctively flew to the hilts of their daggers. "How dare you speak thus!" one of them shouted, his eyes blazing protectively.

Unfazed, Tabitha met his fiery gaze. "And to whom is it I speak?" Eyes narrowing dangerously, her gaze came to rest upon the woman in the gilded litter. "Clearly, you're not who you say you are!"

One of the menservants approached Tabitha, his knuckles whitening around the hilt of his dagger.

"Wait!" Sarah cried, fluttering out of the litter in a graceful yet agitated manner. "Don't harm her!"

Tabitha glanced at the woman, surprised.

Drawing alongside her manservant, Sarah touched his tensed arm. "Please, allow me a moment to speak with this young woman."

The manservant's eyes flashed angry fire, and Tabitha was momentarily reminded of Zev.

"Please," Sarah commanded the manservant, clearly accustomed to giving orders. "I shall join you in a moment."

Bristling, the manservant turned and joined the servants near the litter.

Taking Tabitha's arm, Sarah drew the young widow further into the shadows.

"You are Tabitha, the widow of the courageous evangelist," the woman said, her dulcet tone laced with sympathy.

"I already know who *I* am," Tabitha nearly spat, protectiveness welling within her chest until she thought she would burst. "The real question is *who are you*? You're certainly no impoverished Jew named Sarah. Everything about you screams 'Roman.'"

Glancing around to ensure that they were alone,

the tall woman bent slightly to look Tabitha in the eyes. "I am Claudia Procula, the wife of Pontius Pilate, governor of the Judea province." Opening her cloak, the woman revealed a breathtaking Greco-Roman gown gathered at the shoulder with an elaborate golden pin.

Tabitha stared at the stately woman, open-mouthed.

"Perhaps now you can understand my discretion," the woman said quietly, lowering her gaze in something akin to shame.

"You were there when Jesus was crucified," Tabitha said accusingly, somehow recovering from her shock. "Your husband handed Him over on a silver platter, delivering Him to a bloodthirsty mob."

"You needn't remind me, dear Tabitha," Claudia Procula said, clenching her eyes as if attempting to ward off dreadful memories. "Everything changed that day."

"Meaning?" Tabitha prompted impatiently, her heart pounding heavily in her chest. She hadn't yet decided if this woman was an ally...or an enemy.

"The moment my husband surrendered your Messiah, something changed. He became a tormented soul, increasingly violent and brooding... as if a piece of his soul died with Jesus..." Lady Procula's voice trailed off, her lovely eyes troubled and strangely distant. "He frightens me, at times."

"And has he sent you to monitor our gatherings?" Tabitha demanded, her concerns mounting. "Does that explain your veiled presence?"

"Heavens, no," Lady Procula insisted, her bright eyes wide with horror. "My conscience wouldn't permit it."

"No?" Tabitha dared, arching a sardonic brow. "But blatant lies and misrepresentation haven't seemed to disturb you."

"I suppose I should have been more transparent," Lady Procula admitted, releasing a sigh of defeat. "I chose the name Sarah to represent myself because I didn't wish to be entirely dishonest."

"Because Sarah means *princess*?"

"Or *noblewoman*, I'm told," Lady Procula reminded her sheepishly. "That's what I am, after all—the wife of Pontius Pilate, a noblewoman."

"Why are you here, Lady Procula?"

"Please, call me Claudia. Or Procula. Whichever you prefer."

Tabitha stared at the noblewoman, aghast. Had she truly been granted the right to address the famed Lady Procula by name? Royal blood flowed through the veins of this dignified woman, and yet she humbly conversed with a former maidservant without putting on airs or demanding homage.

"You still haven't answered my question," Tabitha pointed out, annoyed that she was actually drawn to this regal woman. "Why are you here?"

"As I'm sure you understand, it isn't safe to reveal my identity," Lady Procula replied, buttoning her cloak with delicate fingers. "My husband would never permit me to attend church meetings. If he ever discovered my secret..." Lady Procula shuddered, shaking her regal head in dismay. "One careless slip of the tongue could result in utter devastation—not only for myself, but for the believers, as well. My husband has become fanatical in his hatred toward both Jews and followers of the Way. How might Pontius Pilate retaliate if he thought his own wife was deceived by this new sect?"

"Your presence has placed all of us in danger," Tabitha hissed angrily, tempted to take the woman by the shoulders and shake her until her teeth rattled.

"No, no," Lady Procula insisted, her graceful features betraying great anguish. "Can't you see? If my identity remains a secret, then the church remains protected."

"For their sake, I hope you're right," Tabitha breathed, shaking her head in disbelief. "Tell me, why do you insist upon attending our meetings?"

"It began as a simple quest for truth," Lady Procula admitted, lowering her regal gaze.

"And then?"

"Then…it became so much more," the noblewoman admitted quietly, her soft eyes glistening with tears.

"So then, is it safe to assume you are now a believer?" Tabitha demanded bluntly.

Lifting luminous eyes to Tabitha's, Lady Procula responded without hesitation, a slight catch in her voice. "After all that has happened, how couldn't I be?"

CHAPTER 42

Tabitha

"The cloaked woman is Lady Procula, the wife of Pontius Pilate?" Standing in the empty lamplit reception hall, Mary stared at Tabitha with round eyes. Excepting Mary's nephew by marriage, Simon Peter, the believers had departed from the grand villa, returning to their own homes.

Tabitha hadn't intended to return to Mary's after uncovering Lady Procula's identity. But she sensed that Mary should be aware of her shocking discovery.

"You're sure about this?" Simon Peter demanded, his arms folded across his chest, his dark eyes glittering in agitation.

"I'm absolutely certain," Tabitha responded stoutly.

"I never could have imagined…" Mary exclaimed, shaking her head in amazement. "Praise God she has accepted the truth."

"Or so she says," Tabitha put in cynically.

"I have spoken with her on many occasions," Mary said quietly. "I believe she is genuine."

"We'd better hope and pray that she is," Simon Peter asserted, deeply unsettled. "This woman has the power to destroy us, Mary."

"No," Mary said firmly, unbending. "God is our defender. What is one woman against the might and power of God?"

"I don't like it," Peter admitted, shaking his head.

"God is at work in this," Mary insisted calmly. "We can trust that."

"So what's our course of action?" Peter asked, his dark eyes shifting in agitation.

"I imagine we should pray about that first," Mary reminded him with a gentle smile. "Will you alert the apostles about this, Peter?"

"Of course."

"Unless the Lord reveals otherwise, let's protect Lady Procula's secret for now," Mary decided softly. "She could be in grave danger, as her husband is a ruthless man. Quite frankly, I admire her courage."

Grudgingly, Tabitha had to agree with Mary's assessment. Lady Procula had risked much in her pursuit of the truth.

Tabitha could only hope the believers wouldn't pay for the fine lady's courage with their lives.

***

Mary

Seated before her vanity in the soft, flickering lamplight, Mary's slender fingers twisted her thick, waist-length tresses into a simple braid. Scarcely aware of the practiced movements of her own nimble fingers, Mary remained lost in thought, contemplating Tabitha's shocking discovery.

To think—all this time, she had been hosting the wife of one of the most powerful men in Judea! She had known the cloaked woman harbored secrets, but she never could have guessed the extent of them! She supposed that explained Lady Procula's unvarying church attendance during the festival seasons, as Pontius Pilate traveled to Jerusalem to keep the peace on such occasions.

Perhaps she should have made the connection, after all.

Sighing wearily, Mary tied the end of her long braid, gazing into the gilded mirror. She was reminded of similar evenings in years' past, when her husband, Mark, had drawn behind her chair, placing both strong hands on her shoulders and stooping to kiss the top of her dark head.

Years after his unexpected passing, Mary still missed him acutely, aching for his warm smile, his quiet confidence, and the strength of his arms.

Tabitha's recent loss had only sharpened Mary's awareness of her own widowhood, flooding her mind with bittersweet memories. How her heart went out to her dear Tabitha! How she longed to banish the girl's pain, to ease her throbbing wounds. If only she could truthfully assure poor Tabitha that the heart-rending pain would soon vanish, that someday all would be well again.

But such promises were untrue. The pain would always be there, a gnawing reminder of unspeakable loss. True, time—and prayer—would eventually ease and dull the pain's burning intensity. But there would always be moments—moments like these—when fresh floods of sorrow poured over one's entire being, reminding them of what could have been, and yet would never be.

But praise God for the hope of the resurrection! Despite the ache of loss, Mary knew the Lord would make everything right when He returned. He would restore all that had been lost. In Him, there was hope and joy and peace amidst the greatest pains.

Precious Lord Jesus, thank You for bearing these burdens with us, Mary prayed, gazing intently at her own dim reflection. *You, too, are acquainted with grief. You know the sting of loss. You sympathize with our hurts, walking beside us amidst our suffering. You will never leave us alone in it.*

Smiling softly, Mary wondered if she looked any older than she had when her husband had passed. Close friends insisted she was still a beautiful woman with striking, exotic features. Mark had prized her beauty, though she knew her character had been even more important to him.

"My lady."

Mary started, jarred by the abrupt masculine voice coming from the doorway. Glancing over her shoulder, her heart skipped a beat at the unexpected sight of Zev, the captain of the household guard, standing upon the threshold of her bedchamber. He stared at her with avid intensity, something burning in his steady gaze that she couldn't quite decipher.

"Something has happened." Heart pounding in her chest, Mary turned in her chair. Zev's shocking presence warned her that something was terribly wrong. *Oh, dear God! Not Tabitha!*

Sensing his lady's mounting panic, Zev held up

a steadying hand. "Your maid arrived home safely, escorted by an armed household guard as you requested."

"Oh, thank God." Drawing a steadying breath, Mary brushed her forehead with cool fingertips. Her own skin felt clammy beneath her touch. "What is it, then?" Perhaps she didn't wish to know. She prayed that whatever had instigated Zev's unprecedented visit wasn't as serious as his presence entailed.

"I must speak with you—alone."

Apprehension rising, Mary's luminous gray eyes tracked Zev's agitated movements as he stepped boldly into her elegant chamber. Suddenly aware of her uncovered head and gauzy nightgown, Mary's bronzed complexion flamed with embarrassment. Her menservants knew better than to approach her here, alone. The only man she had ever been alone with in this room was her husband, Mark.

Her guard shouldn't be In her bedchamber, not for any reason.

"Zev, you shouldn't be here." Rising in concern, Mary glanced about for a robe or covering. Her skin prickled with a strange sense of dread.

"On the contrary, my lady, it is *you* who shouldn't be here."

"I don't understand." This was *her* bedchamber, after all! Stunned by his insolence, Mary stood rooted in place, her lips parted in surprise.

"Then allow me to make it perfectly clear for you, my lady." Zev drew before her, his muscled form towering over her and radiating with raw, masculine power. "You are not safe here."

Mary was beginning to wonder about that herself. Zev was completely out of line, approaching her at night in her bedchamber. What, exactly, were his intentions?

"What do you mean, *I'm not safe*?" Mary managed shakily, stepping back to place some distance between them.

"You are an intelligent, capable woman," Zev said, instantly closing the distance with two large strides. "Surely you know what is coming."

"Tell me," Mary replied, striving for calm.

"The Jews, the religious leaders, even the Romans—they're coming for you," Zev's chiseled features appeared even more uncompromising in the glowing lamplight. "They won't allow this cult to overrun their city. They've already murdered one of your leaders. You may very well be next."

"I doubt they will come after a woman," Mary pointed out.

"You don't know that."

"Zev, I appreciate your concern," Mary assured him, wishing he hadn't planted himself between her and the door, her only escape route. "But this...this... *meeting* is inappropriate. Please, let's step out—"

"Mary, listen to me."

Mary froze, disturbed by his familiar use of her given name. He spoke her name like a tender caress.

"Zev, please." Unnerved, Mary attempted to go around him.

"Wait." Zev gripped her bare arm, staring down at her with burning intensity. Heart pounding, Mary felt the heat of his fingertips pressing into her skin. "Listen to what I have to say."

"Please, release my arm—"

"Not until you've heard me out."

Mary stared at her guard, wide-eyed and speechless. With one snap of her fingers, she could have him arrested for such inexcusable boldness.

Had he gone utterly mad?

"This is not the time or place for a hidden conference, and I am not properly attired—" she said tersely, her eyes falling upon the robe draped upon the bed. Could she reach it?

"You're beautiful," Zev breathed, allowing himself a bold perusal of her face and form. "You needn't cover yourself for my sake."

Horrified, Mary shook her arm free from his grasp.

"Come away with me," Zev declared, taking her hands captive.

"Zev!" Attempting to jerk free of his grasp, Mary gazed up at him imploringly. His grip was stronger than iron.

"You're not safe here, at least not now. If you refuse to relinquish this stubborn faith of yours, then you must flee to safety—at least until all this blows over."

"It won't," Mary declared, looking him squarely in the face. "This persecution will only increase, Zev. But I will not leave Jerusalem unless the Lord directs me otherwise. I must stand firm despite opposition."

"Have you ever considered that perhaps this *is* the Lord's direction, Mary?" Zev demanded, his eyes hardening. "I can protect you. Let me take you to safety."

"Even if I wished to leave, that would be entirely inappropriate," Mary reminded him, peeved.

"Not if I make you my wife."

Staggered by his proclamation, Mary stared at

him in disbelief. *His wife!* Why, it was unthinkable! Heart pounding, she prayed desperately for the Lord's wisdom in dealing with this impossible man.

"I want you for my wife, Mary. Surely you know that." Steadying her, Zev gazed into her eyes, his own filling with tender longing. "I've waited for you all these years, longer than any man should wait for a woman." Cupping her face in one strong hand, Zev's dark eyes searched hers.

Mary had never seen her hardened guard as he now appeared, his heart bared before her, his eyes beseeching her to acquiesce. Shaken, Mary realized that his manly features were almost handsome in the soft glow of the lamps, his typically fierce gaze caressing the gentle curves of her face.

"Marry me," Zev put in persuasively, growing even bolder in his perusal. "I swear, I'll make you the happiest woman alive."

Zev's ardor was like a dash of cold water. In rising panic, Mary realized he still held her hands captive. "Release me, Zev. Release me now!"

"Stop fighting this, Mary. You want this, too. I know you do." Zev leaned in close despite her resistance, intending to kiss her.

"Stop!" Mary cried, breaking free from his grasp and shattering the serenity of her peaceful chamber.

Zev froze as if he'd been struck, his fists clenching dangerously at his sides as his eyes narrowed in rising fury.

"You need to go. Now." Trembling, Mary reached for her bedpost to steady herself.

For one long moment, the two measured each other from a distance, clearly testing the grit of the other.

Sensing Mary's unwavering conviction, Zev clenched his jaw, outraged. "You are a foolish woman."

"Leave," Mary commanded, ready to summon help if necessary.

Turning to depart, Zev paused beneath the threshold, his dark eyes conveying his disdain. Coldly, he cast a final remark over his broad shoulder. "Have you rejected my proposal because I'm a household guard and you are a lady of means?"

"You know me better than that, Zev," Mary shot back, struggling to maintain her composure. "I have denied your proposal because the Lord commands us not to be unequally yoked. Even entertaining the idea of marrying an unbeliever would displease God."

"This dead Rabbi to whom you've pledged undying loyalty—can He take you in His arms and sweep you off your feet, Mary?" Zev scoffed, arching a sardonic brow. "Can He make you feel alive in every sense of the word? Can He fill your entire being with wild sensations and desperate longing?"

Mary stared at the guard, openmouthed and speechless.

"When you crawl into that bed tonight lonely and cold, just remember—*you* denied yourself the pleasure of a man's adoration and unwavering devotion," Zev said through clenched teeth. "May the Christ you serve so faithfully take pleasure in your stubborn piety."

Mary watched in horror as Zev turned sharply on his heel, stalking out the door. Crumpling onto the canopy bed, she wrapped her arms tightly about her trembling form, fighting for composure.

Zev's brash proposal had shaken her to her very core.

Her heart broke anew for the man she once trusted with her life, for he had hardened himself against his only hope of salvation. Would her refusal to marry him only further harden Zev's heart against the truth? Gazing heavenward, Mary's eyes glistened with unshed tears.

Lord God, what am I to do with him now?

CHAPTER 43

Tabitha

Jarred by a slight rap at the door, Tabitha raised list-less eyes toward the threshold. She knew it wasn't Mary on the other side of the door since her former mistress had already paid her a visit. Candace, Kelila, and many of the church women also visited regularly, dropping off freshly baked bread and steaming pots of food. Most of it often remained untouched, left to congeal on the low wooden table.

Sighing, Tabitha pulled herself up from her mat, shoving aside her clay mug of lukewarm water. Why couldn't everyone just leave her alone? Couldn't they see she didn't wish to be disturbed?

Swinging open the door with a less-than-hospi-table expression, Tabitha's eyes widened in surprise. "Dorian?"

Shifting uncomfortably, the very last person Tabitha had expected to see cleared his throat in discomfiture. "May I have a word with you?"

Blankly staring, Tabitha eventually found her

tongue. "Of course," she managed, a dull ache grasping her chest at the sight of Stephanos' former tutor and friend. It seemed as if everything in her life invited piercing memories. Would these excruciating reminders ever cease?

"Please, come in." Suddenly remembering her manners, Tabitha swung the door open a bit wider.

"It wouldn't be proper," Dorian responded in his crisp, even tone. "But thank you, my lady, nonetheless."

"Oh, I suppose it wouldn't," Tabitha murmured, nettled. In the past, she had gladly invited men into her home, as Stephanos had been present, as well. There was nothing improper about that. But now... now she was alone, without a chaperone, guardian, or husband.

She supposed Dorian was right. Her agitation was cut short when Dorian spoke again, his tone laced with urgency.

"My lady, there is something you must know."

Incredulous, Tabitha gaped at the stoic Dorian, her avid curiosity slowly overtaking her dismay. The stony-faced manservant had spoken more words in these few short minutes than he had in all the months she had known him.

Oh, good heavens! She thought, her heart racing in near panic. *What if Amal and Daphne have sent Dorian to summon me?* She couldn't possibly face them now! She wasn't ready. How could she be a witness to them when her own faith had been shaken to its core? She just couldn't see them, not now.

Maybe not ever.

"My master and my lady have not been informed of this visit," Dorian said staidly, laying her fears to rest. "I came because—as previously mentioned—there is something you must know."

Sensing the urgency in Dorian's crisp address, Tabitha slipped out the door, stepping gingerly into the courtyard. Closing the protesting door behind her, she squinted against the glaring afternoon sunlight. Ensconced within the dimly lit house for days on end, the brightness was shocking, nearly unbearable.

Everyone practicing evil hates the light and does not come to the light, lest his deeds should be exposed... Cringing inwardly, Tabitha dismissed the Savior's remembered admonition as inconsequential. After all, *she* wasn't practicing evil...was she?

True, her faith was battered, her hope destroyed. She preferred to withdraw deep within the shadows of her dim, lonely house. There, she was free to nurse her bitterness, fanning the steadily building flames of hatred and animosity she harbored against her husband's killers. There, she evaded her duty to console others—brothers and sisters also deeply grieved by Stephanos' untimely death. There, she was relieved of her promise to Stephanos—to carry on with the Lord's mission, whatever the cost.

Defensive, Tabitha engaged in yet another silent battle with her own contrary thoughts. How was *she* supposed to console others when her own heart had been torn to shreds? How was she to strengthen the faith of others when God had allowed the unthinkable to transpire in her own life?

Fleetingly, she thought of the small child Stephanos had entrusted to her care. She hadn't even bothered asking Mary about the little girl. Perhaps Luke, the kind physician, had successfully identified the child. Perhaps she'd been returned to her errant mother.

If the poor woman hadn't already succumbed to her wasting illness.

Detesting the guilt sweeping over her in tidal waves, Tabitha refused to be goaded by...*what?* Her conscience? Surely not the Holy Spirit! How could the Lord possibly accuse her now amidst her great anguish and unspeakable grief?

Do not despite the chastening of the Lord, nor detest His correction; for whom the Lord loves He corrects, just as a father the son in whom he delights...

Come now! Tabitha thought, irked beyond measure as the ancient proverb surfaced in her heart. What did Solomon know about this kind of grief, anyway? The man had everything he could possibly want!

No, she refused to be condemned for her raging emotions. Her feelings were perfectly natural, given the circumstances! Surely her actions—or lack thereof—were understandable and entirely justifiable...weren't they? Hers was a righteous anger kindling against depravity of the highest degree.

"My lady, are you all right?"

Deeply involved in her own silent argument, Tabitha had completely forgotten about the fact that she stood in the afternoon sunlight with the Greek manservant! Jarred by his officious inquiry, Tabitha squinted against the sunlight to meet his solicitous gaze.

"My lady?"

"You needn't call me that," Tabitha managed a bit testily, massaging her aching temples. "I have no power over you. I was a servant, as well, before I married Stephanos." Voice catching slightly, Tabitha looked away. First, she had been a daughter. After her parents' violent demise, she had become an orphan, then a maidservant, and eventually—wonder of wonders—a wife!

But what was she *now*? Just one more poverty-stricken widow among thousands in this merciless, godforsaken city.

"You said you must tell me something important." Tabitha sighed, unsettled by Dorian's unblinking stare. "I hope Amal and Daphne are well."

"As well as can be expected," Dorian replied, his expressionless eyes betraying the slightest flicker of sympathy.

"Will they be returning to Greece soon?" she asked wearily.

"I suppose, after their time of mourning," Dorian responded politely.

"I see."

"Pardon my inexcusable boldness, my lady," Dorian said formally, clearing his throat once more. "But you don't seem well."

Tabitha stared at him in dismay. Her husband—the light and love of her life—had been murdered in cold blood and violently stripped from her! Her entire world had been shattered, crashing down around her ears! What, exactly, did he expect from her? A song of joy? A happy dance?

"That is to be expected, naturally," Dorian plunged ahead, clearly unaccustomed to such frank conversation. "But—I beg your pardon, miss—you seem to have lost more than a husband. You seem to have lost faith, as well."

Tabitha stared up at the solemn Dorian, utterly dumbfounded. What did a Gentile manservant know about *faith*? He had some nerve!

"Please, my lady, don't lose heart. Your husband possessed a way about him, as did you—it was disarming."

Shaken from her dismay, Tabitha glanced up at the tall, richly clad manservant through a sheen of tears.

"You must know, my lady, my young master's death—it was not in vain."

Stunned, Tabitha dashed at her tears. Surely he didn't mean...

"I was there at the synagogue that day."

"What?" Tabitha whispered, shocked. "But...but why?"

"Your husband invited me, my lady. I heard his final message and witnessed his dying words. I was shaken by it, utterly shaken."

Dropping her gaze, Tabitha's tears fell from her eyes, splattering upon the sunbaked tiles below her feet.

"I've known nothing but service my entire life, you see," Dorian explained, his sober eyes begging her to understand. "Only then, when my young master willingly laid down his own life for the life of the world, did I realize the living God has been preparing me for a far greater purpose all along—to serve Him by serving others."

"Does your master know?" Tabitha managed through her tears.

"Not yet," Dorian confessed. "He is drowning in something far worse than grief, my lady—*regret*. Perhaps your God will grant me the wisdom to help him."

Tabitha wasn't the least bit moved by Amal's regret. He deserved to suffer after treating his son with such contempt!

"It must have been difficult breaking the news to Amal and Daphne." Tabitha sighed, feeling sorrier for the manservant than for the bereaved parents.

"Your former mistress, Mary, found them first," Dorian admitted, his gaze dropping to his expensive leather sandals. "I roamed the city for hours, pondering all that I had seen. I must confess, I didn't know how to tell my master and my lady about their son's death. Your friend did me a great kindness by finding them that day. Despite her gripping anguish, she bore herself with great strength, going to great lengths to comfort my master and lady."

Despite her gripping anguish... Gaze dropping in shame, Tabitha realized she hadn't once considered how her husband's death must have impacted Mary. She had loved Stephanos like a son, working alongside him each day in business and in the Lord's work. She, too, must be grieving—though one would never know.

What a pillar of strength Mary proved to be time and time again! If only she, Tabitha, could boast Mary's relentless tenacity.

"Thank you for coming to me with this," Tabitha said quietly, torn between relief regarding Dorian's newfound salvation and sorrow over her great loss. Couldn't Dorian have found the Way without Stephanos having to die? Why such drastic measures? Why such a great price?

"I hope this brings you some form of comfort," Dorian offered quietly. "Your husband was zealous for the salvation of souls."

Too zealous, Tabitha thought, aching inside.

"I have spoken with your husband's good friend, a man called Philip. He has agreed to mentor me in the way of salvation."

Nodding woodenly, Tabitha was relieved that Dorian had possessed the foresight to seek guidance in his new faith. In her present state, she wouldn't have thought to suggest it.

"I suppose I must be going now," Dorian said, formal to the last. "Good day, my lady." Offering a polite bow, Dorian swept his Roman cape over one shoulder before turning on his heel and letting himself out the gate.

Leaning against the doorpost, Tabitha watched him go, feeling numb inside. She knew she should be rejoicing with the angels in Heaven over the repentance of another lost soul. With tears burning her eyes, Tabitha battled against swelling grief. As Dorian had aptly stated, Stephanos had not died in vain.

But even that fact brought little comfort.

CHAPTER 44

Mary

Releasing a low whistle, Barnabas leaned back in his throne-like chair, his abundant sea of light brown curls bobbing as he shook his head. "I can see your predicament, dear sister."

Pausing before an impressive arched window lined with elegant tiles, Mary brushed aside the sheer Babylonian tapestry fluttering in the dry afternoon breeze, observing the bustling Upper City street beyond her brother's office window.

"You say this happened just last night?" Barnabas pressed, folding large hands upon his sprawling desk.

"Yes," Mary admitted, her cheeks flaming in mortification. "I knew Zev harbored fond feelings toward me, but I never imagined..." her voice trailed off in embarrassment. "But now...now I'm not sure what to do with him."

"I see," Barnabas responded, his tone tinged with genuine understanding.

"My initial impulse is to release him from my employ." Mary sighed, turning around to face her brother. "He has placed me in a dreadfully uncomfortable position."

"But you're concerned for his salvation," Barnabas surmised, gesturing toward the upholstered chair across from his ornate desk.

"Yes," Mary admitted, gracefully lowering herself onto the chair her brother had indicated.

"You did well, Mary, to decline his proposal," Barnabas assured her. "Our Lord is clear in His command—we are not to be unequally yoked. It is a terrible mistake to marry someone hoping to change them or win them to Christ. That rarely happens."

"I agree," Mary said with great feeling. "Even so, I fear I may have forever closed his heart to the truth."

"You are not responsible for Zev's choices, Mary," Barnabas reminded her. "But I do see your point. You fear that firing your guard will be a poor witness, possibly pushing him even further from the truth."

"Exactly," Mary said, thankful for her brother's practical, affirming presence. "I also fear that his emotions have rendered him incapable of his position. He is an excellent guard, but his ever-present anger gets the best of him. And my refusal to marry him only complicates matters."

"Have you prayed about this?"

"Without ceasing," Mary admitted. She had been so consumed in prayer that she'd hardly slept.

"May I ask you a very personal question, dear sister?"

"Of course," Mary assured him, somewhat perplexed.

Shifting a bit uncomfortably in his chair, Barnabas leaned forward, his soft brown eyes locking with hers. "Are you attracted to him?"

"To *Zev*?" Mary gasped, appalled. "Heavens, no!"

"Are you sure?"

"Of course I'm sure!" Stunned and flustered, Mary stared at her brother in protest.

"You needn't look so appalled," Barnabas grinned, releasing a good-natured chuckle. "It's perfectly natural for a woman to be attracted to a man, especially one who has diligently guarded her family for over a decade."

"But *Zev*?" Mary declared, peeved. "*Really*, Barnabas!"

"I only ask because I need to know all the facts before doling out advice," Barnabas explained in his practical way. "I wouldn't wish to offer any counsel that might place my sister in the way of temptation. If you are even remotely attracted to this guard, it might be wise to part ways."

Blushing deeply, Mary quickly stilled her twisting hands in her lap. She couldn't help but recall the ardor in Zev's dark eyes, the passionate promise in his husky voice. His powerful build and fierce persona might prove alluring to some women. But to *her*? Not only was she dedicated to the memory of her late husband, but she was entirely committed to the Lord. She hadn't the least desire to stray from His will, nor any intention of being sidetracked by an inappropriate suitor!

"First," Barnabas said, drawing Mary from her brooding reverie, "I recommend we earnestly seek the Lord in this matter. I will pray in agreement with you, Sister."

"Thank you, my brother," Mary said earnestly. "I

knew you would."

"In the meantime, I would set some firm boundaries in place," Barnabas continued in his practical way. "Didn't you say your maid is currently tending a lost child?"

"Yes," Mary answered. "Rhoda is quite taken with the little one. She hasn't let her out of her sight."

"Move both of them into your sleeping quarters," Barnabas wisely suggested. "Your staff won't think anything of it. They all know you are a hopeless mother hen."

"That's an excellent idea," Mary agreed, chuckling her amusement. "And my maidservant will provide additional accountability."

"Yes," Barnabas replied. "Until you've reached a decision concerning your guard, carefully avoid compromising situations. Keep attendants nearby at all times."

"Thank you for your wise counsel, Barnabas." Mary smiled, relieved. "I will do as you say."

***

Zev

"Another." Slamming down his clay mug, Zev's flashing eyes dared the tavernkeeper to deny his request.

Measuring the guard's powerful form, the silent attendant reached for the empty mug.

Once the vessel had been refilled and placed—with some reluctance—before him, Zev raised it to his lips, threw back his head, and drained it in one fluid motion. Slamming the mug down along with several coins, he shot a dark stare toward the keeper of the bar before sliding off the rickety wooden stool and roughly shouldering his way through the hordes of disreputable patrons within the seedy establishment.

Annoyed, Zev banged open a dilapidated wooden door, slipping into a cobblestoned court now cast in dark shadows and hazy torchlight. Contrary to its elusive promise, strong drink had done little to numb his rising passions. His rage had been steadily growing, seething just beneath the surface, since Mary's lofty refusal of marriage the previous night.

Clenching his teeth, Zev recalled her scathing rejection: *I have denied your proposal because the Lord commands us not to be unequally yoked. Even entertaining the idea of marrying an unbeliever would displease God.*

Somehow possessing the sense to assign another guard to his post, Zev had stormed off after the humiliating encounter, intending never to return. Even now, he stood by his rash decision. If Mary was too dense to recognize what she had in him, then she didn't deserve him. Not as a lover. Not as a guard. Not even as an old family friend.

Had she even bothered inquiring about his absence? Had she even noticed? Did she even care?

Shaking his head in fury, Zev's lips formed a thin, grim line as he stole through the decrepit outer court, passing beneath a crumbling stone archway with flickering torches mounted upon either side. Eager patrons hurrying to enter the establishment slipped nervously past him, his dark countenance warning them to keep their distance.

For all Mary's prestigious head knowledge, fancy

learning, and profound business acumen, his lady was a fool. He'd offered her his heart on a silver platter, and she'd carved it up like a roasted pheasant on a feast day.

Dark eyes narrowing in fierce indignation, Zev ran a hand through his closely cropped hair and down the back of his neck. Perhaps *he* was the fool for baring his heart and soul before that self-righteous shrew.

"*Shalom.*"

Halting just beyond the crumbling archway, Zev's body tensed in warning as a heavily cloaked figure emerged from the shadows of a crumbling stone colonnade.

Cocking his head to one side, Zev's hand instinctively came to rest upon his dagger.

"Ah, there's no need for that."

The voice sounded vaguely familiar—masculine, young but seasoned. Full of purpose, rather like his long, determined strides.

Grimly, Zev watched as the mysterious figure drew before him, remaining partially hidden in contrasting shadows. Throwing back his hood, the stranger's hardened features were somewhat illuminated by the burning torches mounted behind the wary guard. His expression was veiled, enigmatic.

Saul of Tarsus.

"Fancy meeting you here—on this side of town Zev smirked, still on guard. Unlike his religious peers, Saul was burly and strongly built, an entirely different breed. Somewhat uneasy, Zev observed that his stance and bearing resonated with carefully restrained power. "I hardly recognized you without your prayer boxes and all those lovely little tassels."

Saul's dark eyes hardened along with his firm jawline.

"What do you want, Pharisee?" Zev spat out, his tone rancid with condescension.

Surprisingly, the gravity of Saul's mission trumped his pride, for he responded with a faint, predacious smile. "You are the captain of the guard posted at the villa belonging to one Mary of Jerusalem, yes?"

"Go on." Zev arched a sardonic brow, amused at the direction this conversation was taking. "Tell me what you want."

"I have a proposition for you."

Ripe for the plucking after his fallout with Mary, Zev eyed the holy man with suspicion...and growing interest. His hard mouth tipped slightly as he responded without hesitation.

"I'm listening."

CHAPTER 45

Tabitha

Tabitha awakened with a start.

Heart furiously pounding, she sat up on her sleeping pallet, her clammy skin breaking out in a miserable cold sweat.

Another nightmare.

The dreams always came upon her in the dead of night, so dreadful, so *real*. Always, she heard her husband's anguished groans, the ungodly roar of a depraved, bloodthirsty mob, the deep, throaty laughter of a darker presence, gloating in satisfaction...

Breathing rapidly, Tabitha drew her blanket tightly about her trembling form. Apart from her pounding heart, all was quiet, all was still. Silver moonlight streamed through the latticework, slanting across the hard-packed floor in fascinating geometrical patterns. One lone oil lamp flickered dimly upon a low table near her sleeping place. Everything was as it should be. Even so, fear and rage unlike anything Tabitha had ever experienced welled up inside her, urging her to vent her malice, to avenge her husband's unmerited demise.

When is the last time you prayed?

Mary's honest inquiry sharply surfaced in her mind, unwanted and unbidden. Shaking her head fiercely, Tabitha buried her face in the soft folds of her blanket. How could she pray when God had turned a deaf ear to the deepest prayer of her heart? How could she trust that He had her best interest in mind after all she'd been through, after all He'd willingly *allowed* her to go through? She couldn't help but wonder if He even cared about her at all.

What I am doing you do not understand now, but you will know after this.

Slowly lifting her tear-stained face, Tabitha contemplated the gentle promise whispering to her heart: Jesus' promise to His disciples in the Upper Room the night of His arrest.

"How can I *ever* understand this?" Tabitha whispered, wondering why she even bothered seeking answers when there was no comfort to be had. "How could You let this happen? I thought You were in control. How could You give the enemy free rein? *How could You?*"

Let not your heart be troubled; you believe in God, believe also in Me.

"But how can I believe You, Lord, when You have taken the most precious thing in my life?" Tabitha argued, somewhat relieved that the still small voice remained. "What did Stephanos do to deserve that, Lord? Why did You take him? Why?"

In My Father's house are many mansions; if it were not so, I would have told you. I have prepared

a place for him, beloved. And I have prepared a place for you.

But I wasn't ready to lose him. Eyes welling with tears, Tabitha clutched at her heart in anguish. *I need him here. I need him now. My world is empty without him, Lord!*

This world is not your home.

Then take me from it, as You did my husband! Tabitha's heart cried, overcome with grief. *Take me now, God! I don't want to be here anymore. I don't want to be here without him!* Tabitha waited, half expecting God to strike her dead—if not in answer to her request, then to punish her unspeakable insolence!

Instead, the gentlest of breezes wafted through the house, whispering against her hot, tear-streaked face.

I will come again and receive you to Myself; that where I am, there you may be also.

"I want to go now," Tabitha whispered, dashing angrily at her tears.

Be strong, beloved. You know the way.

Catching her breath, Tabitha wrestled against her anger and doubts. She couldn't deny the Lord's presence—even here, even now. But she couldn't trust Christ's love, not anymore. She knew better than to voice or even silently ponder such irreverent thoughts, and she wouldn't dare utter her suspicions before the Lord. She didn't wish to contemplate the dire consequences should she be so brash.

But she should have known that the Lord knew her heart, inside and out. She needn't voice her brooding thoughts aloud, for He already knew them, every single one of them.

I have inscribed you on the palms of My hands,
My daughter. Look at My hands. Look at My feet.

Choking back a sob, Tabitha buried her face in trembling hands.

If ever you doubt My love for you, remember
the cross, beloved.

Oh, God! Oh, God, I am undone.

I can put you back together, My child. I can
make you whole.

Weeping uncontrollably, Tabitha tossed aside her covering, pulling herself out of bed. She couldn't stay here anymore, drowning in debilitating sorrow and self-pity. God had provided comfort within the body of Christ, and Jesus had shown her the way to healing. She had simply been too angry and stubborn to accept any source of comfort, to receive any guiding counsel.

But it was time to seek the Lord, and she knew she needed help.

***

Having prepared herself for a nice, long argument with the insufferable Zev, Tabitha was surprised when one of the younger guards greeted her at the gate without a qualm. Having been escorted through the torchlit outer court, Tabitha paused before the wide double doors, balancing her heavy satchel on one shoulder and taking a deep, steadying breath.

She'd scarcely released her calming breath when the gilded double doors burst open as if by their own accord. And there stood Mary in her elegant nightdress, her thick, waist-length braid draped over her shoulder. Lifting her dainty oil lamp, her shining countenance was illuminated, alight with the deepest kind of joy.

"How...how..." Tabitha stammered, stunned by Mary's unexpected appearance. It was the middle of the night, for heaven's sake! "How did you know I was coming?"

"Need you even ask?" Mary smiled knowingly, opening her arms to the heartbroken young woman.

Dropping her satchel with a heavy *thud* upon the paved stones, Tabitha went into Mary's motherly embrace, weeping hysterically into her delicate nightgown.

"Shhhh," Mary soothed, stroking the girl's lovely golden tresses. "Be still, beloved, be still. You are home now."

***

Tabitha resumed her former duties with ease, relieved to have her hands busy and her mind occupied. Surrounded by believers and close friends, the days now passed far more quickly. She realized she was incredibly blessed to have a place to go, along with an instant source of employment. Most were not so fortunate. Mary had even tidied and lavishly furnished Tabitha's old room, believing in faith that the young woman would soon return.

After several heart-to-hearts with her wise mistress, Tabitha eventually felt capable of evaluating her priorities and organizing her responsibilities. First was her duty to God. Tabitha had returned to the body of Christ, even participating in prayer and worship. Still, she sensed a slight rift in her once vibrant relationship with her Maker. She had a sneaking suspicion it was her own unresolved anger muddying the waters, but she wasn't ready to relinquish that yet. How could she? That was simply asking too much.

There was also the matter of her in-laws, Amal and Daphne. She had yet to visit them, offering her condolences. Truth be told, she didn't feel the least bit sorry for them. Amal had stomped all over his relationship with Stephanos, prizing money and power far above his only son. And Daphne had stood idly by, too docile to intervene. Even so, Tabitha knew how Stephanos had longed for their salvation, so she resolved to reach them—for *his* sake, not theirs.

She had also considered their stoic Greek manservant, Dorian, with his elaborate robes and dignified manners. She hadn't bothered to express her happiness regarding his conversion and intended to right that wrong against him. He needed to know that she welcomed him into the body of Christ with open arms. She also planned to speak with Philip about Dorian. Even though the young deacon was probably far ahead of her, she needed to know that the manservant was fully equipped to continue in his new faith after returning to Greece. Stephanos would have done everything in his power to ensure this, so she intended to do the same. She feared for Dorian, returning to a pagan, idol-saturated city so soon after his conversion.

There was also her outreach to local widows and orphans, which had completely fallen by the wayside since her husband's death. Now widowed herself, Tabitha realized she could sympathize with the bereaved women of her community unlike ever before. Many of them were far less fortunate than she, struggling to feed and clothe broods of children without the strength and support a husband provided. Now, she was more determined than ever to reach them.

Tabitha had also considered the house she'd shared with Stephanos. It wasn't right for the place to remain empty and vacant when there were so many in need, but the thought of surrendering the home she had shared with her beloved tore at her heart. Even so, she had pondered several viable possibilities. At first, she'd thought to sell the house, donating the proceeds to the church as many others had done. She'd also considered gifting the house to a family in need, or even renting it to tenants on a monthly basis, providing a steady stream of income for the rapidly growing church.

Reluctantly, Tabitha had taken these considerations to Mary, implicitly trusting her instincts. After all, Mary was a capable businesswoman, honoring God in all matters of business and commerce. Impressed, Mary had urged her maid to earnestly seek the Lord's guidance regarding her situation. *He will show you what to do,* she'd insisted.

And then there was the matter of the poor, discarded child she had discovered on her doorstep. Though she preferred to leave the child in the care of an adoring, doting Rhoda, Tabitha knew that was not a permanent solution, and she felt responsible. Stephanos' final commission still rang in her mind, depriving her of sleep and haunting her waking moments: *I entrust her into your care.*

"You appear deep in thought."

Turning from the window overlooking the blooming outer court below, Tabitha smiled faintly as Mary approached her in the Upper Room.

"I suppose I am."

"Anything you'd like to discuss?"

"I was just thinking about that poor little girl."

"Ah, I see," Mary mused, drawing alongside her maid at the wide, rectangular window.

"I should be readying the room for this evening's service," Tabitha murmured, propping her broom against the wall. "Forgive me, my lady."

"What did I tell you, dear one? You needn't call me that anymore."

"You are my mistress again, are you not? And I am your maid. It's only right."

"We are all one in the body of Christ, Tabitha."

"But that doesn't mean I cannot address my lady with respect," Tabitha reminded her evenly.

"What troubles you about the child?" Mary asked kindly, dismissing the former subject.

"Everything," Tabitha said. "We know next to nothing about her, and yet she needs her mother. She needs her home."

"I'm afraid that is no longer an option," Mary said sadly, her gray eyes betraying her sorrow.

Tabitha glanced up, surprised. "What do you mean?"

"Tobias eventually located Luke, the kindly physician. He recognized the child immediately."

"Then what are waiting for?" Tabitha exclaimed, peeved that everyone was dragging their heels. "Why is the child still here?"

"Tabitha, the child's mother was one of Luke's patients."

Was? Tabitha stared at Mary, detesting her mounting sense of dread.

"Luke did everything in his power to save her—even treating her illness free of charge—to no avail," Mary explained sadly. "Recently returning for a follow-up appointment, he discovered the mother already dead. Since the child was nowhere to be found, he assumed his patient must have secured a home for her daughter, knowing her time was near."

Tabitha blinked in surprise, a familiar, unpleasant knot coiling in the pit of her stomach. Life was cruel.

"Luke didn't even know the child's name," Mary said. "She should be called by her name. The whole situation breaks my heart."

"So what must be done?" Tabitha asked dully, numb to the ever-present anger now lodged in her heart.

"The toddler needs our love and assurance more than ever," Mary responded without hesitation. "I know several families who would gladly receive her as their own, but we are all seeking the Lord in this matter. He knows what is best for the poor child. May His will prevail."

Directing her attention back out the window, Tabitha hoped Mary wasn't privy to her deep inner struggle. Despite her initial resistance, she couldn't help but be drawn to the nameless little girl. They had much in common, for they had both suffered unspeakable losses. The child must miss her mother as desperately as Tabitha now longed for her husband. Feeling a sharp stab of conscience, Tabitha supposed she could now relate to the child's ear-splitting screams and raging tantrums. She was sorely tempted to follow suit, shouting out her rage to a cold, unfeeling world.

She should have been more compassionate, more understanding, toward the little one.

"Have you any thoughts regarding this matter?" Mary asked gently, interrupting Tabitha's brooding thoughts.

"No, none at all," Tabitha responded a bit too quickly.

Mary's slender brows lifted in surprise. Wisely, she held her tongue.

The truth of the matter was, Tabitha had far too many thoughts concerning the orphaned child—all of them vying for her attention. She just wasn't ready to address any of them. Not now.

Not yet.

CHAPTER 46

Tabitha

Readying herself for bed, Tabitha sat gingerly on the edge of the plush mattress Mary had provided for her. Tabitha had never slept on something so luxurious, and she couldn't help but wish she'd been granted the opportunity to share the pleasure with Stephanos.

Twisting her thick tresses into a simple braid, she allowed her gaze to sweep somewhat listlessly over the well-furnished room. Mary had gone out of her way to make the chamber warm and inviting, scattering thick Persian rugs upon the stone floor, hanging graceful tapestries, and mounting gilded lamps upon the walls. The intricate vessels cheered the small chamber with a cozy glow, reminding Tabitha of previous nights spent in her former house, wrapped snugly in her husband's arms.

Blinking back tears, Tabitha wondered why nightfall always ushered in the most dismal of feelings, arousing her fears, doubts, and anxieties anew.

"May I come in?"

Glancing up in surprise, Tabitha saw Mary standing in the doorway, looking regal and lovely even after preparing for bed.

"Of course, my lady," Tabitha responded, mustering a brave front. "You needn't even ask. This is *your* home."

"And yours, as well," Mary reminded her gently, crossing the short distance between them and lowering herself onto the bed beside her maid.

Noting the sealed scroll in Mary's hand, Tabitha's curiosity was instantly aroused.

"How are you, beloved?" Mary asked, her luminous gray eyes earnestly searching Tabitha's.

The genuine sympathy reflected in her mistress's features struck a chord in Tabitha's heart. Determined not to make a fool of herself by shedding more unproductive tears, Tabitha cleared her throat a bit gruffly. "I'm thankful to be here, my lady."

"And we're all thankful to have you, Tabitha, every single one of us."

Swallowing the lump in her throat, Tabitha forced what she hoped was a smile.

"Do you still wish to continue making garments for the orphans, widows, and the destitute of this region?" Mary asked frankly, changing the subject.

"I do," Tabitha readily responded. She couldn't bear to think of those poor women suffering as she did, aching for their dead husbands even as they frantically scraped and clawed for crumbs to feed their children. Providing beautiful, quality clothing for them and their little ones was the least she could do to ease their inexplicable burdens.

"You will bless so many," Mary told her, squeezing her hand in a motherly fashion. "That being said, I've made arrangements to have your mother's loom delivered within the week."

"Mary, you shouldn't have," Tabitha gasped, both awed and relieved.

"Nonsense," Mary responded emphatically. "There's plenty of room for it. We can place it in that corner there, where you kept it before you wed."

As her gaze traveled toward the corner Mary had indicated, Tabitha's heart constricted sharply in her chest. How many hours had she worked at her loom in this very chamber, constructing the wedding gown she would wear for her handsome bridegroom? How many nights had she lain in bed, dreaming of a future with the man she loved more fiercely than life itself?

She never could have imagined it would end like this.

"I have something for you," Mary said softly, raising the slim scroll in one hand.

"What is it?" Tabitha asked, eyeing the scroll with a hint of suspicion.

"Stephanos asked me to give this to you at the proper time if…" Closing her eyes, Mary's voice quavered slightly, uncharacteristically, trailing off as she gathered her composure.

"If *what*?" Tabitha demanded, her strained voice sounding odd in her own ears.

"If anything ever happened to him," Mary finished with great effort. "I believe you're ready to see this now."

Tabitha felt as if the air had left her lungs. Quivering inside, she reluctantly accepted the proffered scroll, her entire being filling with dread…and the faintest sense of hope.

"I will leave you to it, beloved. And I shall be in my chambers if you need me." Gracefully, Mary rose from the bed. Placing a delicate hand upon Tabitha's shoulder, she offered a gentle squeeze before slipping from the bedchamber without another word.

Tabitha's hands shook as she inspected the scroll bearing her husband's simple seal, her hazel-green eyes stinging with tears. She knew she should break the seal and open the letter—she *needed* to open it, *longed* to open it—and yet her entire being revolted at the awful realization washing over her like a tidal wave.

Somehow, he had *known*.

Overcome with grief, Tabitha wept inconsolably, her shoulders shuddering in response as she clutched her husband's final farewell close to her aching heart.

***

Tabitha

Standing before a familiar set of intricately fashioned double doors, Tabitha drew a steadying breath.

She wasn't ready for this.

But Stephanos' letter had galvanized her into action, reminding her for whom he had lived... and died. She wasn't ready to process *all* that he had written in the poignant letter he'd penned so carefully, undoubtedly praying his adoring young wife would never have to read it. But she could not ignore his request to win his parents should he be taken before their conversion.

Before their conversion. His letter had sounded so *certain*, as if their conversion was guaranteed! Hadn't Stephanos known who he was writing about? Amal was about as malleable as a stone wall! How was she supposed to win *him*?

Be still, beloved. No one can come to Me unless the Father who sent Me draws Him.

Releasing another shaky breath, Tabitha drew comfort in that fact. Her role was simply to *obey*; God would do the heavy lifting, the part she was unable to do.

Tabitha was about to utilize the bulky, gold-plated knocker when the doors creaked open before her.

"Dorian," Tabitha said politely, hoping she sounded pleased to see him. Her aching heart and raging emotions greatly complicated her task.

"Good morning, my lady," the Greek manservant replied crisply, his handsome features devoid of expression. "My lady will be overjoyed to see you."

She will? Startled, Tabitha allowed Dorian to usher her through the vestibule, into the grand foyer overlooking a serene, pillared atrium with a wide, rectangular skylight cut into the roof and a soothing fountain splashing amidst a glistening pool of blue water.

"Please allow me to escort you to the Lady Daphne," Dorian said, his controlled voice betraying the slightest hint of relief. "She has long desired to see you."

"Dorian, wait."

Dorian's expression revealed his surprise as he paused before the row of wide marble pillars guarding the tranquil, Roman-style atrium.

"I owe you an apology, Dorian." Releasing a nervous sigh, Tabitha had already decided to swallow her pride and plunge right ahead with her explanation. Better to get it over with.

Dorian stared at her somewhat incredulously.

"You see, the day you visited me, I was entirely

consumed with grief…but I was even more consumed with *myself*," she admitted, inwardly battling her own pride. "I wallowed in self-pity after losing Stephanos, and I must admit, it's a temptation I still face every single day—every single moment."

Silent, Dorian studied her with those fathomless hazel-tinged eyes.

"That day, I should have welcomed you into the body of Christ with open arms," Tabitha confessed, forcing herself to meet his unnerving gaze despite her embarrassment. "Instead, I remained aloof and uncaring. Not once did I consider inviting you to prayer service or suggesting that you speak with one of the apostles or elders. You, a brand-new convert, had to find your own way. It must have been very difficult. And for that, I am truly sorry."

Tabitha's confession was followed by a long, awkward pause. For what felt like an eternity, Tabitha remained rooted in place, the gentle splashing of the fountain filling her senses. Had she made a terrible blunder, speaking so frankly to the reserved servant?

"Think nothing of it, my lady," Dorian eventually spoke. To Tabitha's immense shock, the man-servant's husky tone indicated that he was deeply touched. "Your grief is perfectly understandable."

"I'm so thankful the Lord led you to Philip," Tabitha admitted, warmed by Dorian's obvious gratitude. "Has his instruction proven helpful?"

"Immensely."

"Good," Tabitha responded with a decisive nod.

"Now, we'd best locate Lady Daphne," Dorian informed her, once more becoming the stoic man-servant. "Come along, shall we?"

CHAPTER 47

Tabitha

"Tabitha, my darling! How I've longed for you, daughter!"

Astonished, Tabitha felt frozen in place as Daphne nearly turned over her ornamental chair on the balcony in her haste to reach her. Swiftly closing the distance between them, Daphne gathered her daughter-in-law in soft arms.

When Daphne finally withdrew, her pale cheeks were streaked with tears. "I went to your house three times, but I couldn't find you. I've been worried sick for you, my daughter."

Risking a glance toward Dorian, who was staidly resituating his lady's chair upon the sprawling balcony overlooking the red-roofed structures of Jerusalem's many elite, Tabitha assumed he hadn't yet shared his conversion experience with Amal and Daphne. Had he done so, he would have surely offered to consult Mary about Tabitha's whereabouts, setting his lady's mind at ease.

"You needn't have worried about me," Tabitha managed, somehow finding her voice. "I have returned to the house of Mary, my former mistress."

"Mary of Jerusalem?" Daphne asked, surprised. "I knew Stephanos worked for her. You do, as well?"

"I am honored to serve such a kind, generous mistress."

"I must agree," Daphne said, surprising her. "I will never forget her kindness, coming to us after Stephanos..." her voice trailed off as she looked away, blinking back tears.

Tabitha's heart went out to her—the first hint of sympathy she'd known for her in-laws since her husband's passing. "I owe you an apology, Mother," Tabitha said frankly, her conscience throbbing. "I should have come to you after his death. You should have heard it from me."

"I can't even comprehend what you must have gone through, Tabitha," Daphne said, waving aside her daughter-in-law's concern. "I understand, and you needn't apologize, my daughter."

"But I must, nonetheless," Tabitha insisted, taking her mother-in-law's hand. "Please, forgive me. I was selfish, barricading myself in a locked house to avoid all human contact. But you were grieving, too...and you needed me."

"In a way, I am thankful the Lord withheld human comfort. For in so doing, God Himself has consoled me," Daphne said, arousing Tabitha's suspicions. What, exactly, did she mean by that? Tabitha certainly intended to find out!

"Dorian, please see to some refreshments." Tabitha suspected Daphne's command was provided to distract the manservant rather than to provide nourishment.

"As you wish, my lady." It was obvious Daphne's request hadn't fooled him, either. Turning sharply on his heels, he left the two women alone on the well-furnished balcony.

"Do come and enjoy this spectacular view," Daphne invited, sounding a bit distracted.

Drawing obediently alongside her mother-in-law, Tabitha placed her hands upon the smooth marble balustrade encircling the elongated balcony. The Greco-Roman style hanging terrace was a luxurious affair with an elegantly latticed covering overhead, trellises abounding with twisting vines and seasonal flowers, lush, upholstered couches, and potted palms. And she had to admit, the panoramic view of the holy city glistening in the golden sunshine was, indeed, a stunning sight to behold.

"My son was not deceived." Daphne's soft eyes remained fixed upon the courtly cityscape, her quiet tone boding no argument.

"Mother?"

"Stephanos believed that Jesus of Nazareth was the long-awaited Messiah," Daphne mused, her eyes glistening beneath a soft sheen of tears. "He was right, wasn't he? *You* were right."

"Yes, Mother," Tabitha confirmed, her heart doing a funny little flop within her chest. Was this to be the moment she and Stephanos had longed for, prayed for, all this time? "Jesus truly is the Messiah, the Promised One of God."

Grasping the balustrade with white-knuckled hands, Daphne's dainty amphora earrings bobbed in unison as she shook her head. "My son tried to tell us in so many ways," she admitted, her expression clouding with grief. "*You* tried to tell us," Daphne said, turning troubled eyes upon her attentive daughter-in-law. "And yet, Amal and I didn't even recognize our need for a Savior. Why would we long for a Messiah to break the yoke of Roman bondage when we richly benefited from the thriving economy of this booming empire? In our minds, we were not in need—we led lavish lives, delighting in our prosperity. But we were *wrong*." Daphne's eyes kindled with newfound understanding as she gripped Tabitha's shoulders, turning her daughter-in-law around to face her. "We *were* in need. Had we only known that the Messiah had come to free us from *sin*—not the Romans—then perhaps we would have recognized our need for a Savior."

Tabitha stared at her mother-in-law, blinking in disbelief. "Are you saying you believe that Jesus is the Son of God, Daphne?"

"I am," Daphne responded without hesitation. "All this time, I've been apathetic—disbelieving, really—about the prophecies regarding a Messiah. If He came to free us from the Romans, what would *truly* be accomplished? We would gain a temporary sense of freedom, perhaps—only to be enslaved again by yet another powerful empire over the course of time. It's happened repeatedly, after all—from the birth of our nation until now. But a Messiah coming to free us from *sin*, purging us of our unrighteousness, mending our broken hearts and banishing our fears? The results of such a Savior would indeed prove lasting, eternal."

Tabitha could hardly believe what she was hearing. How Stephanos would rejoice! "And your husband? Does he believe, as well?"

"I'm afraid our son's demise has only bolstered Amal's disgust toward the Way," Daphne said, her voice catching in sorrow. "He is filled with rage, Tabitha, and drowning in guilt. I don't know how to help him."

"Only God can help him," Tabitha said, a bit more sharply than she intended. Despite her best efforts, she couldn't seem to muster the slightest iota of sympathy toward her greedy, domineering father-in-law.

"Will you pray for my husband, Tabitha?" Daphne pleaded, her eyes welling with tears. "If he continues down this current path, he will perish in his sins."

Perhaps that's what he deserves! Tabitha's entire being rebelled at the prospect of *praying* for the man who had disinherited her beloved husband. Fleetingly, she remembered both Mary and Stephanos urging her to pray for Saul, another human being she detested with all her might.

Swallowing the bile rising in her throat, she forced herself to meet Daphne's hopeful gaze. "We can both pray for Amal," she managed, deciding it would be far more palatable to pray for Amal than for Saul. All her "prayers" for Saul involved hellfire and brimstone, along with hopeless agony and eternal torment.

But Stephanos had prayed earnestly for his father's salvation, believing God to work a miracle in the stubborn man. She would intercede on behalf of Amal for her *husband's* sake.

"Do...do you think it is all right for me to pray, Tabitha?" Daphne asked meekly, shaking Tabitha from her brooding reverie.

Tabitha stared at her mother-in-law, befuddled.

"Why wouldn't it be?"

"Well, because I don't know if...if I am saved," Daphne admitted, her eyes filling with tears.

"Oh, Mother," Tabitha chuckled, taking the woman's hands in her own. "Don't you remember what I told you long ago when you visited me? *If you confess with your mouth the Lord Jesus and believe in your heart that God has raised Him from the dead, you will be saved.*"

"I *do* believe," Daphne affirmed with an emphatic nod of her head.

"Then pray with me," Tabitha told her, inwardly pleading with God to guide her in this monumental endeavor. Truthfully, she didn't feel worthy of leading her husband's beloved mother in her prayer of repentance. After all, she hadn't even dealt with her own seething anger, now her constant companion. Who was *she* to lead someone else in a prayer of salvation?

Even so, *someone* had to do it.

Fleetingly, she considered summoning Dorian. At the moment, he was far better suited to the task than she! As far as she knew, he wasn't harboring any burning hatred toward anyone! But alas, Tabitha didn't wish to place him—a brand-new believer—on the spot. That aside, it wasn't her place to inform Daphne about his life-changing decision. That was up to him.

Sighing impatiently, Tabitha knew what must be done.

Lord God, be merciful to me, she prayed. *You know Daphne's heart...and mine. Help me guide her in this confession of faith, granting her comfort in this sacred moment.*

"I don't even know what to say," Daphne interjected nervously. "How is one to become a follower of your Christ?"

"Unlike many other faiths, there are no magic words or secret formulas," Tabitha assured her, forcing a smile she was far from feeling. "God knows the intentions of your heart. But we must still go before Him, confessing our sins and our need for Him. If you're not sure what to say, Mother, then repeat after me."

Clasping hands, the women stood upon the magnificent balcony, their heads bowed, foreheads nearly touching as Tabitha led her mother-in-law in a heartfelt prayer of confession, repentance, and acceptance of Jesus Christ as her personal Savior and Lord. Reverently, Daphne repeated Tabitha's simple prayer word-for-word, cleansing tears streaming down her pale face.

"I feel as if a weight has been lifted," Daphne breathed, gathering her daughter-in-law in an affectionate embrace. "Thanks to you, my daughter, I will see my loved ones and my children again."

"Thanks to the *Holy Spirit* who has drawn you, not *me*," Tabitha reminded her, wishing she felt more triumphant than she did. Instead, a gnawing sense of resentment reared its ugly head against her new sister in Christ.

"Praise God," Daphne breathed, dabbing at her tears with an elegantly embroidered handkerchief. "He truly works in mysterious ways, doesn't He? The death of our dear Stephanos only confirmed my mounting suspicions, Tabitha. This life is broken, imperfect, and fleeting. It is eternity that truly matters."

Forcing a lopsided smile, Tabitha silently chided herself for her own cursed selfishness. Daphne had just made a decision worthy of a heavenly celebration, and yet she could barely rally even a hint of sincere gladness. Heart aching, she knew that Stephanos would have willingly and gladly surrendered his life to save Daphne...but what about *her*? *She* had loved him faithfully even when Daphne had remained indifferent and aloof, comfortably barricaded within her luxurious seaside manor in distant Greece! But she, Tabitha, *needed* Stephanos, her husband! She had next to nothing, while Daphne had everything a woman could want—and now salvation, besides! What more did *Daphne* need?

Life was unjust.

True, Stephanos would have laid down his life for his mother in a heartbeat, but *she* did not share his selfless sentiments. Why did Stephanos have to lose his life in order for his mother to find hers? Couldn't Daphne have accepted Christ any other way?

Taking a deep, calming breath, Tabitha offered a half-hearted prayer for help. For Stephanos' sake, she mustn't reveal her bitterness to Daphne. Remembering the mistake she'd made with Dorian, she turned to the beaming woman. "Please join us for prayer and worship at Mary's villa this evening, Mother. It's very important to study the Word together—"

"Oh, Tabitha, I wish I could!"

"And why can't you?" Tabitha nearly huffed, miffed.

"Amal would never permit it," Daphne responded, oblivious to Tabitha's deep angst. "But even if he did, he has made plans to return to Greece, Tabitha.

The arrangements have already been made. Thank God you visited me today, for we must leave upon the morrow."

"Tomorrow?" Tabitha gasped, stunned. She couldn't help but wonder what might have happened had she clung to her stubborn pride and rebellion by refusing to visit her in-laws. Perhaps Daphne would have been forced to return to Greece without the assurance of salvation! Mary had presented Stephanos' letter—urging her to reach them—just in time.

"Tabitha, I'm afraid this is goodbye," Daphne whispered tremulously, her brown eyes clouded with tears.

Taken aback, Tabitha reached for the marble balustrade to steady herself, feeling as if she'd been punched in the gut.

She hadn't expected this at all.

"But how will you carry on your faith in Greece, alone?" Tabitha managed, surprisingly concerned for her.

"Not alone."

Both women turned in bewilderment as Dorian strode upon the balcony, a large silver platter laden with delicacies in hand.

"I beg your pardon, my lady," Dorian said, his eyes flickering briefly toward Tabitha, "but I couldn't help overhearing. You have accepted Stephanos' Messiah."

"I have," Daphne responded, stunned by her favored manservant's uncharacteristic boldness.

"As have I," he said huskily, setting the tray upon an impressive wooden stand.

"Oh, Dorian!" Daphne gasped, overjoyed. "Praise God."

Glancing back and forth between wealthy mistress and faithful manservant, Tabitha wondered if perhaps the Lord had plans for them far greater than they could imagine. Perhaps their faith would eventually take root amidst a land of pagan idols, reaping an abundant harvest among the lost.

"What is going on here?"

All three turned to see Amal standing beneath the balcony's colonnaded entrance, his countenance fearsome to behold.

CHAPTER 48

Tabitha

"What is *she* doing here?"

Shocked, Tabitha realized *she* was the one Amal referenced with such unveiled loathing. Glancing toward Daphne and Dorian, Tabitha decided their sheepish expressions might have proven rather comical under different circumstances.

"Well?" Amal demanded, his dark eyes traveling between the three of them.

Never one to back down, Tabitha turned and faced her father-in-law head-on. "I came to visit your wife," she said coolly, struggling against her keen dislike for him. "I didn't know your permission was required...sir," she added demurely.

"Why are you here?" Amal demanded accusingly. "You didn't bother coming until now! Were you hoping for a gift or a handout before we departed?"

"Amal," Daphne pleaded, mortified.

Amal halted his wife's protest by raising one uncompromising hand. "We lost our only son, and a *stranger* had to locate us to inform us of his passing!" Amal stormed, his kindling anger like a tangible presence between them.

"You lost your son *years ago* by your own greed and obstinance!" Tabitha shot back, uncowed.

"Leave." Amal's scowl deepened. "You are no longer welcome here."

"Amal!"

"Quiet, Daphne!"

"Amal, Tabitha is *family*," Daphne protested in disbelief.

"Not anymore," Amal growled, his flaming gaze coming to rest upon the lovely young woman beside his wife. "Have you forgotten our son is *dead*, Daphne? She is no longer any relation to us." Ignoring his wife's quiet weeping, he turned flashing eyes upon Tabitha. "*Leave*, or I shall have you detained."

Turning toward her weeping mother-in-law, Tabitha took her trembling hands. "Shhh," she soothed. "I will write, Mother. We'll keep in touch."

"Over my dead body," Amal hissed, coming at her with sparking eyes.

"If you insist," Tabitha replied with icy sweetness, standing her ground. "Although I'm sure it needn't come to that."

"*Get out.*"

Leaning in to kiss her mother-in-law's damp cheek, Tabitha returned Amal's hard stare before striding calmly beneath the arched colonnades upholding the impressive balcony. "Be strong in the Lord, Mother," she encouraged, pausing beneath the central arch. "This isn't goodbye. We will see each other again, be it on this earth or in the kingdom."

"Farewell then, my daughter," Daphne managed

through her stream of tears.

Allowing her father-in-law a final glance, Tabitha's hazel-green eyes glowed with avid intensity. Proudly lifting her chin, she turned on her heels and slipped out of sight.

***

"My lady! My lady, wait!"

With one hand on the gleaming gilded knob, Tabitha paused before the stately double doors, catching her breath in dismay.

Less composed than she had ever seen him, Dorian hurried toward her, appearing relieved he had reached her in time. Adjusting the disheveled mantle pinned at his shoulder, he looked as if he'd made quite a mad dash to the first floor. He must have taken the winding marble steps at least two at a time!

"You needn't have troubled yourself, Dorian," Tabitha muttered, still heated from her infuriating encounter with Amal. "I can see myself out. Surely you don't wish to incite your master's wrath against you."

"My deepest apologies regarding that unseemly episode, my lady," Dorian stated fervently, catching her off guard. "You must forgive my master. He is simply overcome, beside himself with grief."

"He looked just fine to me," Tabitha remarked curtly.

"So it would seem," Dorian supplied, his striking eyes scanning his surroundings with a hint of apprehension. "But I've known him half my life, and I can assure you: he is angry—and afraid. He is

SEEKING THE TRUTH | 443

lashing out at all the world, I fear."

"Perhaps that is so," Tabitha said, her conscience pricking at her own angry manner. "You know him far better than I."

"He is a hard man," Dorian admitted, his tone low. "But he's not all bad. Perhaps, in time, he will come around."

Tabitha thought that was highly unlikely but held her tongue. She'd already done enough damage today. She cringed anew, wondering what Amal must think of her now. She'd done very little to suppress her rising temper on the balcony.

But the man was *impossible*, simply infuriating! She was quite certain Amal could pique the most benevolent of saints! Why, that man could ruffle the feathers of the most placid, tranquil dove! Even so, deep down, Tabitha knew she was still accountable to God for her own actions—regardless of Amal's inexcusable behavior.

"Please pray I didn't just undo all Stephanos' prayers and efforts regarding his father's salvation," Tabitha said glumly. "I don't even know what got into me up there, Dorian. Lately, I hardly recognize myself. One moment, I'm submissive, humble, and eager to obey, but then the next I'm completely flying off the handle."

"You are *grieving*, my lady," Dorian responded knowingly, his typically veiled hazel eyes reflecting more compassion than she'd previously seen in them. Bending to levelly meet her gaze, Dorian said in his serious manner, "But it shan't always be this way, my sister. In time, this, too, shall pass."

For some reason unbeknownst to her, Dorian's quiet charge struck a chord deep in Tabitha's heart.

Looking down at her own sandaled feet, she furiously blinked away the tears stinging her eyes. She didn't wish to make a fool of herself. She'd already done that once today.

"Thank you, Dorian," Tabitha said once she'd managed to compose herself. "You sound as if you are speaking from experience."

"Who among us hasn't known sorrow?" Dorian said, his mouth tipping enigmatically.

Tabitha was sorely tempted to pry, but somehow resisted the urge to do so. Dorian was a terribly private man. He certainly wouldn't welcome an interrogation. Instead, she admitted anxiously, "Daphne says you will be leaving tomorrow, but that concerns me. I know very little about these things, but isn't it dangerous to set sail this time of year?"

"My master has arranged to winter in a vacation house in Caesarea Maritima," Dorian explained, and Tabitha detected a slight cringe in his tone.

"I see," she responded brittlely. "So he isn't leaving Jerusalem to handle pressing matters of business in Athens. He just doesn't want to be here." *As far from me as humanly possible*, she thought, peeved. Most likely, he feared her influence over Daphne, sensing his wife's great interest in the Jerusalem church.

"Caesarea's magnificent port rivals his own in Athens. My master harbors many important contacts in the city and has already arranged to meet with them during his stay," Dorian amended, though his argument was weak in Tabitha's opinion. "While there, he desires to review his affairs in the port city."

"Dorian," Tabitha said, attempting to dismiss her seething irritation toward Amal, "if you can locate faithful followers in Caesarea, please do so. And take Daphne to meet with them. Accountability is extremely important, especially to those new in the faith."

"I will do my best," Dorian promised, and Tabitha saw that he meant it.

"During His ministry on earth, Jesus visited Caesarea Philippi. But I don't think He entered the port city of Caesarea Maritima," Tabitha said, disheartened. It was unlikely Dorian would encounter any believers there.

Suddenly, she thought of Lady Procula and her countenance brightened. The noblewoman resided in the seaside palace of Pontius Pilate when they weren't visiting Jerusalem for the great feasts! Perhaps Daphne and Dorian wouldn't be the only believers in Caesarea Maritima after all! But just as quickly, Tabitha remembered the gravity of Procula's situation. Unfortunately, her conversion remained a secret.

But with Daphne's status and influence, perhaps it wasn't entirely far-fetched to hope the wife of a high-powered shipping mogul could arrange a meeting with the governor's wife. After all, Pilate's home base benefited greatly from Amal's flourishing industry. Perhaps Lady Procula would recognize Daphne's faith. Or—better yet—perhaps Daphne would speak of faith herself. Sensing the light of Christ in Daphne, would Lady Procula feel safe disclosing her secret to her? What if the two aristocratic women became friends and confidantes?

"The Lady Procula—wife of Pontius Pilate—is a kind, fair woman," Tabitha said, hopefully planting a seed in Dorian's mind. "She might prove a worthy companion for Daphne during your stay in Caesarea Maritima."

"I shall keep that in mind." Dorian looked surprised, undoubtedly wondering how she—a widowed maidservant of extremely low status—knew anything about the famed Claudia Procula. But he didn't ask any questions.

Furrowing her brow, Tabitha considered Daphne's options in Greece. Her chances of encountering a believer in Athens were next to nothing. Tabitha resolved to keep in touch with Daphne and Dorian at all costs. She would speak about this with Mary, as well, along with Candace, Simon, Kelila, and Philip. Undoubtedly, there were dozens of believers who would gladly correspond with Daphne and Dorian once they'd returned to Athens.

Suddenly remembering Amal's threat on the balcony after she had promised to keep in touch, Tabitha's countenance clouded in dismay. *Over my dead body,* he'd declared. The pig-headed lout would probably burn all her letters before they ever reached his wife!

As if sensing the direction of her thoughts, Dorian spoke up, warily scanning the perimeter to ensure they remained alone. "You needn't worry about losing contact with Daphne, my lady," he added crisply, his nonchalant manner returning as he reached for the door. "I oversee all my master's correspondence," he added, his eyes sparkling with a hint of mischief.

"Dorian, you are something else," Tabitha laughed, realizing for the first time how much she would miss this wonderful new brother in Christ. "Thank you, truly. With all my heart."

"It is my pleasure to serve you, my lady," Dorian

replied, grandly sweeping open the imposing bronze doors.

"I will miss you." Blinking back tears, Tabitha paused on the threshold, lightly touching his forearm. "Safe travels, my brother. May God be with you."

"And you, as well."

Tabitha couldn't be certain, but she thought she detected a slight sheen of tears reflected in his eyes as she departed.

CHAPTER 49

Mary

"My lady, may I have a word with you?"

Glancing up from the open ledger upon her desk, Mary's heart lurched slightly as the captain of her guard appeared beneath the bibliotheca's pillared entrance. Silently thanking God that Tobias stood at her elbow, Mary wondered about Zev's request.

Tobias glanced at her in surprise, his neatly oiled mustache twitching in question. Undoubtedly, he wondered why the guard found it necessary to interrupt Mary's busy workday. "I will wait outside, my lady."

"Tobias, please remain with us," Mary quickly spoke up.

"I would prefer to speak with you alone," Zev put in curtly.

"I'm sure you understand why accountability is preferable," Mary replied evenly, refusing to be cowed. Though she longed for Zev's salvation, she would not place herself in a compromising situation again.

"Very well," Zev replied, failing to mask his annoyance.

"What would you like to discuss with me?" Mary asked her guard, wondering if she really wished to know.

"Your safety, of course."

This again, Mary thought, carefully concealing her displeasure.

"First, please allow me to extend my humblest of apologies," Zev implored, sounding uncharacteristically genuine. "I regret to say, my behavior toward you the other night when we were alone...well, it was inexcusable."

Mary stared at her guard incredulously. Though she had been seeking the Lord earnestly on behalf of her stubborn captain of the guard, the last thing she had expected was a formal apology! Could this possibly be an indication that the Lord was working in his heart?

Suddenly realizing Zev was still awaiting her response, Mary shook her head as if attempting to clear her own stupor. "Thank you, Zev," she managed, her cheeks turning scarlet as her overseer glanced questioningly between the two of them. "I accept your apology and appreciate your humility."

"In that case," Zev continued, clearly relieved to move on, "is it safe to assume my job remains secure?"

"Of course," Mary replied, although she didn't appreciate being put on the spot like that. But unless the Lord directed her otherwise, she didn't see any reason to release Zev from her employ—if his apology was sincere and his behavior followed suit.

"Then as the captain of your household guard, I'd like to suggest reinforcing security on the premises," Zev said directly, his steely eyes boring into hers. "Though I cannot agree with or accept your hazardous faith, I recognize certain measures can be taken to protect you, as well as the church you insist upon housing here."

"What kind of measures?" Mary asked, saddened by his statement.

"Guards should be stationed in the Upper Room—not only during your services, but when the apostles and church leadership meet, as well. Of course, I will be your first line of defense stationed at the main gate. But I recommend multiple layers of security in case the first or second level is breached."

"I see," Mary mused, considering his suggestion. She had stationed guards in the Upper Room before, when persecution seemed inevitable. Zev's suggestion was entirely practical.

"Just say the word, and I'll set the plan in motion."

Glancing at him in surprise, Mary saw the eagerness in his eyes, the readiness of his stance. Her beloved Mark had trusted Zev with the lives of his cherished wife and son when he traveled for months at a time. And Zev had proven himself trustworthy through it all. Saddened, Mary wondered why the Lord had placed this man in her life when he stoutly refused God's mercy at every turn. She had always known him to be a steadfast, powerful man, fully committed to whatever he set his mind to. But alas, it would seem he had set his mind against the truth, displaying the same unwavering steadfastness in his refusal to believe.

"You may reinforce our household security however you see fit," Mary replied quietly, attempting to mask her keen disappointment. "You have valiantly protected my family for many years, Zev. I trust your judgment."

"As you wish, my lady," Zev replied, his dark eyes flickering slightly in response and causing Mary to wonder what he must be thinking. In his usual, efficient way, Zev turned on his heels and left to perform his lady's bidding.

***

Mary was utterly delighted when Luke, the kind physician, paid her an unexpected visit shortly before the celebrated Feast of Lights. Having ushered him into the quiet bibliotheca, Mary sat behind her desk, spellbound, as he pleasantly described the adventures of his journey from Antioch and updated her about new patients and perplexing medical cases, both in Jerusalem and abroad.

"It was a wise decision to travel overland rather than setting sail this time of year," Mary observed, folding her hands on her desk.

"Ah, I've made a few risky decisions in the past, experiencing a squall or two on the high seas," Luke responded, his warm brown eyes sparkling with fun. "Once, I was quite certain we'd be shipwrecked. And though I thoroughly relish adventure, I'd prefer to forgo such excitement in the future."

"Hopefully it is safe to assume your days of risking shipwreck upon the high seas are far behind you," Mary smiled, amused. "It sounds like you've learned your lesson."

"Enough about me," the modest doctor said,

leaning forward in his chair, his dark eyes gleaming with interest. "How are *you*, Mary? I've been worried for you and the others after the senseless murder of your young deacon."

Mary's gray eyes sobered as she nodded her understanding. "We belong to Christ and by His power, we will overcome."

"But is that an answer, really?" Luke prodded, his scientific mind ever seeking answers. "I have no doubt you will overcome, as you are the strongest woman I've had the honor of knowing. But how do you fare in the face of all this...trouble?"

"I have peace," Mary responded honestly, her eyes softening in the gentle lamplight as she sensed the young doctor's concern for her and for those she loved. "Peace that surpasses my own understanding."

"Ah, and I suppose that peace comes from the Christ you serve so faithfully?"

Mary smiled, for there wasn't a trace of malice or even sarcasm in the doctor's tone. Only avid curiosity, as he had displayed from the very beginning. "Absolutely," she responded without missing a beat.

"Incredible."

"It is."

"And that poor child? The girl you asked me to identify?" Luke inquired hopefully. "How is she? Have you located a decent home for her?"

As if in answer to his casual inquiry, the slumbering villa resounded with shrill, ear-splitting screams that echoed and reverberated off the cold, frescoed walls.

"As you can see," Mary responded rather wanly, "we've experienced a few rough nights with the little one."

Luke's brown eyes widened in alarm as the girl's piercing cries filled the night air, easily carrying throughout the large villa. Shifting a bit uncomfortably, Luke noticed the brazen cries were growing nearer rather than more distant.

Tabitha entered a moment later with the screaming, resisting toddler in tow. Shifting the child's weight on her hip, the pretty maidservant was clearly engaged in a battle with the little one and appeared to be losing. Wrapping her arms tightly about the small, writhing form, she paused in the wide, pillared entrance, glancing over her squirming bundle toward Mary's sprawling desk. "She's been like this all evening, my lady," Tabitha gasped, winded. "We can't get her to bed down for the night. Rhoda suggested we seek your guidance."

Rising from his chair, a rather nervous-looking Luke bowed respectfully toward the flustered maidservant, his eyes shifting toward the wrestling toddler in amazement.

Noticing him for the first time, Tabitha's cheeks colored in embarrassment. She must look a sight indeed! The dark circles under her eyes, along with her deepening pallor, disheveled garments, and honey-gold hair sticking out in all directions, evidenced the intense struggle in which she had been engaged.

"Master Luke," Tabitha nodded politely, wondering if she could be heard above the child's incessant screams. Turning toward her mistress, she added, "I do apologize, my lady. I didn't know you had company."

"It was an unexpected—though *welcome*—surprise," Mary smiled warmly.

"Forgive me for troubling you, my lady—"

"Nonsense," Mary declared, holding out her arms to the wailing child. "Bring her here, beloved."

Tabitha was only too glad to comply. Crossing the room with the speed of an athlete, she deposited the flailing, writhing bundle in Mary's open arms.

"There, there, my darling." The child quieted almost instantly, nestling her tear-drenched face against Mary's soft shoulder.

"Remarkable," Luke breathed, watching along with Tabitha as the child cuddled happily in Mary's welcoming embrace. "If I may be so bold," Luke ventured, his gaze shifting between Mary and her lovely maidservant, "have *you* considered adopting the girl, Mary?"

Tabitha stared at the young doctor in disbelief. How could he even suggest such a thing? Mary was nearly buried alive in work already! Did he really expect her to take on the monumental task of raising a stranger's child as her own?

"Actually," Mary replied, gently rocking the little girl in her lap, "I've considered it repeatedly—upon numerous occasions."

Tabitha's attention snapped back to her mistress in shock.

"She certainly seems to trust you," Luke observed, immensely relieved the child's screaming tantrum had abated.

"She does," Mary agreed, gently smoothing the girl's wispy brown hair in a motherly manner. "And yet, as much as I long to adopt her myself, I have no peace about the matter."

"It seems to me a perfect fit," Luke pronounced, drawing a look of annoyance from Tabitha.

"That's what makes my uneasiness all the more strange," Mary said, resting her cheek upon the child's head. "But it is entirely possible the Lord has a better plan in mind for her—a home more suitable to her needs, and most importantly, to her spiritual growth."

Luke clearly disagreed with Mary's assessment, though he was too polite to press the issue any further. Instead, he turned his attention upon the disheveled maid at Mary's elbow. "Tabitha, isn't it?"

Blushing in dismay, Tabitha responded with a subtle nod. Though she had always admired the kind, humble doctor, she was somewhat displeased to see him this evening. Recalling Mary's playful comment of years gone by, she blushed even more deeply. *He is an exceptional young man,* Mary had declared about the handsome young doctor in the presence of both Rhoda and Stephanos. *Had he chosen to follow our Savior, Tabitha, I would arrange a betrothal for you this instant.*

At the time, Tabitha had been utterly mortified. Marriage had been the last thing on her mind! If only she had known what she knew *now*...if only she had been granted more time with her beloved Stephanos.

Thank goodness the doctor hasn't become a believer yet, she thought, relieved. Otherwise, she might be in danger of her lady's meddlesome and unwanted matchmaking! Cheeks blooming in horror, Tabitha suddenly realized her own selfishness, for she had been *glad* a kind, compassionate, and decent man hadn't yet accepted Christ as his Savior simply to avoid her own discomfort!

Was there no end to her selfishness and self-pity?

"It is a pleasure to see you again, Tabitha," Luke said warmly, interrupting her silent lecture.

Smiling weakly, Tabitha was spared the discomfort of further conversation when a tall, powerfully built, cloaked figure entered the bibliotheca like a specter from the night. Alarmed, Tabitha—along with the startled doctor—looked to Mary in question.

Pausing rather theatrically below magnificent, painted pillars, the specter's cloaked head turned, surveying those gathered in the large, lamplit office library.

"My, it's crowded in here. Apparently, I wasn't the only one with this idea."

Instantly recognizing the striking voice as belonging to Alexander, Mary's informant, Tabitha's heart constricted in her throat. His presence bode ill tidings. She wasn't ready to deal with another debilitating blow.

Oh, God, what now? Whatever it is, spare us, Lord.

Sensing the tension mounting in the air, the toddler, formerly slumbering in Mary's lap, lifted her curly head, whimpering in fear.

"Tabitha," Mary said, her voice calm yet authoritative, "please put this little one to bed."

Though desperate to hear whatever news Alexander planned to share, Tabitha was relieved to escape the confines of the tension-thick chamber. Dutifully taking the whimpering child from Mary, Tabitha hoisted her onto her hip. Offering both the doctor and the informant a reluctant nod, Tabitha fled the office library with a protesting child in tow, battling against the paralyzing fear rising in her chest.

CHAPTER 50

Mary

"Alexander," Mary said in greeting, rising from her throne-like chair. "Please, join us."

Without removing his hood, Alexander's head cocked instinctively toward the young doctor.

"This is Luke, the physician," Mary explained. "He has been an absolute godsend on numerous occasions."

"A Gentile?"

An amused smile flitted across Luke's comely features.

"I assure you, he can be trusted," Mary told him, smiling to herself. She found it amusing that Alexander, a Greek, would be wary of a Gentile.

"Ah, very well." Throwing back his hood, Alexander flashed his roguish grin. "If *you* say he can be trusted, well, I'll trust you."

"You have my word."

"And mine, as well," Luke supplied graciously, extending his hand in greeting.

"One never can be too careful," Alexander shot back, firmly grasping the doctor's hand.

"Do I want to know what's going on here?" Luke ventured with a nervous chuckle. "For a moment there, I feared we'd stumbled upon a dark apparition or a hired assassin."

"Alexander is my informant," Mary explained to the confused doctor. "Please allow me to formally introduce you." As she did so, Mary couldn't help but compare the drastic differences between the two men. The pair was as contrary as night and day—Alexander with his strikingly handsome countenance, swarthy complexion, and brazen demeanor stood in stark contrast to the pleasant, ambitious young doctor with his friendly bearing and studious curiosity.

"Pleased to make your acquaintance," Luke affirmed after Mary's brief introduction, mildly studying Alexander's imposing form.

Alexander was less forthright, remaining somewhat closed to the newcomer.

"So how did you become an informant?" Luke inquired with great interest.

"For your own sake, the less you know about me, the better," Alexander responded wryly. "If you don't *know*, you can't *tell*—should you ever be detained and questioned."

Chuckling in amusement, Luke received a pointed look from Alexander. "Oh, you weren't in jest."

"I was not."

Clearing his throat in surprise, Luke shifted a bit uncomfortably.

"So tell me," Alexander mused, sizing up the young doctor. "What led a successful and undoubtedly wealthy Gentile physician to embrace a Jewish

Carpenter from Nazareth?"

Cringing inwardly, Mary prayed Luke had not been offended by Alexander's scathing sarcasm. Reasonably so, Alexander remained suspicious, and she couldn't blame him. Daily, he placed his life on the line, shielding believers from the schemes of wicked men.

"A worthy question," Luke agreed, and Mary thanked God for his good humor. "To be frank, I am not a follower. I am, however, a very good friend of our dear Mary. I remain in her debt, as do my patients. She funded the start of my medical practice."

"He's not one of us?" Alexander demanded of Mary, his countenance fierce.

"Not yet," Mary replied lightly, unperturbed.

Luke returned Alexander's fiery glare with an easy smile.

"I assume you have come bearing ill tidings?" Mary asked Alexander forthrightly, coming around the desk and between the two men, providing a bit of distance between them. "Are we in trouble?"

"Aren't we always?" Alexander quipped in his sardonic manner.

"What now?" Mary asked, steeling herself for further calamity.

"I'm afraid Stephanos' untimely death has only fueled Saul's bloodlust," Alexander stated grimly, his glittering gaze flitting between Mary and the astonished doctor. "Tonight, Saul of Tarsus persuaded the high priest to organize yet another 'emergency' meeting of the Council. He has convinced the Sanhedrin that the city will remain unstable, ripe for revolt, until every last believer has been exterminated."

Luke drew back in horror. "The believers pose no threat to the Sanhedrin, nor to Rome!"

"You don't have to convince me," Alexander scoffed.

"On what grounds has this Saul of Tarsus presented such astounding accusations?" Luke asked in disbelief, his practical mind demanding an explanation.

"There have been 'incidents' on the streets, in the synagogues, near the Temple..." Alexander mused, his dark eyes flashing fire. "And it's getting worse. Saul has convinced the religious leaders that the Romans will take notice, intervening with force, if the problem—which is *us*, by the way—persists."

"I'm well aware of such *incidents*," Mary spoke up, shaking her regal head in dismay. "Jews and Romans alike have become increasingly violent toward believers, spitting, throwing rocks, and hurling dust at us in the markets and on the streets. But, Alexander, not once has a believer instigated a confrontation or even responded in retaliation."

"*You* know that, and *I* know that," Alexander responded, a muscle jerking in his chiseled jawline. "But the Sanhedrin remains under Saul's hypnotic spell."

"This is outrageous," Luke declared, the first time Mary had seen the calm, composed doctor ruffled about anything. "Something must be done about this!"

"Any suggestions?" Alexander quipped a bit snidely. "Saul has the Sanhedrin in his pocket."

"We must alert the believers," Mary said quietly. "I will host a special meeting tomorrow evening."

"It might be in everyone's best interest to leave

the city, at least for a time."

"It might," Mary agreed sadly. "The Lord will guide each family in the way they should go. Some may be called to leave, others to stay."

"And you?" Luke ventured quietly, the concern evident in his brown eyes. "What will you do, Mary?"

"Whatever God asks," Mary replied, touching his arm in reassurance.

"Your informant may be right," Luke told her earnestly.

"*May* be right?" Alexander repeated, annoyed.

"Perhaps you should leave the city for a time, Mary."

"I will take it before the Lord, my friend," Mary promised. "But for now, let's focus on alerting the others so they, too, can seek the Lord and make informed decisions."

"The threat of imprisonment surely hangs over your heads," Luke said, "but perhaps you can take comfort in knowing the Sanhedrin has no right to capital punishment. You needn't fear for your lives."

"Ah, and how would you explain what happened to Stephanos?" Alexander shot back, perturbed.

The doctor fell thoughtfully silent, mulling over the information he'd been presented.

"Luke is correct when he says the Sanhedrin has no legal right to capital punishment," Mary said gently, sensing Alexander's mounting ire. "Unfortunately, we've seen firsthand how easily they find ways around that statute."

"Undoubtedly, the death penalty will prove more challenging for the Sanhedrin to enforce, and we can thank God for that," Alexander conceded grimly, his stark features even more striking in the waning lamplight. "More likely, believers will be fined, lashed, beaten, or imprisoned. But we must brace ourselves, Mary. Some of us will be murdered if the Sanhedrin can get away with it."

The silence that followed was heavily laden with tension. Mary knew the believers must be on guard—not only against the Sanhedrin, but against rising tensions within the body, as well. Apprehension often bred arguments and ill tempers. The enemy would undoubtedly come against them by means of infiltration, as well, stirring up trouble on the inside even as the Sanhedrin came against them from the outside.

"The entire city knows of our church gatherings here," Mary quietly observed, turning to meet Alexander's purposeful gaze. "Should we designate another meeting place, somewhere hidden, underground?"

"You, Mary, were discussed at length during the Council meeting," Alexander divulged, obviously amused. "Honestly, according to Gamaliel and the high priest, you are untouchable. I don't think they would dare arrest followers here amidst a peaceful public gathering."

"But why not?" Mary asked, staring at Alexander in shock. "Why am *I* untouchable?"

"You have something akin to diplomatic immunity, Mary," Alexander grinned, enjoying the Sanhedrin's predicament. "You dominate the oil industry in Jerusalem, not to mention in the nearby provinces. That aside, you have enough money, power, and influence to cause quite a stir, and they know that. Not to mention, the Temple compound depends upon your groves to produce ritually pure olive oil. And your brother, Barnabas, has been wise to maintain his connections within the Levitical community. By some miracle, he still has the ear of his former instructor, Gamaliel, which drives Saul utterly mad."

"I see," Mary replied, fascinated. "Perhaps we can use these facts to our advantage."

"Amen to that," Alexander agreed, his tone resonating with purpose.

"Then if you are certain, we will continue to meet here for the believers' safety."

"Are you sure about that, Mary?" Luke spoke up quietly, his soft brown eyes reflecting his concern for her. "It could be dangerous."

"But it is far more dangerous to fear man above God," Mary assured him, her mind already made up. "Unless the Lord has other plans, we will continue to meet in the Upper Room."

"Please, take no offense, Alexander," Luke dared, pacing the elaborate tile floor. "But what if you're wrong about Mary's standing with the Sanhedrin? Are you placing her in danger?"

"We're *all* in danger, or hadn't you noticed?" Alexander shot back, peeved.

"Very well."

"I must go," Alexander said darkly, clearly wrestling with deep emotion. Reaching into a satchel slung over one powerful shoulder, Alexander produced an armload of slim parchment scrolls. "I was one of the functioning stenographers when Stephanos was tried before the Sanhedrin; therefore, I copied his final address meticulously, word for word, and I've spent the last month producing copies to keep on file—one for you, Mary, plus one for each of the Twelve, as well as one for Tabitha and a few extra to spare."

"Oh, Alexander." Tears sprang to Mary's eyes as she accepted the pile of scrolls. "You have no idea how much this will mean for us, for Tabitha."

"If you don't mind my asking, why Tabitha?" Luke interrupted, perplexed.

"Tabitha was married to Stephanos," Mary said, turning soft eyes upon the surprised young doctor.

"I had no idea," Luke breathed, running his hand down the back of his neck. "Had I known, I would have most certainly offered my condolences. How is she, Mary?"

"She's wrestling with grief, as can be expected," Mary replied sadly, while Alexander's pointed look warned the young Gentile against any bright ideas.

"I see," Luke responded, his eyes filled with pity. "Alexander, may I be so bold as to request a copy of your deacon's final speech?"

Mary and Alexander stared at the physician in surprise.

"He was an eloquent speaker, a force to be reckoned with," Luke explained, his tone begging them to understand. "I'd like to know what he lived and died for."

Placing the pile of scrolls upon her desk, Mary turned to face her informant in question, seeking his permission.

"I don't know what on earth you'll do with it," Alexander shrugged, looking over the intelligent young doctor. "But, sure. Why not?"

Gingerly retrieving a slender scroll, Mary held it out to the physician.

"Thank you most kindly, both of you," Luke said

with great feeling as he accepted the parchment scroll, tucking it away in his leather medical bag for safekeeping.

"I have entrusted these scrolls to your care, Mary," Alexander resumed, his dark eyes flickering with hidden emotion. "Now our brother's final message shall be preserved for all time."

"Praise God," Mary breathed softly, brushing at a stubborn tear. "Thank you, Alexander."

"And now I really must go," Alexander told her, his tone laced with regret.

"I understand. God be with you, my brother."

Taking powerful strides, Alexander paused beneath the pillared entryway, his dark eyes glistening with intensity. "From this point forward, everything changes, Mary. I know you – —you won't turn anyone away. But keep this in mind: every new face presents a new threat. Our enemies may be hidden in plain sight. How can we truly know who comes seeking the truth, and who has been sent as a wolf in sheep's clothing?" He paused, allowing the gravity of the situation to fully sink in. "You will remain in my prayers, Mary."

"And you, in mine."

"Be strong in the Lord." Drawing his hood over his head, Alexander slipped into the darkness of the open court, blending with the night.

CHAPTER 51

Mary

Having first consulted with the twelve apostles, the six remaining deacons of the Jerusalem church, and the Lord's brother, James, Mary sat on a bench beside a very quiet Tabitha, listening as Simon Peter addressed the entire church assembly from the wooden platform. Frankly and honestly, Peter presented the facts to them, openly relaying the grave danger they now faced.

How strange it felt, meeting with armed guards stationed before the entrance! Excepting Zev, her guards were believing men. Perhaps they would benefit from the apostle's faith-filled sermons. She certainly hoped so.

Precious Lord, Mary prayed silently as numerous questions and concerns were voiced from the congregation, *please grant us a spirit of faith and power rather than fear. Please grant each of us wisdom, leading us and guiding us as You see fit.*

Mary sat, listening, with her hands folded in her lap as the remaining apostles joined Peter on the platform, patiently bearing with the believers' concerns, offering sound counsel and godly wisdom. Families with young children and those caring for infirm or elderly relatives wondered aloud if they should relocate to safer regions. With tears in their eyes, parents discussed selecting guardians for their children, since imprisonment—even death—had suddenly become a very real possibility.

Numerous questions arose, some of which seemingly possessed no answers. Should believers keep their faith a secret at a time like this? Should those with young children refrain from evangelizing for the sake of protecting their little ones? Could the children be trained to locate their assigned guardians if their parents were unexpectedly victimized? And should assets and property be sold to produce extra funds in case of sudden emergencies?

As the believers continued speaking frankly among themselves and seeking guidance from the apostles, Candace, seated on the bench in front of Mary, turned to face her, cradling a sleepy, bleary-eyed Rufus in her arms. "Simon and I are in agreement," she whispered, her soft eyes betraying the pain in her heart. "Should anything happen to us, will you receive our boys, Mary?"

Luminous eyes filling with compassion, Mary squeezed Candace's shoulder in understanding. "Absolutely," she responded without hesitation. "You have my word."

From the corner of her eye, Mary noticed Tabitha's head come up. Was she wondering why her dearest friend hadn't asked her to take on the children? Surely Tabitha understood that Candace's selfless nature wouldn't permit her to thrust such a huge responsibility upon Tabitha during her time of grief.

"Naturally, our first thought was to ask Kelila and Philip," Candace explained, also sensing Tabitha's hidden reaction. "They are family, after all. But they will be newlyweds, surely desiring to raise a family of their own. And, Tabitha," she added gently, "I wouldn't think of asking you to take on such a task right now. You need time to grieve, time to heal."

Tabitha said nothing, appearing to stiffen on the bench.

"But, Tabitha, if anything happens to me and my dear husband," Candace continued with a hint of mischief, "you'd best remember my boys consider you an adoptive aunt! There will be no riding off into the sunset for you," she teased, her brown eyes sparkling despite her deep concerns. "You will always be an incredibly special part of Rufus and Alexander's lives."

Tabitha simply nodded, offering a very faint smile.

Giving Tabitha's knee a playful squeeze, Candace turned back toward the platform to heed the active question-and-answer session between the believers and the apostles. As the darkness thickened beyond the rectangular windows overlooking the outer court, the Upper Room basked in the rosy glow of flickering candles and glimmering oil lamps, bathed not only in the cheerful firelight but also the presence of God. After every imaginable question had been raised and addressed, the apostles led the gathering in heartfelt prayer, beseeching the Lord to lead and guide each individual family.

"The Holy Spirit will lead you, each and every one of you," Simon Peter said after nearly an hour of fervent prayer. "Some of you have undoubtedly received answers as we sought the Lord in prayer tonight. Others will receive your revelation as the Lord sees fit. But let us never forget," he added, his sober gaze sweeping over the tense gathering, "our times are in God's hands. And we, too, can seek Him just as our ancestor, the mighty King David, once did. Please, bow your heads and pray along with me."

Mary watched as the apostles on the platform placed strong arms about each other's shoulders. The congregation followed suit, taking the hands of the believers seated on each side of them. Seated on the end of the bench, Mary took Tabitha's cold hand in her own before gracefully bowing her head.

"Oh, God," Peter cried, surrounded by his brothers in Christ, each of them praying silently in agreement, "*deliver me from the hand of my enemies, and from those who persecute me. Make Your face shine upon Your servant; save me for Your mercies' sake. Do not let me be ashamed, O Lord, for I have called upon You.*"

Encouraged, Mary's heart responded as the congregation rippled with softly spoken *amens*, dispelling the spirit of fear attempting to settle over the righteous gathering. *Thank You, precious, Father,* her heart cried. *Here, fear has no place. Here, in Your sacred presence, the enemy must flee in sheer defeat. Here, bathed in Your Holy Spirit, we are safe.*

Quoting the righteous prayer of David, Peter's powerful voice wafted over the congregation, strengthening the hearts of many. "*Let the lying lips be put to silence, which speak insolent things proudly and contemptuously against the righteous,*" he prayed, his voice resonating with authority. "*Oh, how great is Your goodness, which You have laid up for those who fear You, which You have prepared for those who trust in You in the presence of the sons of men!"*

Mary smiled to herself as the entire assembly stirred with passionate agreement, the Upper Room resounding with firm *amens*.

"You shall hide them in the secret place of Your presence from the plots of man," Peter cried out with great conviction, raising strong arms in worship. *"You shall keep them secretly in a pavilion from the strife of tongues."*

"Amen!"

Opening his eyes, Peter's burning gaze swept over shining faces, now strengthened in the everlasting, never-failing Word of God. *"Oh, love the Lord, all you His saints! For the Lord preserves the faithful, and fully repays the proud person."*

"Amen, amen! Praise God! So be it!"

Mary's heart responded along with the rest, filled with faith, abounding in peace.

"Be of good courage, and He shall strengthen your heart," Peter declared, and Mary imagined he spoke with the passion and fervency of the one who had penned the ancient psalm. *"All you who hope in the Lord."*

***

Late into the night, Mary sat before the elegant, marble-topped vanity in her bedchamber, brushing her lush, waist-length hair with long, graceful strokes. Kissed with waning candlelight, her exotic features were illuminated in the shimmering glass as she reflected upon all that was discussed during the prayer meeting that night.

So much had happened in such a short period

of time. The shocking martyrdom of their beloved Stephanos had only served to embolden their enemies, particularly Saul of Tarsus. Setting aside her ornate ivory brush, Mary folded her hands in her lap, gazing distractedly at her own sober reflection. After the prayer service had ended, many believing families had lingered to discuss their plans of action. Many had decided to simply pack up and relocate, taking their elderly, infirm, and little ones with them.

Though Mary couldn't blame them, she wondered if perhaps their decisions were motivated by a lack of faith. And yet the families she had spoken with hadn't seemed afraid. Some even seemed excited, anxious to take the gospel to new places, regions where it might be received with gladness rather than hostility.

Several paces behind her, gentle Rhoda was singing sweetly over the sleeping orphaned child, a Scriptural hymn about the might and power of their great God triumphing against His foes. Her quiet song seemed to soothe the anxious toddler now sleeping tranquilly in her cozy little bed.

"*Though an army may encamp against me, my heart shall not fear; though war may rise against me, in this I will be confident...*"

Closing her eyes, Mary exhaled slowly, basking in the peaceful promise of the ancient psalm. She decided Rhoda's song was quite fitting for the occasion.

Like Mary's heart within her aching chest, the church was breaking apart, piece by piece, before her very eyes. The believers were scattering like hens after seed, fleeing Saul's coming rampage.

Thank God the apostles feel called to stay, Mary

thought, pressing delicate hands against her throbbing heart. *And James, the Lord's brother, will also remain.* To Mary's profound relief, Simon and Candace also believed the Lord had directed them to remain in Jerusalem. Mary assumed Candace's lovely young sister and Philip, her betrothed, would also stay.

True, many believers had chosen to remain in the city. And for that, Mary was grateful. She cherished her church family as if they were her own kin, her own flesh and blood, now aching to see so many of them preparing to set out for a new life, one that no longer included her.

Righteous Father, I know you work all things together for good, Mary prayed, grasping at her faith like a lifeline. *But this? Your people are being scattered abroad, hunted down like beasts of prey. What good can come from this, Father? Help me understand.*

Mary waited, wondering what kind of answer she had expected to result from her presumptuous request. Sensing nothing, she plunged ahead with her heartfelt confession.

Father, I trust Your will; truly, I do. But please, help my unbelief. My heart is breaking inside my chest. Your church is being torn apart. Some will go to the outlying regions of Judea, others to Galilee and possibly even Samaria. How shall we remain banded together when separated by so many miles? How shall we stand united amidst this great dispersion?

And then an entirely unexpected revelation hit Mary with the force of a ton of bricks. Straightening in her regal chair, Mary's eyes snapped open in disbelief as her Savior's words sprang to mind as vividly as if they now floated before her upon the still, night air.

But you shall receive power when the Holy Spirit comes upon you; and you shall be witnesses to Me in Jerusalem, and in all Judea and Samaria, and to the ends of the earth.

"In Jerusalem...and in *all* Judea...and even Samaria..." Mary whispered, her heart pounding furiously in her chest.

Go therefore and make disciples of all the nations, baptizing them in the name of the Father and of the Son and of the Holy Spirit...

Go therefore and make disciples of all the nations...all the nations! Suddenly, it all made sense.

In faith, she had asked. In His mercy, God had answered.

Oh Father, why do I even bother doubting Your wisdom? She thought, her lips lifting in a soft smile of thrilling wonderment.

Even now, God's perfect plan was being carried out! Ruthless men had unintentionally brought about the fulfillment of prophecy, the very thing her Lord had predicted before returning to His Father in Heaven!

Chuckling to herself, Mary bowed her head in heartfelt worship. She couldn't wait to tell the others, especially Tabitha...if the grieving young widow was ready to receive the shocking revelation.

But for now, she would be still, resting in the all-consuming peace her Savior had so graciously supplied.

CHAPTER 52

Philip

Philip stood enshrouded in darkness, standing before an open door. Suddenly, shafts of blinding light exploded from the formerly unassuming doorway, knocking him off his feet. Stunned to his very core, Philip pushed himself up on one elbow, slowly, cautiously rising to his full height.

The opened door remained before him, flooding his field of vision with fair, ethereal light, beckoning, inviting him to enter. Cautiously glancing both ways, Philip allowed himself a nervous peep through the open door.

Gently rolling hills, lush and verdant, stretched forth beneath a cloudless sapphire sky. As if experiencing an instant, lightning glimpse of an entire province, Philip saw stone houses and open courts, bustling markets sheltered beneath colorful awnings, stately looking synagogues, thriving orchards, and dusty, well-traveled streets. Sheep grazed upon a distant hillside, bleating in contentment as their little lambs skipped about. Blinking in amazement, Philip wondered about the mysterious land he now beheld just beyond the open door.

And then he saw His blessed Savior, seated beside an ancient stone well, deep in conversation with a bold-looking woman bearing a heavy earthen jar, her dark head uncovered, her dress—along with her manner—both colorful and flamboyant.

The woman at the well.

Jesus, Philip's heart responded, his entire being rejoicing at the sight of his Lord. *Jesus, how desperately we miss You, Lord. The sound of Your voice and contagious laughter, the kindness reflected in Your gentle eyes, Your soothing, healing touch.*

See, I have set before you an open door...

Philip shot up in bed like a lightning bolt, drawing a ragged breath. Heart pounding furiously in his chest, he breathed in the fresh night air, struggling to regain his bearings.

Instinctively, he knew he had experienced a vision. The mysterious land, a foreign people, the sight of His beloved Jesus seated beside a familiar well...

Throwing aside his covering, Philip rose from his bed. Crossing the small chamber he had faithfully prepared for his lovely bride-to-be, Philip paused before a neatly latticed window. Pushing open the wooden shutters with trembling hands, he gazed upon a vibrant moon, rising steadily in the velvet night sky.

Philip had thought he'd *known* what the future held for him—for him and his beautiful bride. How many hours, weeks, and months had he invested in this perfect little home, lovingly fashioning every latticed window, every seamless doorframe, every shelf and cupboard, every single detail! For months, Philip had dreamed of lifting his bride in strong arms, carrying her over the threshold, taking her hand and leading her to this very bedchamber outfitted with the finest furniture he could afford. Here, they would have begun a life together. Here, they would have raised a family in the fear of the Lord... in Jerusalem, the holy city.

Oh, Lord, what shall I tell my betrothed? What on earth would Kelila have to say about all this? She, too, had spent months planning a life with him in Jerusalem.

Gazing out the narrow window, Philip raised questioning eyes toward Heaven, shaken to his very core. The supernatural vision had gripped his heart, setting his entire being ablaze with swelling apprehension...but also with resolve.

Thy will be done, Lord. Recognizing the eternal call of God, Philip bowed his head in acceptance of his divine orders, pondering all that had been revealed to him, hardly believing *he* would be the privileged one taking the gospel of Jesus Christ to the most unexpected of places.

Soon, he would go to Samaria.

***

Kelila

"I think it's wonderful!"

"You *do*?" Philip stared at his betrothed, open-mouthed.

"Of course!" Kelila declared, her dark brown eyes sparkling with excitement. "Philip, you were right all along!"

"I was?"

"Yes! The Lord *does* have a calling for us, Philip! And now He's shown you exactly what it is. Now, we can truly begin to plan!"

Standing with Kelila in the open outer court adjoining Simon and Candace's house, Philip shook his head in absolute amazement. Despite the immense relief welling inside his chest, he couldn't help but think Kelila's response was simply too good to be true. Did she fully understand what he was saying? Would she still feel this way once the reality of it fully sank in?

"Kelila," Philip said slowly, taking her delicate hands in his. "Do you realize what this means?"

"Tell me," Kelila smiled, more radiant than Philip had ever seen her, especially as golden sunlight streamed down upon them as if pronouncing the Lord's mercy and favor.

"It means we must *leave* Jerusalem," Philip explained gently, his brown eyes tenderly searching hers. "It will be difficult at first. Our friends are here. Our church is here. Your family, Kelila—Simon and Candace, Alexander and Rufus—desire to remain here in Jerusalem. When we journey to Samaria, all these things will be left behind."

Tears sprang to Kelila's eyes as the full impact of their calling began to sink in. For the briefest moment, Philip wondered if she had changed her mind. What if she refused to go to Samaria? What if she called off their wedding?

Then Kelila smiled through her tears, her dark eyes filled with peace.

"What is it, my love?" Philip asked, his heart

aching just a bit.

"I love you, Philip," Kelila said, draping her arms over his shoulders and clasping her hands behind his neck. "Soon, you will be my husband. I support you in your calling."

"I know it is so much to ask," Philip said hoarsely, torn between his love for God and his desire to please this beautiful woman. "But, Kelila, if you've changed your mind about me, about *us*—"

"Hush," Kelila teased, placing a slender finger against his lips. "Not for a moment, Philip."

"But your life, everything you *love*, Kelila, it's all here in Jerusalem—"

"I love *you*, Philip," Kelila reminded him, her shining eyes confirming her declaration. "And I love God. Is God confined to *this* city, unable to breach its borders? Of course not! God is in Samaria, too, Philip, and now He has asked us to join Him there."

Blinking back tears, Philip silently praised His gracious Father for this remarkable, godly woman. She was no longer the selfish, willful girl he'd met at the fruit vendor's booth. No, Kelila was fast blossoming into a mature, powerful woman of faith.

How he loved her!

"Besides," Kelila grinned with a playful tilt of her head, sending her lush black waves cascading over one shoulder, "we can visit Jerusalem anytime we'd like! And my family can visit us in Samaria once we get settled in! Oh, what fun! Wouldn't the boys just love to travel?"

Philip stared at his betrothed in awe. "Kelila, you amaze me, beloved."

"Have you so soon forgotten the pledge of Ruth the Moabitess?" Kelila demanded, her eyes growing uncharacteristically serious. "I stand by her wisdom, Philip, and her vow shall become my own to you."

Philip knew he should say something, but his lips refused to form the words. He was utterly overcome, disarmed by her wisdom, grace, and beauty.

"Don't you remember?" Kelila prodded, stepping even closer.

"Of course," Philip responded hoarsely, gazing into the exquisite face he adored.

"*Wherever you go*, Philip, *I will go*," Kelila promised, tenderly touching his bearded face. "*And wherever you lodge, I will lodge. Your people shall be my people*—even the Samaritans!" she laughed, and Philip couldn't help but chuckle along with her. "And, after all, your God is already my God."

Pulling his bride-to-be close, Philip buried his face in her neck, dampening her lush raven-black tresses with his tears.

"*Where you die, I will die, and there I will be buried*," Kelila continued, wrapping slender arms around him. "*The Lord do so to me, and more also, if anything but death parts you and me.*"

When Philip pulled away, his eyes were shining—not only with traces of happy tears, but also with boundless joy. "I believe it's about time to make you my wife, beloved."

Flashing her famous smile, Kelila gazed up at him, playfully batting long lashes. "What's taking you so long, anyway?"

"You'd best prepare yourself, beloved. It could be any day now." Planting a firm kiss on her smooth forehead, Philip turned to depart.

CHAPTER FIFTY-THREE

Mary

Standing upon the hanging balcony overlooking the spacious outer court and the great stone fountain below, Mary's solemn gray eyes scanned the distant horizon as dusk settled upon Jerusalem, once a shining city upon a hill, a gleaming beacon of light—now, an enemy fortress harboring agents of darkness.

Alexander's dreaded prediction had been realized with alarming speed, for Saul was attacking God's church with a vengeance, arresting both men and women, throwing them in prison, and relishing their torture. Some, in the throes of unbearable agony, had even denied their faith to obtain a swift release.

Oh God, my God, Mary prayed, visualizing the faces of precious brothers and sisters now in chains, *I saw great potential in Saul. These many years have I prayed for him earnestly, believing You were at work.*

Clutching at her heart with trembling hands, Mary stood rigid and still upon the balcony as warm tears slipped beneath her closed lids.

How could I have been so wrong?

Ambushing believers with calculated fury, Saul always seemed to know where to find the ones he sought, and always far removed from Rome's watchful eye or witnesses' prying gazes. Only days prior, he had descended upon a secret location where several deacons rendezvoused at the house of unbelieving relatives. Beating down the door, Saul and his cronies had dragged the deacons away in chains.

How had he possibly known where to find them?

Clenching the elegant railing with tense, white-knuckled hands, Mary lifted her face against the wind as evening breezes tugged at her thick, long braid.

Her brother had paid her an unexpected visit the night before. With tears in his eyes, Barnabas had promised to depart for Cyprus, taking John Mark with him, if anything happened to her in Jerusalem. Recalling his desperate entreaties, Mary's gaze swept over the dim city, landing near the district housing Barnabas' opulent neighborhood.

I fear for you, my sister, Barnabas had admitted, his soft eyes spilling over with concern. *Come away with me now—both you and John Mark—if only for a time. Allow me to protect you.*

Though she cherished her brother's tenderhearted concern, Mary had stoutly refused.

Someone must remain on the front lines, she thought, squaring her shoulders in resolve. Though many believers had been called to relocate, she was not among them.

She would stand and fight.

The faintest hint of a smile lurked about Mary's lips as the Spirit stirred within her heart. Her enemies hadn't the slightest idea what they were up against.

They didn't know her God.

***

Alexander

Alexander awakened to a sound akin to a battering ram, splintering wood, pounding footfalls, and his wife's terrified screams.

Plunging out of bed, Alexander reached for the flickering lamp on the bedside stand as armed guards bearing sputtering torches barreled into the small bedchamber, spears glistening.

Even in the dark, Alexander recognized the guards from Caiaphas' own employ, their features cast in the torchlight's writhing shadows.

"What is the meaning of this?" Alexander demanded, coming around the bed as his wife cowered behind him, hastily shrugging into a modest robe and reaching for her shawl.

"You're under arrest," one of the guards huffed, taking his lamp while another grasped him roughly by the shoulders and spun him around to bind his wrists.

"For what charge?" his wife, Mara, demanded in outrage.

"Trust me, woman, you don't want to know."

"I work for your superior," Mara shouted, boldly facing the slew of guards. "I'll have you prosecuted for this!"

"Bind the woman," the first guard ordered tersely, offering Mara a fiendish smile. "You're coming, too."

"Mara, *go*!" Alexander shouted as an officer hauled him toward the door.

"I won't leave you!" Mara screamed, her face streaked with tears.

"Go, *now*!"

As several guards pushed their way toward Mara, Alexander sprang into action, plunging his powerful shoulder into the nearest guard's. With a loud grunt, the soldier staggered forward, sending his torch plunging onto the bed.

The straw mattress erupted in flames, forming a partial barrier between Mara and the armed men. The guards drew back, outraged.

"You filthy dog!" one of them shouted in fury.

As the flames spread across the bed, licking at the walls and the ceiling, Mara pressed herself flat against the farthest wall. Alexander had successfully separated her from the guards—and himself. Now, the large, open window behind her was her only escape.

"Alexander!" she cried, devastated.

"Mara, *go*!" Alexander shouted as the guards hauled him out the bedroom door, cursing him with every breath. One of the men kicked him behind the knee, almost bringing him down. "Get out! *Now*!"

"I love you, Alexander!" Mara wept, planting both hands on the windowsill and hoisting herself over the ledge. "I'll find you! I'll get you out!"

Daring a glance over his shoulder, Alexander saw his wife disappear through the square opening just as one of the guards roughly shoved his head down, pushing him through the remainder of his modest house and out the main door.

Bursting out of the house and into the balmy night air, Alexander's gaze instinctively swept the perimeter as a chill winter breeze teased the foliage underfoot and the palm fronds overhead. A breathtaking display of glistening stars rivaled the beauty of a tranquil silver moon. Had it not been for the shouting of the guards and the putrid smell of smoke lingering in the air, one might have mistaken it for yet another peaceful evening.

Pushed along by two armed guards, Alexander was brought face to face with a heavily cloaked man of low stature, yet powerful build, appearing like a specter of death in the silver moonlight, his broad legs splayed, his feet firmly planted upon the gravel walkway.

Throwing back his hood, the cloaked figure studied Alexander as a predator might size up its prey. Hard, uncompromising eyes narrowed in disdain as Alexander was forced roughly to his knees by several guards. Glancing over his prisoner's head, the cloaked figure—clearly the ringleader of the surly band—surveyed the small house now being consumed by writhing amber flames. Dark eyes hardened in fury, sparking with burning hatred.

Saul of Tarsus.

Alexander wasn't the least bit surprised to see him. In fact, he'd been expecting him all along.

God, guide my wife to safety, Alexander prayed. *Deliver me from the evil one.*

With a loud hiss, red hot flames burst forth from the open windows of the small house, sending shards of pottery, splintering wood, and glowing embers dancing and fluttering upon the evening breezes.

Turning his attention back to Alexander, Saul's ruthless eyes hardened along with his jawline. "I should have known it was you all along."

"You'll have to be a bit more specific," Alexander quipped rather drolly. "What have I done to deserve such special treatment?"

"You know exactly what I'm talking about."

"I can't read minds, you know. But I appreciate your vote of confidence."

Planting his hands firmly upon his knees, Saul bent so he was eye level with the fearless informant. "When I get through with you, you're going to wish you were dead."

"I'd expect nothing less from you," Alexander replied, flashing a sardonic grin.

Straightening to his full height—which was rather unimpressive, in Alexander's opinion—Saul turned to face the guards flanking him from behind. "Lock him up, men. We'll deal with him at dawn."

CHAPTER 54

Mary

Unable to sleep, Mary roved about her quiet villa, careful not to disturb the slumbering staff. Armed with a brightly burning candle, she traveled a cool, frescoed hall, pausing on the threshold of her son's private bedchamber. Lifting her candlestick a bit higher, Mary observed her sleeping son upon his bed.

Heart twisting inside her chest, Mary leaned against the doorpost, poignantly watching him sleep. He appeared so tranquil, so carefree. At fifteen years of age, he was beginning to look very much like his handsome father.

Lord God, protect this precious son of mine. Bowing her head, Mary prayed over her only child, earnestly beseeching the Lord on his behalf.

Feeling drained, she turned and ambled back down the hall. Taking a broad marble stairway, Mary descended to the first floor, emerging in the vast, lamplit reception hall. The mosaic floor felt cold upon her bare feet.

Suddenly, an explosion of sound erupted like a shock wave in the outer court—a woman crying out, followed by furious pounding upon the bronze double doors.

Heart racing and adrenaline kicking in on overdrive, Mary hastily deposited her candlestick upon a nearby stand, flying across the reception hall and entering a narrow, frescoed vestibule.

More shouts, followed by a loud scuffle and a woman's muffled screams.

Flinging open the double doors, Mary stood rooted upon the threshold, heart pounding like a battle drum in her chest.

Zev stood in the outer court, one powerful arm imprisoning a tall, slender woman as he attempted to drag her from the courtyard. She struggled violently against him, her garments and shawl askew, desperately striving to pry off the hand clamped firmly over her mouth.

The woman looked to Mary, wild-eyed and frightened.

"Mara!" Mary cried out, staring at her guard in shock. "Zev, release her this instant!"

"You know this woman?" Zev demanded, tightening his grip around Mara's waist.

"Of course, I do. And I demand that you release her!"

Grudgingly, Zev acquiesced.

Rewarding Zev with a cold glare, Mara stumbled across the courtyard, taking Mary's shoulders in an iron grip. "They took him!" she sobbed, doubling over in anguish.

Casting a severe warning glance toward Zev,

Mary redirected her attention toward the weeping woman. "Mara, what has happened?"

"It's that despicable Saul. He's arrested my husband!"

Oh, God, no. Please. Fleetingly, Mary wondered if her heart had stopped. *Not Alexander.*

"When?" Mary managed, steadying Mara as best she could. "Tonight?"

"I escaped," Mara gasped, pressing the heels of her hands against her eyes. "But they took my husband and our house is burned to the ground. Oh, Mary, what can we do?"

Glancing over Mara's shoulder, Mary was unsettled by the odd look upon Zev's face.

"Mara, please. Come inside."

"Shall I escort you both, my lady?" Zev inquired, his voice sounding strange in Mary's ears.

"No," Mary responded quickly, feeling uneasy. "Please remain stationed at your post."

Turning from the grim-faced sentry, Mary quickly drew Mara inside the ornate vestibule, promptly closing the door behind them.

"Your guard is a brute!" Mara pronounced angrily, adjusting her disheveled shawl.

"Oh, Mara, forgive me, dear sister," Mary breathed, touching the young woman's tearstained face. The red imprint of Zev's hand was still visible upon her fair skin. Mary's delicate brow furrowed in anger. Tonight, Zev had gone too far. "His behavior was inexcusable."

"Oh, enough about him," Mara plunged ahead, near panic. "What can be done for my husband, Mary? We must help him!"

Closing her eyes, Mary sought the Lord for answers, receiving none.

"Well?" Mara demanded, nearly beside herself with grief. "We can't just let them take him!"

"What's going on?"

Both women glanced up in surprise as Tabitha entered the narrow vestibule, armed with a dimly lit oil lamp.

Glancing between the two troubled women, Tabitha's countenance paled. "Oh, no. Mara, I'm so sorry."

"Mary, Tabitha, you have to listen to me," Mara said, her eyes boring into her friends'. "Alexander believes we're dealing with a double agent. He told me just this evening, before they came for him."

Mary and Tabitha blinked in surprise.

"A double agent?" Mary repeated blankly.

"Someone on the inside," Mara insisted fiercely. "Possibly someone in this very house."

"Mara, I think that's highly unlikely," Mary soothed even as she began to second-guess herself. She'd known and relied upon her staff for years, many of them for over a decade! Surely they could all be trusted.

"How else would Saul know where to find those in hiding?" Mara pressed. "The deacons he just arrested—Saul couldn't have possibly known where they were staying, Mary—not without an *informant*! And my husband? His cover was flawless. He would've fooled me too if I wasn't married to him!"

"I'd have to agree," Mary admitted, deeply troubled. If Alexander had successfully gained the trust of the high priest himself, what could have possibly tipped Saul off?

Inexplicably grieved, Mary realized Mara must

be right. Someone had betrayed them—multiple times.

"If we don't find out who's doing this, more will be arrested, possibly even killed!" Mara insisted, her features tight with grief. "Mary, we can't let this go on."

"No, we can't," Mary agreed.

"Who would do this to us, my lady?" Tabitha demanded, ready to put an end to it right then and there.

"Oh, Tabitha, I wish I knew."

"What about that Gentile doctor?" Mara suggested, clearly suspicious. "Alexander says he's an unbeliever."

"Luke would never do such a thing," Mary assured her, alarmed.

"Then who?" Mara demanded. "Who is it?"

"Let's review the facts," Mary suggested, striving for calm as both women waited expectantly for answers. "Whoever it is, he or she has access to this house...to our prayer meetings and even our secret conferences with the apostles. That alone rules out Luke, the physician."

"But only our fellow believers have that kind of access," Mara pointed out.

"And the guards," Tabitha added practically.

Mary's countenance paled as the answer came.

Tabitha recognized that look. "You know who it is!"

"Oh, dear God," Mary breathed, reaching for the wall to stabilize herself as the color drained from her face. "How could I be so foolish, so naïve?"

"Mary?" Tabitha looked at her lady in question.

Releasing a tremorous sigh, Mary glanced knowingly between the two women, her eyes filled with pain…and remorse.

"Mary," Mara said slowly, planting a firm hand on her friend's shoulder. "What is it?"

Mary could have easily wept. Turning aside from the two women, she crossed the lamplit vestibule, pushing open the heavy double doors.

"Where are you going?" Tabitha demanded, frightened for her lady. Never had she seen such a look upon Mary's face.

"I know who it is," Mary declared fiercely, slipping into the night.

***

"How could you do this to us?"

Zev spun on his heel as his lady slammed open the iron gate, her gray eyes blazing with angry fire… and pain.

"What are you talking about?" Zev demanded gruffly, his grip tightening upon his glistening spear.

Observing the threatening gesture, Mary cried, "What are you going to do, Zev? Thrust your spear into my heart and then vanish into the night?"

Lifting his kindling torch, Zev studied her coldly.

"You might as well!" Mary nearly wept. "It would hurt far less than your hateful betrayal!"

"My betrayal? Have you gone mad?"

"Perhaps *you* have! Zev, I trusted you with my life—what's more, with the life of my son! How could you do this?"

"Do you even hear yourself, Mary? You are babbling like a mad woman. You don't even know what you're saying!"

"Oh, I wish I didn't, Zev," Mary replied, her tone dangerously quiet. "I gave you a second chance. And I stood up for you, Zev, even when others felt I should release you from my employ. How could you then stomp all over my kindness and mercy? I extended an olive branch, Zev, and you trampled it into the ground."

"Is there trouble, my lady?" Daniel, a young, believing guard, drew alongside her, concerned.

"I should say so," Mary stated with dangerous calm, her eyes boring into Zev's. "I must ask you, Daniel—was it Zev who stationed you in the Upper Room, commanding you to remain when the believers, church leaders, or apostles met?"

"Yes, my lady," Daniel responded hesitantly, clearly confused.

"And did Zev demand a full debriefing following any such meeting?"

"He did," Daniel replied slowly, clearly wondering what had so riled his typically composed mistress.

"I imagine you were thorough in your reports, Daniel."

"As I was commanded to be," Daniel replied, his eyes drifting between Mary and his captain. "My lady, may I ask what this is about?"

"This is about the fact that Zev has betrayed us, Daniel," Mary replied, her tone tinged with ice.

"This woman's gone mad!" Zev's eyes flickered slightly even as he maintained his innocence.

"Why did you do it?" Mary demanded, striving to maintain control. "How much were our lives worth to you, Zev? The promise of wealth? A few paltry coins?"

Zev's eyes hardened as a knowing smirk tight-

SEEKING THE TRUTH | 493

ened his features. "More than you'd ever dream of paying me."

"Oh, Zev." Gazing up at the guard through her tears, Mary wondered if this was how her Savior had felt when Judas stood before Him, having betrayed Him with a kiss.

"I suppose this is goodbye, then," Zev mused, his tone and manner laced with sarcasm as he thrust his flaming torch toward Daniel.

"I should have you arrested," Mary breathed as Daniel accepted the steadily burning torch, drawing protectively alongside his mistress. "Fortunately, you have no power over us once released from my employ."

Zev's smirk deepened as he turned to go.

"Zev."

The guard paused halfway down the cobbled way, casting a sardonic glance over his shoulder.

"You can tell your *boss* I'd wish him better luck next time—if I actually meant it."

Eyes kindling with hidden fury, Zev's jawline hardened in disdain. Shaking his head slowly as if pitying their ignorance, Zev turned his back upon them and vanished into the fog.

CHAPTER 55

Alexander

Seated with his back pressed against a cold stone wall, Alexander wondered what cruel tortures Saul was devising for him. A public beating, or flogging, perhaps? Better yet, maybe the Pharisee planned to feed him to a pack of wild dogs. That would prove interesting, he was quite sure.

He'd seen it done before, though it was the Romans who favored that inventive method of capital punishment.

Well, he liked dogs. Perhaps he could charm the rabid creatures before they had ample opportunity to devour him.

With a small smile, Alexander lifted his wrists, now draped in heavy iron chains matching the set biting into his ankles. He knew he should be concerned—maybe even near panic—and yet...he wasn't. Instead, he felt enveloped in the strangest sense of peace. As if imposing angels stood guard about his small holding cell, daring the enemy forces to engage.

At the far end of the dank chamber housing the tiny cell burrowed far beneath the house of his master, Caiaphas, a door creaked open on reluctant hinges.

Fascinated, Alexander rose, thankful the length of his chains permitted him to do so. Saul had promised—almost gleefully—that soldiers would retrieve him at dawn to obtain a confession and dole out his punishment. Based on the inky darkness just beyond the narrow vents stationed high above his cell, he supposed dawn to be several hours away.

Gripping the iron bars in a somewhat relaxed manner, Alexander listened as soft, padded footfalls approached his fortified cell. As a somber form approached him, Alexander deciphered the familiar outline of a Pharisee donning traditional, tasseled robes. In one trembling, outstretched hand, the Pharisee bore a dimly flickering oil lamp to light the way before him.

"*Shalom*, my good man," Alexander called with his usual dry humor. "To what do I owe the pleasure?"

"Shhh!" the Pharisee hissed, his dark eyes shifting in obvious fear as he paused anxiously before Alexander's cell. "Don't speak."

Alexander stared at the Pharisee in surprise. Though the puny flame from his small lamp did little to illuminate his features, Alexander sensed the Pharisee was young—very young. Everything about his manner and bearing conveyed his deep anxiety.

"I've come to release you," the Pharisee whispered

hoarsely, clearly scared out of his mind.

"Have they dropped the charges against me?" Alexander asked, stunned.

"Of course not," the Pharisee hissed, producing a heavy ring of large, wide-toothed keys from the pouch about his waist. Slipping a key into the lock, he turned it as quietly as possible, grimacing when the metal bolt slammed open.

"You're helping me escape?" Alexander stared at the Pharisee in utter shock.

"The evangelist was a good man," the Pharisee responded as if that explained everything. Kneeling, he unlocked Alexander's ankle shackles, then rose to remove the chains about his wrists. "Though we didn't agree doctrinally, what they did to Stephanos—it wasn't right," he explained, his voice catching. "And now they want to kill you, too."

"*Kill* me?" Alexander repeated in surprise. "Well, that isn't very sporting."

"Put these on," the young Pharisee commanded, shoving a pile of neatly folded garments against Alexander's broad chest.

"Did you fold these yourself?" Alexander inquired, shaking open the loose folds. "Nice work!"

"Just put them on."

"These are a *Pharisee's* robes!"

"How else do you intend to slip out of a *high priest's* house, unnoticed?"

"Good point, although Caiaphas favors the Sadducees," Alexander acknowledged wryly, slipping the first rough layer over his head. "Thanks to the master's secret councils, Pharisees and Sadducees alike have been coming and going throughout all hours of the night."

Clearly, the Pharisee wished Alexander would hurry up. His eyes darted about his surroundings, betraying his anxiety.

"This getup is downright scratchy," Alexander observed, shrugging into a heavy outer robe. "No wonder the Pharisees are so grouchy and bad-tempered."

His rescuer was not amused.

"Am I breaking one of your laws by wearing this?" Alexander quipped, fumbling with the fringed tallith.

"Don't ask," the Pharisee responded, and Alexander thought he detected a hint of humor in his tone.

"How do I look?" Alexander grinned, rotating and extending his arms to grant his rescuer the full effect.

"Ridiculous," the Pharisee responded curtly. Taking Alexander's arm, he dragged him down the length of the musty corridor. "But never mind. We must make haste."

"Pardon my asking—but won't the guard stationed beyond that door wonder why only *one* Pharisee went in, but *two* came back out?"

"I happen to know that the guard on duty has a weakness for strong drink. He keeps a flask with him to pass the time."

"So...?"

"*So* I slipped a little something in his flask before he left for work today." Guiding Alexander down the narrow hall, the Pharisee pushed open the sturdy prison door, revealing a guard slumped over on the floor. "Don't worry—he'll revive in a few hours."

"Devious." Alexander's respect for the nervous Pharisee heightened considerably. "I like it!"

Swiftly, the Pharisee tucked the heavy ring of keys into the slumbering guard's pouch. Straightening, he faced Alexander head-on, his face etched in shadow as torches burned steadily behind him. "You know Caiaphas' house like the back of your hand. Select the best route of escape and don't look back."

"If I do, shall I turn into a pillar of salt?"

"Are you always so flippant?"

"I have my moments."

"*Go!*"

"But, wait. First, I must thank you, my friend," Alexander insisted, placing a firm hand upon the young man's shoulder. "You've taken an incredible risk to free me. Surely you will allow me to repay you for this unspeakable kindness—"

"You can repay me by not getting caught. Now *go!*"

"As you wish," Alexander responded, sensing the urgency in the young man's tone. "But should you ever desire to learn more about what Stephanos lived and died for, please join me at the house of Mary. We'd be delighted to have you."

The Pharisee stared at him in exasperation.

"All right, all right! I'm leaving." Ceremoniously adjusting his billowing robes, Alexander assumed the pious air of a Pharisee, mentally calculating the best means of escape. Ascending a narrow, torchlit stairway leading to the ground level, Alexander glorified Almighty God for His unspeakable mercy—and His sense of humor. Straightening his distinguished-looking garments, he pressed his hands together in the self-righteous gesture he'd so often observed in laughable amusement, thoroughly enjoying the ironic ruse.

The apostles were going to love this story.

***

Tabitha

Dawn was fast approaching when a sharp, unexpected *rap, rap, rap* at the door jolted Mary, Mara, and Tabitha from their fervent prayer vigil.

"Who could that be at this early hour?" Mara asked dully, her bleary eyes betraying her extreme fatigue.

"Whoever it is, Daniel must have permitted him to enter the outer court," Mary observed, releasing Mara and Tabitha's hands. Had one of the apostles learned of Alexander's arrest? If so, had they come bearing news?

"Who's Daniel?" Mara asked, her mind hazy and clouded.

"Daniel is the guard Mary has assigned to take Zev's place," Tabitha explained, seated on a low stool before the women's straight-backed chairs. "At least, temporarily." Just thinking of Zev's infidelity filled her entire being with fury. Had she known of the guard's defection, she would have confronted the traitorous sentry herself!

God, rain down curses upon his proud, ugly head!

Rising in her typically poised manner, Mary crossed the large reception hall to answer the door.

Cheeks flaming, Tabitha realized that should have been *her* task to perform. Had she not been so busy calling down fiery curses upon their enemies, she wouldn't have irresponsibly left the job to her exhausted mistress.

Embarrassed, Tabitha watched as Mary disappeared into the dark vestibule. A moment later, Tabitha heard the heavy doors creaking open, followed by a sharp gasp from her mistress.

"My lady?" Tabitha asked, instantly on her feet.

Mara, too, straightened in her chair, troubled.

Mary came around the corner before Tabitha could reach her, leading a tall, broad-shouldered Pharisee by the arm.

Shrinking back in alarm, Tabitha stared at Mary, wide-eyed and openmouthed. Judging by his imposing build, this religious leader was not Nicodemus or Joseph of Arimathea, both of whom were followers of the Way.

Since when had Mary become so chummy with a *Pharisee*?

And then the Pharisee drew back his heavy cloak and tasseled tallith, flashing a broad, familiar grin.

"Alexander!" Instantly, Mara was on her feet, rushing for her husband with arms outstretched, weeping almost hysterically.

Alexander swept up his wife in strong arms as she buried her face in his neck, sobbing in relief.

As Mary stood beside the reunited couple, her eyes glistening with tears, Tabitha watched from a distance, a dull ache claiming her chest.

She wanted to be happy for Mara. She really did. But deep inside, she felt nothing save raging jealousy.

Why had God spared Mara's husband but taken *hers*?

It wasn't fair, nor was it just.

Quietly, Tabitha turned on her heels and slipped out of sight.

CHAPTER 56

Mary

Tabitha's silent withdrawal wasn't lost on Mary.

After congratulating Alexander on his miraculous escape, Mary insisted the couple remain with her—indefinitely, if need be.

"I'm afraid our presence here will only endanger you, Mary," Alexander said, his arm wrapped protectively around his wife. "Besides, I think it's about time we took a little vacation from Jerusalem."

"At least remain here with me until you've decided when and where to go," Mary insisted. "No one knows of your presence here. You will be safe."

"Your guard let me in."

"Daniel has no idea who you are," Mary assured him. "And we discovered the man responsible for turning you in. I assure you, he has been dealt with."

"I'd like to hear more about that," Alexander commented a bit brittlely.

"And I'd like to hear all about your miraculous release," Mary said, smiling. "But right now, you and Mara must rest. Please allow me to escort you to a guest room. There will be plenty of time for discussion in the morning."

"It's nearly morning now," Mara laughed, leaning contentedly on her husband's arm.

"And I don't expect to see either one of you before noon," Mary replied firmly, her tone boding no argument.

After the young couple was comfortably settled in a luxurious guest room, Mary turned, making her way briskly down a frescoed corridor.

Praying silently, she called upon the Lord for guidance. Sleep would have to come later, despite her keen exhaustion. For now, there was a far more pressing matter at hand.

***

"Tabitha?" Mary entered Tabitha's dimly lit chamber with caution, her luminous gray eyes alight with sympathy and understanding.

Sprawled across her bed, Tabitha pushed herself up on her elbows, her long hair falling over her shoulders and partially obscuring her tear-streaked face as she gazed up at Mary with fierce, red-rimmed eyes.

"Oh, beloved," Mary said, going to her. Lowering herself onto the narrow mattress, Mary reached for the brokenhearted girl.

"I'm fine, really." Jerking away, Tabitha straightened, angrily flipping her honey-colored tresses over one shoulder.

"You don't look fine."

"Well, clearly not as *fine* as Mara fares this night,"

she spewed bitterly, her fists clenching angrily at her sides.

"You're wondering why the Lord spared Alexander, but not your dear Stephanos."

"Look, I know I should be happy for her," Tabitha spat out, rising anxiously from her bed and pacing about the room like a caged tigress. "But it's just not fair. It isn't right, Mary. What did Stephanos do to deserve *stoning*? If God could so easily spare Alexander, why not Stephanos, as well?"

Mary knew they would never fully understand, not on this side of Heaven. But she wasn't sure if Tabitha was ready to receive the small bit of understanding that had been granted to her.

"Let me guess," Tabitha spewed, pausing angrily before her mistress. "*God has a plan*, right?"

"You know that He does," Mary responded gently, her heart breaking for her dear maid.

"Well, maybe I don't want to be part of it anymore," Tabitha hotly declared, crossing rigid arms over her chest. "You'll recall that before accepting Jesus, Mara was no saint. By her own admission, she turned from the God of her fathers, remember? She even married a Gentile soldier and got a divorce! And yet God chose to lavish mercy and favor upon *her*, while snatching away *my* husband? *Why?*"

Mary waited quietly, allowing Tabitha the freedom to voice her pain.

"Unlike Mara, *I've* served God faithfully my entire life, and yet He stood idly by while my husband was tortured and stoned to death," Tabitha fumed, her countenance fierce. "Where's the justice in that, Mary?"

"When I lost my husband, Mark," Mary said, her

soft eyes resting upon Tabitha with understanding, "I felt just as you do. My entire life, I'd striven to serve God, to honor Him in my thoughts, deeds, and even in my finances. But when Mark was taken, I felt as if my entire world had spun out of control. I didn't understand why the Lord hadn't intervened. It wouldn't have been difficult for God to save Him. He is, after all, the God who spoke the entire universe into existence. Surely He could have prevented one man's heart from failing him."

Tabitha stood before Mary, breathing heavily. Somehow, her lady's quiet voice, laced with compassion, held Tabitha's raging tongue in check.

"But then God reminded me that this life is *temporary*, fleeting. Truly, we are here one day, but gone the next like a vapor or a puff of wind. But everything that happens *here* is to prepare us for the *next* life, Tabitha—everlasting life with our heavenly Father. There, He will right all wrongs. There, every knee will bow, and every tongue will confess that He is fair and just and good. And though the enemy rages against us now, God is the Master of taking what was meant for evil and using it for good. This, in turn, will result in the salvation of millions."

Tabitha looked away, unconvinced.

"Have you read your copy of Stephanos' final sermon, Tabitha? The one Alexander delivered for you?" Mary asked very gently.

By the look in Tabitha's eyes and the stubborn set to her jaw, Mary knew she hadn't.

"Please do. For in it, your husband reminded us that nothing can happen without God's permission." Ignoring Tabitha's mounting consternation, Mary resumed her quiet exhortation. "From the beginning of time, God has worked all things together for our ultimate good. And He continues to do so, even now. Just as the Lord reminded me when my beloved Mark passed from this life, God has *good* plans for you, Tabitha—plans of peace, not of evil. Plans to give you *hope*, a future. Can you believe that?"

"What *good* has come from losing Stephanos?" Tabitha demanded angrily.

"The salvation of his mother, Daphne," Mary gently pointed out. "And the salvation of her trustworthy manservant, Dorian. In addition to those blessed victories, we may never know the full impact of Stephanos' final testimony, Tabitha. Perhaps dozens more have accepted Christ due to his courage and conviction in the face of certain death."

"But did he really have to *die*?" Tabitha cried out, further chagrined. "If those stubborn people had simply accepted Christ sooner, then perhaps he wouldn't have had to perish."

"Stephanos would have gladly laid down his life, even if it meant but one soul would join us in the Kingdom of God," Mary patiently reminded her, though she knew her words supplied little comfort.

"But he shouldn't have had to!" Tabitha cried fiercely. "Let those people find Christ some other way."

"Tabitha, do you remember our Lord's great commission?"

"Of course I do," Tabitha huffed, turning away in frustration.

"Tell me what it was."

"Surely you know it better than I do," Tabitha snapped, annoyed.

"Humor me, Tabitha."

Tabitha rewarded her mistress with a hard glare.

"Please?" Mary implored, her soft eyes reflecting her understanding.

"He told us to make disciples of all the nations," Tabitha ground out, peeved.

"And have we done so thus far?"

Tabitha stared at her blankly. "What do you mean?"

"Have we taken the gospel to all the nations?"

"We've preached the Word faithfully, without ceasing!"

"Here in Jerusalem, yes," Mary agreed quietly, sadly. "But have we done as our Lord commanded? Have we taken the gospel throughout all of Judea and Samaria and to the ends of the earth?"

"The gospel is well on its way *now*, with our church family scattering like frightened mice," Tabitha retorted. "Many of the church leaders are seeking foreign mission fields. Even Kelila and Philip have decided to take the gospel to Samaria."

"And why is that, Tabitha?"

Tabitha stared at her lady in horror, the truth hitting her with the force of a battering ram.

"Jesus' great commission is finally being fulfilled, because Stephanos willingly laid down his life for the salvation of the world, Tabitha," Mary explained, ever patient. "We had become a bit too cozy here in Jerusalem, don't you see? Perhaps we *needed* a little push. Now, in the wake of persecution, many believers have been forced to scatter among the nations, taking the Good News along with them."

"But at my husband's expense?" Tabitha gaped, dismayed.

"We cannot possibly comprehend all the ways of

our God," Mary said, rising to take Tabitha's hands in hers. "But we do know He stands beside us amidst these unspeakable tragedies, shaping and molding them into something meant for our ultimate good."

"I don't want to feel this way," Tabitha whispered, her eyes softening as they filled with tears. "But how can I trust the Lord—and teach others to do so—after all that's happened? I *do* believe He has a plan, but after losing my husband…I'm almost afraid to remain in His will if it's going to be this painful."

"I understand, Tabitha," Mary assured her, and she meant it. "Have you taken these fears before the Lord?"

Tabitha shook her head, her eyes and expression distant. "Perhaps I've simply been walking the wrong path all along."

"You know that isn't true, beloved."

"I feel lost, Mary. I don't know how to find the way again."

"Oh, but you do, beloved," Mary reminded her, tipping Tabitha's chin with a gentle finger. "Don't you remember how the Apostle Thomas felt when Jesus told him He must return to His Father? He said, 'How can we know the way?'"

Tabitha closed her eyes, weeping softly.

"And how did Jesus comfort our dear Thomas, beloved? What did He say to him?"

"'I AM the way…'" Tabitha whispered, warm tears spilling over her cheeks.

"Amen," Mary softly agreed. "And He still is. Tabitha, Jesus *is* the way—*the only way*—to healing. And yet, in your hour of greatest need, you have distanced yourself from Him. It is entirely understandable, for your wounded heart is anxious to trust again. But you *must*, my dear girl. Jesus wants to comfort you. He wants to be your Healer."

"But I don't feel Him near me," Tabitha whispered through her tears. "I cannot feel His presence or His leading."

"Sometimes, beloved, one must simply *obey* first. The feelings often come *later*," Mary reminded her, smiling warmly. "But even then, when the feelings do come, we cannot be led by them. We must cling to the unchanging Word of God, for it is the same yesterday, today, and forever—regardless of our fickle feelings."

Obey first. Looking away, Tabitha's heart constricted in her chest. For even now, the Holy Spirit tugged gently at her heartstrings, placing a knowing finger upon the one secret sin she had been nurturing since her husband's treacherous passing.

"What is it, beloved?" Mary asked, carefully watching her maidservant's troubled expression. "Come, sit with me," she invited, gracefully lowering herself upon the edge of the bed.

Dropping her gaze in resignation, Tabitha reluctantly joined her mistress. "Perhaps I haven't sought the Lord because...because I feel unworthy."

"Tabitha, we are *all* unworthy," Mary reminded her. "Jesus loves us despite our weaknesses and grants us strength to overcome."

"I know He does," Tabitha said, releasing a shaky sigh. "But, Mary, I have so much hatred in my heart. Every day, it grows. Sometimes, the ferocity of my own emotions and the darkness of my thoughts frightens me."

"You are struggling with hatred against Saul and those who murdered your husband," Mary stated with understanding.

"Yes," Tabitha admitted, grieved. "Sometimes, I simply daydream about inflicting vengeance upon Saul and his murderous men. I couldn't care less about the salvation of my husband's killers, Mary. If I'm entirely honest, I don't even *want* them to be saved. I want them to suffer." Burying her face in her hands, Tabitha groaned in anguish. "How can I possibly overcome this?"

"Tabitha, beloved." Taking her maidservant's trembling hands, Mary met her weepy gaze. "By your own strength, you cannot overcome this. But by the grace of God, you can. Remember, we overcome evil with good."

Blinking back her tears, Tabitha nodded slowly, hesitantly.

"Our enemies have mastered the art of hatred, but they know nothing of God's love," Mary spoke with quiet, fervent conviction, arresting the attention of her brokenhearted maid. "Only love can transform hate, Tabitha. And this is why our Savior tenderly reminds us to love our enemies as He did—as Stephanos did."

"Oh, God, grant me the strength to do it." Tabitha swiped at her tears, shaking her head in amazement.

"He will, beloved. But, Tabitha," Mary said, her tone so serious Tabitha's tears instantly ceased. "I want you to consider this: Perhaps there is a reason the enemy has targeted you with such relentless fury. Perhaps, just perhaps, he knows the Lord has a mighty future for you, one that will impact lives for all eternity."

Tabitha stared at her lady in wonderment as strange little tingles skittered up and down her spine. Not once had she considered this. And yet, it made perfect sense.

"I will leave you alone to consult the Lord in this matter," Mary smiled, patting Tabitha's knee in a motherly manner. "Beloved, should you need anything—anything at all—you know where to find me."

Tabitha watched as Mary rose from the bed. Crossing the room with her usual grace and poise, Mary slipped beyond the stone doorway, pausing long enough to cast a tender smile over her shoulder.

Glancing toward her small bedside table, Tabitha's teary gaze fell upon a slender parchment scroll, its seal unbroken. Releasing a silent prayer of heartfelt repentance, Tabitha reached for the scroll, gingerly breaking the elegant wax seal.

Tucking her legs comfortably beneath her, Tabitha drew a deep, steadying breath, carefully unrolling the rough parchment.

At long last, she was ready to receive her husband's final message.

CHAPTER 57

Tabitha

After hungrily devouring Stephanos' last sermon, Tabitha spent the following hour in the presence of the Lord, fervently seeking His guidance in a spirit of repentance. Consumed with exhaustion, she eventually dropped onto her cozy bed, spent with tears of contriteness...but also gladness.

The Lord would surely restore her. She knew it, deep in her heart. At times, the narrow road ahead would prove trying, even challenging, but for the first time since her husband's death, Tabitha was ready to resume her walk with God.

Hours later, Tabitha awakened, utterly amazed.

Unlike the gripping nightmares following her husband's violent departure, Tabitha had awakened to an entirely different dream. In it, she saw Jesus standing at the right hand of God, arms outstretched, smiling warmly as He ushered her beloved Stephanos into His shining kingdom. Though she hadn't been able to see past the brilliant, blinding light enshrouding the throne of God, Tabitha's wide eyes had tearfully absorbed every detail of her Savior—His gentle eyes, His welcoming smile, His nail-scarred hands and feet. And though Jesus appeared much as He had when He was on the earth, there was a resounding power, a new strength, about His person. Tabitha thought He was beautiful in every way, resplendent in His shining robes.

And despite His awesome majesty, there her Savior stood, welcoming her beloved husband with tears shining in His eyes.

Sitting up in bed with a sharp gasp, Tabitha blinked back tears of wonder and joy. Raising her eyes heavenward, she shared a secret smile with her loving Savior.

For the very first time since tragedy had struck, nearly ripping her heart in two, Tabitha clearly saw the unfading beauty of the life her husband had lived, the sacrifice he had made. Shaking her head in wonder, Tabitha realized she couldn't possibly fathom the treasure awaiting him in Heaven.

And had it been up to me, she thought, ashamed, *I would have robbed him of the joy set before him. I would have stripped away my husband's privilege of suffering for Christ, of laying down his life for Him. I would have robbed him of his reward.*

Swinging her legs over the side of the bed, Tabitha dropped to her knees, bowing her head until her smooth forehead touched her clasped hands upon the bed.

Precious Lord, after You went to the cross, how could I possibly doubt Your love? She prayed, her heart breaking inside her chest as she remembered her Savior as He had appeared in her dream. Such love shining in His eyes! Such great mercy etched upon His every feature! *Forgive me, Lord. I want to walk in Your will, not mine.*

Rising a bit unsteadily, Tabitha spun on her heel, finding herself face to face with her own reflection glistening in the elegant mirror mounted upon the opposite wall. With an unwelcome shiver, she recalled the Spirit's startling admonition, the revelation she had received shortly before her husband's death: *The devil has asked to sift you as wheat.*

Eyes widening in amazement, the truth hit Tabitha like a ton of bricks—the truth she had been seeking all along, despite her searing anger and harassing doubts.

Oh my, she thought, stunned by her shocking realization. *It wasn't the loss of my precious husband that nearly destroyed me,* she thought, blinking at her own startled-looking reflection. *It was my burning hatred toward those who killed him.*

Lifting her arms—and her gaze—heavenward, Tabitha remembered the words once spoken by Mary, the mother of her blessed Savior, a kind, patient woman filled with the power of the Holy Spirit, brimming with wisdom and profound understanding. *"Behold the maidservant of the Lord,"* Tabitha declared with a smile, willingly committing her cause into the hands of her capable Creator, her hazel-green eyes reflecting a powerful purpose. *"Be it unto me according to Thy word."*

***

Candace

"There," Candace stated with satisfaction, carefully draping her younger sister's bridal attire over a rickety, straight-backed chair. "We have packed your belongings, prepared your ointments, perfumes, and bath salts, and altered your lovely gown, Kelila. The only thing left to do now is wait for your handsome bridegroom."

"Isn't it exciting?" Kelila nearly squealed, scooping up her three-year-old nephew and clutching him close to her heart despite his writhing protests. "Philip promised he would come for me any day now!"

Smiling to herself, Candace watched as Kelila lowered a squirming Rufus to the ground, playfully swatting his backside as he hurried away to join his brother in the outer court. Nearly two years had passed since Kelila had shown up on their doorstep, rocking her cozy little world with a grand—though completely unexpected—entrance!

But my, how things have changed since then, Candace thought, smiling through her tears. Kelila—once a willful, selfish girl—had blossomed into a mature, godly young woman. Almost effortlessly, the vibrant Kelila had become a cherished member of the family. Now, Candace wondered how she would possibly manage without the girl's cheery laughter filling the house.

"I just can't believe we'll be leaving for Samaria so soon after the wedding," Kelila was saying, smoothing the folds of the cream-colored, velvety gown.

"How soon after the ceremony will you depart?" Candace asked, attempting to keep her tone light. She surely didn't wish to dampen Kelila's happiness. The Lord had led her sister to a wonderful, godly man. Despite her inner struggle, Candace truly did rejoice for them.

"Well, after the vows are exchanged at Mary's

villa, there will be a small celebration for family and close friends, as you already know."

"Yes," Candace smiled, happily anticipating the marriage supper Mary had arranged for them.

"We plan to spend our wedding night in the lovely little house Philip built for us," Kelila explained, blushing prettily. "And we shall remain here in Jerusalem for the week, celebrating our marriage with family and friends. After that, Philip says we must leave for Samaria."

"I see."

"Oh, Candace," Kelila said with tears in her eyes, "I can't quite explain how happy and anxious and scared and delighted I feel—all at the same time!"

"What do you mean, dear sister?" Candace asked, concerned for her. "Is everything all right? Has Philip said or done something to give you pause, Kelila?"

"Oh, it's nothing like that," Kelila laughed, brushing aside Candace's concerns. "I can't wait to marry Philip. But, oh, how I shall miss you and Simon and my dear, sweet nephews." Looking away, Kelila blinked back a sudden rush of tears.

"Now, stop that," Candace teased, forcing a brave smile. "You know we are going to visit you the moment you get settled in!"

"And we shall return to Jerusalem at least three times each year to celebrate the pilgrimage feasts with you," Kelila reminded her, feeling a little better. "In fact, we'll probably come around so often you'll have to bolt the door to keep us out!"

"You may have to do the same in Samaria," Candace confided, chuckling in amusement. "I will truly miss you, my sweet sister. But Simon and I support your mission wholeheartedly, and I admire your courage, Kelila."

"Philip believes our testimony shall remain un-hindered in Samaria," Kelila told her, a mischievous glint in her dark eyes. "After all, our persecutors refuse to set foot in Samaria!"

"I hadn't thought of that," Candace smiled, re-lieved her sister would be far removed from the trouble brewing in the holy city.

"Who knows?" Kelila grinned, swooping in to en-circle her sister in an unexpected embrace. "Perhaps you'll love Samaria so much, you won't ever want to leave!"

Candace couldn't help but admire her sister's en-thusiasm. "I suppose we shall find out soon enough," she smiled wanly.

CHAPTER 58

Tabitha

The promise of spring was in the air, calling to mind new life, new hope, and new beginnings.

It was a fresh, invigorating day, with a brisk but pleasant breeze rustling through the verdant greenery climbing long, painted trellises and spilling over elegant urns scattered about the lovely, open-air court nestled safely within the heart of Mary's villa. Brilliant golden sunlight streamed down upon the scene, warming the cold stone tiles underfoot and the vibrant canopies suspended overhead. Tiny, bright-eyed birds flitted somewhat reluctantly from branch to branch, eyeing the bubbling fountain below with interest.

"Thank you for inviting me to join you for breakfast, my lady," Tabitha said sincerely, seated across from Mary in the lush inner courtyard. The cozy table between them was piled high with tantalizing refreshments, beckoning the women to partake of its delights, inviting them to break their fasts of the previous night.

The kitchen staff had truly outdone themselves. Tabitha knew she and Mary couldn't possibly consume all this food! Had Mary supplied her chefs with special orders today?

"I am honored you have joined me." Mary smiled graciously, knowingly observing the lovely young maid before her. "Tabitha, you look changed, beloved."

"I *feel* changed," Tabitha confessed, her heart swelling with relief. "And by God's grace, I *am* changed."

"Tell me what happened." Mary leaned forward in her chair with rapt attention.

"The Lord visited me in a dream last night, Mary. Perhaps it was merely a vision; I can't be sure. Either way, I was reminded of His great love for me, for Stephanos. Surely, His will can be trusted."

"Praise God for His abundant mercy," Mary breathed, toying with the long golden stem of her goblet. "I am so very proud of you, beloved."

"You shouldn't be," Tabitha admitted, shaking her head with a wry smile. "It took months of resisting the Spirit's leading for me to finally submit, kicking and screaming and carrying on like a stubborn child." Fleetingly, Tabitha thought of the poor orphan upstairs with Rhoda. Perhaps she, too, would experience the Lord's peace someday.

"But ultimately you accepted the Spirit's leading, Tabitha," Mary reminded her, smiling warmly. "It took some time, but God's will has prevailed in your life."

"May it continue to do so," Tabitha said with great feeling. She didn't wish to feel separated from her beloved Savior, not ever again. "David's psalm of repentance has been fresh on my mind this morning. I have offered it back to the Lord in prayer. Truly, His Word is strengthening me."

"I know the psalm of which you speak," Mary replied with understanding.

"*Create in me a clean heart, O God, and renew a steadfast spirit within me,*" Tabitha quoted with quiet conviction. "*Do not cast me away from Your presence, and do not take Your Holy Spirit from me. Restore me to the joy of Your salvation, and uphold me by Your generous Spirit. Then I will teach transgressors Your ways, and sinners shall be converted to You.*"

"Amen," Mary said wholeheartedly. "And, Tabitha, I believe you *will* teach others the ways of God. By His grace and His powerful anointing upon your life, many shall be converted."

Tabitha could only smile, her shining countenance brimming with the joy and peace of God.

"The Lord has granted you peace," Mary observed. "It fairly radiates from your person."

"If that is so, then it's truly a testament to God's transforming power. Just last night, I nearly gave in to despair."

"Cling to Him, beloved. He will supply the strength you need for each new day."

"It's as if all my fears and doubts have faded into the background, Mary—only because my eyes are fixed upon Jesus," Tabitha explained, shaking her head in wonder. "Years ago, I sat upon the steps of the Synagogue of the Freedmen, telling the children about Simon Peter's encounter with Jesus during the great storm upon the sea."

"Ah, when our dearest Peter found himself walking upon the water," Mary chuckled lightly, remembering the story well.

"At the time, Stephanos joined me on the steps. I was a bit annoyed with him," Tabitha admitted, smiling at the distant memory. "Somehow, he always seemed to steal my thunder without even trying."

Mary smiled through a faint sheen of tears. She knew what Tabitha meant.

"The children were enthralled by Peter's story," Tabitha smiled, her eyes distant. "Seeing this, my wonderful Stephanos—always the evangelist—took the opportunity to drive home a very important lesson: When we focus on the storms of this life, we lose sight of the only One who can calm the storm. The moment Peter took his eyes off Jesus, focusing on the raging, crashing sea, he sank beneath the churning waves."

Mary nodded, remembering the humiliation in Peter's eyes when he had first relayed the frightening ordeal.

"But despite Peter's crisis of faith, Jesus was right there in front of him, His hand outstretched, just waiting to pull him back up," Tabitha mused, her eyes sparkling with wonder. "And He's always there, Mary—always waiting for us to reach for Him, to take His hand so He can pull us above the crashing waves."

"Amen," Mary affirmed with great conviction. "Praise be to God."

"Had I taken the time to contemplate my husband's teachings, I would have remembered his powerful admonition," Tabitha explained. "We must always remember to keep our eyes fixed upon Jesus, even amidst our darkest storms."

"You have learned a very powerful lesson, Tabitha," Mary said, rejoicing for her maidservant. "And I have no doubt this experience will equip you to serve others with grace and understanding in the future."

Tabitha's eyes flickered slightly, arousing Mary's curiosity.

"What is it, beloved?" she asked gently. "There's something more, something you haven't yet shared with me."

"I suppose there is," Tabitha admitted, shifting a bit nervously in her chair.

Mary waited patiently, praying silently as she did so.

"I had thought...had *hoped*...well, that perhaps the Lord would grant me the privilege of bearing a child to carry on my husband's legacy," Tabitha explained, blushing as she voiced the deepest longing of her heart.

"I see," Mary said softly, her eyes clouded with tears of understanding.

"It would have been so perfect, so sentimental," Tabitha admitted, lowering her gaze in shame, "to discover I was with child, to know I carried his legacy within my womb, to have a sweet little one to remember him by."

"I can understand your longing, beloved," Mary assured her, placing her hand comfortingly upon her maid's.

"Though I don't understand the Lord's refusal in this matter, I will still trust Him, Mary," Tabitha said, slowly lifting her head as her eyes glinted with purpose and determination. "He wouldn't have denied my request without reason."

"My lady?"

Mary's head came up as Rhoda emerged from beneath a row of stately pillars, escorting the loudly protesting orphan by the hand. "Good morning, Rhoda! I see you've brought a sweet little friend."

"Our sweet little friend is refusing to eat breakfast this morning," Rhoda confided, clearly at her wit's end. "Have you any suggestions, my lady?"

Breaking free from Rhoda's grasp, the little girl toddled over to Tabitha's chair, holding out her arms to her.

Gazing upon the orphaned little one with her outstretched arms, large brown eyes, and soft, curly tendrils of brown hair framing an impish little face, Tabitha was taken aback as a shocking revelation dawned...

Stephanos *had* indeed given her a child!

I entrust her into your care...

Glancing across the table at Mary, Tabitha saw that Mary's wide gray eyes reflected the same stunning realization as her own.

Shaking her head in absolute wonderment, Tabitha scooped up the little girl, cuddling her close to her heart. "You just want to be loved, don't you, little one?" Tabitha was even more amazed when the child responded, burying her face in the folds of Tabitha's soft garment.

"I believe our gracious Father has answered your request, beloved," Mary pronounced, her eyes shimmering with tears.

Rhoda, too, appeared to understand, smiling broadly as she nodded her wholehearted consent.

"Today, the Lord has given you a new home and

a new name, beloved." Turning the child around in her lap, Tabitha offered the orphan a gentle smile. "You will be called *Laurel* in remembrance of your father, Stephanos." So, too, would the child's name reflect upon her grandmother, Daphne.

"Laurel," Mary repeated, utterly delighted. "How fitting!"

"Laurel—like the beautiful leaves gracing a victor's crown," Tabitha mused, gently stroking the child's smooth brown hair. "The name *Stephanos* references a wreath or crown of victory, so my husband was aptly named, for he received the crown of life—attaining the ultimate victory through Christ Jesus, our Lord."

"Praise our great and glorious God," Mary declared, smiling at the unlikely pair seated across the table. "Yet again, He has exceeded our wildest expectations."

"His perfect plan was there all along," Tabitha exclaimed, flooded with a peace so profound it surpassed her own human understanding. "He was simply waiting for us to find it."

CHAPTER 59

Kelila

Philip and Kelila wed in a lovely, quiet ceremony before family and friends in Mary's stately villa. Kelila had hardly recognized the Upper Room, arrayed with decorative garlands of vibrant greenery and fresh flowers, outfitted with fine linen tapestries and a petal-strewn walkway leading to the platform up front.

Yet again, Mary had completely outdone herself.

Hours later, Kelila stood within her own flower-strewn bedchamber, clasping hands with her new husband, gazing into his soft brown eyes with wonder and excitement and tender longing.

"I can hardly believe we are married, my love," Philip breathed, gently pressing his forehead against hers. "Kelila, you are radiant, my darling, beautiful in every way."

"I wondered what this would be like—being alone with you, Philip," Kelila admitted with a nervous smile. Alone in their own little home—even if it was a temporary one!

"How do you like it so far?" Philip teased, playfully nuzzling the curve of her neck.

"We've only just arrived," Kelila grinned, draping her arms over his broad shoulders. "I can still hear our friends outside the house!"

"But they can't hear us," Philip reminded her with a mischievous smile. Soon, their family and friends would scatter after escorting the brand-new couple to their bridal chamber. But for now, it felt good to be reminded of how very *loved* they were. They would not begin this marital journey alone.

"Philip," Kelila said, her tone and expression serious.

Philip leaned in close, attentive to his wife's concerns.

"Mary gave me a very generous gift today," she explained, her dark eyes begging him to understand. "With your permission, I would like to send the amount I took from my father—including restitution—to board a ship and travel to Jerusalem without his consent."

"Of course," Philip promised, his eyes softening with understanding. "I admire your willingness to right the wrong committed against your father."

"It's the right thing to do," she agreed reluctantly. "Although I doubt it will change his opinion of me." Smiling wryly, she added quickly, "I'd like to entrust the remaining sum to your care, Philip, to distribute as you see fit. I know the unexpected funds will prove incredibly helpful as we set off for Samaria to build a new life from the ground up."

"That was, undoubtedly, our dear, generous Mary's intention," Philip smiled fondly.

"Well, now that we've gotten *that* out of the way…" Kelila's dark eyes grew playful once again. Placing her hands against his solid chest, she flashed her most radiant smile. "Aren't you going to show me how happy you are to take a wife?"

"That's exactly what I intend to do, my beautiful." Taking Kelila in his arms, Philip bent to kiss his adoring bride.

***

Tabitha

Standing before her husband's grave with young Laurel settled comfortably upon her hip, Tabitha gazed at the dry dirt mound bearing a simple marker, recalling the anguish she had experienced the day he was buried.

Today, with warm, golden sunlight streaming down upon her head and shoulders, Tabitha realized one never would have guessed she now stood in a place of death. Despite the sea of unmarked graves stretching before her, Tabitha was filled with an inexplicable sense of peace.

One day, Lord, she thought, cheek to cheek with her newfound daughter, *this place of death will spring to life as your saints explode from their graves, summoned by Your fiery presence, the voice of an archangel, and the trumpet call of God! Soon, You shall return for us, banishing death forever.*

"Preserve him for me, Jesus," Tabitha whispered, her luminous eyes fixed upon her husband's sun-baked grave. "I want to stroll through flowery meadows with him, hand in hand…with *You*, Lord, by our side. Preserve him for that day."

Oh come, Lord Jesus. Come for us soon.

Alerted by a stream of pebbles loosened from uneven, rocky ground, Tabitha turned, protectively clutching her child close to her breast.

There stood Saul of Tarsus, his countenance strangely veiled.

Instinctively, Tabitha's gaze flitted to the lethal dagger strapped at his leather belt. Sporting common attire, Saul appeared even more fierce without the flowing robes of a religious man.

Knowing a moment of very real fear, Tabitha swiftly relinquished herself—and her child—into the hands of God. She couldn't help but wonder what had driven Saul to this place of desolation. Would he be defiled for setting foot within this desert field of lonely graves? She didn't know.

Clearly, the rigid Pharisee hadn't expected to encounter her, either. He studied her with unyielding dark eyes, the same eyes that had studied her husband with hatred and burning intensity in the Synagogue of the Freedmen.

How can I love my enemies, Lord? Feeling the familiar bile rising in her throat, Tabitha knew a moment of panic. Shutting her eyes, she desperately beseeched Almighty God for help. *I cannot forgive this man, Lord, who earnestly sought the death of my husband. Help me, God! Help me now!*

And then the answer came like a soothing balm, settling over Tabitha like the divine cloud which had guided the Israelites across the harshest and most unforgiving of deserts. Basking in the magnificent peace of God, Tabitha knew what she was called to do.

Without a word, Tabitha approached Saul of Tarsus, gingerly stepping over jagged rocks and the dry, uneven terrain. Standing fearlessly before her persecutor, Tabitha adjusted Laurel's weight on her hip, gazing up into the hardened face of a murderer—the man who had orchestrated her husband's demise.

"I forgive you, Saul." Lightly touching his arm, Tabitha felt Saul's taut muscles tense beneath her delicate fingertips. His dark eyes hardened in disdain...or was it something else?

"You didn't know what you were doing," Tabitha said quietly, her hazel-green eyes brimming with unshed tears. "But someday, you will...in time."

Quietly stepping past him, Tabitha abandoned the vast sea of graves, leaving behind her malice and bitterness, as well. Such qualities reigned in places of death, not within the hearts of God's children.

Slowly turning his head, Saul watched as his victim's young widow gracefully picked her way up the steep terrain, cuddling her little child close to her heart. His conscience pricked, catching him entirely off guard.

Saul hadn't realized the evangelist had a child.

Turning back toward the grave of one seemingly insignificant dead Jew, Stephanos' final words rang through the sea of desert tombs, searing Saul's impenetrable heart with white-hot heat, filling his entire being with trembling, quaking rage... and a paralyzing sense of dread.

Lord, do not charge them with this sin.

Saul's hard mouth formed a thin, grim line as his penetrating gaze swept over the evangelist's unimpressive resting place. Instinctively, he knew his sleepless nights would be forever haunted by the evangelist's final words.

And now, his widow's reaction.

CHAPTER 60

Tabitha

Cradling little Laurel close to her heart, Tabitha stood upon the balcony adjoining the Upper Room, gazing upon the breathtaking silhouette of a hostile city cloaked in the magnificent russet-colored hues of a brand-new sunrise. She couldn't imagine a grander city—nor a city more hopelessly mired in the futile traditions of men.

Saul of Tarsus continued to rage against the church of God with calculated fury, but Tabitha was not afraid. Remembering the words Stephanos had spoken over the ruthless Pharisee, she prayed earnestly for his restoration as her gaze swept over the red-roofed structures of Jerusalem's many elite.

With arms draped trustingly about her mother's neck, Laurel, too, studied the glistening city with keen interest. Still, the child had not spoken, but Tabitha had faith that she would...in time. Rather than fretting about her daughter's traumatic scars—including the girl's refusal to speak—she chose to pray for healing instead.

Oh, Lord, how happy I am to walk in Your will! Tabitha thought, flooded with relief. For after weeks of earnest prayer, the Lord had graciously revealed her next step, filling her entire being with apprehension... but also an unlikely, abiding sense of peace.

"In faith, I will embrace Your plan, Father," Tabitha whispered, considering the wonders Almighty God must have in store for her...and for her precious Laurel. Glancing warmly at her beautiful daughter, Tabitha flashed a confident smile.

"God has answered us, dear one," she said happily, receiving a shy grin from the little girl. "Soon, our adventure begins."

Absorbing the stunning beauty of the only city she had ever known, Tabitha whispered a quiet farewell. For soon, she would set out on a life-changing journey, reluctantly leaving the ninety-nine in search of the one lost sheep.

A LOOK AT BOOK SIX:
SEEKING THE TRUTH

Get carried away by the captivating display of unwavering faith and strength in this compelling tale of the transformative power of God's love.

Tabitha, a courageous young widow, sets out on a mission to share the message of Jesus Christ with her sceptical uncle, Joram, in the ancient seaport town of Joppa, when—despite Joram's bitterness and sarcasm—her unwavering faith and infectious joy touch the lives of those around her.

In another corner of the world, newlyweds Kelila and Philip embrace their missionary calling as they arrive in the village of Sychar. But when Kelila's dreams of a peaceful life clash with Philip's sacred purpose, she's led to a path of self-discovery and surrender, where she must learn to let go of her own desires and embrace the greater plan that God has in store for her.

In Jerusalem, Mary struggles with her beloved son as he begins to drift further and further from their faith. Concerned he is far more interested in the pursuit of fleeting pleasures than the way of everlasting life, Mary must put her faith in the Lord and pray for His guidance.

Embracing the Life is an inspiring tale of divine plans, unwavering faith, and the power of hope amidst religious upheaval and the sinister forces of darkness seeking to destroy the light of truth.

AVAILABLE SEPTEMBER 2023

ABOUT THE AUTHOR

Rachael C. Duncan is a passionate follower of Christ. Her goal is to reach as many people as possible for the sake of Christ and His kingdom. She believes that God has gifted each of His children with different gifts to be used to strengthen the body of Christ and fulfill the Great Commission. (Matt. 28:19-20; 1 Cor. 12)

Rachael was blessed to be raised in a strong Christian home, and she accepted Jesus Christ as her Lord and Savior at a very early age. Since then, she has determined to live her life in accordance to His Word and to share the love of Christ through the gift of writing.

Rachael has been passionate about writing since she was a small child. She especially loved writing plays and short stories. At the age of fourteen, she wrote her first play, which was performed as a dinner theatre production by a local school.

She has been actively involved in both women's and children's ministries for over a decade. Currently, she enjoys teaching a weekly girls' Bible study, writing plays for a local homeschool group, and participating in local ministry outreaches for women and children.

Rachael currently resides in Texas with her husband and their first "child"—a playful rescue puppy named Riley! In addition to her writing, she is an enthusiastic "keeper of the home" and "helpmeet" as well as being actively involved in ministering to the women and children God has placed in her life. (Titus 2:3-5; Gen. 2:20-23)